Sincerely Yours
Bella Z. Spencer.

Tried and True,

OR

LOVE AND LOYALTY:

A Story of the Great Rebellion.

BY

MRS. BELLA Z. SPENCER.

SPRINGFIELD, MASS.:
W. J. HOLLAND.
1867.

SAMUEL BOWLES AND COMPANY,
PRINTERS AND BINDERS.

Preface.

I VENTURE before the public once more, in the character of an author, with much diffidence, and shall depend largely upon the truthfulness of the narrative, for public favor, apart from any claim to literary merit. Frequent visits to the Army of the South-west during the war, together with unusual advantages for becoming familiar with the singular events which marked the progress of our national strife, have placed me in possession of the plot, and nearly all of the details, of this story. I spent several weeks at Paducah in 1862, leaving it after the battle of Shiloh; and it was while traveling thither, I first came to know the heroine of my story. Afterwards I met her at Corinth, at which place I spent a part of two summers—the first before the battle of Corinth—the second in the year following, while General G. M. Dodge was there in command, and with whom my husband then served as Chief of Staff. While there, and afterward when in Tennessee and Alabama, life at head-quarters with Mrs. Dodge opened to me facilities for gathering the materials used in this work, which I could not have gained in any other position. Many visits were made to the sick and wounded, and the miserable Refugees who swarmed through our lines. Many were the long horseback rides into the country, passing fear lessly beyond our pickets to any place which our fancy might select; and it is to such a life I owe what knowledge I possess of the suffering, wrong and oppression of a people whose position was worse than that of the slave.

In the narrative, I have touched but lightly upon the condition of the Refugees. Here, however, I feel constrained to say a word in their favor, hoping to win for them a sentiment of pity, at least, from those who may read. It is true that many of them seemed ungrateful for the care bestowed upon them. If they were not, ignorance must be their excuse for the lack of expression to their feelings. But, in the majority of cases, I found no cause for complaint. They were ignorant indeed—driven from their homes in the most forlorn and destitute condition, while the fact that their husbands, sons, brothers, were in the rebel army, served to cut them off from all sympathy. Often the fact that those men were not left to choose, seemed to have been forgotten; and a *conscripted* rebel was as much a rebel as those who had willingly taken up arms against the Government. We did not pause to remember that their helpless position rather rendered them subjects of pity than distrust, depending, in most cases, upon the wealthy planters for the very roofs which sheltered them. They were too poor to emigrate when the hour of danger drew near, and had no other alternative for persecution and abuse than to allow themselves to be driven forth like cattle to the slaughter, leaving their families behind. Then, as our army advanced, and those who had the means fled before it, the wretched beings, who had no friends and no means for following, were forced to remain and share the traitors' fate. Sickness, want, even starvation, came upon them, when the hand of humanity was withheld. They were compelled to leave their homes, and wander friendless through the land. Still worse was it for those who had braved the rebels and entered the Union army. Their houses were burned—the one cow and few pigs slaughtered—if they had a horse, it was taken from them, and thus were they set adrift upon the world. Perhaps the clothes they wore were all that was left them upon earth, and thus they came through our lines, weary, foot-sore, ragged, with babes dying upon the breast, and little children famished for want of food. What wonder if they died by dozens! What wonder if many seemed ungrateful, when help was extended to them with doubtful sympathy, and few would believe their story of loyalty! Surely it was not on those—poor, ignorant, lowly—the burthen of treachery should have rested. They were the victims, and no thought of chiding ever entered my heart, if they failed to utter the thanks which I knew it must be hard to feel under the circumstances. It seems to me I could not have been grateful for what they received; and yet the majority *were* grateful in their way. A poor woman's "I don't know what we'd 'a' done ef it hadn't 'a' been fur you," was equivalent to the heartiest expression of thanks. And who could doubt the sentiments which made them cling tearfully to one's hands and garments when the hour of parting came, sobbing out blessings and prayers that alone could have arisen out of gratitude? I do not exaggerate when I say that the Refugees were more pitiable than the Negroes.

While in North Alabama visiting my husband's regiment, which was composed mainly of native Alabamians, just before Sherman took the field for the great campaign, I saw, on the banks of the Tennessee River, the ruins of "Passiver Hall"—abandoned by the rebels, and burned by them to prevent its falling into our hands when we took possession of that country.

As much as possible, I have avoided going into the revolting details of the cruel abuses of the slave. Every southern sympathizer will deny the truth of those stories, and every northern heart is sick of contemplating them, even through the medium of the pen. This much I must say, that even Mrs. Stowe's representations—claimed to be the *exceptions*—cannot give any exaggerated idea of the truth.

Up to my sixteenth year, my home, from early childhood, was in the South, and in the midst of slavery. What knowledge I claim is personal; and it is because of this knowledge I am now, and ever have been, a decided republican. It was bad enough before the war, and extended throughout the South. After the war began, those who kept their slaves with them, were often fiendish. Two strong cases were brought to our notice in Middle Tennessee, while we had our head-quarters at Pulaski. Mrs. Bane, whose husband commanded the Fiftieth Illinois Regiment in the Sixteenth Army Corps, was then at Lynnville, and one day when Mrs. Dodge and I drove up to see her, we found a queer, bright little specimen of humanity in her house, in whom we became greatly interested. That little creature, the daughter of a pretty mulatto woman, was left friendless and alone in the world. Her master, also her father, was in the rebel army. Her mother had been tied across a barrel by a brutal overseer, and beaten severely, and then left in that position all night. When morning came, she was dead. The mistress, a very short time afterwards, while angrily flourishing what they call a "bull whip" on those plantations, over a couple of small negro boys, fell dead with it grasped in her hand. Thus little Georgie was cast adrift upon the world, and as Mrs. Bane was about to leave the place, with no prospect of being settled for some time, we took the child with us to head-quarters where we kept her until we were sent North, and Mrs. Linton, another of our corps ladies, took her home with the intention of rearing her with the care her intelligence required.

The other instance was in Pulaski, the town we occupied, and the lady was a Mrs. Jackson, who ostentatiously came out upon the sidewalk to welcome our troops when they entered the place, claiming to be loyal. She sent invitations frequently to General Dodge and his officers to dine and take tea with her, until she had won the confidence of nearly all in her professions of loyalty. But a short time after I joined Mrs. Dodge there in 1864, news was brought to the General that she was cruelly abusing a negro girl, whom she had beaten shamefully, then locked in the smoke-house, and kept upon bread and water for forty-eight hours! She sent numberless notes to the General pleading excuses, and begging for interviews, until he ordered a stern and prompt cessation of the correspondence through his Chief of Staff.

I might give many other such instances, with authentic names, dates, etc., were it necessary; but too much of this is known to allow the matter now to drop ere the negro shall have accorded to him all rights before the laws of his country. Perhaps many will think that, since the institution of slavery has been abolished, cruelty is at an end. If so, the following paragraph from a letter just received by my husband from the surgeon of his old regiment, a native Alabamian, and still a resident there, may not be devoid of interest:

"The rebels here are rebels yet, and we find as much disaffection as ever. Union men are scarcely safe in the country. They have arrogated to themselves a great deal, and are very sanguine of another revolution, which shall, somehow, end in the re-enslavement of the negroes. Meanwhile, they so manage matters, that the negroes who are able to work, are in the horrible position of slaves without masters—slaves as to their labor and treatment, without the benefits which the interests and cupidity of their masters formerly secured to them in the way of medical attendance, good food, clothing, etc. The weak, infirm, aged, and the women and children who cannot work, are turned adrift to shift for themselves or starve. The Union men who lift their voices in their behalf, are marked, persecuted and threatened with death. Doctor I. W. Stewart and his father-in-law, Emory, are displaying more cruelty to the negroes than I have ever before known in this country. A few days since, they tied one across a log, and well-nigh beat him to death for the most trivial offense, such as would not have been noticed in a state of slavery. They threaten me with death because I am known as the consistent friend of the Government and the Freedmen, and we are all expecting to be obliged to make up a party and leave the country for a home somewhere in the West."

Such is the present state of affairs in the South, where the men who have dared to remain loyal, cannot go back to their homes in peace, though peace has been declared. If, therefore, any attribute to the coloring of imagination the events of the story which I have given them, it is still within their power to prove, by personal observation, the entire truthfulness of the pictures drawn.

For the description of the battles of Shiloh and Fort Fisher, I am much more largely indebted to the author of "Sherman's Campaigns" and Mr. Abbot, than to my own ability. All the events of Fort Fisher I owe to Mr. Abbot, though it is not in his words that I have given them. The description of Shiloh in "Sherman's Campaigns," by one of his officers, being the finest I have anywhere seen, I have taken the liberty of adding to it the meager contents of my private memoranda, as made from accounts of various officers at the time of the battle. Here, also, I have changed the phraseology somewhat, perhaps to the author's disgrace, but in using it, surely I may lay claim to a high appreciation of his more accurate knowledge of the position of the forces, than it was possible for me to gain without being engaged in the strife—which, luckily, is not a woman's province. For the description of Corinth, I have depended entirely upon memory, touching more upon the individual results than the general strife.

If, from the whole combined, I have been enabled to interest the readers, and give a correct picture of life during those "stormy times" which can only be remembered as a dream by those who were not personally involved in them, I shall feel satisfied with the hope that my work has not been wholly without purpose. B. Z. S.

PHILADELPHIA, *April*, 1866.

Contents.

CHAPTER IV.

SURMISES AND QUESTIONINGS NOBLY MET.

CHAPTER V.

LIFE AND DEATH IN A MILITARY HOSPITAL.

CHAPTER VI.

HOSPITAL LIFE AT PADUCAH.

CHAPTER VII.

DEFYING A HOSPITAL KNAVE—A LITTLE PROGRESS IN LOVE MATTERS.

CHAPTER VIII.

TAKING A YOUNG SOLDIER HOME TO DIE—RUMORS OF A BATTLE.

CHAPTER IX.

THE BATTLE OF PITTSBURG LANDING.

CHAPTER X.

GOING TO THE BATTLE-FIELD.

CHAPTER XI.

INCIDENTS AND HORRORS OF A BATTLE-FIELD.

CHAPTER XII.

AMONG THE WOUNDED AND DYING.

CHAPTER XIII.

PRISON PENS AND REFUGEES.

CHAPTER XIV.

ESCAPING FROM PRISON.

CHAPTER XV.

PLEADING FOR THE LIFE OF A REBEL PRISONER.

CHAPTER XVI.

REFUGEES AND THEIR PITIFUL CONDITION—DISAPPOINTMENT AND FAITHLESSNESS.

CHAPTER XVII.

A SERIOUS COMPLICATION AND ITS RESULT.

CHAPTER XVIII.

A HOME OF AFFLUENCE—ITS BEAUTIES AND ITS BLEMISHES.

CHAPTER XIX.

SOME OF THE WORKINGS OF THE "PECULIAR INSTITUTION."

CHAPTER XX.

MORE DETAILS OF LIFE AT PASSIVER HALL.

CHAPTER XXI.

SHARP PRACTICE AND BRUTAL DOINGS.

CHAPTER XXII.

CHAPTER XXIII.

CHAPTER XXIV.

CHAPTER XXV.

CHAPTER XXVI.

CHAPTER XXVII.

CHAPTER XXVIII.

THE CAPTURE OF FORT FISHER.

CHAPTER XXIX.

AN UNLOOKED FOR DENOUEMENT.

CHAPTER XXX.

THE LAST ACT IN THE TRAGEDY, WITH BRIGHTER CLOSING SCENES.

CHAPTER I.

A NIGHT ON THE MISSISSIPPI.

NIGHT was closing in, gloomy and cheerless. A pair of dark, earnest eyes looked up to the starless sky with a wistful yearning in their depths that seemed both to plead and question. But it was a girlish face, over which the black plume of her hat drooped softly; and the slight figure around which she drew her shawl with a shiver, was tall and graceful. Only for the earnest eyes, and the quiet dignity of manner, there would have been little by which an observer might trace indications of an unusual strength of character; yet this tall, pale girl, who stood upon the guards of the steamer that gloomy evening in March of '62, was destined to fill no insignificant position in a land struggling for liberty and peace.

Standing a little distance from her, a young Federal officer seemed to watch the shore with its dark, panoramic beauty, as they passed down the Mississippi. But, oftener, his eyes were bent upon the sweet face upturned so wistfully in the dusky light. He noted the luxuriant sweep of golden brown hair from the white temples; the rounded beauty of the delicate features; the full lip, warm, and firm, and tender. The face was pale now, but a passing change of feeling could bring the warm, bright color into the cheeks, glowing vividly through the transparent skin, like the rich bloom of a ripe peach.

One little hand was ungloved and rested lightly upon the guards, white and soft, and dimpled like a child's. Perhaps this Federal officer had a weakness for pretty hands, for his eyes fell to where it rested more than once, and a pleasant smile crept about his handsome mouth as he made a mental observation with regard to the fact that she wore no ring upon the third finger.

Both had stood there for an hour; both had watched the steeples of St. Louis fade from sight, and listened to the clanging machinery as they steamed onward; but neither had spoken or given a sign. In truth, she was so deeply absorbed in her own thoughts, she was unconscious of his close proximity; and he was too much of a gentleman to force himself upon her notice by any remarks, without an introduction. As she shivered and drew her shawl about her, evidently preparing to retire within her state-room, which opened directly behind her, he was casting about in his thoughts for a means of gratifying the strong desire that had found a place in his heart. He wanted to know her, to hear her speak, and watch her face while talking. Those black eyes, he felt assured, would be glorious in the light of any wakened interest.

As she turned away to enter her room, he heard her sigh—one long, weary sigh, that made him feel strangely sad in remembering it. He unconsciously echoed the quiet plaint of a doubting heart, as he paced slowly down the guards to the gentlemen's cabin, where a number of men were busy with cards.

"Have a game, Captain?" asked one of the gentlemen, looking up as he entered. "Take my place; I am tired."

"No, thank you; I never indulge in such amusements."

He passed on quietly to where the Captain of the boat sat over a paper, with a cigar between his lips, and took a chair beside him.

"We seem to be going on nicely. What time do you expect to make Cairo?"

"Sometime to-morrow night, if no accident occurs to prevent. Anxious to get there?"

"Rather. My men are at Bird's Point, and I have not seen them for some time. When our brave Lyon fell, I was badly wounded, and am only now fit for service again. It has been a sore trial to me to remain idle all this time. But then; 'they also serve who stand and wait.' Perhaps my confinement has not been altogether useless. I have had time for reflection, and I feel that I am a better man now to stand up for my country's weal, than I was before."

Captain Norris looked at him sharply, puffing at his cigar with a zeal worthy a better occupation.

"Strange," he said at length, "how hot young blood is. Not one of you, man or woman, in the bloom of life, who are not willing to give up all for the cause you espouse. I suppose if death should meet you to-morrow, you would not shrink from it, urged on by your present hope of glory."

"Sense of right, sir!" answered the young man, with a glow upon his fine face. "I should not scorn the glory if fairly won in my country's service, however. No man could ask higher honor than to be crowned with the approbation deserved in her defense. But I hope no selfish wish for personal aggrandizement actuates me in the course I am pursuing. Nay, I am sure it does not."

Captain Norris smiled a little doubtfully. He was older and less enthusiastic; but he was a loyal man, if practical and worldly; therefore we will not judge him too harshly.

"Well, well! I hope it will all turn out right—that your good arm may help to save our land, and our dear land may gloriously reward you. Heroes and heroines! Of these there will be many before this war is ended. Cast your eye up the cabin. Do you see a young lady going to the piano? That girl will be a heroine, or I am greatly mistaken. You would not think it, unless you could hear her talk; but let her once speak on the subject, and you forget her baby face, and fancy it is a strong man's spirit speaking through her lips. She is going to give herself to her country in her way—to attend the sick and wounded wherever she can do so properly. I can't say that I approve of women exposing themselves to sickness and danger, and above all to harsh criticism. But if any one is fit for the duty, she is. Young, lovely, fearless; and so truly dignified, no man would dare to approach her, save with profound respect."

"Who is she, and where does she come from?"

"Her name is Harmon, and I think she is from the East. But I really cannot say with certainty that it is so. She is not at all communicative about herself. She came to me for passage down the river, and put herself under my care. I think she intends to stop at Cairo, but she may go from there to Mound City, or elsewhere, if she thinks she may be needed more."

At this moment a sweet, clear voice floated down the cabin. Both gentlemen remained silent, listening, and looking at her where she sat in the distance with a group of little children gathered around her. She sang gaily, piece after piece, amid evident signs of delight; and then, as a finale, came the ever sweet and stirring air from Trovatore: "Ah! I have sighed to rest me." When it was finished, there was a general rousing from a profound silence, for even the card-players had stopped to listen. Captain Norris drew a long, deep breath, and Harry Wilfer rose to his feet, pacing slowly across the cabin with his hands behind him, a habit of his when deeply moved. The fresh, sweet tones of the woman's voice, bearing their involuntary burthen of sadness, had struck down to the depths of his heart. With eyes fixed as wistfully upon her, as hers had lately been upon the starless sky, he finally resumed his seat, watching intently as she played with the children, and dreaming out her future.

"She sings splendidly. Would you like an introduction, Wilfer, and ask her to sing again after tea? Come and I will take you up now."

"Thank you. I wanted to ask it, yet hesitated. Do you think it will be agreeable to her?"

"Doubtless. No fear of her being over-fastidious, as the life she has chosen will throw her unavoidably in contact with officers. But I will first ask her permission, certainly."

The old gentleman made his way through the crowded cabin to the young lady's side, and from his post of observation, Captain Wilfer saw him bend with stately grace over the fair young head. She lifted her face earnestly, seemed to consider the request, then answered him with evident reluctance. With another bow Captain Norris left her, and came back to where the expectant young officer stood anxiously waiting.

"I have her permission to introduce you after supper," he said with a smile. "Until that time, she has promised to amuse the little ones."

Both gentlemen reseated themselves, and Captain Norris resumed his paper.

Following his example, Harry Wilfer leaned back in his chair and divided his time between his paper and the scenes going on in the cabin. There was but one that possessed great interest for him, however, and he was rather suprised himself, at the rapidity with which this interest grew upon him. He could not keep his eyes from the group of children of which the strange girl formed the centre; and as their merry shouts of laughter came ringing down through the cabin, he longed inexpressibly to draw nearer, and hear what was going on among them.

At length unable to resist the temptation, he rose and went outside, passing along the guards to the other end of the boat. Through the side door he entered the apartment occupied by the stewardess, and begged her permission to sit down there with his paper, a privilege she granted under the potent spell of something he slipped into her black hand. Smiling broadly, she wheeled a chair beneath the chandelier over the cabin door, and he took it in quiet satisfaction, seeing that it commanded a full view of the group he had come to watch.

Miss Harmon was seated upon an ottoman, half a dozen little ones upon the carpet at her feet. One small child with golden curls clustering around her beautiful head, nestled lovingly in her arms, her great eyes uplifted to the lady's face watching the motion of her lips as she told a marvelous fairy story, to which many older people listened with scarcely less interest.

Captain Wilfer listened also, almost breathlessly, as she went on in her sweet, low voice, that could change so wondrously with every phase of feeling. It was a fascination to watch her features in their varied expressions, each eager face changing with their changes, as the children gazed up at her, lost in the adventures of her story. Now and then some quaint little bit of humor crept into the narration that had the power to draw shouts of silvery laughter from the rosy, parted lips; and at such moments her eyes would dance gloriously, while the full mouth was drawn down into an amusing gravity of expression that was irresistible.

Perhaps it was the magnetic power of his intense gaze, that drew her attention to Captain Wilfer. He had forgotten himself, and sat with his eyes fixed full upon her face, when she glanced toward him suddenly, and became slightly disconcerted. The next instant she went on steadily, but the wonderful charm was broken, and she closed the story with a rapidity that proved but too surely he was the unlucky marplot to the children's pleasure.

A chorus of childish voices begged her to remain, when she had finished, and "tell them another story." But she drew each little one to her, kissed it softly, murmuring a word in the ear that seemed to reconcile the small petitioners, and then gently withdrew from the circle.

Captain Wilfer sighed with a sense of deep regret, but remained in his seat. To leave it would show too plainly why he had been there, and he did not wish her to understand that the act was a premeditated one. Still making use of his paper, he was entertained by a series of discussions among the ladies on board, all more or less favorable to the young stranger. With her lovely face and manner, it was no wonder if she favorably impressed beholders—and the interest she exhibited in the children around her was sufficient to win a place in each mother's heart. Yet, in spite of all this, curiosity was the strongest element expressed, and he heard, with a half scornful smile, the various conjectures and remarks, that passed freely around, when her presence no longer restrained them.

From what he could learn in this way, he found that no one knew anything about her, save that she designed giving herself up to the service of her country. They had even ventured to ask her questions about herself, but she declined with quiet dignity to answer them, saying in the hearing of several, "that her personal history could be of no possible service to any one, and she was not vain enough to suppose any real interest could attach to her—a perfect stranger. Curiosity she never stooped to gratify."

After this decided rebuff, they were refrained from questioning her faults and contented themselves with surmises.

Evident preparations for a summons to supper, caused the Captain to rise and go back to the gentlemen's cabin. As he passed the door of Miss Harmon's state-room, the sound of a smothered sob came to his ear. He did not dare to linger and listen for a repetition of that painful sound, though the impulse seemed almost irresistible. With quick, irregular strides, he hastened on, a nameless pain at his heart which kindled his cheek, and knitted his brow in spite of his efforts to appear calm. The opportune sounding of the gong for supper, and the confusion which followed, gave him opportunity for composure, and he took his place near the head of the table, by Captain Norris' courtesy, waiting the signal for the gentlemen to be seated.

One chair at the Captain's right hand remained vacant for several minutes after the others were seated, and the young man's eyes sought Miss Harmon's door involuntarily. Would she come out before all these people and take her place to be stared at? While he was debating the question within himself, she glided quietly to the table, pale and calm, as if no passion had stirred her sobs into audible sound five minutes before. Perhaps, after all, he was mistaken. But, looking more closely at the drooping eyes, he detected a slight flush upon the lids which confirmed the fact of her distress, and he was filled with wonder and conjecture—quite as curious as the women at whom he had smiled derisively only a short time before.

"What a combination she must be," he thought, remembering the different phases he had witnessed in the brief space of his own observations. First upon the guards, with that wistful, doubting expression; then at the piano, full of music and mirth, following it by only a change of effort to please in the same vein. Then the quick withdrawal, the sudden anguish, which he felt alone could wring from her sounds of such woeful import. Now the quiet, placid brow and eye and lip, kept under a control that was marvelous! He could not believe that the emotion had passed. It was only held in check, and his regards took a reverential tone, holding her power in the highest honor and respect. To know such a woman, would be happiness beyond any he had ever known. From that hour he resolved never to yield his purpose, until he had won the right to be called her friend, or lost the interest which spurred him on to such a purpose.

CHAPTER II.

BURNING OF A MISSISSIPPI STEAMER.

It was growing late. Across the sky drifted great masses of clouds, black and lowering. Fitful gusts of wind swept across the deck where Captain Wilfer walked heedlessly, his head bent, his hands behind him. Few persons were astir on board, and he should have been asleep; but a haunting spell was upon him. His was a quiet, undemonstrative nature outwardly, but feeling with him was deep and strong. He had gained the wish which a few hours before had thrilled him with anticipated pleasure in the fulfillment, yet he was not satisfied. He had been presented to Miss Harmon; had sat and conversed with her for half an hour. Her beautiful eyes had rested steadily upon his face, and he had been granted the privilege of drawing her out—making her speak of her wishes, feelings, likes and dislikes. All this but deepened the spell so suddenly woven about him; yet in the memory of each recalled word, tone and action, was a sense of pain. Through all, her stately chilling grace had seemed to place an inseparable barrier between them. With seeming frankness, she was yet ice and rock to him. No action of hers escaped the analysis of his absorbing interest. With almost jealous watchfulness, he had noted the difference between her treatment of others and of himself. The warm, bright smile that wreathed her lips when the kind old Captain spoke to her, turned cold as her glance wandered back to his own face. For the one it was sunlight alone; but for the other, sunlight upon glittering frost. The perfection of her manner left him nothing with which to find fault. But she had made him feel that she divined his interest and would repel it. He had not offended her by his evident admiration. Had that been true, her lofty nature would have scorned the mockery of a politeness she might easily have declined to extend to him. Nor was it indifference. That would have rendered her as frank and cordial with him as with others. It was a something not to be defined by words. For reasons of her own, she evidently desired to keep him at a distance—to rear a barrier between them, over which he might not dare to pass. It was not that she feared him as one with evil intent. There is a magnetic influence emanating from the pure mind which makes itself felt irresistibly; and by that nice tact which seems to belong only to refined and intelligent women, she had made him understand that she comprehended no wrong motive in his seeking her acquaintance. There was no gleam of scorn for the lightness of a nature content with the pleasure of an hour—no intuitive shrinking of a pure from an impure nature. Why then did the glance of her eye, the chill of her manner, say: "Between you and me there is a great gulf fixed."

All his nature was stirred from its habitual quiet. He could not rest. For the first time in his life he had met one whose power could enthrall him; and in proportion as she withdrew from him, he seemed to become more deeply involved in the strength of this new-born passion. His judgment told him that it would be well could she check his interest, as was her evident intent. Their duties were before them; their paths would lie apart, and to each was allotted a course that might not be crossed by the other. And yet, it would be a pleasant thing to have the sympathy and counsel of such a woman, through all the coming years of strife. He would have been more than glad to watch her labors—to aid her, perhaps—to feel the influence of her life near him, though he might not share any part or feeling of that life. Of another, he might have accused himself of extravagance in this spontaneous faith which he found flowing out to her—faith in her nobility of character—her strength of purpose—her tenderness of heart. How could he judge of her heart? By the simplest evidence. It had been indisputably proved by her attention to the little children, who were drawn to her as if by magical influence.

During the early part of the evening, the same little golden-haired beauty who had sat upon Miss Harmon's lap while she recounted the fairy story, stole up to her and crept into her arms. With the sweet face pressed against the stranger's bosom, she sat contentedly for ten minutes—then the waxen lids drooped, and she was soon locked in peaceful slumber. Captain Norris was talking to him, and Captain Wilfer was listening silently to what he said, while his eyes wandered to the pretty picture before him as often as politeness would allow. He saw her looking down into the infantine face with such an intense, wistful gaze, it seemed as if the whole soul of the woman was in her eyes. Suddenly she bent her head and pressed a quick, passionate kiss upon the child's parted lips. The little creature stirred, started up with an eager, frightened gaze, when, seeing Miss Harmon's smiling face above her own, she sank back quickly, an expression of satisfaction upon her features. Nestling against her in perfect confidence, with her tiny hands clasped over the lady's slender fingers, she relapsed immediately into slumber.

Captain Norris was still talking, when Miss Harmon raised her head again calmly, and turned her eyes toward the speaker. But Harry Wilfer had seen one shining tear fall upon the baby's curls, and how quickly the head drooped lower, that her face might be out of sight—hiding her emotion with a determined will. Five minutes later, she was conversing with both in steady, even tones, and one wondered, while each was charmed by her sweetness and intelligence.

As Captain Wilfer recalled all this, in his lonely walk upon the deck, it was no wonder if the thoughts this woman drew forth, were intense and calculated to disturb him. Anything mysterious fretted his open, candid nature. Admitting that it was no business of his to pry into the secrets of her life and motives, he was still very desirous to gain the knowledge she sought to conceal. At that moment, he would have thought no sacrifice too great that could purchase the privilege of sitting beside her, and hearing, from her own lips, all about herself—the strange life out of which such a character had been formed.

Suddenly the Captain was aroused from his thoughts by a startling sense of something wrong. A strong smell of fire came from below, and through the darkness he could detect a denser gloom at one side of the vessel, like a huge volume of smoke. At the same time a half-suppressed murmur of voices reached him, which soon rose and swelled into clamorous confusion. The boat was on fire, crowded with hundreds of helpless souls, upon the brink of destruction!

With a bound, Harry sprang up the steps to the pilot house, and asked hurriedly:

"How far are we from the shore?"

"Only a short distance. I cannot run her in further on account of the narrow channel. I will do the best I can, and may God help us!"

The man's voice was deep and hoarse with suppressed excitement. Scarcely able to discern his course, he had striven faithfully to guide the boat along her dangerous way; and now destruction was upon him in a sudden and appalling form. Before Captain Wilfer had reached the lower deck, a broad, lurid glare shot up, revealing to the pilot his position in fearful distinctness. Hoarse cries came from every part of the vessel, mingled with the shrill screams of women and the cries of little children. They nerved him to almost superhuman efforts, and he turned the wheel with a desperation which brought her to, headed directly to the shore. The flames were creeping up the sides and along the stern. He had seen that at the first glance, and sought to bring his vessel round so as to give a better chance for taking off the passengers.

Bells rang sharply, and were responded to with promptitude—but the rapidity with which the fire gained every part of the fated steamer was terrible. Those who had any presence of mind for action, had succeeded in lowering the boats, while the passengers rushed to them frantically. With wild shrieks many had leaped into the river, and were struggling for the shore. With a sick sensation at heart, Captain Wilfer saw some go under, and knew that they would rise no more; but there was no time to lose in watching aimlessly. He had spent no idle moments since discovering the fire, and after he had gained the lower deck to ascertain the position of the fire and calculate the time left for preparations, he turned and hastened above, charging the men to remain at their posts and answer the pilot's signals for the proper management of the steamer.

Through the hurrying, affrighted mass of beings, he made his way back to the ladies' cabin—his thoughts upon Miss Harmon and her safety. She was standing in the middle of the floor; a life-preserver fastened about her waist, and her busy fingers binding others around such of the children as she could gather under her protection. With lips compressed, and face pale as marble, every feature seemed rigid with a fixed purpose. Captain Wilfer caught her eye, and heard her say in quick, sharp, ringing tones:

"Help these women all you can. I have promised my aid to the children, and may save some of them. Do not fear for me; I can swim. Give your help to others."

She had divined his motive even then, and declined to be the object of his care. Glorious in her royal beauty now, she stood as a queen to command, and he obeyed with confidence in her power, not only to help herself but to help others. When the last life-preserver had been disposed of, she grasped two of the smaller children in her arms and cried out to the almost paralyzed mothers to follow her with the remainder. Captain Wilfer anticipated her object and was at her side immediately.

"Let me go before, Miss Harmon; I will take off one at a time. We are close to the shore, and it will take but a few moments."

"Then hasten. The flames are growing upon us fearfully. If we cannot remain, I will seek the water and try to sustain them till you return to help me. Oh, God, aid us to save these helpless children!"

The intensity of her voice thrilled him as he sprang into the water, with a terrified child clinging to his neck. Its wild scream was immediately smothered in the waves, and the mother sprang forward frantically—then fainted upon the deck. Some one went to her assistance and Miss Harmon noted it thankfully. Her hands were full, yet she longed to tender aid to such helplessness. In her own superior strength, she did not forget how others were constituted, and there was no contempt for such in her mind—she could only pity, and try to encourage the timid and fearful ones.

Two or three gentlemen, noting her position, came forward with a ready will to help. They had not been idle; but now all they could do was to leap into the water and bear, each, with them, one of the children which she had in charge. With suspended breath she committed them to the mercy of stronger arms, and watched their course by the lurid glare in agonized suspense. At the same time others were urging the affrighted women to make the attempt to reach the shore by jumping into the river. Placed thus between two destructive elements, it was difficult to act with courage, but they were soon driven to it by the scorching heat of the advancing foe. The flames rapidly enveloped the whole of the steamer's stern, and were leaping to the pilot house. Several barrels of oil stored among the freight had aided in their advance; but the bow of the boat was protected by huge walls of grain piled from floor to ceiling of the lower deck. They did not take fire so easily, and served as a partial screen, at the same time protecting the boilers from immediate contact with the destroyer. In the first discovery of the danger, water had been thrown over it also, which served somewhat to retard the flames. But now they were drawing nigh, and the brave girl shuddered to feel the hot blasts upon her cheeks, while two little ones yet clung to her dress.

"Here, jump into the boat, my good friends," cried Captain Norris as the men rowed alongside again, after leaving its last load in safety. He stood up panting and drenched, with a face as pale as ashes. Nobly had he acted his part, and Astria Harmon could but do him honor even then, in her heart, when peril was most imminent. He handed them down in safety, while the wind tossed his gray hair from his white temples. With an exclamation of joy, she saw that the last one was rescued, and she only with one child now remained. The others had been taken into the boat by the mothers, until there was no room for more. This one was the golden-haired pet of the evening, who clung to her so eagerly that she resolved to lose her own life ere she would abandon the helpless, confiding child. Mrs. Oliver, the mother, had been borne away in one of the boats with her other two children, and when she hesitated in anguish, lest Lily should be lost the brave girl bade her go, and trust her child to her care.

"I will save her or lose my own life," she said, and the poor woman went, believing she would do as she promised.

"I am afraid we cannot wait for the boat, Miss Harmon," said Captain Norris at her side, as the smoke and heat began to suffocate her. "Take to the river, and I will help you all I can. My strength is almost gone, but we can keep up till assistance can reach us. You are not afraid?"

"No; I am ready. Go you first, and I will follow. If anything should break my hold on the child, be prepared to catch her."

The next moment he rose after his leap into the river, and looked around for Miss Harmon. She had followed him closely, with one fervent, audible prayer for help, and came up near him, bearing her struggling burthen along with one arm, while she swam with the other. They were close to the steamer, but they did not see the violent rocking of the whole mass, which tossed the stream into a miniature ocean. Loud cries of horror came from the shore, and there was a chorus of shouts which they could not distinguish in the roaring sound that filled the air. Captain Norris had gained her side and gave her the aid of one hand to bear up her burthen. She swam away bravely, and he kept up, exhausted as he was, for some yards. Then hearing his laboring breath, she spoke:

"Tread water awhile—it will rest you. Surely they will meet us soon."

"I hope—"

He did not finish the sentence. One great booming sound broke apparently over their heads, and a shower of flying pieces of the ruins descended upon them. A fragment struck the old gentleman upon the head, and with a low cry he sank from sight.

"Oh my father, he is killed," she gasped, still struggling upon the lashing waves. She felt the tiny fingers of the child clasped with incredible force around her wrist, and gave thought to her, hoping against the fate that threatened both with death, when a stunning blow upon the back of her own head deprived her of motion. She knew that she was losing consciousness—that the child was sinking with her, gasping and struggling for the frail life she had so hardly striven to save; but she was powerless to move, and they went down, down into utter darkness. Then all was blank.

BURNING OF THE STEAMER MEDORA.

CHAPTER III.

AFTER THE DISASTER.

HARRY WILFER succeeded in reaching the shore in safety with his charge, and placed her in the care of those whom the boat had just brought from the burning steamer. Turning at once with the intention to return for another, he saw Miss Harmon standing upon the deck, a group of women about her, several children clinging to her dress, and one pressed within the shelter of her arms. She was looking for him, the safety of others uppermost in her mind, and he responded to the mute, yet powerful call, with a swift bound which brought him to the water's edge. His foot struck against some object, wrenching it with a violence which drew from him a sharp cry of pain, and deathly faintness followed. When he struggled to rise in desperation, he grew dizzy and blind, falling unconsciously against the bank of the stream.

No one heeded him in the intense excitement, and when he recovered the deck was deserted—not a soul remained on board. But the red glare illumined the scene with appalling, yet grand distinctness, and he saw a boat nearing the shore, freighted with a number of passengers. Two figures near the vessel attracted his attention, struggling outward from the place of danger. And while his eyes rested upon them, a hoarse roar, and mighty trembling sound, seemed to shake the very air around him. The cries of those nearest to where he lay, confirmed but too surely the terrible fear that he felt. In one moment the boilers would explode, and those struggling creatures must perish!

"It is Captain Norris and that brave girl who has done so much for our women," said a man's voice in the crowd. "Oh, is there no way to help them?"

"God pity them—none!" was the response, and in the same instant his despairing cry was followed by the explosion which sent the soul of one noble being to eternity, and spread destruction on all sides, hurling the fragments over the river and upon shore. Then a man's figure was seen to float away and sink, but the woman struggled on with her burthen, and Harry Wilfer made one wild, desperate leap into the water. The frenzy of his excitement bore him up, and he swam vigorously till within a few yards of her, when a floating object struck her head violently, and she sank, drawing the child with her beneath the waves.

They rose again within reach of his hand, and he grasped her desperately. Almost at the same instant the smallest boat shot alongside of him, and strong hands lifted them into it—the girl with the child clasped tightly in her arms. When they had reached the land and laid them down upon the barren soil—so cold and bleak on that fearful night—one was pale and limp, the last spark of life flown from the tiny frame. The other was white and rigid—with teeth firmly set as in a mighty struggle with the destroyer.

Willing hands were stretched forth and sought to bring them back to life, but the bereaved mother gave one wild, hopeless cry, as the body of her child was placed in her arms, and fell forward upon the ground, sobbing frantically. The scene was one to remain fixed in the memory of a beholder through a life-time. Some had been killed and many wounded by the fragments which were hurled upon the shore, and now there were wails for the dead, and cries of suffering from the living, that would have melted the most stoical heart.

"Oh, God, where art thou?—or art thou pitiless thus to strike thy helpless creatures from life!" moaned Mrs. Oliver in her anguish.

"Nay, are you not afraid of this questioning?" asked another who bent over her in the effort to comfort her.

"How can I help it? This was my pet—*his* idol—my youngest born. He is sick unto death, and I was taking his children to him for a last good-bye. Now he will never, never see her—his darling Lily? Oh, my child, my child! How can I tell him that she is dead."

"If he is so near to death, he will see her soon in a better world," murmured the gentle voice, and then there was only a smothered sound of sobs under the mother's bowed face.

Captain Wilfer turned back from this scene to where Miss Harmon lay, attended by a physician and several ladies, who were giving her what assistance was in their power, his heart beating violently when he heard the excited exclamation:

"See! her fingers have relaxed and she is moving! She lives! Oh, it is such a pity she could not have saved the child—she risked so much for it!"

He could not help it—shattered with the shocks of that fearful hour, and the pain of his sprained ankle. With feelings strung to such fearful intensity, these words had a mighty effect upon him, and with one irrepressible sob, he laid his head upon the ground and wept.

As the flames of the burning vessel abated and the light began to grow dim, it was proposed to build a fire on shore, and a dozen men were busy instantly, bringing such material as they could find, while others went off in a boat to get firebrands to light it from what was left of the fated MEDORA. It was no easy matter to light the damp, sodden mass which had been thrown together; but at last a flame kindled and grew slowly, until a broad, friendly gleam rewarded the labor, and groups clustered around it gratefully—women and children still sobbing. Then they waited for the morning, watching for the signal lights of some steamer which could relieve them in their doleful condition.

The doctor, who had been busy with Miss Harmon, had her placed near the fire and left her in the care of others, while he went to Captain Wilfer in answer to a suggestion made by some one who noted his pain. In a few moments he had stripped the stocking from the swollen member, and set the dislocated joint skillfully.

"You are in bad luck, Captain," he said regretfully. "I am afraid it will be some time before you are able to take command of those men at Bird's Point. This foot will have to be nursed well for a month, at least."

The young man groaned.

"Too bad, too bad! but others have fared much worse. I will try to be patient."

"That is right. It is sometimes braver to be still than to act. Your time will not be wasted, I hope. Something will come to you that may make you glad of having received this check to your active career. At any rate, since it has happened, it is well to believe it."

"Yes. I have been in a good school, and from experience learned how much better it is to submit to our fate than to struggle against it, especially when it meets us in such shapes. It is not easy to bring ourselves to it always; but if we watch the course of subsequent events, we are pretty sure to see in the end what has been gained by it."

"You are learning philosophy at the proper time, young man. Live up to what you preach, and your head will whiten with old age, not with care and worse than useless fretting."

"Call it faith rather than philosophy," answered the Captain, slowly. "I do not claim the latter, but the former I strive to retain, simple and pure. As far as I can see my way, I will walk fearlessly, doing the best I can. When a blow falls upon me in the darkness and I cannot see the source, I must wait for the dawning light to reveal it. The night may be long and wearisome, but the morning will come at last."

Doctor Hart looked at the young, earnest face, as the red light gleamed upon it, and wished there were more of the same kind in the world. So simple and candid, and yet so manly was the sufferer in every way, the world-worn, weary observer of the faults, foibles, and evils of human nature, felt an involuntary and strong sentiment of respect spring up within him, and it gave a hearty ring to his voice when he said, a few moments later:

"There, that is the best I can do now. I wish it could be better, but no man can work without the means. I hope that it may be in my power yet, if a boat comes to rescue us from our disagreeable and unhappy plight. If we go down the river, I shall be able to attend you at Cairo for a while. Now I must leave you and go to others. Some time during the night I will come back. I want to know you better."

"Thank you! I shall esteem it an honor. You are not altogether a stranger to me, Doctor. I have seen and heard of you in St. Louis. Will you add another to the favor just done me, sir?"

"With pleasure."

"Let me know the extent of the injuries under which the lady you have just left is suffering."

"The only injury is upon the head, and is not at all serious. She was stunned and the over exertion—the intense excitement of the night, with the shock, were too much for her nerves. In a short time she will rally, for she has a good constitution. Interested there?" he added with a quizzical smile.

"Very much," replied Captain Wilfer in a simple, serious way which checked further questions. The Doctor said no more, but grasped his hand in a friendly pressure and then left him to perform like offices of kindness for others.

That was a miserable night upon the bank of the Mississippi where through the long hours the sound of sobs and cries never ceased. A few were mute and patient; many full of complaints and fretting; but the magnitude of real woe in their midst, made it a night of unutterable horror to all. Sitting with his back against a fallen tree where he could command a full view of the various groups about the fire, Captain Wilfer fixed a scene upon his memory that could fade away only with life. Such of the gentlemen as had been fortunate enough to escape with their coats had given them up to make beds for the wounded. With one of these and a life-preserver for a pillow, Miss Harmon lay a short distance from him, her large black eyes staring vacantly into the fire, her face very pale and quiet. She was yet too weak to rise, though the ground was drenched with the late rain, and the night was cold. His heart ached to see so many helplessly stretched upon the wet earth, and to feel that nothing more could be done for their relief. A few yards from where she lay, sat Mrs. Oliver with her two children sleeping upon her knees. They had shivered and wept until the warm rays of the fire soothed them, and with their poor little faces buried in her lap, had forgotten their troubles. The mother was very still, her head bowed down upon her breast for a long time. Once she raised her face and looked toward the spot where the dead had been placed to await removal, and a spasm of anguish swept over it heart-rending to behold. Then the face was buried in the trembling hands, and sobs shook the poor woman's frame from head to foot. Miss Harmon heard the smothered sound and looked at her compassionately a moment. At first she did not seem to recognize her; but suddenly a thought flashed through her mind, and she raised herself partially in her eagerness. Seeing who it was, she fell back with her hands over her face, large tears slowly trickling through her fingers.

"Oh, my Father, couldst thou not have spared me this last!" she breathed so lowly that he could just catch the words; and Harry Wilfer's eyes grew moist, as they had many times before that night. He knew how hard it was for the woman who had risked her life to save another, to witness the hopeless anguish of the mother for her lost one, and could understand the emotion which she did not seek or think to conceal. In every woman's nature there is a tender chord of sympathy that may be touched by the suffering of man or beast; but nothing so deeply moves the soul of compassion within her as the tears of a mother for her sick or her dead. And perhaps this woman, on whose face his eyes rested so earnestly in his mental questionings, had some dear memory which strengthened the native sentiment of loving pity toward her kind—the memory of some cherished pet sister or friend which had been recalled by baby Lily's blue eyes and bright hair. This may have drawn her more closely to that especial child, giving her strength to battle with death for the precious life sheltered within her arms—for the sake of something lost out of her own existence.

With all these speculations running through his mind, he had little thought how nearly he pressed upon the truth—or by how strong a memory she had been moved to act. He could sit there while the fire flickered, and the night waned, watching her face with the wet lashes lying upon the white cheeks: but he could not see the struggle that was going on in her heart—how she was striving against the bitterness of a rebellious impulse. No shadow of a mental query was upon her face, which darkened her soul as she lay thinking in silence of her failure.

"Is a blight to fall upon everything that I touch? Shall I never be able to do good to any one without bringing greater evils upon their heads than they have ever known? What is my sin that I should be thus hardly punished? Where shall I turn—what shall I do? Oh, my God, if I could dare to ask a boon of thee when thy hand has been laid so heavily upon me, I would beseech thee to show me thy purposes. I am blind and cannot see. In my nature thou hast made me strong and impatient. If I have no help from thee, I shall rebel against the evils that oppress me. Why stoop in anger to so frail a thing as I—thy helpless creature? Or, if thou canst bend to me in wrath, why not show me the cause for my punishment. See, oh see, how impatient I grow, and cannot help it. Have pity, oh my Father, have pity."

Did that mute, yet almost passionate prayer find its way up through the starless night to One who seemed so far away to many who sat cheerless and heart-sick under the weight of a mighty blow? Doubtless, even though no visible or tangible response lifted the shadows from the oppressed soul.

All over our beloved land were scenes—not only like unto this, but worse. While she moaned and cried in bitterness of spirit, Captain Wilfer thought of the dead and the dying from battle-fields already drenched with human blood—and of the desolated hearts and homes that would no more glow at the sound of returning footsteps. The measure of a nation's woe was broad and deep—but not yet was it filled. The sacrifice was only begun. Ten thousand—nay, thrice ten thousand lives would not purchase the return of that peace which had so suddenly taken its flight. He could look to the end with hope, but his was not a mind so easily lulled to rest as to give credulity to the glowing predictions which had so often been repeated around him. One of the few who realized the purpose, passion and resources of the South, he saw in prospect a long and fearful conflict, for which he had striven to fortify himself by faith, prayer and steady action. And in this type of noble manhood, we have painted but an outline of ten thousand glorious dead, whose names to-day stand not upon the roll of fame—whose deeds are known only to the hearts that loved them best, and hold them most sacred in remembrance.

Just as day was breaking over the dreary landscape, a steamer turned a point in the river and came into full view. One great, joyful shout of welcome went up, and tears fell afresh from eyes that had done little else than weep all night. Signals were answered, and the steamer slowly came to shore a hundred yards below the charred wreck of the Medora, where the water was deep enough to land her. Ready hands extended aid to all, and the wounded were soon removed to more comfortable quarters. The dead were reverently placed upon the lower deck and covered over for removal to a proper resting-place, while the living went sadly, almost silently on board, after their first burst of joy. In less than half an hour from the time the vessel landed, she was, with her added passengers, steaming down the river toward Cairo. Accidents such as have just been recorded never fail to create an excitement; and at this time, when the country was rife with growing discord, everything startled us into extravagance of action. The passengers vied with each other in their attentions to the unfortunate beings thrown thus upon their mercy, and while busy tongues kept up an unceasing chatter, trunks were depleted to supply them with proper apparel. Purses were made up for a number of those who had been left destitute, and kindnesses showered upon them all in every shape.

Miss Harmon was among the number destined to become the recipient of charitable favors, though she shrank sensitively from the many questions with which she was overwhelmed. The story of her bravery spread throughout the boat, and for the time being she was a heroine for whom no one could do too much.

"All this attention oppresses you, I am afraid," said an earnest-faced woman beside her as she bent over the sofa where Miss Harmon reclined wearily. "Shall I relieve you?"

"O, if you can, I shall be so thankful!"

"Then, if you can walk, come with me into my state-room. There is a wide berth there, and you may lie down in peace while I keep watch over you."

"You are very kind. How shall I thank you? Perhaps the others may think me ungrateful, but I hope you will not. No words can express my obligation."

"That is understood. What can be expected of you but to rest? This is your right, and I will try to secure it to you. Rise and let me support you."

This conversation had been carried on in an undertone, while a crowd clustered around them; but no objections were made if any understood their import. Grateful for the ability to escape, Miss Harmon rose and suffered herself to be led away to the stranger's room, where her weary head pressed the pillow with a sense of inexpressible relief. Her new friend was quietly attentive, bathing her face and smoothing her hair with a soft, soothing touch—which, while soft, was full of character in its steadiness and confidence. There were no wavering, fluttering motions, so painful to a nerve-shattered person. Every step, tone, look and touch betrayed a clear head, unwavering purpose and sympathetic nature. When she had made her charge comfortable, she retired and closed the door upon her, leaving her to the luxury of a coveted hour alone with her own thoughts.

Mrs. Noble was a bride—had been married quietly in church one morning early, stepped into the carriage with her newly wedded husband, and started for the field where his command awaited him. He was an officer, holding the rank of Major in a western regiment, and had been home on a brief leave of absence after the fall of Donelson. While there, he had been married to his betrothed of a few months, and was now taking her with him to Paducah, where he intended to leave her while he went to Pittsburg Landing. As she emerged from her state-room, Major Noble met her with a smile.

"At the good work already, little wife?"

"I could not help doing this. The poor thing looked so wan and distressed, it went to my heart to see her. You know every room is crowded, and there was no hope of getting a place for her for some time, if at all. I could not enjoy keeping mine when one who had acted so nobly as she did last night, was in need of rest and quiet. Did you hear how she tried to save somebody's little girl, and how many more she did succeed in saving by her calmness and bravery? O, it was grand!"

"Yes, I have just had the whole story from Doctor Hart, whom I know. There seems to be a peculiar interest about her that excites much attention. No one knows anything about her—where she comes from, who she is, or what her circumstances may be. Did she accept the purse made up for her?"

"No. She took the dress and shawl proffered to her by some of the ladies gratefully, but refused the money positively, saying she had need of but little, and that she thought she could readily supply her needs at Cairo. For awhile the people so urged and worried her, I could scarcely bear it. At length I determined that I would not, and took her to our room."

"Right; and you can find out who she is."

"Ah, you are curious. I thought men were free from that most ridiculed of all weaknesses in woman."

"There is something better than curiosity, little wife, and that is sincere interest. If her aims be what I have been led to believe, we may be a great help to her. But for your sake, I prefer to know something about the persons we may be led to befriend."

"Certainly, that is but right. I will not question her, however, George. If she chooses to tell me, it is well. If not, we must accept her silence or let her go. I never could pry into people's secrets."

"No dear, but you may win confidence by your own true womanliness, which must meet a response where there is a like character to deal with. I leave you to your own judgment, and shall be satisfied with the result."

He drew her arm through his own, and passed out upon the guards, after first having closed the door to secure their guest from officious attention. Muffling her more closely in her shawl to protect her from a keen north wind, they paced up and down the guards outside, where they could watch the shore as they swept onward toward their destination.

And while they walked, a woman came out and sat down upon a stool not far from them. She was broken down with grief, and wept piteously, bowing her head upon her hands as they rested upon the railing of the guards.

"That is the poor woman whose child was drowned in the young lady's arms. Oh, how my heart aches for her! What can I do to give her any comfort?"

"Let her alone now. A good cry will help her more than attentions which would only worry her. No doubt she came here to escape all those eyes that were watching her in her distress. While she gave her children their breakfast, I observed that she could with difficulty restrain her emotion. Then some lady took charge of them and they fell asleep upon a sofa. For awhile she can be free. Give her the benefit of this freedom."

With a delicacy that proved true kindliness and sincerity of nature, they turned away and seemed not to observe the stricken woman, though her sobs smote very painfully upon Mrs. Noble's ear. It was not in her nature to witness distress without an effort to relieve it. After a little time the sound of a room door opening behind them caused both to look round, and they saw Miss Harmon emerge from their stateroom and walk straight up to Mrs. Oliver. The next moment she had fallen upon her knees at her side, and with her arms thrown around her person, laid her head upon her shoulder.

"Oh, believe me," she said brokenly, "I tried my best! I promised you to save little Lily, but God chose to frustrate my designs. If I could give my life to bring back that sweet child to you, I would do it. My heart will break to think how I failed when I strove so hard to save her for you. *How* can I comfort you?"

There was no response save the clasping of one fair hand in her rough palm, and a sound of deeper sobs. Tears rolled rapidly over Miss Harmon's face and fell upon her dress, but there were now no audible sounds of the agony she could not repress. To the eyes that witnessed the scene, the tears, the white face, the broken words, and the attitude had spoken enough, and they could not bear it.

"She will do harm to both," Major Noble said in a low tone. "Go, dear, and take her back to bed. Such scenes are not calculated to make a man very stoical," in testimony of which assertion, he brushed the tears from his cheeks which had gathered there.

Mrs. Noble obeyed him and went to her charge, over whom she bent persuasively for several minutes before she could induce her to go back to her room. Finally she allowed herself to be taken away, and once more laid down, with her face turned to the pillow. Mrs. Noble left her alone then, and went to Mrs. Oliver, by whom she drew a chair, and sitting down, took her hand in her own quiet way, and soothed her into a partial resignation.

CHAPTER IV.

SURMISES AND QUESTIONINGS NOBLY MET.

"Miss Harmon, you have not thanked me for saving your life."

"I do not thank you."

"Why?"

"Because I cannot feel glad that you kept me from a sleep that would be more desirable than you can know. You look astonished, but since you force me to speak, I must be candid. If you had remained silent, I should have left you to your own thoughts, and allowed you to think me heartlessly ungrateful. Now you will be shocked and more curious than ever. I cannot help it."

"Do not try. I was too strongly tempted to make you talk, to preserve the delicacy which I usually hold dear. For an hour I have watched you as you sat in that large chair, silent and thoughtful. You did not seem conscious of my presence; yet I felt that you knew I was here upon this sofa and suffering. You are not without feeling, as I have had many proofs in the last twelve hours; and I knew from Doctor Hart that you asked who saved your life in that dreadful moment when the fragment of the exploded boat struck you. So I thought as I lay here watching you, that you were not glad, both by your face and by your silence; and I wondered at it, for you are young, strong and full of purposes that may be worked out grandly. I resolved to make you tell me why you do not thank me, even at the risk of appearing impertinent. If you say anything it will be in candor, I am assured. Will you tell me now?"

"You have a right to ask this much, since you *have* saved my life, and I will tell you," she answered gravely. "I am alone. The friends who are not dead, are worse than dead to me. They are rebels, and I am a wanderer from home, almost penniless, and with scarcely a hope for the future. It requires more courage to live than to die under some circumstances. My life is an instance of this. I have been strong enough to maintain it—even to form plans for the future by which I may make it endurable. If there are times when my weak, womanly nature shrinks back from the path marked out, and my heart longs for a sympathy it cannot know, the fault rests not wholly with me. I think I know myself. To-morrow I shall regret that I spoke to you in this way. My duty is before me, and I know I can discharge it, in spite of the difficulties which may—nay, will surround me. To be idle, would drive me mad. I am selfish in wishing to give myself no time for anguish. Yet I do hope to do good, and to carry out a principle of right, maintained thus far, through untold trouble. Do not attach too much importance to my bitterness. By to-morrow I shall have conquered it, and will be full of ambition and of will. It is but a passing weakness."

"I believe it. Did anybody ever tell you that you are a strange woman?"

An expression half haughty, half painful, swept over her pale face.

"Yes. It has been the bane of my life to feel and be told that I am unlike others. I do not wish it, or court this singularity. Aware that I have been created differently, I must meet my fate, and act myself. There is no help for it."

"You think me rude for asking you such a question?"

"Rather. I allow you to take some liberties because I can give you nothing else in return for your kind intentions. Personal questions are not pleasant to me, however."

"So I perceive. But if I were not rude and unusually forward in my address you would not heed me. Being odd yourself, you must be approached by odd ways. I could not feel satisfied to have you leave me without a word or look—so I forced both from you."

"It had been kinder to let me alone—both to yourself and me."

"You are mistaken. It will do both good. I get some information that I want, and give you a knowledge of others, who are as selfish as you. Think less of yourself, and you will be less unhappy."

"I have not to learn that lesson."

"Then you are worse than I thought. There is an excuse for the ignorant in the sins of omission. What can you say in extenuation of yourself?"

"That, however good the will may be, the ability is not always equal to its behests. It is an easy thing to talk; it is not always easy to act, if the action must go against inclination. Where heart and brain each claim, as it were, an individuality it is like the man and wife who each pulled the end of the rope their own way, and gained nothing in consequence. Brain says go; heart says stay; and if we go for the brain, the heart will ache or break. The rule works as hardly the other way."

"There must be some remedy for so perplexing an evil. What is yours?"

"The head must win the heart, or the heart must win the head. They must work together. Sometimes the winning is harder work than that which follows."

"Most true. You are learning that life is not a mere farce, as some people choose to call it, but a season for earnest thought and action, where we must suffer much if we gain much. It may even prove that the gain is never perceived until the freshness of existence has passed away. Do you realize fully all the difficulties with which you will have to contend in the path you have chosen? Are you strong enough to meet and conquer them?"

"With God's help I hope to be," she replied earnestly. "Yes, I fully comprehend the magnitude of my undertaking. A very few, if any, will understand me. I shall be subjected to curiosity—impertinence perhaps, at times. The sight of suffering and death must become familiar to me. I must do my duty without hesitation, where a clear head and stout heart will be indispensable. My path will lie not only through thorny, but noisome places. To society I must be steel—to my country warm, tender and faithful. I am not romantic or fanciful. What I choose is from a sense of duty—not an enthusiastic hope of making a heroine of myself. There are no claims upon me, and none to care where I go, or what I do. Being thus thrown upon myself, I choose to give what strength I may possess to the best purposes within reach. Out of this life I hope to gain comfort. If I have deeper and still more selfish motives than I have placed upon the surface for your sight, it does not matter. They are my own and sacred. Does your foot pain you?"

This sudden question was caused by an instant corrugation of the forehead indicative of pain, which she detected as she glanced at his face to note the effect of her words.

"An occasional twinge, but no severe pain. It was a thought which disturbed me. Do you intend to remain at Cairo long?"

"It depends upon circumstances. As the army moves further south, I shall hope to keep pace with it and prove useful."

"You will not camp out?"

"Certainly not. I shall not be so near as you imagine to our troops; if at times I should be, it will be in a very quiet, retired way—at some farm-house or village. Do not think I intend to familiarize the army with my person, like the angels of mercy in sensation novels. If I familiarize myself with the wants of the army it will be a far different thing."

"In the meantime how do you propose to support yourself? Pardon me if I seem rude; but you have lost everything by last night's accident, and must have means to live. I understood that you had declined the purse made up for you."

"Yes. I hope I am not yet an object for charity, however. If in a strait, surely I may claim what I need from the Government, since my wants will be moderate. But I have a means of taking care of myself. Why you choose to ply me with questions is best known to yourself. I have said before that they are not pleasant. You will admit that I have been amiable in answering them so far; but if you please, I prefer now to be excused from answering any more. Shall I get another cup of tea for you, Captain Wilfer?"

"No, thank you. I have offended when I did not mean it. Let me crave your pardon and set myself aright in your eyes. Believe me, it is not mere curiosity, but deep interest, which prompts me to ask such questions as I have put to you to-night. And let me add in all kindness, that you will find many more as much interested and less fearful to offend than I am. Your course is a noble one, and commands my deep respect. I shall look upon it, if permitted, with earnest hope for your preservation and success. But one of your greatest trials will arise from the interest that you will create wherever you go. No man will be able to look upon your face, or hear you speak, and pass you indifferently. What I say may offend now, but you may remember it at some time with a different feeling. I desire mainly to prepare you for whatever may come. You will have need to be forever watchful."

She looked startled, and for a moment half irresolute. The idea had at once been seized which he intended to convey, and it confused her. But after a little thought the cloud lifted, and her face wore again its habitually calm, collected expression.

"I understand and thank you, but have no fears. I shall not sleep upon my post in an enemy's country. We are approaching Cairo. Are you able to walk out and see it as we land?"

Major Noble, coming up at the moment, offered his arm, and the young man rose reluctantly. Mrs. Noble took Miss Harmon's arm and followed the gentlemen out upon the guards. It was easy to see that Captain Wilfer regretted the interruption to a conversation he had forced upon her; but Miss Harmon felt glad to escape from it, and hailed the gleaming lights of dismal Cairo with more of joy than is usually felt in approaching it. He had not spoken to her all day, though he lay upon a sofa close to where she sat in a large chair for two hours. When tea was served, she quietly rose and brought his cup and plate to the sofa, insisting that he should not move; and it was then he had opened the conversation which has been recorded, while she sat thoughtfully beside him, holding his plate of toast.

"A sad, yet beautiful sight," remarked Mrs. Noble in a hushed and tender tone. "I wonder how many hearts yearn to-night toward the spot where those camp-fires glimmer, and the forms pass to and fro like the fire-worshipers before the shrine. See the light slanting in bars across the waters, as the glare of their funeral piles fell upon Omen's sea! Many a brave soul would to-night cry out, if death came, as did Hafed in his enthusiasm, 'Now, Freedom's God, I come to thee!' happy to die in defence of a cause so noble as the battling for freedom."

Miss Harmon said nothing, but the light in her eyes, which spread over her earnest face, spoke more eloquently than words. Here was beginning the reality of a new phase of life for her. As she recognized it, she grew more and more silent and thoughtful. Each looked upon camp and river and leaden sky overhead. The little steam-tugs hissing and sputtering as they darted back and forth from point to point, seemed things of life, swelling proudly beyond their natural dimensions with the importance of the duties that were entrusted to them. Subdued as she was, Miss Harmon could not help smiling when Major Noble remarked upon them as reminding him of small people who make a great noise over little things. The fancy had struck her in the same way. Yet when he turned to her a moment later, she answered his look by a defence:

"Small things are often of very great importance. We are apt to think 'fussy people' of very little consequence, and the character enables them to pass unnoticed where greater people would not dare to venture, thus giving them opportunities which others might not embrace with any degree of safety. I dare say these same little steam-tugs are by no means unimportant parts of our present national machinery."

"You are right. They dash about from place to place rapidly, and carry dispatches of great importance. Is it your habit to put in a plea for everything which appears to be depreciated?"

"There is nothing so small or useless as not to serve some good purpose. At least, I can take courage from believing so."

"Neither man or woman need ever seek for courage from such things," spoke Captain Wilfer, gravely. "The beings formed in God's own image, endowed with a portion of his divinity, stand in his sight, large to do well. He creates us great in ourselves, because we are a part of himself; and he gives us the power to grow in greatness to the end of our days. The strongest stimulant we need, is to stop and think what we are—then set forward with a will to accomplish some purpose. Living so, how can we look upon ourselves as 'little things.'"

"Surely," said Mrs. Noble, "we cannot arrogate to ourselves this 'greatness' if we realize his full power over us. What are we in his hands? Helpless things, utterly tossed by circumstances as a thistle-down is blown before the wind. In his sight, if we try to be Christians, we are as nothing."

"Pardon me, madam, but I think you mistake your Creator, and do him great injustice in such thoughts. You will acknowledge that every life has its earnest, all-important purposes. These purposes are not small, and *require* no small strength, ability and courage to accomplish them. He would never create insignificant creatures to do his mighty works, and I hold that as his instruments, we are great; and, being great, largely responsible. The Christian who realizes this, will think well of himself for the sake of what has been to him entrusted."

"I never took such a view of it, yet I must say I like your idea, novel as it is. Yours is the best plea I have ever heard for self-esteem. What do you think of it Miss Harmon?"

"That the man who feels thus, has more than the outline

of a grand and glorious life foreshadowed," she answered in a low, yet clear and positive tone. Both gentlemen looked at her with deepening interest; and one was inspired to a sort of enthusiasm for noble deeds, though his lips uttered nothing.

A short time passed in silence, and Major Noble proposed that they should go on shore. Captain Wilfer was removed first, but before the officers who came for him, conveyed him away, he had a moment's time to speak with Miss Harmon.

"I know nothing of your plans, or where you intend to go from here. I think you said you did not yourself know. May I ask one favor before we part to-night? It is to keep me advised of your whereabouts, and if ever you need a friend's assistance, to call upon me as you would upon a brother. In this I have no wish save to serve you as a woman whose purposes I honor. The memory of your face, and your character as I understand it, will be to me a refreshing power. I shall be a better man for what you have made me see and feel. Never forget how much you hold in your hands, for *your* power is greater than you know. My address is on this card. If by any chance I should fail to see you again at this place, pray let me hear from you?"

"I will promise nothing, Captain Wilfer. It is not right that I should. If our paths should ever cross in the future, I shall be glad to see you—glad to aid you if you need my aid. But I must never go beyond my duty, and trust that you will remember me with no more than a passing thought. Shall I say good-bye, now?"

She held out her hand, and he took it respectfully. Had he followed his impulse, he would have raised it to his lips, but he dared not thus express the deep emotion which he could with difficulty control.

"It is useless to say that I regret your denial, since I could only make the request from a strong desire to have it granted," he said slowly. "And to say that I can remember you only with a passing thought, would not be true. It is impossible. I am more interested in you and your future than I dare to express; but I must accept your decision. May you be successful and happy. Should we ever meet again, I shall pray that the shadow may be lifted from the fair, sweet face of one who has known sorrow but too early. God bless you, and good-bye."

Miss Harmon bowed in so stately a manner as to appear cold, and he sighed in turning away, chilled to the heart. Had he looked back in passing down the cabin, he might have seen a different expression in her face—an expression of mingled gratitude, pity, and regret.

Cairo is not a pleasant place at any time, and our friends found it almost intolerable, when, after walking through the deep mud upon the levee, for some distance, they arrived in a most miserable plight at the St. Charles Hotel. No mode of conveyance was provided for strangers; and as it was quite dark, they were forced to make their way as best they could, by the light of a borrowed lantern. Then, after having reached the point for which they aimed, and climbed the broad stairway to the parlor floor, they found that every room was engaged, and no hope of any kind of accommodations in the house. The reception room and parlors looked utterly cheerless and dimly lighted; but half warmed, with soiled carpets and tattered furniture, the prospect was anything save inviting. Mrs. Noble laughed cheerily, however, and put her little feet upon the stove hearth with a merry declaration of independence. Her husband looked grave and annoyed, and with a woman's ready tact she sought to dispel it, while Miss Harmon gently drew Mrs. Oliver to one of the two sofas in the room and made her lie down.

"Rest," she said kindly, "and I will try to take care of your children until a room is vacated; then you shall have a better resting place."

Mrs. Oliver's eyes filled as she looked up into the face of her benefactress. Some thought had swept suddenly through her mind of which she repented, and she spoke deprecatingly, as if she had given utterance to it in words.

"Never think I blamed you. All that a body could do, you

have done for me, and I do n't want you to think me ungrateful. Do n't let me hurt your feelings. I could not help the thought, as you said it, as how you 'd failed before. Thank you kindly for your offer, and I 'll try to get some sleep, for I 'm a'most heart-broke. Oh, Lordy, I wonder what folks have to suffer so much for?"

She turned her face toward the back of the sofa, and was silent, leaving her little ones to the care of Miss Harmon without another word. Astrea sighed bitterly, and with pale, compressed lips, bent to gather the children closely to her upon either side, as she sat upon a low chair near the sofa. They had been hastily clad in various garments, the gifts of strangers to the unfortunate, and with the events of the last night still brooding over them, looked forlorn and desolate enough. Major Noble went out to make some inquiries at the office, and his wife dropped her assumed gayety instantly.

"Come here, little boy—what is your name?—and sit upon this chair beside me. I will take your head in my lap, and you may go to sleep. The lady will take care of your sister, but both of you will wear her out. Will you come?"

"Do I tire you," he asked simply, looking up in Astrea's face.

"No, my dear, you do not."

"Then let me stay with you. I like you the best. You tell such pretty stories. Tell me one now, won't you?"

Mrs. Oliver stirred uneasily upon the sofa, as if the child's request had recalled too keenly the scene of the night previous; but when Miss Harmon hesitated painfully, fearing to cause distress, she said in a quiet tone:

"Never mind me, lady, if it 's not asking too much of you. The poor little things hain't much to comfort them."

So she sat holding the two little curly heads upon her knees, and repeated a long, marvelous fairy story, which served to interest not only her small audience, but to divert her own mind from painful thoughts. By the time she had finished, a servant came in to inquire if a Miss Harmon was there?

"I am Miss Harmon," she said. "What do you wish?"

"Only to say that a gentleman has kindly vacated his room, and places it at your service, as he expects to leave soon, and a few hours will not make much difference. It is ready, and I will show you to it, if you please."

"Thank the gentleman in my name, and say that I accept it gratefully, for a bereaved woman and her little children. Come, Mrs. Oliver, and I will go with you and assist in putting the bairns to bed."

She made no remonstrance, and in a few moments they were in a small room upon the parlor floor, where stood a wide bed, a wash-stand, and a chair. Miss Harmon took the little girl and undressed her, tucking her under the covering with the kindness of a mother. When the three lay calmly upon the couch with a grateful sense of rest, Astrea knelt at their side and offered up a simple, earnest prayer. Then she went back to Mrs. Noble and they talked together for an hour before the Major came in.

"At last I have obtained a resting place for you," he said in evident relief, laying his hand fondly on his wife's shoulder. "You will take Miss Harmon with you and I will sleep here on the sofa or the floor until morning, which is not far off. Nay, never look so deprecatingly at me, Miss Harmon. This is only a very small part of what we must endure for our country's sake. There will be many nights when we shall have no other covering than the sky—no other pillow than the damp earth. My little wife expects this for me, and she is now having the initiatory lessons in a soldier's life."

Mrs. Noble looked up into the pleasant, manly face of her husband with a proud smile, then, without any show of hesitation, turned her lips to the hand resting upon her shoulder.

"I shall have the comfort, come what may," she said quietly, "of knowing that I never stood between my husband and his duty."

They rose, and preceded by the Major retired to a room some one else had vacated for the accommodation of the ladies. Evidently it had been known that Miss Harmon had given the room provided for her comfort to one more in need, and the possessor of the one now placed at their disposal, was for "the ladies"—which the Major was only too glad to accept.

After seeing them safely inside the door, the gentleman bade them good night and went to his sofa in the forlorn parlor. In less than half an hour all had fallen into peaceful slumber.

"You will go with us to Paducah," Mrs. Noble said to Miss Harmon at breakfast the next morning.

"When do you leave?"

"This afternoon there will be a boat, and then we expect to go up the Ohio. From what I can learn, we are sadly needed there—two or three hospitals and not a single Union woman to attend to the wants of the sufferers. The inhabitants are terribly rebellious. I want you very much, for the Major will have to go straight to Pittsburg Landing, and I shall be entirely alone. It is not brave to dread it, I know, but I do dread the first few days exceedingly."

"I cannot go with you; I will come as soon as possible. My first duty is to Mrs. Oliver. Her husband is at Mound City, and dying. She is striving to get his children to him for a last good-bye; I must assist her all in my power. Poor creature! I have just been in to see if she had a palatable breakfast, Major, and her face is the saddest proof of misery I have ever looked upon—so wan and hopeless."

"You do right to stay by her in her trouble," he said earnestly. "I will procure for you a military pass, and when you have done all you can for her come to my wife. At all times, as a servant of my country, you must command me in any way that I can serve you. Promise that you will not hesitate."

"I will not, indeed, and thank you most gratefully."

Soon after the above conversation Mrs. Oliver with her little ones, accompanied by Astrea Harmon, set out for Mound City on a small boat which ran between that place and Cairo. And on the following morning soon after daylight, Mrs. Noble found herself occupying a rather dreary-looking room in the St. Francis Hotel at Paducah.

CHAPTER V.

LIFE AND DEATH IN A MILITARY HOSPITAL.

THE sun came forth and was shining brightly when the two women arrived at Mound City and walked up to a small hospital to inquire for William Oliver. A boy not above seventeen or eighteen years of age sat upon the steps with a blanket drawn closely around him, seeming to enjoy the warmth and brightness of the spring day. To Miss Harmon's question, he answered readily.

"Don't know, Miss, but the steward can tell ye in a minit. That's him just gone inter the hospital—that feller with the red head."

Astrea looked, and saw a large, rough looking man passing along a row of berths, visible through the open door. Mrs. Oliver stood pale and trembling at the entrance, while Miss Harmon followed and accosted the steward.

"William Oliver?—No. 40. I'm afraid he's dead, Miss. When I saw him an hour ago, he seemed to be a breathin' his last. Come this way an' I'll see."

She went with him through a little side door, and saw in a small room four or five berths, on which lay men in the last agonies of death. The steward pointed to one with the No. 40 on the foot of the berth, and turned abruptly away.

The occupant was not dead, but lay with closed eyes, breathing faintly. She laid her hand upon his forehead, and called in a low voice:

"Mr. Oliver, are you asleep?"

He stirred, then opened his large, brown eyes with a wondering gaze.

"What is it? Has Lizzie come?"

"Do you mean your wife?"

"Yes. Did she bring the children?"

"She has come, and the two eldest are with her. Shall I bring her to you now?"

"O, yes. Why did she not come at first?"

"I wanted to see if you were asleep. Now be calm, and she will come in one minute. You know it will not do for you to get excited, don't you?"

"O, I won't; tell her to come quick."

Astrea went out, and approached the woman with a smile. The strained, agonized expression passed from Mrs. Oliver's face when she saw it.

"He is here, and awake, waiting anxiously to see you. Come darlings, and see papa."

Leading them all to the door, she gently put the wife forward first, holding back the children, to give their mother time to greet the man she had come to see die. With a bitter cry she sprang forward and fell upon her knees beside him, covering his white face and thin hands with kisses. Her sobs mingled with the moans of the sufferers around them, and amid it all, the faint, broken voice of the husband was almost lost. Astrea caught a few words, and tears rained over her cheeks silently.

"I thought you'd never come, Lizzie. Where's the baby? Didn't you fetch her along?"

A prolonged cry answered this query, but before Mrs. Oliver could speak, Astrea stepped forward and presented the children, who still clung to her hand.

"See, here are two of your bairns. They have come such a long way to see their poor sick papa, and now they want him to speak to them."

"My boy," murmured the man, his eyes lighting proudly. "This is my little man, and he's going to be a soldier. Here's chickey, too, who always sings for papa. Kiss me, dearies."

The boy went up to his father and gravely kissed his lips; but the little girl shrank timidly back. Astrea lifted her up and held her over the berth. As the soft, shy lips touched the sick man's mouth, two large tears stole down his thin cheeks.

"She don't know me," he said huskily; "I've been gone such a long time. Wife, where's Lily?"

"Oh, William, don't! I couldn't bring her, I couldn't! I did try, but God wouldn't let me. Don't ask me about Lily."

"*You* tell me," he said, looking at Miss Harmon wistfully. "Tell me if anything has happened to her. I can bear it."

"We left her at Cairo. One night after dark we got there, and when we went to the hotel, some kind friends took little Lily while she slept, and cared for her. The next morning we went to a quiet little graveyard, and put Lily to rest—safe from all troubles in this wearying world."

Over the sick man's face swept such a radiant light, Astrea looked down at him in wonder.

"I shall not be alone, when I get there," he murmured. "She will meet me—my pet birdie; I dreaded to go all by myself, but now I shall have her. Poor Lizzie! You were afraid to tell me. Don't cry. I am sorry for you, but you'll have two and I'll have one. After awhile you'll all come to us."

"Oh, don't leave me! you won't die, you won't die, William! I can't give you up—oh I can't, I can't!"

The sick man struggled visibly for calmness, but Astrea saw the grey hue spreading fast over his face—precursor of that death which was inevitable. In alarm she strove to quiet the frantic wife by urging upon her the necessity for calmness, but in vain. Mrs. Oliver sobbed and wrung her hands, utterly overcome with grief, and the children awed and frightened by the scene, wept piteously with her, while the husband and father lay breathing out his life. The shock of excitement had been too great, and consciousness soon deserted him. Out of this state he never woke again; but just as the sun set, his spirit passed away, and his widow and orphans were left helpless, thrown upon the charity of the world.

Miss Harmon found a shelter for her charges that night under the roof of one of the citizens of the place. For the dead was prepared a private soldier's coffin, and the day succeeding, they bore him back to Cairo to a grave beside his child. Then Astrea placed Mrs. Oliver and her children on board a steamer bound for St. Louis. The Captain promised to give them the kindest attention, and she turned to say good-bye with a heavy heart, reluctant to leave one so helpless, to the mercies of a heartless world.

"When you get home, send a letter to me at Paducah, Kentucky," she said while holding Mrs. Oliver's hand. "I have put my address upon this piece of paper, and, if I am not there, will send for your letter. As soon as I am able to do it I will send you the remains of your husband and child, that you may have the poor comfort, at least, of weeping over their graves. I can do no more for you now, save to pray that God will guard you safely home. Good-bye."

"Good-bye, dear angel," sobbed Mrs. Oliver, sinking upon her knees and holding one little hand in both her own. "I can't thank you—I don't know how, for words ain't strong enough. But He'll bless you a thousand fold."

With an impulse of deep pity, while her tears fell fast, Astrea stooped and kissed the woman's forehead, raised her tenderly, and turned away to press a parting kiss upon the lips of the little ones who clung to her sorrowfully. As soon as she could break away from them, Astrea left the children, and without looking back, ran down the stairs, across the plank and up the levee toward the St. Charles. From the parlor window, a short time after, she saw the boat leave the wharf, and steam up the river toward St. Louis.

The remainder of the day was passed drearily, waiting for a boat to take her to Paducah. But it was night before a vessel came, and then it was only a government boat, stripped of every convenience, and devoted to the transportation of troops and stores.

"Surely you will not venture on that," said the clerk who

came at her request, to advise her of it. "The trip would be very unpleasant."

"I shall have worse things to bear, doubtless, before this war ends. Yes, I will go on that. Will you send some one with me on board?"

"Certainly, I will go myself; but I should think it better to wait. Captain—"

"What were you going to say?"

"Only that Captain Wilfer charged me particularly to see you comfortable, and I think he would scarcely approve of this, if he knew it."

"He has nothing to do with me or my movements, I choose to go, and it does not at all matter what he thinks or how he feels about it."

She raised her face haughtily, and turned to the door. Her heart was not the strong, ungrateful thing that she made it appear to this man, who was looking at her in curious surprise; but she hoped he would give an account of both her words and manner, and that it would serve to check an interest which was but too apparent.

The Ohio River was full of floating ice, which had been loosed and broken up by the rains and warm sunshine of the few days previous. Perched upon a hard berth in a comfortless state-room, Miss Harmon lay all night and listened to the heavy dashing of the ice against the boat, and the jests, laughter, and songs, of the soldiers in the cabin. They were gay and light-hearted in the face of all discomforts, and amused themselves with cards till nearly dawn, little dreaming that a fair young woman was lying within sound of their voices, who would gladly have exchanged places with any one of them, in the hope that a friendly ball might hurl her with one swift stroke from a life that was almost too oppressing to be borne.

At daylight she was out, watching for the first glimpse of Paducah, but it was more than an hour ere a turn in the river brought her in sight of it. In the morning beams, as the smoke curled up towards the clear sky and the quiet of early day brooded over it, it seemed scarcely possible to believe that it had lately been the scene of the wildest excitement, when the Federal troops took possession of the place. One of the fairest and most prosperous of southern towns its position was an important one, almost immediately at the mouth of the Tennessee River, and rendering access from it, easy, to several important points. Its citizens were bitterly ultra in their southern proclivities, and she did not anticipate a pleasant sojourn there; but she saw before her a field of labor to which her steps had been directed as most needing her; and forgetting self as far as she could, the advance was made bravely. It was almost a defiant feeling with which she first set her foot upon the main street and looked up at the windows of the St. Francis Hotel, where she must remain a while. She remembered as she walked up to the ladies' entrance, a time when she had gone across its threshold under far different circumstances; but she dared not think of that now! Choking down the sob which rose in her throat, she lightly mounted the stairs, passed down the hall to the parlor, and ringing the bell, asked for Mrs. Noble. That lady had just risen, and sent for her at once to come to her room. The servant led her back the length of the same hall she had just traversed, and paused before a door at the farthest end. Astrea looked at the number, and pressed her hand over her heart with a spasm of pain.

"The same—the same," she murmured under her breath, "Oh, fate, into what strange paths art thou leading me!"

In response to the servant's tap upon the door, it was immediately thrown open, and Mrs. Noble's arms clasped her warmly.

"O, I am so glad you have come! You cannot think how much you are needed. I have not had one moment's time to worry since the Major left me. My hands are full, and I have half cried my eyes out in seeing the misery there were none to relieve. To our poor boys, your face will be welcome as an angel of mercy. I was just getting ready to run up to the hospital when you sent for me."

Mrs. Noble ran on breathlessly while leading Miss Harmon to a seat, and assisting to remove her wrappings. She did not notice how Astrea's eyes wandered round the room, scanning various articles of familiar furniture, now soiled and faded. She could not know how a mental inventory was taking place, and the lonely woman was saying within herself, "there is the chair he sat in,—the same sofa he lounged upon. Before that window we stood together and looked out upon the shining river. Alas! what changes have come since then!"

Aloud, she said in calm enquiry:

"How many hospitals have you found here?"

"Three. They are the churches of various denominations which our Government has deemed it expedient to use, as we can find no better buildings at present. From this window you can see the Presbyterian Church hospital, only a little more than a square distant. The others are farther away. There being three, if no other lady comes to help us, we shall have to take one, each, and give a day to the other alternately. While there is enough to keep any three women busy in either one of these hospitals, there are extreme cases in all that must have proper and prompt attention."

"You propose to board here?"

"Yes, and you will remain with me, won't you? The Major said that he should feel so much easier about me if you were here and would room with me. If you will only stay, I will try and make it as pleasant as I can for you."

Miss Harmon smiled. She knew it was only a delicate way of providing a temporary home for herself, but she did not hesitate to accept the kindness thus offered. It was pleasant to think that she was not forced to wander forth in search of an abiding place. To have lived alone long in a large hotel, even had she been able to afford the expense, would have been out of the question. Sharing with another lightened her responsibility, and at the same time furnished her with a sweet companion. Already she had began to grow fond of Mrs. Noble, in her simple earnestness and warm enthusiasm. The sad accident which had spread such a gloom over the lives of many unfortunate beings, had drawn together two women, young, fair, sincere and energetic. Each recognized in the other tenderness, purity and power, and at once felt that influence which was destined to ripen into a friendship earnest and lasting.

"You have not promised that you will remain with me," remarked Mrs. Noble, as she went on with the completion of her toilette.

"I will promise, if that is what you wish. It will be delightful to be permitted to share your home for the time being. Only I must have one condition attached to my acceptance. Whenever I become troublesome, in your way, or disagreeable, turn me out without hesitation. I will not allow myself to discommode you in any way whatever, if I know it."

"Very well; I accept the condition. You will want to bathe your face and brush your hair; then I presume you would not object to breakfast."

"Not very obstinately. To tell the truth, I feel rather faint with need of it. Having had nothing since noon yesterday, I have just commenced to realize that people must attend to physical demands if they hope to feel either well or cheerful."

Putting aside her hat and gloves, she let fall about her the long, heavy waves of golden brown hair which almost enveloped her person. Mrs. Noble cried out in delighted admiration, and gathered the soft masses in her slender fingers caressingly.

"O, how beautiful. I passionately love fine hair. It always seems to me the lovliest feature man or woman can possess. With no other charm than this, you would be lovely in my eyes. But it so happens that you are more generously endowed, and I have lost my heart completely, as I do with all beautiful things, animate or inanimate. Do not smile that way, or I shall feel as if you pitied me for my weakness."

"Nay, the love of the beautiful which has been given us, is rather a virtue than a weakness. Through it we are led to all good and noble things. It is beauty of principle and character which wins honor and esteem; and the beauty which pleases the eye, not only makes us happier, but naturally causes us to trace beauty to its original source. I love it, too, and I am grateful that God has endowed me with the powers of appreciation which I possess."

"Are you not grateful that he has endowed you with beauty's self? You cannot but know that you are beautiful."

"Once I was grateful, for it made me happy. Now it does not give me pleasure, and I cannot be thankful. On the contrary, it makes me feel uneasy and fearful. I must guard every word, tone and look, as never a prisoner of state was guarded, lest I do or say something that will leave me a prey to self-reproaches and regret. Beauty of person is sometimes a curse. Were I as plain as many whom I envy, I could pass quietly and unnoticed wheresoever it pleased me. As it is, I cannot."

"You are not vain, at least," answered Mrs. Noble, in admiration of Miss Harmon's simple candor. "And your principles will save you from the consequences of a beautiful face. You have the strength to carry out your own will, and if you once get in the way of considering things in the light you expressed but now, I do not see what you have to fear. Yet why should you guard yourself. Perhaps this sweet face, aided by your own true womanliness, may win for you one worthy, even, of your heart. It is not impossible nor improbable."

Astrea Harmon faced her suddenly, her features set, almost rigid with the strain of self-control.

"If you could know what you are saying, I am sure you would never again repeat what has escaped you. It can never be, Mrs. Noble. I cannot win, or be won. Let this pass now and forever. Perhaps at some other time you may know, but not at present. Now our duties are before us; let us perform them, and leave the past to bury itself. It has not been a happy past for me, and I would flee from it. It may be that it has robbed my future of all promise or hope; but if so, I will try to bear it to the end, patiently."

Then silence fell between the two, and neither spoke again until Astrea announced herself ready for breakfast.

Very few people were in the dining-room when they entered. A few moments after they were seated, a lady came in with two children, and languidly took a place at one of the tables but a short distance from our friends. All her movements were slow and deliberate, conveying at once the impression of a very indolent, but very obstinate nature. Turning her blue eyes upon the quiet little party, around which the colored waiters gathered with alacrity to take orders, she stared them in the face scornfully, curling her pretty lip in utter defiance of common politeness.

"Do you know that lady?" asked Astrea, quietly, while her dark eyes shone with a dangerously angry light beneath the lashes purposely drooped over them.

"No *lady*, I should say, to judge by appearances. I believe she is the wife of the proprietor. She is the heroine of a very pretty little romance—is quite celebrated for her independence of action! Just before the Federalists drove the Confederates from this place, Beauregard was riding through the streets, when she rushed out, seized his hand, and drawing him down as far as she could, threw her arms about his neck, and gave him her blessing in the shape of a kiss! I cannot say how her young husband liked this proof of admiration for another in the main street; but I suppose he imagined it merely an exhibition of feeling produced by intense patriotism, and so forgave it."

Astrea laughed, a low, sweet laugh.

"Let her do her worst now. At first I was disposed to feel insulted and angry at the stare she inflicted upon us. But I should feel ashamed to resent anything from one who can so far forget what belongs to true, modest womanhood."

"She has behaved very rudely to me since I have been here. Yesterday as I happened to pass her in the hall, she gathered aside her skirts and swept by me with the scorn of an insulted queen. I did not mind it, however. Since we have possession of the place, and the power all in our own hands we can afford to be magnanimous."

The words were scarcely uttered, ere something whizzed

by Mrs. Noble's ear and struck the wall behind her. One glance showed the person of whom they had been speaking, standing face to face with them, her lovely features marred with intense passion. A fork quivering in the wall, explained the expression she had chosen to give her wrath. For one moment she gave vent to a perfect torrent of vehement abuse, then drew her children from the room. The servants seemed amused at the scene, but dared not say a word. The anger of their mistress seemed to afford them infinite delight since they understood its cause.

"Fortunately she did not strike you," said Miss Harmon with a deep breath of relief, "what a termagant she must be! I tremble to think of the injury she might have inflicted."

Mrs. Noble only laughed.

"I am afraid I deserved it, for I spoke loud enough for her to hear me, purposely. It was neither right or generous to retaliate upon her in such a manner. All my life, I have made it a rule never to retaliate, till now, and this shall be a lesson to me."

"I am strongly tempted to report her. A woman who would do as she has just done, would hesitate at no step which would inflict an injury on us or our cause. We are not safe under the same roof. Of course I am not afraid of her, but such a course as this carried out openly, is intolerable."

"Let her alone; she will not dare to do anything more rash right here in the face of our power. She is not so far disgusted with life as to wish to part with it. A little storm like this, is nothing to be wondered at occasionally. Southern blood is hot, and when forced to boil in silence for a time, it is its nature to run over sometimes. I dare say she will be all the better after this, for the little thunder-gust with which she has honored us."

"It is to be hoped she may; and if not, she may shortly find herself in a less agreeable position than the one she now occupies."

It is probable this last implied threat was repeated to her, for when the ladies encountered her near the door in going out an hour later, though she did not seem to notice them, her manner was quiet and lady-like.

"'Thus conscience doth make cowards of us all,'" laughed Mrs. Noble as they turned up the street to the hospital. "Her ladyship has taken the alarm. Do you know I think yon ought to have been a man, Miss Harmon? You would have made such a splendid commander. One glance of those black eyes—one tone of that determined voice, would be enough to bend an army to your will."

"Nonsense. Do not begin thus early to shake my confidence in you by exaggeration and fulsome flattery. I warn you that I am as you but a little while ago declared—free from vanity; and you may find me over nice in my criticisms. Sometimes I am betrayed by my impulses into being very severe."

"O, well, *be* severe; I shall not mind it. You are only a woman, and no larger than I am. As you have the right to speak, so have I, and it is as well to express as to think what I have just said," returned Mrs. Noble, lightly.

"But you do not think that. You have exaggerated largely. Besides I am not sure but I shall quarrel with you in regard to the expression of our thoughts. We think and feel many things that it would not only be unwise, and unkind, but sheer folly and madness to express."

"There! I own myself vanquished at the first onset. It *would* be madness, and I do not want you to believe it my habit. Usually I am quite discreet. Verily I do believe that it is your coming which has put me into such good spirits. I feel like taking everything gaily, lightly. Pardon me if I seem too light under the circumstances."

Miss Harmon looked into the dancing brown eyes—at the full mouth, wreathed in smiles, and her own face relaxed, a lovely light dawning upon it. Involuntarily she slipped her arm through Mrs. Noble's, and drew it close to her side. Whatever her faults might be, it was easy to see that her nature was as her name—noble.

CHAPTER VI.

HOSPITAL LIFE AT PADUCAH.

TIME passed away rapidly, and the labors of the two ladies were earnest and untiring. And it was during those memorable weeks at Paducah, the character of our heroine passed through the furnace of hard, practical tests, and came out pure gold. She shrank from nothing, and never ceased in her efforts to bring relief. The more delicate sharer of her labors, would watch her in wonder, as she went from berth to berth, cheerful, smiling and ever ready to humor the whims of the most capricious of her charges. No complaints ever escaped her lips, though too often the pale face and dark eye testified to the utter weariness of the overtaxed frame.

In the kitchen she had defied the German cook who had crowned himself king with his immense paper cap, and reigned right regally in the face of his black scowling brows and broken mutterings. No fear of spoiling her delicate fingers withheld her from making toast, or preparing a cup of tea for the longing invalid who waited and watched her coming with child-like impatience. And when it was done, she would sit down upon the berth and taking the weak, helpless head of the soldier upon her arm, convey the refreshment to his lips as a mother would feed her child. Nearly every eye watched for her coming in the early morning; and faces that could smile, always smiled her a welcome. When she left the hospital at noon and night, regrets, coupled with blessings, followed her. People unaccustomed to such duties, can have no conception of what this woman endured. The long days when she took no rest, nor even allowed herself to wander a step from her chosen path. Out of chaos she had brought order; and through that order, preserved the lives which were the sole lights of many homes. Her daily routine was so systematic, that she was enabled to do much good. First on coming in the morning she bathed the faces and brushed the hair of those who were unable to help themselves; saw that they had their breakfast and administered their medicines. After that, of warm, sunny days, the floors must be washed nicely, and the windows set open to keep the air pure; the berths must be changed and the patients kept neat. It was one of her theories that no sick person could recover without pure, fresh air and surroundings, and she persisted in her course in spite of the remonstrances of the steward, who looked upon her as one deranged. As for the physician in attendance, he did not care, and let her have her own way without molestation. Between them there was natural antagonism. His indifference to the welfare of the men under his charge, had roused her indignation to an expressive point, and she had taken him to task with a severity which he called presumption, but which was no more than simple justice. No man has a right to trifle with human life, and least of all, that life on which he depends for his own freedom and protection. While her heart yearned over the soldiers who had left fair homes and loving friends for the battlefield, sickness, danger and death, he looked on them carelessly, treating them as little better than animals which may be used for the advantage of man, without regard to the feelings which the poor brute has no power of expressing. He could hear moans of pain and cries for help without a show of sympathy. He could look upon the agonies of death without a tear; and when he went his regular rounds to prescribe for his patients, the sight of an empty berth served only to add a smirk of satisfaction to his homely features, which said plainly as words could convey "One less to be bothered with."

"I thank God from my heart, that all men are not like you,"

she said to him one day in her indignation. A cold and unfeeling remark to a man suffering with inflammatory rheumatism, had fallen upon her ear, and she could not refrain from resenting it.

"Why, fair lady?" he asked with a half-sneering smile.

"If they were, I should lose my faith both in God and man. You have the heart of a stone and the manners of a heathen! I am sorry to be betrayed into any unlady-like vehemence, but your conduct deserves it. Here are more than a hundred men, helpless in your hands, and with no friends to aid them if I do not. I protest against your cruel neglect and indifference. It is my intention if you continue in this way, to report you and have another surgeon appointed in your place. I owe it to these poor men whom I consider nothing less than your victims."

"You had better let me alone, or you may get into trouble," he answered rudely. "I have let you alone because I saw that your presence was beneficial; but as soon as you interfere with me, I am free to confess that I will not tolerate it. Attend to your own business, and we shall get along without trouble."

"No, Doctor Grey, we shall never get along without trouble while I can find reason for such charges as I intend to repeat. I do not mind the pitiful meanness of the course you have taken in claiming the credit of all well doing here, and boasting of the order, cheerfulness and improvement of your hospital and patients. That is more of a personal affair, and for myself I claim nothing but the consciousness of duty well done. But I do object to the indifference you manifest in not seeing that your orders are carried out. You order a certain diet for a patient, and never know if he has had it—whether it could be procured; and if not, its place supplied with something else that will not injure him. I have been culpably remiss in my common duty to humanity, in leaving unsaid so long, what I am saying now, because I disliked to come in actual contact with you. Yet if another could see what I have seen, I think they would sustain me in my present action. Go look at the tea which has come to your store-house for daily use; you will find it literally baked to the box—black and mouldy. See the meat—one living mass!—and the coarse brown sugar that is to be stirred into that tea with iron spoons. A palatable dish, truly, for a man worn to the verge of the grave by fever, and who requires the best of nursing and the most delicate, nutritious food to win him back to life. When I first came here the provision made was even worse than now, for the bread was coarse, brown loaves, toasted at morning into a black, bitter crisp. Fried bacon, and corn bread, made with water and a little salt, half-baked and disgusting, to vary the diet! I could not feed a dog on such food without a sting of conscience that would forever cure me of the cruelty. Yet you let it go on from day to day, and with all my most strenuous efforts, I cannot remedy the evil alone."

"What can I do? If the Quartermaster's department furnishes no better rations, we cannot draw them. Your complaint is needless, I think."

"No; if Government furnishes nothing better, you can refuse to draw it, and draw the equivalent in money instead. With that money, if you cared for the lives of these men, you could buy palatable food in the country—fowls, butter, milk and eggs. These luxuries never come into the building except in small quantities—not half enough for the most reduced, yet they might easily be procured."

"You had better procure them, then."

"I will, if you will draw the money and place it at my disposal."

"How am I to know that you would use it for the purpose you claim?"

"I am not at all surprised at your question since you must judge the principles of others by your own. Yet if you are fearful, I am not unwilling to account for the use of the funds you place in my hands. The purchaser can take receipts for everything he buys, and thus show the use which has been made of it. All I wish, or care for, is to see the men properly provided with not only delicacies, but the necessaries of life."

"I cannot believe the need is so extreme as you represent."

"That doubt confirms my charge of unpardonable carelessness. If you had given the matter any attention, you would have known that it is even worse than I have stated. Come and look at just what has been brought here to-day. It is a sample of the provisions for the last two weeks—nay, even longer for it was so before I came. Men have actually starved to death right under your hands, and you never heeded it."

"That is a strong assertion."

"True, nevertheless. If you do not give a man food that he can eat, he will of course die in the course of time. Disease may make his death more rapid, and you will say he died of that disease. But I know better now, and I will not longer see this go on without an effort to change the tide of destruction."

"As you will, I will see what can be done at the Quartermaster's. Don't make any more fuss about it. I hate fussy women."

Miss Harmon's lip curled; she felt humiliated to have been forced to stoop to a passage at arms with a man so coarse and heartless. But she had excited his fears, and her only hope had lain in that. With a cowardly dread of dismissal from the service, seeing the power she had over him, he concluded it to be the best policy to yield, though it galled him to have a woman command his actions in any degree. Her charges had not been made without a confidence in her ability to prove them, and in proving them she could effect his ruin. Doctor Grey felt, as he strode through the deserted streets to his boarding-house, that he had been outwitted, and the knowledge did not at all serve to sweeten his temper.

The effort was made and succeeded. The money was drawn and sent to her; but whenever her name was mentioned by officers or citizens, in terms of admiration, a shrug of the shoulder, an expression of the face, or a subtle insinuation did its work of revenge by exciting curiosity, suspicion and distrust. From this time forth, no step was unwatched—no action on which comments were not made, and construed as best suited the evil-minded ones, ever ready to crush and trample innocence under foot. When, far into the night, her lamp burned steadily, there were those who saw and reported it, making it a matter for speculation and gossip. Sometimes when she walked upon the street, on her way to and from the hospitals, she was obliged to notice that people whom she had known and spoken to, purposely avoided her. But while she wondered, this did not trouble her. "To the pure all things are pure," and she had no idea of the evil a wicked man was working out for her.

Mrs. Noble shared this ostracism in a measure, and being entirely unable to divine the cause, was worried and fretted by it, but she finally set it down as the work of their fiery little hostess, and gave it no further thought.

"Whether it be true or not, I will think so," she said. "Who else would try to injure us? If she can wield this influence, however, among our own people, their good opinion is scarcely worth having. We will do that which we know to be right, and—'*Honi soit qui mal y pense.*'"

So ended the subject for a time. At the close of the third week of their residence in Paducah, Major Noble came down the Tennessee River on furlough, to pay them a visit. One was delighted and happy, the other pleased and glad to see him.

The same day of his arrival, after a long chat with the ladies, he went out and remained for an hour. When he returned, he looked puzzled and disturbed.

"What is it, George?"

The quick eyes of the wife at once detected that he was troubled.

"I scarcely know. Where is Miss Harmon?"

"In her own room, I suppose. She will occupy the one next to ours while you stay."

"Do you think her entirely honest, dear? I mean in all her dealings. You look shocked at the question, but let me explain. By her own confession, she lost everything she possessed by the boat accident; and for her transportation here, you are aware that I gave her a pass. Yet I find that she has regularly paid her bills in the hotel, and appears to have plenty of money. By a mere accident I learned that funds had been placed in her hands for the use of the men at the hospital, and I feel deeply troubled about it. How can you explain the matter?"

"I fear I cannot explain it, George, but never doubt her. She is as true as steel, and an angel in goodness," cried the little woman warmly. "If you need proofs, look here. In this drawer is a purse where she keeps all the money that is sent to her, and here are copies of the receipts of all her expenditures. I have seen everything, and know that her course is honest and irreproachable. O, you do not know how good she is. Many a time, when I am too weary to sit up, she sits here writing letters and copying receipts, far into the night, after a hard day of toil. I cannot comprehend how she endures it, but she does, and it has become such a custom now, I cannot sleep unless I see her first at her little table with all her writing paraphernalia before her. Then I forget everything while she works on. It shames me to remember it, but indeed I could never do half she does and live, though I work just as earnestly and as willingly."

"You leave me more than ever puzzled. Can you tell me what she writes?"

"Letters, of course, as I said before. Sometimes she will bring home a dozen to answer, and when she goes out in the morning, she fills her little bag with them and herself drops them into the post-office. May it not be possible that she has friends who supply her wants? She receives a number of letters from the North. It pains me to find you growing suspicious under the very first thing which you cannot understand. Be more charitable; it is so unlike you to be otherwise. For all the world I would not have her know that you have asked me such questions. She is honor's self-embodiment."

"God grant that you may be right. I do not willingly distrust any one, least of all a lonely woman, among strangers and without protection. She is such a strange, strong, beautiful creature, one cannot help observing her closely, and indulging in much of speculation. That woman has had a history, or I am greatly mistaken; and if we could know it, it would be better for all, perhaps. I confess that my interest has been deepened by Captain Wilfer's growing passion. Since his regiment arrived at Pittsburg Landing a week ago, he has fairly haunted me, and has been constantly asking questions about you. I knew he only wanted to know what Miss Harmon was doing, and I humored the poor fellow by reporting everything you wrote to me concerning her. His heart is gone fifty fathoms deep in love."

"What a pity!"

"Why, pray? Is there anything so very bad in a young, unmarried gentleman falling in love with a young, unfettered lady?"

"No, but she said something to me the day she came that I must remember. I hinted at her eventual union with some brave man, and she said quite impressibly, that she could neither win or be won. From her manner, I gathered that some tie binds her—something in her past life would render it dishonorable in her to accept attentions from gentlemen with a view to marriage. More than this, I do not know."

"Do you think it best that I should give Wilfer the benefit of your surmises?"

"Perhaps it would be wiser; it may save her from annoyance, and both from pain."

Here the conversation ended, for the object of their discussion tapped upon the door for admittance. She came to ask of the Major some information with regard to military tactics, and they urged her to remain and sing for them. She did not refuse, but readily took up Mrs. Noble's companion, the guitar, and began to play. Major Noble regarded her attentively, as she sat before him, with her pure face slightly uplifted, and her dark eyes fixed upon the wall. There was a change in her person. The slight form had grown slighter, and the red no longer played under the transparent skin of her cheek. An habitual paleness made brow and cheek and neck white as alabaster. Dark circles were under the eyes, and the mouth looked sadly weary.

"She is killing herself," he said in silent comment. "There is lack of rest, and mental disquiet shadowed upon her face. We must try to change all this."

"You are threatened with a battle at Pittsburg Landing, are you not?" she asked when she had finished a song and laid the instrument aside.

"Yes; it may be soon—it may not be for weeks; but I am persuaded that we shall have a battle, and a hard one."

"How I should like to be a man, and to take a part in it!" she said, her eye kindling.

"I told you, you ought to be one," laughed Mrs. Noble, "but got a lecture for my pains. Are you not already doing your part? Why long for more?"

"Because I long for the excitement of a more active life."

"I should think you are having enough of that, to judge by your wasted face and figure. My dear girl, you are trying to do too much."

Astrea shook her head.

"No, Major Noble; it would be harder work to remain idle. I want to be busy, that I may forget, sometimes, to long for what I cannot hope to attain. Perhaps the time may come when it will be different."

"Is there anything in which I can help you. I am at your command at all times."

"Thank you, but not yet. Perhaps, some day, but not now. Time is not ripe for action. I appreciate your kindness, and when the hour comes in which you can serve me, I will come to you gladly. Until then, let me go on in my present path."

"Without questioning, I suppose?" he remarked, smilingly. He would not show her how eagerly he longed to make her speak more of herself.

"Yes, if you can be so kind. It may be cowardly, but I confess to a shrinking from the pain questions would cause me, and I need all my strength."

In a moment she looked into his face with a searching glance, and added:

"I know I have not the slightest claim upon your confidence without a return of that sentiment; yet I would fain beg you to have faith in me, Major Noble. Let my actions regulate your treatment of me, and if I prove worthy of distrust, then distrust me. On the other hand, if I prove worthy of your confidence and esteem, give them to me as generously as you can. I have not much to comfort me in this world."

The lady's lips trembled, and her hearers were touched inexpressibly by her sad appeal for sympathy. It was not like her to bend toward others and sue for a sentiment that might not be given spontaneously. Mrs. Noble better appreciated the humility of the haughty spirit, and assigned the cause to the affection which she had herself inspired in Miss Harmon's breast. The latter was so grateful for the love and confidence her new friend had bestowed upon her, she could not bear to feel that the husband lacked in the feeling, though, with a woman's penetration, she had at once divined his discontent.

"Will you allow me to ask you just one question and not think me rude?" he asked after a moment's hesitation. "It pertains wholly to affairs here."

"Certainly."

"How is it that I find your board bill settled? I intended to pay it for you when I settled for my wife, as a sort of recompense for your companionship. You have cheated me out of the pleasure and I feel disappointed."

Astrea's face flushed crimson—a vivid, painful flush, filling Mrs. Noble's heart with compassion; but she answered readily:

"I could not think of allowing you to pay me for being the recipient of your wife's favors, Major Noble. The obligation is all upon my side. You know me poor, and cannot understand how I have managed to defray my expenses; and if I refuse to explain, I suppose you will think that you have a right to question my integrity. If that is the case, ask your wife what she knows of the disposition I make of that which is intrusted to me."

"I have done that already."

"Then you did doubt my honor," she said quickly, a proud look in her eyes.

"No, Miss Harmon, I simply could not understand it. You lost all you possessed by the burning of the Medora, and I know that you refused the purse made up for you. What am I to conclude?"

"This: that I have an honorable and legitimate means of supplying my small wants, and if you cannot take my word, painful as it will be to me, I must withdraw from the protection of one who will not accord me this much of confidence without proof positive."

"I must believe you, Miss Harmon, and humbly crave your pardon for wounding your feelings. It was farthest from my wish either to wound or offend you."

"Let it pass, I am assured of you good intentions, even while I am so proud that I am forced to resent anything like interference in my private affairs." The haughty expression melted from her face into a gentle smile as she held out her hand, and their mutual compact sealed for future trust and friendliness, the matter dropped. After this Major Noble saw little of our heroine during his stay. A number of sick and wounded had been brought down from Donelson, which required an extra demand upon her time. Before he rose in the morning, she had breakfasted hastily and was away. Her dinner hour varied according to circumstances, and she did not take tea until everybody else had finished, and consequently ordered it to her own room. By this means, if he had felt disposed to trespass further upon her patience with questions, he had no opportunities for doing so, ere his furlough expired.

"Give Captain Wilfer to understand the state of affairs," Mrs. Noble said to him at parting. "I have thought of it all, and believe it the kindest to both, to make him feel that he can have no hope of winning her." But the lady's good intentions were frustrated, for Major Noble had not been gone an hour, before Captain Wilfer made his appearance in Paducah.

CHAPTER VII.

DEFYING A HOSPITAL KNAVE—A LITTLE PROGRESS IN LOVE MATTERS.

"I HAVE good news for you, Miss Harmon," said Doctor Grey that evening as he came in to make his usual visit. "And having good news to relate, I should like to have you reward me by telling me what, of all things you can imagine, would at this moment please you most."

"To hear that you were dismissed the service," she answered curtly.

A general laugh responded, for a dozen men had heard his request and her answer. He scowled, but said dryly:

"Well, I cannot quite gratify you in that way, but the next thing to it will be to leave, I suppose, and I expect to do that to-morrow. To-day's mail has brought me a Colonel's commission from the War Department, and I am to repair at once to the field for active duty."

"Then you will have an opportunity for pursuing your favorite employment in a more legitimate manner."

"In what particular do you mean?"

"Killing men."

"By Jove! woman, you have a tongue like an asp," he blurted out hotly. "I pity the man who is to take my place, for I believe in my heart that you have a spite against the whole profession."

"There you are mistaken. For the faculty I have the highest honor and esteem. No class of men does so much good, or claims warmer appreciation; I only object to a few unscrupulous exceptions."

He held a memorandum in his hand, on which he was penciling orders for the night.

"I would like to know why you hate me so," he said, without looking up from his occupation.

"I do not hate you; I despise you too thoroughly for that. People who excite contempt, cannot go deep enough for hatred. It takes a nobler caste of humanity to rouse so grand a sentiment."

He winced visibly, but laughed as if he wished to be considered taking what she said as a jest.

"You call hatred a grand sentiment?"

"Yes. The grandest of all sentiments is love—the next its opposite—hate."

"I'm sure—where are you going?"

"About my duties."

"Why? Cannot you spare me one moment on my last evening in your kingdom?"

"No. I feel humiliated already, by deigning to exchange words with you," and she was gone, busy at the farthest end of the room in a moment. For a while she kept out of his reach, but in leaving the building, he determinedly followed her, and with the venom of a small, vindictive nature, gave utterance to a threat.

"Doubtless we shall meet again before this war ends, and if so, I shall hope for the opportunity to repay some of your favors. Be assured that I shall not let a chance pass me."

"It would not be like you to do so, and I do not expect it. The man who can willfully see his fellows die, without thought or care, and then strive to cast suspicion upon the woman who had the spirit to speak in their behalf, would stop at nothing."

He started, and her full, dark eye, fixed upon his, made him recoil. "You are generous in your accusations, at least," he said, recovering himself.

"I could be more generous, even, for I have traced, unintentionally, more than one attempt to do me injury, to its proper source. Do not think your actions of so much importance as to believe I care for them in the least, when they are intended to affect me. I mention it merely to show you that I am not ignorant of your movements, and that will explain my professed contempt." Without another word, she turned from him abruptly and hastened to the kitchen. He slammed the door after her angrily, and strode down the street. It was a long time before they met again, and then it was under far different circumstances.

When Miss Harmon returned to the hotel awhile later, she found an unexpected visitor. Mrs. Noble had gone in to tea, and beside her sat Captain Wilfer, chatting pleasantly. Astrea would not have liked to own the sudden fluttering of her heart as her eye met the earnest glance he bent upon her in his greeting. She was compelled to face him at table, and bear the scrutiny of two pairs of eyes, consequently the need of guarding herself was imperative. It would never do to show surprise or embarrassment; so she sat down, and with seeming carelessness, passed the compliments of the season, asked him about his lame foot, and whether he was ready so soon for field duty. No particular interest being manifested in all this, he looked grave and dissatisfied, for he had hoped against Mrs. Noble's assurance, given him during the day, that she would show some feeling either of surprise, pleasure or annoyance. Anything would have been preferable to such entire coolness—such perfect ease as this. Well was it for her that he could not feel the sick sensation in her heart—hear the burden of the sigh strangled in its birth: "more weary struggling." The pain it cost her to render herself so utterly indifferent, to all appearance, had for the first time wakened the fear that she might care for him more than she desired. Only misery could come of it. What could she do?

The three formed a triangle, and kept up a continuous stream of small talk for five minutes. In the midst of it, Astrea's busy brain had divined a plan and determined to carry it out. That plan had the power to lift the weight from her heart and light her face with the real brightness of relief; and as her spirits rose, her admirer became more and more miserable. Mrs. Noble was right. His hopes were indeed vain! What a foolish thing it was, to come here and place himself under the spell of her penetrating power! How could he listen to her voice, see her smile, or look upon the beauty of her peerless face without becoming more hopelessly enslaved? Love makes strange havoc of man's reason, sometimes, and Harry Wilfer had ceased to strive with himself for the belief that he did not love Astrea Harmon—cold, proud, willful, beautiful woman! Was she not tender, and loving, and kind as well? Oh, why could she not be all this for *him?*

He was a stranger to her, comparatively. What could she know of his position, character or past life? How could she care for him without a better knowledge? He did not expect it, so he reasoned, but he had hoped for a little show of interest, in spite of the repulses she had given him during their short acquaintance. Sometimes the very strangeness of events, engenders interests that are not imagined or acknowledged until after the lapse of certain time for reflection. He had dared to hope this might be the case with Astrea Harmon, and she would treat him more kindly in a second meeting. Now that he sat with her fair, still face before him in the repose of a brief respite from talking, he wished himself back in his camp, stretched out upon his blanket, with his face upturned to the stars. They, too, were cold and still and beautiful, but they were steadfast, and as much his as another's. Nay, they were more his, accordingly as he loved them! and their companionship never left such sickening sensations of pain and disappointment in his heart as he now felt. She had asked how long he expected to remain. He remembered that, when she said to Mrs. Noble as they rose from the table:

"I suppose you can spare me for a few days, can you not? To-morrow I must go to Cincinnati."

"To Cincinnati! What takes you there?"

"I expect a boat will," smiled Miss Harmon. "And *I* shall take with me on the boat, a poor boy who must die in a short time, and he wishes to go to his mother. She has been an invalid for years, and there are no relations beside. These are the last of a large family, and it would be hard if he should die and be buried away from her."

"When did you make this decision?"

"This evening. He has moaned so bitterly for several days I have had a ceaseless heart-ache; and his pleadings to go home have almost set me wild. There is no other to trust him with, so I have concluded to go myself."

"And you go to avoid me," thought Captain Wilfer. "I wish I could feel as cold and careless."

The ladies invited him into the parlor, and Mrs. Noble opened the piano. Astrea declined to sing on the plea of weariness, but she talked to him freely, always speaking of other things, seldom of herself. When he got up once to examine a painting upon the wall, she voluntarily became more genial, and opened a conversation upon art which occupied them for some time very pleasantly.

"You admire paintings?—but I fear you will derive little pleasure from the contemplation of that picture," she remarked with a quiet smile. "It is a trial to see copies of our favorite works of art thus mutilate the idea of the artist. I wonder how Rembrandt would feel to see this burlesque upon one of his favorite landscape scenes? There never has been a shadow of justice done to the wonderful power he possessed of blending and contrasting light and shade in the copying of that picture."

"Rembrandt is a favorite of yours, I may infer."

"Indeed he is! How could one help admiring him? There are others as dear, though I could almost worship the memory of Raphael, with his exquisite beauty and tenderness, combined with a severe dignity, a matchless power with which none could vie. Paul Veronese, in his way, claims as strong a feeling, in spite of his inconsistencies. I always smile at the daring disregard of probabilities manifested in his productions;

but his works enthrall me, nevertheless. Then Hogarth, the eccentric, comes in for his share of regard. I like the truthful, willful spirit, which dared to paint life from its striking realities, regardless of the world around him. To those who look upon life as a very good and pleasant possession, I suppose his satire and sarcasm would not prove at all improving or instructive. They would consider him too severe, and therefore condemn him. But those who *know* life, will sympathize with him and call him truthful and honest. I once saw in Rome a copy of his 'Strolling Actresses,' which amused me greatly. The scene is a great barn, turned into a theatre. The party gathered together in it to dress for the performance, was never equalled in fancy or reality. 'The Devil to pay in Heaven' is the play they are about to exhibit, and it is said the object of the satirist was to ridicule those artists who strove to ornament the parlors and halls of those days with mobs of the heathen divinities.

"The *dramatis personæ* are principally ancient deities of the first order. Jupiter, Diana, Apollo, Flora, Night, Syren, Aurora and Cupid, figure on the play-bills. These personages are accompanied by two eagles and a ghost; two dragons, two kittens and an aged monkey. Juno sits upon an old wheelbarrow which serves her for a triumphal car, and with one arm uplifted she rehearses her part, while Night, dressed in a starry robe mends her stockings! The Star of Evening rising over the head of Night, is a burnished tin mould used in baking tarts. A young girl with one eye and a dagger fixed in her mantle by way of a skewer, represents the Tragic Muse. She is cutting poor pussy's tail to obtain blood for some solemn purpose, and smiles in delight as it drops into a broken dish. On a Grecian Altar lies a loaf of bread and a tobacco pipe, while two little devils are quarreling over a pot of ale, out of which one is striving to drink.

"Diana occupies the center of the design. The inspiration of her part comes upon her while she is dressing, and with her hair full of flowers and feathers, and one foot on her discarded crinoline, she rehearses her speech with extravagant enthusiasm. While the others are quite plain, the artist has shown his capability for beautiful creations in the face and form of Diana. Flora sits at her toilet, homely and awkward. A wicker basket contains her regalia, and she smooths her hair with a piece of candle, looking into a broken looking-glass the while. Apollo and Cupid are trying to bring down a pair of hose hung out to dry on a cloud; but the wings of Love cannot raise him, and he is obliged to use a ladder. Aurora sits on the ground with the morning star in her hair. She is in the service of the Syren and offers Ganymede a glass of gin, which he swallows in the hope of curing his aching tooth. The woman who personates the Bird of Jove, is feeding her child; a regal crown holds the sauce pan which contains the milk, and the little creature, frightened, cries lustily. A monkey in one corner sports a long cloak, a bag wig and solitaire, while he amuses himself with dipping into water the plumed helmet of Alexander the Great. The scene is comical in the extreme. One kitten touches an old lyre with evident skill, while the other rolls an imperial orb; cups and balls intimate the sleight-of-hand pursuits of the company; and as a moral, two judges' wigs and an empty noose are near. On the pulpit cushion is a mitre filled with tragedies and farces, revealed by the light of a dark lantern. Beside them a portly hen has found for herself and brood, a roost, on a set of unemployed waves, manufactured to perform the part of a storm at sea.

"Hogarth was forty-eight years of age when this picture was produced, and his fame established, with wealth enough to support a certain style of living easily. Otherwise, he might have failed to attain what his work was now bound to furnish him with, since his fellow artists accorded him praise with such jealous reluctance."

"He has in you, at least, a graphic describer of his excellencies," remarked Captain Wilfer. "But was he not a better engraver than painter?"

"I think not. He did engrave many of his favorite designs, unwilling to trust them to others; but as a painter I like him best."

"You spoke of Raphael; do you remember the disappointment of Sir Joshua Reynolds when he first visited the Vatican?"

"Ah, yes; but that was because of his inability to appreciate the great master. He himself acknowledged that he expected to find beauties superficial and alluring; or rather, if he had found what he expected, they would have been superficial. Afterwards, like many another who had failed to see the grandeur of his conceptions at first, Reynolds became one of the most devoted worshipers of his genius. As a man, I do not so much admire Reynolds. He was too vain and self-conceited; yet his appreciation of art redeems him. I remember being very much charmed with descriptions from his private diary of the works of Titian, Correggio and Paul Veronese."

"The same fault extends to many others of your acknowledged favorites; even Hogarth was not free from it."

"O, you mistake! Hogarth with his rough, honest ways, his homely face, his rude manner, his hatred of vice and folly! The vanity of human nature leads us to express our weakness for self in dress, show and various pretentious ways. To Hogarth you can ascribe none of these; for he was culpably careless in his appearance, and thought so little of people's opinion as not only to go where he pleased, and to dress as he pleased, but to satirize them mercilessly."

"Certainly, you have vindicated him from the charge of vanity," said Mrs. Noble, who had been an interested listener thus far. "If you will allow so humble a personage as myself, however, to take a part in your learned discourse, I shall claim the liberty of defending Reynolds. Cunningham does not give him such a character as you ascribe to him. I think you must have some of your favorite Hogarth's envy, to stimulate your prejudice. Hogarth was a coarse, rude man, while Reynolds was polished and refined. It puzzled me to understand why you should prefer the former above the latter, whe I know you prize refinement and cultivation so highly."

"Because the first was a true man and a true artist, while the other was cold, selfish, and by far too ungracious with his brother artists to win a very warm degree of esteem from me. He preferred the society of literary men to his brothers in art, and was careful never to allow any professional man to gain anything from him, after his studies in Rome. He admired and venerated the severe dignity and exquisite beauty of Michael Angelo and Raphael; but while he talked of the 'grand style' and the 'great masters,' he chose a style for himself altogether different, and that neither divine or lofty. I admit skill, by which he acquired wealth and fame, but who was ever the better for it, whom he might have benefited? He remained silent, and his brother artist must toil on without any aid from his hand. A truly noble nature would not have proved so averse to imparting something of his superior knowledge to others. On the contrary, he not only kept his own counsel, but attacked others bitterly; and he attacked to injure, that he might himself rise. Hogarth attacked to improve, and he gave his brethren the benefit of his long studies and his genius by writing very valuable works upon art. He represented life; gave an image of man; exhibited the workings of the heart; recorded the good and evil of his nature; set before us the very creatures with which the earth is peopled; shook us with mirth; saddened us with reflection; melted us to tears; pleased us with skill and threw over us the spell of power. All this proves him nature's nobleman, in spite of his coarseness, which I choose to call honesty rather. He never, like Reynolds, preached one thing and practised another; he was too straightforward for that. With every conceivable difficulty my hero was forced to contend, but, dapper little man that he was, he stood up sturdily with a courage and a spirit that became grand; while enemies were all around him, ready to find fault and pick him to pieces. Fortune was more gracious to your favorite; he was gifted with fine appearance, rejoiced in the circumstance of good birth; had a polished education and every attribute to popularity apart from his profession. There was not so much of merit in his fame. He ought to have been all that partial historians claim for him, with every auxiliary to a grandly beautiful life at his command. While I admire his pictures, and give him due credit for the good in him, I must still yield appreciation to the hated, annoyed and struggling ones who have left glory upon their names, a laboriously acquired right."

"All artists have to labor; the most gifted and fortune-favored have been forced to labor indefatigably for all that they have attained."

"True. Nothing of lasting worth is achieved without it; and he who reaches eminence without any aid save his own industry and ambition, deserves the greater credit. If he must win the goal through ranks of contending foes, then thrice glorified is that man in my eyes."

"Then the fortunate of earth's children must go their way, and in you the lonely and oppressed will find a sympathizing friend."

"I should be regardless of truth to deny it Captain Wilfer, though in the acknowledgment I may be charged with affectation. I do not wish to arrogate to myself the title of philanthropist; I shall be content with a more modest and unpretending name."

"You could not have a nobler ambition than to win such a title. It is seldom that we find young ladies who will not rather shrink from than seek their friendless fellow-mortals. I often wonder, in not finding more like you, when woman's nature is so universally acknowledged tender and generous. Why is it that there are so few really benevolent people in the world?"

"There are more than we recognize. The really benevolent work out their ends in silence, and only God and their own hearts know the ways or the results. We must ourselves reach a high standard in the scale of being, before we can see the numberless ranks of good people that surround us. What we do see are only the 'surface crowds' who have really never known suffering, or have been afflicted so lightly as only to drive them within themselves, finding cause for fretting, pining and complaint—seeing in their own cases the 'bitterest sorrows known,' while the remainder of the world have no conception of what sorrow is. It is singular to observe how selfish small woes make the majority of a certain class. I think deep sufferings and great afflictions are almost sure to make the victim generous, charitable and sympathetic."

"The inference is plain," said the Captain with a thrill in his low voice, meeting her glance with one of undisguised feeling.

She blushed and turned away her head, partially to hide her mortification. The next moment she was paler and colder than before.

"We are becoming personal," she said with a freezing ring in her voice. "I do not intend you to understand that my sorrows have been heavier than the sorrows of others. The world is full of greater suffering than ever I have known, doubtless."

"Was ever so strange a woman created?" thought the Captain, smarting under the sudden change. After having kept away from personal allusions so long, she had betrayed herself unconsciously into opening the door of her heart, until he could catch a glimpse of the beautiful light within; but an unguarded sentence thrust him from the threshold, and the winds blew cold and chill around him. The light and warmth were closed from his sight, and he must wander away hungering. Was not this woman in all her generosity more than cruel to him? She might at least, vouchsafe to make him understand *why* he was not permitted to be her friend, if no more. In this case, of the two she was wisest, notwithstanding his superior knowledge of the world. He would not stop to reflect upon it, else he must have owned that the lover can never become simply the friend of a young and lovely woman.

Mrs. Noble saw the embarrassing restraint that had fallen upon the two, and came to the rescue with one of her gay sallies which brought a laugh from both. She had such a quaint way of saying things sometimes, her presence was invaluable. The restraint melted away at once, and the three laughed and jested merrily, ere they separated for the night. Captain Wilfer accompanied them to the door.

"Miss Harmon, as I have yet three or four days to spare, will you not allow me to make the trip to Cincinnati? I should take great pleasure in relieving you, when I know that you cannot be spared without detriment to others. Besides, I am sure that I could make a capital nurse. Let me take this extra duty off your hands."

"You are kind and I thank you; but you could not do it. The boy is entirely helpless, and you could no more take care of him than you could of a baby."

"You will not undertake it alone?"

"No, I shall take a nurse along to help me. Good-night."

"Good-night, Miss."

He turned away and walked rapidly down the hall. The request had been preferred under a desperate impulse. If she would only let him help her in some of her undertakings, he might at length win a little kindness at her hands—he would be so unfeignedly sincere in his efforts to aid and not annoy her. But this keeping aloof, these eternal repulses were exasperating. The disorder grew upon him. The Captain Wilfer of a few weeks before, and the Captain Wilfer of to-night were two different beings. The one was a cool, calm, earnest, dignified man, the other more resembled a hot-headed, obstinate boy, devoid even of proper pride and self-respect! By the time he reached his own room, he was thoroughly angry with himself.

"Why would you not let him go?" asked Mrs. Noble when she had locked the door and thrown herself upon a sofa to watch Astrea unfasten her luxuriant hair, "I am sure it would have been a kindness to let him do it, and spared you to me and your hospital. How I am to get along without you is a mystery."

"The time will be very short, and I ought to go. You should know that it will not do for me to accept anything from Captain Wilfer which would place me under obligations to him, as such a service certainly would. I had hoped that you would help me to get rid of him."

"And I have endeavored to do so, but the man is mad, evidently. I see no other hope for you than to make him understand your reasons for repulsing his advances."

"No, Mrs. Noble, I will not be forced into laying my heart and life bare to any man for the sake of freeing myself from his attentions," she answered proudly. "It must be enough that I choose to treat him civilly, without giving him encouragement. A man of proper feeling and self-respect will withdraw when he sees that he is not welcome as a suitor—not force himself upon a lady who shows him by every action that his presence is painful. I confess myself surprised and disappointed in Captain Wilfer."

"Ah, don't be severe, Astrea! Surely the woman who wakens so strong a sentiment in an earnest man's heart as love, should have some pity, at least."

"Have I done this willingly? Is the fault mine that he cares for me, or I cannot encourage him?"

"Of course it is not. Yet I think I should be a little like him, with such a nature as I have. We are not alike, you and I, and you cannot understand, perhaps, how absolutely necessary it is for me to see my way clearly. I must *know* why this must be so, and that must not be so! I cannot take a mere 'yes' or 'no,' without explanation. You could let people pass to and fro forever, asking no questions, content that they should go their own way, and attend to their own affairs; but that is because you wish to be let alone yourself. Am I not right? I dare say, however, you have some little curiosity where you are interested."

"No. If those who interest me, tell me of themselves, I

like it; if not, I charge them with nothing unfair, and never feel dissatisfied with their course. We have no right whatever, to that which is not spontaneously given. I could never take the smallest degree of pleasure in a thing wrung from any one."

"You *are* peculiar! but never mind. You shall not be teased. Keep your own counsel till it pleases you to impart what you know. I long to hear you tell me. Don't sit up to-night, will you?"

"For awhile I must."

Then they were silent. Mrs. Noble assumed her white wrapper, brushed her hair, read her Bible and knelt down for a few minutes in prayer. Ten minutes later her regular breathing announced quiet sleep, while her companion sat before the table, her long hair sweeping around her like a veil, and the pen rapidly passing over the paper beneath her eyes. It was past midnight when she sought her place by Mrs. Noble's side and wearily dropped upon the pillow. Soon she slept too, but that sleep was restless and broken with feverish dreams.

CHAPTER VIII.

TAKING A YOUNG SOLDIER HOME TO DIE—RUMORS OF A BATTLE.

NOTWITHSTANDING the anger with which Captain Wilfer had arraigned himself before his keener, better judgment, the morning found him watching for Miss Harmon, that he might see her safely on board the boat that was to take her to Cincinnati. He took a position commanding a view of the hall, and as he paced back and forth with his hands behind him, watched the door anxiously. Anger was useless, and he smiled scornfully at judgment in his mental revolutions at this moment. What did it signify if he was silly and boyish? Better men had been made foolish before him by beautiful and willful women. Why should he loathe the chains in which he found himself bound helplessly? He had not sought them, nor could he shake them off. The spell had been woven about him without will or wish, and no coldness could chill the warm, rich love born of this woman's beauty and power. No ordinary woman could thus creep into his heart with unwilling strength and steal away his self-control; and as his sophistical reasoning took this form, he began to grow proud of his thralldom. Then, out of love and pride, came a resolve deep and earnest. If it was in the power of man to win and bend her by the force of a sincere and ennobling passion, he would yet become her master. This should be the one great aim of his life. A little while since, and ambition had been his ruling passion; but now ambition was secondary to love, and it was a new sensation. Hitherto the blind god had kept far away from him, and he had passed unscathed by beauty and brilliance. Now freedom was gone, and he was compelled to own himself the slave of one who showed him, by every sign in woman's power, that his suit was disagreeable and painful to her.

While he walked slowly, meditating upon his mortifying position, the ladies had taken an early breakfast, and Miss Harmon came out ready for her journey. A messenger had already been in to inform her that her charge was safely on board the boat and waiting. She had only to follow, and in half an hour, would be steaming up the Ohio River.

Captain Wilfer was at the head of the stairs, lifting his hat with a graceful morning salutation. No anxious face, or expression of disappointment now. He was taking a new course, and it best suited him to be polite without any special show of interest.

"I had an early walk, Miss Harmon, and happening to be in the hotel just now, I will ask your permission to see you safely on board. Let me carry your traveling bag."

She gave it to him quietly, walking beside him in silence until they reached the boat. Then the only acknowledgment she made was in cold and frigidly polite terms. He had not expected anything else, but it exasperated him to find her so unmoved when it might be the last time she should ever see him. Was he not going to the field, where a battle was imminent; and could she remember this in connection with any man without a show of feeling or interest? His own resolution to preserve a cold and polite demeanor melted with the thought, and he changed his plans accordingly—so vacillating does love make us. The longing to hear one word of earnest encouragement from her lips had grown in the moment when about to part, stronger than any other, and he could not leave her without it. As he hesitated in putting his thoughts into words, she looked into his face, and there read what he could not express. Her features assumed a soft and sweet gravity as she held out her hand frankly, answering his thoughts.

"Captain Wilfer, you are going forth to a mighty work—to danger,—perhaps to death. As a loyal man I know your duty will be well done, and I bid you God speed with a sincere wish for your success. As a servant of our beloved country, I shall ever remember you kindly. May your life long be spared and a useful career before you lead you on to glory and triumph. If it will be any comfort to you in the hour of battle to know that others remember you prayerfully, believe that I shall not forget you. Good-bye."

Did her eyes really grow humid? Was there a tremor in her voice in uttering those sweet words? He could not doubt it, but it was for the soldier—not the suitor this emotion was shown. She made him feel that, yet his heart thrilled with a sense of delight which gave rise to the thought, "When I am more worthy of you I shall hope to win you. If ever man earned the love of glorious woman, I will claim the right to yours." Aloud he said modestly:

"Thank you for the assurance. It will indeed be a comfort to me to be so remembered, and I shall treasure this promise with deepest gratitude. The time is coming when we shall need the prayers of our friends; and those who stand afar off to look on, will do well to keep in mind the imperiled ones whose ways are through dangers, and will bring to many death. Yours will be no careless eye to see our danger—and no lukewarm prayers will fall from your lips. To think of your earnest patriotism alone, would nerve me to action; to know that you give a thought to me, and have confidence in my sincerity of purpose will add tenfold to my power. For these words, so kindly spoken, I thank you again, and leave you a better man for having heard them. God bless you."

She did not withdraw the hand he held when he bent to kiss it. Something of his own spirit was in her, and she could not deny him this last encouragement to duty. The next moment he was gone, and she sat down thoughtfully beside the sick boy whose large eyes had scarcely left her face during the brief interview. All his medicines, water, sponge, and ices had been placed near him, so that she might give him the best of care; but when she sought to wet his lips, he turned his head away quickly, saying with child-like directness:

"Don't. I don't want anything now. Who was that gentleman that just now went away?"

"Captain Wilfer, an officer in the Federal army."

"Do you like him?"

"Yes, rather. We must like good people."

"Then you must be very good."

"Why?"

"Because everybody likes you so much. I like you, and all the boys like you up at the hospital. I saw a fellow cry like a child last night when the new nurse you sent there came to him. He said it wasn't you, and he did not want anybody but you. I guess the Captain thinks a sight of you, too. He looked at you as if he did."

Miss Harmon's color rose, for those large penetrating eyes were watching her closely. Ill as he was, he evidently took delight in making her feel that he divined the true state of her suitor's feelings.

"You ought not to talk, Frankie; it makes you so weak. You are panting now from the exertion of saying so much. Be quiet, my boy."

A quiet light dawned in the boy's eyes. "I know. You don't want me to talk about him because it makes you blush. I guess you like him, too; I wish you didn't, though."

"Why?"

"I'm jealous. When I get well, I want you to like me better than anybody, and come and live with my mother. She's splendid. Won't you?"

Astrea's eyes filled with tears, and they dropped on the little thin hand she held.

"Dear Frankie, I do love you very much, and I wish it could be—that—that—"

She could not finish the sentence, and he demanded eagerly.

"Could what? Tell me."

"You could get well, dear boy—for your poor mother's sake."

"You don't think I will?" very wistfully. Was it kind to feed him upon false hopes, and let him pass away without thought or preparation? His only wish had been to go home, and now that the hope of seeing his mother was so near realization, his spirits rose into a confidence painful to dissipate. She knew that he could not long enjoy the attainment of earthly aspirations, and sorrowed for him as only those can sorrow who have tested the bitterness of disappointment in all dearest things. Gentle she was, always, but doubly gentle now, looking at the wan face and wistful eyes.

"Do you think, Frankie, you would be afraid to go away from the earth if God should please to take you?" speaking softly.

"I don't know. I don't want to go. Not that I'm afraid, but—my mother!"

How the weak voice faltered! She bowed her head to the boy's pillow and strove to say quietly, keeping back her tears,

"Your mother will not miss you long, perhaps, and it is a pleasant thing to think that when you meet again there will be no more parting or suffering. I want you to think about death, dear Frankie, because it is a calm, sweet sleep that will come to you soon. Think of it without dread or fear, for there is nothing awful in it. God loves his children, and calls them home to happiness and rest. Those with whom they cannot stay on earth come after them, and oh! the joy of being reunited forever! I would like it, Frankie. If I could give you my health and strength for your weakness and nearness to that happy change, I think I could be selfish enough to want to take your place. If life on earth is sweet to the young, how much sweeter must be life in heaven, where only pure happiness is known. When you go, you leave all ills behind you, while men will say of you, 'he was a brave, noble boy, whose life was given to his country, when stronger and more able men held back from their duty.' Does this thought give you any pleasure?"

"Yes," and the kindling eye and cheek told her that the effort had not been made in vain to turn his thoughts into a proper channel. Soon he turned his cheek to the pillow of his cot and closed his eyes. Seeing his lips move, she bowed her ear and caught fragments of a childish prayer, learned, doubtless, at his mother's knee. After that he lay silent for a long time, and finally slept.

The river being high with the Spring floods, their progress was slow; but time did not hang heavily. When awake Frankie loved to hear her read to him from her little pocket Bible, or to sing for him as she had often done at the hospital. Sometimes she talked to him in such a sweet, earnest way about death, all its terrors vanished, and he awaited it in peaceful, calm content. It was singular, how she could win people to her own way of thinking in whatever she strove to attain. Herself longing for rest, and seeing in it nothing to dread, she had made death appear not only beautiful, but desirable to this boy just in the bloom of early youth. He no longer thought or cared to live on earth after she had painted the other life in such exquisite colors. Only he wished that his mother and Astrea could go with him. Was it wrong if she murmured to herself in reply to his wish:

"Oh, if it could be!"

Yes. She knew that it was not right—that the ceaseless longing for death was little short of rebellion against the will of Him whose purposes she could not yet understand in her afflictions. If her daily cries for strength and patience seemed unheard, it is no wonder that she grew faint and weary in the struggle: yet God requires of his children a blind faith which questions not his ways. She had not reached this state. It would be long before she could reach it in her conflicting emotions. Strangers looked with interest at the fair young face, and many flattered her as people are wont to do when they see the young and lovely sacrificing youth and beauty to humanity. Some censured and criticised her course as improper, not hesitating to speak their thoughts in her hearing, little aware of her utter indifference to all that they chose to utter. While she and her charge were objects of curiosity and interest to all, she would sit for hours beside the cot, and when not reading or talking to him, give way to thoughtful questionings and conjectures. How many miles of fair southern land she traversed in fancy, during those watchful hours! How many dear familiar scenes and faces were recalled! What spasms of anguish swept over the fair face while the cry in her heart grew more intense. "Give me patience. I cannot bear it! Lost to me—torn from me—all that I love. I cannot even know if sickness, or death comes to my darling. Oh, help me to wait and be strong. Have pity on me, oh my Father. Look into my torn heart—see how I suffer, and be merciful!"

Meanwhile Mrs. Noble left alone with her duties performed them steadily, sad and lonely in her friend's absence. On the third day a matron was established in each of the hospitals, with assistants who were competent to give them all the aid they required, and she found herself at liberty to take some rest. Captain Wilfer had returned immediately to Pittsburg Landing, from which place letters came almost daily from her husband. He reported the Captain moody and almost morose, shunning society, and giving all his time to the study of military tactics, that was not employed in active duty. By this she inferred that he was striving to overcome his passion, and for his sake, grew more at ease on the subject. After awhile it was abandoned, and ceased to be discussed in their correspondence, other things arising of more immediate importance. So sped the time away until that eventful 7th of April, a never-to-be-forgotten day in the annals of American history.

A calm, quiet Sabbath dawned over Paducah. White clouds drifted over the clear sky slowly in broken masses, adding to the beauty of the day. The two ladies had been to visit the hospitals and returned, after the morning service by the chaplain; and now they sat quietly before the window, looking out in silence.

No sweet chimes of Sabbath bells broke on the air here. The hum of business was hushed; no sounds disturbed the almost oppressive stillness. Toying with the leaves of her prayer book, Mrs. Noble said dreamily:

"One could almost wish something to happen such a day as this. I feel stifled, crushed down with an inexpressible weight. I wonder if it is the natural result of a Sabbath without bells. I miss them so very much."

"I do not know, but I imagine it something more portentous. You disclaim superstition—so do I; still I feel as if something unusual is about to happen. In Nature the calm before a storm denotes its power, and we may well dread it."

Her voice was very sad. Since her return from Cincinnati a great change had come over her. The pallor of her cheek had given way to a vivid flush. Sometimes her eyes would flash, and an expression of fierce defiance sweep over her features. She was evidently laboring under some great excitement; whether the result of overwork, or caused by some secret trouble, Mrs. Noble could not tell, and dared not question. Astrea had her own peculiar way of checking inquiries, and if she chose, gave straightforward replies which explained nothing. Had she confessed the truth, Mrs. Noble would have owned herself somewhat afraid of her in spite of her growing affection. And it may be that, perceiving this impression, Astrea had tried to deepen it in order to shield herself from her friend's inquiries into private matters.

But, looking at her now in her quiet mood, with her subdued manner and sad voice, yearning and wistful under the influences of the day, she could not restrain herself, and once more approached forbidden ground.

"How thin and delicate you are growing, Astrea. When you have no color, as now, it is painful to mark the change of a few short weeks. Why will you suffer in silence, accepting no sympathy? It is unnatural. Woman was never created to suffer alone."

"I must be an exception in this, then, as in other things. Not yet can I share my troubles with others."

"Not even for the sake of relief?"

"It would only add to my misery."

"I cannot see how—I cannot understand, but of course you know best. That I love you is a fact you cannot doubt; and I do not know that I have ever forfeited your confidence. You might trust me, I think. To see you suffering and fading before my eyes day after day, almost breaks my heart."

Miss Harmon's eyes met her tearful gaze, wistful and bright.

"Do you care so much for me as that, Helen?"

"I do, indeed. I have no sisters or mother, Astrea, and few friends who understand me. With more of confidence, you could be all the world to me as a friend. I wish you would make up your mind to be less reserved."

"I will soon."

Miss Harmon left her chair, knelt at Mrs. Noble's side and put her arms around her, leaning her head against her shoulder.

"For your dear love, I thank you with all my soul. Nothing on earth beside, can be more precious and ennobling than the love of a good woman, bestowed upon one of her own sex. I do appreciate it, and am profoundly grateful for it. Perhaps in a few days I can tell you all you wish to know."

"Why not now? Has anything of importance occurred since you went away? Ever since your return you have been so flushed, so excited, I feared you were threatened with fever. Is it mental disquiet?"

"Yes, Helen, deep and fearful. I have been tried hardly. While in Cincinnati I heard of one who held my life in his hands once—whom I loved better than my own life! He proved unworthy, and turned my affection into bitterness, contempt—almost to hatred. I should hate him, did not God take pity on me and preserve me from it. I have a ceaseless struggle to control my feelings when I remember who and what he is, and the power he still has over me to make me wretched. Ask me no more now, Helen. I will tell you only this. In the Confederate camp not far from Corinth, is an officer, who, while he has no control over my person, holds, as it were, every tender chord of my heart in his cruel hands; and he is merciless as a fiend! Oh, my God, my God!"

She rose from her kneeling posture and paced the floor rapidly, her breath coming in gasps. The struggle for self-control was intense—hands locked in mute anguish—wrung together with indomitable will. As Mrs. Noble watched her in painful surprise, her own heart ached with sympathy. She had never seen any human being so moved, yet so resolute to conquer herself. And in woman, naturally so dependent and confiding in others, there was something terrible in the fierce determination her face and manner expressed. Finally she sank upon her knees by the bed, burying her face in the covering, while her companion slipped to the floor and bowed her head in silent prayer. Before she had time to rise, Miss Harmon was at her side, calmed magically by the sheer force of a strong will; but her eyes wore a strained, glittering expression and her voice was sharp, and unnatural.

"Come out. The house stifles me. Perhaps we had better visit the hospitals again; the poor boys like to see us, and I forget everything else when I am there."

Without hesitation Mrs. Noble went for her hat, and the two walked up the street together, and turned across to the quiet hospital. Here everything wore the same calm, serene appearance, and an unusual silence pervaded the wards. As they entered the building, clouds drifted over the sun, mellowing the light; but it was pleasant to receive the glad greeting of those who had gratefully acknowledged their care. Mrs. Noble paused to speak to an old man, who beckoned her to come nearer, and Astrea crossed the room to a hypochondriacal patient who lay buried in blankets enough to smother him. In a moment she was heard to laugh merrily, and Mrs. Noble caught the sound of her voice in playful raillery.

"Why, grandmother, you seem to be cold this bright April day. One would think you in Greenland."

"I'm so 'fraid of takin' cold," murmured the man in a whining voice.

"Nonsense, you cannot get cold such a day as this; and what you need is fresh air. Throw off some of those superfluous blankets—take that silk handkerchief from about your head, and breathe the air fearlessly. You are not sick now—only weak, and a little air and exercise will give you a good appetite. Get up and take a few turns around the room, and I will have the nicest of dinners prepared for you presently. All you want is to regain strength. You look much better than you did yesterday—or would, if I could see your face. Do you know what you remind me of, with your nose peeping out of that muffler."

"What?"

"The wolf dressed up as Red Ridinghood's grandmother."

A general laugh responded, and the man got up feebly, dropping his wraps with reluctant hands.

"You are sure I won't take cold?"

"Very sure. What have you eaten to-day? You were sleeping when I came this morning, so I could not ask you."

"O, I haint eat nothin' to speak on at all. Nobody gits anything I kin eat when you aint here. If it hadn't 'a' been for you, I'd 'a' died long ago. You've been the savin' of me."

"Thank you; but I cannot save you yet, if you will persist in this kind of work. You must take exercise and air, eat good food and be cheerful. If you will do this, I will get the Doctor to give you a certificate for a furlough in a week, and you may go home to your friends. I dare say that a certain little girl there would be delighted to see you."

He opened his eyes wide.

"How did you know about her?"

"Jessie? O, a little bird told me. Never mind now; go and take a walk while I see the cook and order your dinner."

"I 'bleve you're a witch," he muttered, his face alive with

pleasure as he reached for his cane that stood by the cot, and slowly started off. Astrea took his arm, steadied him until he reached the middle of the broad-aisle, then left him to himself, and started for the kitchen.

"Come to me soon, won't you?" asked a feeble boy as she passed a cot in going out.

"Yes, in a minute, Willie. Do you want anything to eat?"

"Not now, thank you. I only want to talk to you a minute."

In a few moments she came back and sat down beside him.

"I wanted to ask you about Frankie Hays. He used to be close to me, and I knew he would die soon. Since you came back I have not had a chance to ask you about him."

"He is sleeping to-day in Spring-grove Cemetery," she answered softly. "I took him home in time to see his mother; and a little while later he was gone, very peacefully and happily. The day after his burial, I left the city, but I first saw a little white shaft that bore his name and date of his death, with a beautiful line below which said, 'For his country.' No one will ever look upon that simple record without a thrill of honor for the noble boy who sleeps beneath it. His mother will soon lie by his side, and I am glad to think that none will be left behind to sorrow bitterly for them. Strangers soon forget the poor, no matter how worthy they may be—how different their stations in life may have been. How do you feel to-day?"

"Pretty well. I shall get on nicely I dare say. Everybody is kind to me."

"As they should be. It is little enough we can do, when compared with what you have done. I often wish when I think of those battles where boys like you faced the storm like heroes, I could have been a man to share your danger. Such brave spirits as yours always make me ambitious and enthusiastic."

The youth's eyes kindled.

"You make others feel the same way. Whenever you talk

to me, I always long to be well and go back again to my regiment."

"O, you will be well soon. Now I must leave you and see to others. Do you think of anything you want?"

"Nothing, thank you. I am much obliged to you for coming to me."

She glided away; in a few moments Mrs. Noble saw her administering medicine to some other patients lower down the same ward. After that she saw her take a small tin cup from a cupboard, and disappear. In a moment she came back with it and a small flannel cloth in her hands. The cup contained vinegar and into it she had put a spoonful of cayenne pepper. This she put upon the stove to heat.

"What are you going to do with that, Astrea?"

"Bathe Mr. Nicholls' arms and hands. He is in great pain with inflammatory rheumatism, and I find this remedy gives immediate relief. Did you never try it?"

"No, but I will the first opportunity I have."

Astrea turned back her sleeves, took the cup and flannel, and went to Nicholls. Mrs. Noble followed her, and saw her bare the man's arms, dip the cloth in the hot vinegar and apply it carefully. Mr. Nicholls was groaning very bitterly when she went to him, but as the application brought relief, he closed his eyes with a breath of thankfulness.

"Ah, that is nice! I have not slept since night before last, and am about worn out."

Before she had done, he was in a quiet slumber, and spreading a blanket across his chest to protect his arms and shoulders from the air, she bore the empty cup back to the kitchen.

"How I wish I could be as efficient as you are," said Mrs. Noble when she returned. "With all my experience, I never can be so ready in what I have to do, but always must stop and think, and calculate! You seem to know without a moment's thought."

"That is from habit, however. There is the doctor, and I must speak to him about the amputation which must be performed on John Mason's arm. Poor fellow! We cannot save it for him."

"The doctor's face was grave as she approached him.

"Have you heard the news, Miss Harmon?"

"No. Anything unusual going on?"

"Fighting at the Landing. Rebels attacked them this morning, and seized our camps. The accounts are confused, and may not be true; yet I fear that, so far, it has gone hard with us."

"Oh, do not say it. We *will* not be beaten."

"Not if all men were like you, should we be beaten. You have the spirit of a hero."

"Mrs. Noble! She is going to faint, doctor." She had come near enough to hear what they were saying, and a sudden fear had seized her that for a moment deprived her of strength.

"No, no! It is but momentary. How long did you say they had been fighting?"

"Since daylight, report says. The battle still rages hotly."

"Oh, God protect my darling," murmured the wife, turning her pallid face away. They heard, and uttered a solemn "amen."

Only anxious faces were seen in Paducah that day. Even the rebels, while they exulted, were uncertain and wavering in their triumph, for reports conflicted too much to give them a positive ground on which to stand. In the meantime, let us look upon the field of action, and see what is being done there.

CHAPTER IX.

THE BATTLE OF PITTSBURG LANDING.

Day had dawned clear and lovely. A few fleecy clouds drifted slowly athwart the sky, adding to the beauty of the Sabbath morning. A battle had long been expected, and our officers were looking anxiously for Buell's arrival, growing more and more eager as the enemy grew more bold. On the fourth and fifth the enemy's cavalry had appeared and effected some injury, but made no alarming show of deadly determination. It is doubtful if many in command of the Federal forces, looked upon the dawning of that Sabbath as the dawning of a most eventful day in the history of their struggle for the Union. It is so natural, even with strong indications of the nearness of danger, to fix it farther than it really is from us, by the force of sanguine temperament.

About eight o'clock in the morning, the Confederates opened fire upon General Sherman's division with his artillery, having formed under cover of the brush in a low lying piece of ground, and almost immediately afterwards, the infantry pressed forward across the bottom and up the slopes to the Federal lines. While this advance was being made on Sherman's front, large bodies of the enemy were seen moving to the left in heavy masses, to attack Prentiss. The onset was fierce and determined. Our men being little prepared for the suddenness of the movement, were taken at a great disadvantage. But they rallied with a spirit of patriotism worthy the cause they defended, and for an hour held their ground bravely, then began to give way. Wearied, heated and overwhelmed by overpowering numbers, a sudden panic seized a portion of the troops, and two Ohio regiments—the Fifty-third and Fifty-seventh, broke in disorder, exposing Waterhouse's battery, which had been protected by a brigade of McClerland's division. This division had been promptly moved forward to support Sherman's left, but the enemy's attack had been so vigorous, the three regiments composing it gave way, and the battery was lost. The remainder of three brigades maintained their position for an hour longer, but at ten o'clock the pressure upon Sherman's front was so heavy, it was found necessary to change position and he gave orders to move his line near McClerland's first position, there to continue the defence.

Sherman's line was now upon the Purdy and Hamburg road, and riding across the angle at the intersection of this road with the Corinth road, General Sherman met Captain Beher, whose battery was attached to McDowell's brigade. He ordered it to come into position immediately, and the gallant Captain wheeled to give the order to his men. His face was pallid, his eyes aglow, every nerve strung with a firm purpose as he did so. To him his men looked eagerly for action, when just as the order was received, a ball struck him, hurling him from his horse to the ground. The dismayed drivers and gunners instantly fled panic-stricken, carrying with them one gun and a caisson, abandoning the remaining six to the enemy. Here was a straight, and Sherman was forced to choose a new line of action. Without loss of time he moved promptly forward the still steady portion of his division to the support of General McClerland's right, then seriously menaced by the enemy. At half-past ten a furious attack was made on McClerland's front, and for sometime, our cause looked inauspicious; but an opportune movement of McDowell's brigade against the enemy's left flank, forced him back much to the relief of the hardly tried forces. Sherman here took advantage of the cover which the trees, and a wooded ravine on the right afforded him, and held his position for four hours, most determinedly resisting the efforts of the enemy to drive him back to the river. About half-past three General Grant appeared, and General Sherman and General McClerland greeted him with anxious inquiries.

"How is it?" asked Sherman, riding close to his side and looking straight into the troubled eyes of his superior officer.

"Bad," was the characteristically blunt answer. "We have lost on all sides, and our troops are in lamentable confusion. Resistance seems almost hopeless."

"But we *will* resist?" a fiery gleam in the piercing eyes of the questioner.

"Yes, to the last. Wallace is on his way from Crump's Landing with his entire division, and we must bring our line of defense to cover the bridge over Snake Creek, that this reinforcement may approach. Effect it with as much order as possible."

The change of position was made with a degree of precision hardly to be expected under the circumstances. Many fragments of troops were encountered during the movement and united with the two divisions. Meantime Hurlbut had been too hardly pressed and had fallen back toward the river. But notwithstanding the knowledge of this, the new line of defense was held stubbornly. The troops rallied and fought with exceeding bravery, driving the enemy from McClerland's front, and forcing him back into the ravines for cover.

It was growing late, but the Federal troops to the right now seemed to have gained a decided advantage, having in their front an open space the distance of two hundred yards or more which was not again crossed by the enemy. But the force of the attack upon the left wing was heavy and disastrous. General Prentiss' two brigades had given way early in the morning and drifted to the rear as General Hurlbut pressed forward to their support. By ten o'clock they had melted away—the ground strewn with the dead—while many brave men, prisoners, were forced back to the rear of the contending rebels. Among these, Captain Wilfer stood listening to the still raging storm of battle, and longing impatiently to be with his little handful of men. They had fallen around him like braves, until few were left; but with these he would have fought to the last moment of life, had he been permitted. To some, imprisonment is worse than death, and Captain Wilfer thought as he paced back and forth with his hands bound behind him, a guard upon each side, the ball would have been welcome that brought him death rather than this.

"Oh, to hear the thunders of the cannon, and to know that they need me, yet I cannot go! I must stand almost within sound of their voices, and never move a finger to help them. My God, preserve my country."

Up from a strong man's soul went that prayer. Regardless of those who were around him, he fell upon one knee and lifted his flushed face upwards. The guard turned angrily and spurned him with his foot.

"Git up, ye hypocritical cur, an les' have none o' yer foolery. Yer only beginning to taste southern spirit and power; but wait! Every cussed Yank in the kingdom 'll have to come to this yit." The young man sprang to his feet, his teeth ground together in impotent rage.

"You may insult me," he said, "I am your prisoner, bound and helpless, but you cannot curb thought, nor change my feelings. Before to-morrow's sun shall have set, you will probably be less insolent and assured—if defeat can cow you. As surely as there is a God to defend the right, do I believe he will give us the victory."

"You shet up," scowled the guard doggedly, and hurried him further to the rear.

Stuart's brigade had held the extreme left of Smith's division, until the pressure upon its front, and the exposure of its flank by the disaster to Prentiss, compelled it to take up new lines of defense on the ridges which rose brokenly between our forces and the river. This last position had been held unyieldingly by our men until after six o'clock. The battle had been waged with unabated zeal on both sides for twelve hours. Our troops had been forced from all their camps early in the day with the exception of Wallace's command, which the enemy vainly strove to dislodge. The reinforcements eagerly hoped for, had not yet arrived, with the exception of Nelson's division of the Army of the Ohio. They had crossed the river and come upon the field of action in time only to fire a few shots before our forces were withdrawn for the night.

The scene they witnessed on landing was appalling, and might well have shaken brave hearts, though it had the effect rather to shame and fire the men with a just indignation than to discourage them. A crowd of nearly ten thousand men thronged the landing, hiding behind trees and under the bluffs to escape the bursting of the enemy's shells, crying out to the new arrivals that the Federal forces, had been beaten and imploring them not to advance further. Soon a murmur ran through the ranks of the Ohioans, and then sharp sarcasms and withering jeers answered the cowardly appeals, until the columns had gone beyond their hearing.

After nightfall the rain began to descend in torrents, drenching the wearied troops as they sought rest upon the field where they had fought so nobly. But they were in good spirits, for they knew that the enemy had been repulsed, and that Buell's forces were arriving. Wallace's command would come during the night, and when morning should have dawned again the fresh battalions hurled against the foe, might render their victory complete. The gunboat Lexington dropped a shell into the Confederate camp every ten minutes, until after midnight, when the Tyler relieved her and shelled it at intervals of a quarter of an hour. While those shells robbed the foe of rest, they were inspiring to the hearts of our gallant men.

On the morning of the 7th our commanders were cheered by the accumulation of power around them. The remainder of Nelson's command had arrived and taken a position on the left front. Crittenden's and McCook's divisions followed successively, and extending the line to the right connected with Hurlbut's left. General Wallace came into position on Sherman's right, and they were ready for action. But the enemy was out of sight on our front, and showed no signs of an advance. General Grant, however, fulfilled his promise to the division commanders, and gave orders to move forward and drive the Confederates from the front. By six o'clock the artillery was brought to bear upon the left; and by ten, the consolidating commands were warmly engaged in a contest for the possession of the old camps. With rising spirits, our forces pressed forward until they reached the open fields in front of the log church of Shiloh. Here the position of the Confederates was a strong one, and held stubbornly. For three hours they kept their ground, but after that their zeal began to wane, and their weakness become too apparent. At two o'clock a portion of Beauregard's army was withdrawn, soon followed by the remainder.

Thus was Shiloh won! Shall we pause to calculate at what price? Alas! too surely did the scene upon that field speak of the appalling truth to the sad eyes that wandered over it in search of missing friends and comrades. The dead were strewn thickly over the drenched, trampled earth, amid the ruins of artillery, the lifeless remains of slain animals, the broken and fallen timber mown down by the showers of shot and shell and heavy cannon balls that had sped through the trees and thickets. Well has Bulwer said that "death levels all ranks." Sadly was it exemplified on the field of Shiloh, where friends and foes fell side by side to rise no more; and officers and men slept upon the same lowly pillow. Strangely moving scenes came under the eye, and melted hearts already tender with grief. Wandering over a spot where a certain battalion had been hotly engaged with the enemy, in search of a lost cousin, was a young officer whose open, manly face was an index to the character for bravery and generosity he bore. He was not ashamed of the tears that fell over his cheeks as he peered into one pallid face after another, sealed with that eternal silence which must rob it of expression forever. Before one spot he paused for several minutes, looking upon a strange scene. Near the foot of a large tree upon a mound, were two men with hands clasped, as they had fallen in their last struggle. Both were privates, but one wore the Confederate uniform, while the other was habited in the Federal blue, with a tiny, brilliant flag pinned to the bosom of his coat on the left side. The two dead faces were turned to the sky, and the unmistakable resemblance of feature proved them to be brothers.

What a picture, and what a story it told! Here had been a contest of heart, and brain, and hand. Here, brothers divided by political feeling had met in the storm of battle, and in receiving their death simultaneously by one of those strange coincidences for which there is no law, resentment had suddenly melted, and, with hand grasped in hand, they had breathed out their lives together, reconciled. Yes, if attitudes can speak, theirs told the story of reconciliation and forgiveness—brotherly love revived and sealed by death!

A little further on was another sad picture, telling at a glance how great had been a last want—how life had struggled with death until the latter had gained the victory. It was a youth with soft, sunny hair above an almost girlish brow, in whose side a ball had lodged without having caused instant death. Doubtless the intense suffering and the previous violent excitement had caused a raging thirst, and he had crept several yards, leaving a crimson trail as he moved to where a little rill bubbled along among the bushes. With his left hand he had clutched a clump of alders, while with his right he endeavored to reach down and fill his canteen, which fell from his stiffening fingers into the edge of the water, ere a drop had touched his parched lips. Death came quickly, and he had fallen with his face downward, dying in agony as the rigid features with their contracted lines testified. A young officer who looked upon this scene, here sat down and covering his face with his hands, groaned heavily, and said to himself, "Poor boy. A mother's heart would break to see you now! Oh, black and bitter day to many. How shall traitors account to God for all the misery they have this day created. Oh, the pall they have this day laid upon fond earthly hopes! Who shall find light that has doomed hundreds to walk in perpetual darkness! An hour ago, I was a man and a soldier. Now I have grown womanly and cannot look upon such dreadful scenes." He sobbed aloud, not caring who might hear him. Some one heard and called to him from a short distance. He sprang to his feet at once, moving toward the spot whence the sounds proceeded with rapid steps. There he found an officer leaning against a tree, looking pale and faint. One arm hung helpless at his side, shattered by a ball, and he had bled copiously. With a promptness that was rare under such circumstances, the young officer took his wounded comrade by the shoulder and laid him gently upon the ground. Then he tore off his own coat and put it under his head for a pillow, and without waiting to utter a word he started off on a run toward a group of men at some distance, who were picking up the wounded. When he came back four of the ambulance corps accompanied him with a litter, and the wounded officer was lifted upon it, and borne to the tent of the nearest surgeon. It happened to be the quarters of an Illinois surgeon to which he was taken, and Doctor Raler had just finished amputating a limb, aided by one or two assistants. He was a young man with dark hair, blue eyes and a manly earnest face. Sympathy softened every line of his fine features, and he sighed audibly in turning to his new patient, who had been placed upon a camp cot, and lay pale with pain before him.

"This arm must come off," he said regretfully, lifting the helpless hand, black with stagnant blood. "Poor fellow, his right arm, too! It is hard to deprive men of such worthy members."

The wounded man unclosed his eyes and looked at him steadfastly.

"There is no hope?"

"None. It is the arm or the life that must be sacrificed. Which shall it be? If I leave the first it will cost you the second."

"Take the arm then. For my young wife's sake I must keep my life if I can. Poor Helen! it will break her heart to see me maimed."

"It is bad, yet not worse than the fate of thousands on the field to-day. I saw one young fellow up there in Thayer's command, who had both arms taken clean off by the enemy's balls. One arm is better than none, and I am glad you have one left."

Again the officer closed his eyes. It was hard to give up that which was so dear to him. And what man could resign his strong right arm without a bitter feeling of regret? Major Noble was not so far above his fellows in the scale of humanity as to ignore the pain of the sacrifice, to say nothing of the dread of physical suffering which belongs to human nature. And yet were the same path to be trodden, he knew, as he lay there waiting for the end of the operation, that he would run again the same risks and suffer the same consequences, rather than fail in his duty as an officer and a man.

Doctor Raler kept him in his own tent, and toward night a high fever set in followed by delirium. He called for his wife incessantly, but the Doctor did not approve of the idea of bringing ladies to the field, and hoped soon to send him away where he could get better care. Among the multitudinous duties which crowded upon him, he found time only to pen a hasty note to Mrs. Noble informing her that the Major had been wounded and was under his own especial care; but that was all. Had it reached her, dreadful as it was, it would still have been relief to the torturing suspense in which she lived from day to day. Bad news, it is said, is better than none, and in this case it would have proved true. It is silence after danger which is worse in its lingering torture, than the first fierce blow which smites with weakness but does not kill.

CHAPTER X.

GOING TO THE BATTLE-FIELD.

"I HAVE succeeded at last, Helen, and engaged passage for you up the Tennessee River on a boat sent from Cincinnati for the wounded. There is only half an hour in which to get ready. Can you bear it?"

"Oh yes, I can bear anything, if I can bear this awful suspense. This is Thursday, and since Sunday no word or line. I wonder that I have lived through it. And now, if I should get there only to find him—?"

She could not speak the word, and Miss Harmon went to her, lifted the poor wan face to her bosom silently, comforting her with a mute caress. What words could meet the anguish of an hour like this, with healing. The long nights of speechless pain, when the wife's steps fell ceaselessly upon her ears—and the long days vainly devoted to efforts for patience and hope, had at last exhausted her powers of soothing by words. The pall of affliction was too heavily spread over the sick heart, and she could see that words only tortured her. There was nothing to be done but to wait, and this had been a bitter task for both. Finally Mrs. Noble grew wild and desperate. Two days had been spent in the endeavor to get a passage up the river upon some passing boat, but all had been fruitless, until the afternoon of the second day, when she succeeded in finding accommodations for the journey. Every effort had been made in the midst of crowds where men grouped, clustered and stared at her. Sometimes a rude jest or coarse compliment reached her ear; and those to whom she applied asked her needless and numberless questions, only to detain her, and to refuse at last that which she persistently sought. For herself she could not have borne all this. For another she could bear anything cheerfully, if that other was a woman and in affliction. But it is no wonder if grateful tears, sprang to her eyes when at last a kind man with a gentle voice and earnest manner, bade her bring her friend on board and place her under his charge, accompanying it with a promise to aid her all in his power, to find her husband when they should have reached the Landing. Looking into his face she saw truth and honor stamped upon every feature, and her heart was lightened of a load of heaviness. When all arrangements had been made, and Mrs. Noble reclined upon a sofa in the cabin, Astrea stooped to kiss her forehead.

"God be with you," she murmured. "I must leave you now." Helen clung to her hand.

"I cannot go without you! Come with me."

Astrea looked up and saw the kind old gentleman near them, gazing compassionately at the pleading face of the young wife. He bowed affirmatively.

"You had better go," he said in a low voice. "She will need you to sustain her."

A second look at the sufferer's face, and a thought of what might be her fate when she reached the battle-field, decided Astrea in her course. Her trunk was always packed for removal at any moment and she now sent for it, at the same time penning a line to the matron at the hospital informing her of the cause of her absence.

Long and weary hours were those which followed. Mrs. Noble had exhausted her strength at first by the violence of her distress, and with her face buried in the pillows of the sofa, would lie all day long like one in a trance, save at times when excessive fear gave her unnatural strength, and she would give vent to the most touching expressions of suffering. So the first afternoon and the second day passed. At twilight of the second day's journey up the river, Astrea was seated beside her, holding one hand, while silently studying the faces of those around her. She had said but little, feeling too much depressed for conversation with strangers; but it was natural to make mental estimates of character, measuring the worth of the man or woman by the outward appearance, coupled with words and actions which without being known to any but the observer, never fail to give an insight into the true character of the person observed. There were two ladies from Cincinnati, a Mrs. and Miss Bache, mother and daughter, who had volunteered to assist in giving aid to the wounded. Everything about them indicated their high position in society. They were evidently ladies of refinement and culture; yet there was something repulsive in the manner of both—a self-consciousness amounting almost to arrogance, and an arbitrary desire to bend one and all before them to their own will and wishes, which was galling to those who perceived it. The daughter had her mother's blue eyes and auburn hair, fair round cheek and delicate mouth, with a voice low and clear, and a bearing easy and natural. Only the haughty willfulness of look, and the pleased glance when a circle closed around her, betrayed the disagreeable traits in her character.

There were also three surgeons—two from Cincinnati and one from Covington. In these three Miss Harmon discovered the elements of kindness above all other traits. Doctor Vattier had been noted for his benevolence, and it was the custom of his fellow-citizens to send people in especial need to him, telling them secretly to withhold their names in the matter, but never to fear being turned away without sympathy and aid. This memory had come to Astrea when she heard his name, and she looked with keener interest at the quiet pale face, and light blue eyes. His grey hair added a greater charm to his expression, by making it more placid. It was a pleasant face to look at. This was the man who had met her so kindly at the first, and whose influence had obtained for them comfortable passage. Doctor Blackman was larger, more robust in form, with heavy black hair just sprinkled with silver, and a keen black eye that flashed everywhere, seeing everything. He was generous to a fault, but quick tempered and exceedingly excitable. Added to this, a very sympathetic and sensitive temperament, served to make up such a character as we meet daily, and like well, yet seldom appreciate fully, because of our own inability to make allowance for those qualities which cannot be separated from them and with which we cannot have patience. Had it not been a well known fact that men make mistakes in their vocations the world over, Miss Harmon would have wondered that this man had chosen surgery as a profession. She did wonder when Doctor Vattier told her that he had a reputation for skill above any other surgeon in the West. He had regarded Mrs. Noble and herself frequently, with apparent interest but had made no advance toward acquaintance, seeing the helplessness of the one, and the taciturnity of the other. Sympathy was in every look; if he had not expressed it, the reason lay in his respect for their feelings and wishes to shun intrusion.

The third physician, Doctor Clarke of Covington, was a slender, spare man with black eyes and hair—an active vivacious soul that kept all its froth on the surface, hiding its depths. He laughed, jested and paced up and down the cabin with his hands locked behind him. His fund of anecdote was inexhaustible, and his stories without number. The other ladies regarded him with ill concealed dislike; seeing no deeper than the surface, and they could not, or would not credit him for a sterling worth deserving of respect. They voted him heartless and unfeeling; criticised his light conversation and careless ways mercilessly.

If Astrea made no affirmative response to their censure, it was because she was not ready to pass judgment without further study. Her interest was positive. She felt as if it would be pleasant to know whether they or she were right in their impressions. In his society more than any other, was a young

Englishman who had obtained permission to visit the battle-field, claiming to have been a student of medicine, and who had offered himself as an assistant. His services were accepted, and he was going in that capacity, well pleased to have been allowed the privilege. He was rather short and heavy, with fair hair and side whiskers, a fearless blue eye and intelligent expression, generally—talked with ease and confidence, as one well assured of his own ground, and sufficiently strong to maintain it. Wherever he took a position it was with the will to hold it, whatever opposing power might be brought against him. When Doctor Vattier casually remarked upon this trait to Miss Harmon, her beautiful lip slightly curled with an irrepressible show of feeling as she answered:

"Since he is an Englishman it would be surprising if he lacked in self-esteem."

Doctor Vattier laughed and made no reply, for the gentleman was too near them to render personal remarks safe; so the subject dropped then, to be resumed later. When it had grown too dark for Astrea to pursue her study of faces further, her gaze went back to Mrs. Noble's careworn features, lying against the cushions with the pallor of death upon them. Lights had not yet been brought, according to the request of Miss Bache, so she could but dimly see the drooping of the dark lashes over her friend's white cheeks; or the weary expression about the sweet mouth. While she gazed in silent sympathy, Helen stirred, clasped closer the hand that held her own and drew Astrea nearer to her side. Gradually the cabin had been cleared of nearly all the passengers. Miss Bache reclined in a chair too far down to hear what they might say, and her mother had gone to her room. Doctor Vattier and Doctor Blackman had mounted to the upper deck, while the others sauntered about, leaving only our friends with the young Englishman and Miss Bache in the cabin.

"Astrea," began Mrs. Noble with an effort for calmness. "Do you know I have fearful forebodings of what is to come?"

"You mean that you fear to find your husband has not escaped with life from this terrible battle?"

"Yes, that and other things. These long days and nights have been so horrible! Then the thought of trenches in which friends and foes are heaped indiscriminately, as that man said to me at Paducah, has almost driven me mad. While I have lain here, trying to be still and wait, my brain has been on fire, and I think now—if I should find that God has taken my husband from me, I can never be a good and patient woman again. I was willing to give him to his country for manly service, but not to die. I trusted God for his salvation; hoping and believing that he would be spared, I have been cheerful and willing to do all in my power. Now if I find my trust has been vain, I shall never have faith again, and through all my miserable life I shall wander desolate and doubting. Think how horrible that would be—without faith, robbed of hope and love and light and life!"

"How will it be if you find him wounded, or that he has been taken prisoner? The latter may have been his fate."

"If wounded, I can nurse him back to health, and will feel humbly grateful for his dear life. If imprisoned, then the torture of suspense will go on until he can be exchanged. The thought of those fearful southern prisons fills me with horror and unspeakable distress. To know him in one, would nearly drive me mad."

"Try not to think of it, then. You know all things are probable in time of war, and the soldier's fate is death, imprisonment or wounds, more possible than escape from them altogether. I will hope in spite of the silence which caused us so much distress, that it may not be so bad as you fear. You must try to rise above these feelings, and regain strength. If you should find him in need of your aid, it would be impossible to render it to him in your present condition."

"Only assure me that he is alive, and I can do anything. Oh, it is the fear within me which keeps me prostrate. His loss would lose me all the joys of earth—all my hopes of heaven."

"Child, are you mad to talk so rebelliously? Do you place your husband before your God in your affections? This is all wrong."

"I know it, but I can no more help it than I can still the ceaseless yearning for comfort which nothing but the assurance of his life can give. I have prayed as woman never prayed for patience and strength to bear my burden, as others, oh, so many others, must bear theirs from this time forth. I have thought of every possible thing, and tried to school myself for the very worst; and yet I know if I find myself utterly bereft, that I have not enough of His divine love to give me submission to His will. A fierce rebellion will rise within me, and I may grow mad enough to cast back the life which He has made worthless, since I cannot have to bless me one that is dearer. This is a dreadful frame of mind. If I could get out of it I would, but I cannot."

Astrea bowed her head, an earnest prayer in her heart. It was very difficult to know how best to answer such a confession and remove such a phase of feeling, most effectually.

At this moment the lamps were lighted, and Doctor Clarke entering the cabin, took a seat near them with a book in his hand. Presently Doctor Vattier followed, and Astrea saw him make a sign in answer to one from the young Englishman. A moment later, he came to her and asked permission to introduce the latter.

"He is your guest and I cannot refuse," she answered with great reluctance.

"That is scarcely to be considered a gracious permission," he smiled, "still I accept it, for I think it best to have you less to yourself than hitherto."

As he said this he glanced at Mrs. Noble. Astrea bowed and he withdrew. In a moment he came back with the stranger.

"Mr. Meridan, Miss Harmon." Both bowed, and Mr. Meridan took a chair in front of her. She moved her own seat so as to screen Mrs. Noble's face from his sight, and waited for him to begin conversation. Seeming perfectly at ease, he began as with an old acquaintance. "I have been admiring your beautiful country, Miss Harmon, more than I can well express. There is such a great variety of scenery, one can never weary of it. Like a vast panorama, as we glide by, it seems to move, presenting to the eye new beauty at every moment. I have now been nearly a year in America, and am daily seeing something new. I am in love with it already; if I stay here much longer, it will make me a traitor to my native land, and win me to itself for life, this strange, mixed exasperating America."

"Why exasperating?"

"Because of its social codes mainly. The classes are not set apart with sufficient distinction, and the gentlest blood in the land must mate with the meanest if there is money to back the clown in his assumption of a gentleman's position. Our system of education is different. The lowly cannot rise above their station, and know their place too well to attempt it. Here any man who wills it, may be a king—of a sort."

"And why not, if nature has endowed him with kingly power, rising within himself? I am a true American, Mr. Meridan, and hold those in highest respect who have abilities to lift themselves above the misfortunes of low birth and poverty and ignorance, to position, wealth and knowledge."

"They have not knowledge; that is the worst of it. Not one out of every fifty of your wealthy men, is a cultivated man. They start out with a desire to get rich, and labor to that end until they realize the fulfillment of their desires. When they are so inflated with success that they think themselves the smartest men living, and entitled to the highest respect and honor, they will tell you of their struggles with poverty; regale you with innumerable histories of toil, losses, misfortunes and sufferings, from the first start in life upwards, and then boast of their lack of education. Their libraries are filled with books of which they know nothing; their walls hung with pictures of which they cannot judge the real value beyond the cost in dollars and cents. And yet these men have thrown open to them the best saloons of the land, and they are made welcome among the most aristocratic members of society, because their purses are large, and their bank credit indisputable. Do you think this just as it should be? If they must be admitted to society, would it not be better if they could first prepare themselves by a decent polish at least?"

"Must a man wait to the end of his days for the reward of his labor? Many are old before they can amass wealth, and it has passed beyond their power to become polished and refined. Old habits are too strong upon them. Knowing this, they avail themselves of the privileges of a democratic land, and strive to enjoy their gains as well as they can."

"Would it not be better if they could be content with less in gold and store their minds with more of knowledge?"

"Doubtless, but money making has an incalculable fascination. I find it a passion not only with Americans, but the French, Germans, Italians and Englishmen who make their way to us, are generally seized with the same desire, and often outstrip us in the golden harvest. We are a strange people, because of the strange mixture of national characteristics. Our avenues of trade are open to all, and the one monopolizes an avocation to success who is most capable of using his privileges. He serves well for his claim upon society, and earns it, whether we yield it to him graciously or not. You will see that I own a partiality for 'self-made men.'"

"Evidently, and it puzzles me, for you are cultivated yourself, and one would suppose might naturally shrink from coarseness and ignorance!"

"Mr. Meridan, the rude and honest simplicity of the laboring man is not coarseness in my eyes, and I must esteem those who have good and noble qualities of heart, whether high or low in position. After all, the quality of the heart and mind make the man to honor. If it is not good, his millions will not win from a true man or woman sincere respect, even if he has education and a certain polish called refinement, which passes him with the world of fashion, irreproachable."

Here Mr. Meridan paused before speaking, and looked at her.

"Do all native American ladies reason as you do? Have each and all of you such decided opinions as yours on the various subjects which excite discussion?"

"If they have not, they should have. Surely, if we are women, we should not be excluded from the right of thinking for ourselves—especially since it is our lot, as a sex, to give the first bias and impression to the mind of lordly man."

"Ah, you are sarcastic. Perhaps you are a 'woman's rights' woman."

"No, not in the sense the term suggests. A woman's greatest power and beauty lies in her thorough womanliness. When she departs from that, she becomes unnatural, and must lose respect, consequently her influence for good. I am not a native American, however."

"From whence do you come?"

"England. America is my dear home by adoption. All that I have known of joy or pain, good or ill, has been on her soil. She has sheltered me, comforted me, loved me, and I am grateful—will be faithful. It shames me when I remember that Englishmen have come to this fair land and shared her privileges, received the fruits of her soil, lived under her laws safely and happily, only to turn their backs upon all in the moment of her danger. Had I been a man, I could sooner have faced a whole battalion of the enemy, than to have appealed to the English Consul for protection from the draft! It was a burning shame to me which I shall never forget."

Mr. Meridan winced and looked grave. A smile had gone around the little circle, and he did not relish what it expressed.

"It certainly is to be regretted," he said, after some thought; "but those who have done so, had their own private reasons, and good ones, doubtless."

"Yes, good enough for them, since they were not noble enough to act without the most utter selfishness. They wanted her gold, her lands, her offices of honor and her protection in prosperity, but they did not want to fight for her in her trouble, and would escape it by such a contemptible appeal. I know of only one class of people worthy to be placed in the same catalogue."

"Which class do you mean?"

"Copperheads! I have seen men who were rebels, deep and bitter at heart, denying their politics, sheltering themselves under the Federal Government, and speculating upon Government wares for gold. Such men deserve only contempt and scorn, and I could sooner give my hand in acknowledged amity to an open rebel, than to tolerate the presence of a copperhead."

"Right," cried Doctor Blackman, slapping Mr. Meridan on the shoulder lightly. "I agree with the lady in all the grounds she has taken, and the last especially. I think I should want to shoot my grandmother if she was one of that vile set. Madam, pardon me, but may I ask where you were reared?"

"In the South, surrounded by slaves, and educated in the midst of Southern Institutions."

"Then how does it happen that you are not a rebel yourself?"

"I could not see things in the same light, and in differing, cut myself off from my early life and associations as fully as if the grave had closed over me. I never believed slavery to be right, and secession was with me out of the question. In the midst of the hot-headed and excited masses I was not likely to pass unscathed, with such sentiments as it was known I cherished. The result is my presence here."

"Why, your history must be quite a romantic one," began Mr. Meridan; when Miss Harmon spoke quickly:

"Yes, sir, but I must be excused if I decline to relate more for the benefit of strangers. It is enough that I am homeless and friendless, having nothing left but a desire to serve my country as a woman may."

Mr. Meridan bowed apologetically, and soon after withdrew, feeling his presence distasteful to her. Doctor Vattier followed and took his arm.

"A rather positive character," he said as they paced the

lower cabin slowly. "To look at her face one would not expect to find independence and courage like hers."

"I do not know; we should not too readily deceive ourselves. Certainly the face is very youthful, but strong notwithstanding. She may prove dangerous, and I would advise you to watch her."

"What do you mean?"

"Simply that there have been such things as spies in times of war, who wore feminine apparel and used beautiful faces as passports to places where knowledge was most valuable. Suppose she should prove one of this kind? I would not cast suspicion unjustly upon any woman, but she would alarm me if I was a commander in your army, and she should come much about me. You know nothing about her."

"Enough to claim for her the respect and honor all brave, true women deserve. I cannot permit you to shake the confidence of others in her integrity, while she is under my protection. One moment's thought ought to prove to you the improbability of such an idea. What could she learn from us, or how from us reach the enemy with any information that might prove valuable? You will pardon me for the frankness, but I fear that a personal feeling of resentment is at the bottom of your desire to lower her in my esteem. It is not generous or manly."

"Doctor Vattier, I beg of you not to think so ill of me as that! The thought I spoke arose only from an honest belief that what I suggested might be true. I am not so mean as to retaliate upon a woman by injuring her reputation for loyalty."

The young man's brow had flushed hotly. "Then let it pass. I have not the slightest suspicion of the possibility of such a thing, and could not stoop to watch her, even if I had, knowing how powerless she is. I wonder how we are progressing?" Thus abruptly cutting short the conversation, the Doctor stepped outside and peered through the gloom at the shore, lying in a dark, rugged line against a somber sky. Mr. Meridan feeling anything but pleased, mounted to the hurricane deck, and with a cigar between his lips threw himself upon a bench and strove to soothe his disagreeable feelings.

The day following his stubborn pride forced him to seek Miss Harmon's society. It should not be thought that he was afraid of her, so he broached any topic that promised interest, and found himself well entertained in the fresh, original ideas, which were always expressed readily, but never with arrogance or an undue importance to her own views. Very soon he found himself wondering at her varied fund of information, and the evident study she had given to most of the subjects introduced. The smart of last night's encounter had not lasted long enough to occasion any very deep-seated dislike; but if it had done so, it must have melted under to-day's more genial warmth. As the hours glided by, he constantly wandered away as if in search of change in occupation, but always came back to where she sat beside her friend, as one drawn irresistibly by a new and fascinating power. Astrea experienced but little interest in his society, yet felt it due to herself to maintain her position steadily, as he appeared disposed indirectly to attack her. At least she looked upon his advances in that light, and was constantly prepared for them. She had another reason, also, for encouraging his advances, when she observed that Mrs. Noble had thrown off the languor, which had prostrated her, and listened with unmistakable interest to what they said.

Toward the close of the afternoon on Saturday, quite a little stir was perceptible among the surgeons and their assistants. It was reported that they were nearing the Landing, and then Helen grew strong and restless under the excitement. Heedless of Astrea's entreaties to be calm, she passed from the cabin to her state-room, and from that to the guards and back again, unable to remain still for a moment. Her eyes shone like stars, while her cheeks burned with a bright spot in the center of each. There was not one on board who could look without pity on the poor young wife, thus writhing under the anguish which was consuming her.

"How can I wait? How can I wait? Oh, my God, be merciful!"

Astrea stood at her side just beyond the door, and heard the passionate murmur with starting tears. The setting sun just touched them both, tinging the pale face with a golden radiance and adding strange lustre to the strained, anguished eyes. Softly one arm stole around the quivering form.

"Helen," very tenderly, "words are meaningless to a heart tried like yours; but I believe in God's goodness and I am praying for you all the time."

"Heaven bless you! faithful friend. You are far better than I, and He may hear you kindly. I feel myself too wicked for prayers now."

Her head sank to Astrea's shoulder, and she stood quietly looking at the shore as they passed, for several minutes. The sun went behind the hills, and the gray twilight crept over the earth; the boat steamed on against the current with heavy, monotonous clamor; and finally after a weary and tedious journey, our friends saw them tie up under the bluffs at Pittsburg Landing.

CHAPTER XI.

INCIDENTS AND HORRORS OF A BATTLE-FIELD.

A FULL moon had risen, and the stars shone brightly from a clear blue sky. The silvery radiance was spread over a strange scene, wild and sickening to those who looked upon it from the deck of the Lancaster. Across the river gleamed the red lights of the gunboats, whose long dark lengths were distinctly outlined upon the water. Towering above the Lancaster, were the bluffs, dark and forbidding. Above and beyond them gleamed the camp fires of our soldiers, while upon both sides of the boat as it lay in position directly fronting the bluffs, were other vessels upon whose decks crowds passed to and fro continually. The noise and confusion was great; the mud so deep that the poor laboring animals used to draw freight from the steamers to the top of the bluffs, could scarcely move their burdens. Hoarse cries and curses, mingled with the cracking of whips, and occasional bursts of laughter, filled the air. Here the leaves had already put forth their tender green, and the rosebuds bloomed profusely along the bank of the stream. The faint, sweet breath of early flowers floated to them over the noisome places where the dead still lay unburied. Mrs. Noble shuddered and covered her face with her hands, unable to look longer at the mocking beauty of the night over such horrors. Astrea sickened but would not turn her eyes from the spot where a dozen figures lay distinctly outlined.

"Surely," she said to Mr. Meridan who stood near her, "those men have not lain there until now—since the battle!"

"O, no. I presume they are the rebel wounded who died since the battle. We must not forget all that the Federalists have had to do since that time. The health of the army demands that the dead should be buried as soon as possible. By to-morrow morning they will have disappeared."

Mrs. Noble's hand at this time closed on Astrea's arm so hard as to give her absolute pain.

"Doctor Blackman is coming! He has been to make inquiries for me."

As he approached, she trembled violently. Astrea's heart gave a great throb of delight with the first cheery ring of his voice.

"Mrs. Noble, it will be utterly impossible to get ashore to-night. The mud is almost impassable in daylight, and there are roads only where one can be made. But I have just met the very man of all others most fortunate to see, for Major Noble is at his tent and has been under his care since receiving his wound. He reports him doing pretty well now, though he has had rather a hard time of it."

She scarcely heard the last part of the sentence. With a low cry she sank to her knees and lifted to the starry sky a white face wet with penitential tears, murmuring brokenly:

"My God I thank thee—I am not worthy of his dear life—yet thou hast spared him to me—the faithless one! My husband, oh, my husband."

Doctor Blackman coughed and dashed his hand across his eyes. Mr. Meridan turned away and walked to the other side of the deck.

"By Jove," cried Doctor Blackman, following him, "it is worth while for a fellow to have a wife who cares for him like that! Ar'n't you sorry you're a bachelor?" Mr. Meridan made no reply, and looking at him more closely, the Doctor saw a bright tear fall from his cheek, which he had sought to conceal as unmanly.

"Something good in the chap, if he can cry over a woman's joy in finding what he never saw. After all, I guess the world in general is better than we are disposed to give it credit for being," with which sage and charitable mental comment, he thrust his hands deep into his pockets and marched away. The next moment he had disappeared through the gangway, and was seen busy with the wounded which were already being brought on board.

"Can I be of any service to you, ladies?" asked Mr. Meridan, returning to them and speaking as men speak when it is hard to control the powers of speech and render them effective. Astrea was forced to answer for both, for Mrs. Noble was weeping unrestrainedly.

"Not to-night, thank you, if it is not possible to go to Major Noble. We will go below, and see what can be done there to pass the time usefully until to-morrow morning; then perhaps, we may be only too glad to claim your kind offer of service."

"Command me fully: I shall be only too happy to aid you in any way. If you will allow me to hint it, I fear it is not best for either of you to be here. The air is damp, and you will take cold. Permit me to assist you below, Mrs. Noble."

Immediately upon reaching the cabin, Miss Harmon led her to her room, brought a cup of tea which she drank eagerly, and then made her lie down. Notwithstanding the stimulant which she had taken, the overtaxed woman soon sank into a profound slumber, and her tender nurse left her to sleep in peace while she sought the cabin. Here cots had been hastily thrown upon the floor upon either side and in the middle, leaving two narrow passages between, the length of the boat. Already they were filled with the wounded, whose eagerly expressed wants filled the place with confusion. Previous experience had taught her what was to be done, and she immediately prepared for a night's labor by stepping into her own state-room and assuming a proper dress for moving about among the cots. In a few moments she again appeared with her white arms bared, and a handkerchief bound about her hair, upon which she had dashed water until it was drenched. Several bright drops ran down the smooth skin of her cheeks as she came out into the light.

"Why, what have you been doing to yourself, Miss Harmon?" asked Doctor Blackman, who happened just then to pass her.

"Only getting ready to help you. I have put water on my head to prevent a headache from stooping. You see how much need there is for care. I would not like to have to give up before these poor men get something to eat, and have had their wounds dressed."

"You'll do!" answered the Doctor heartily. "I wish just now, we had a dozen more on board like you!"

"Thank you—so do I, in some respects."

"What particular respects?"

"Willingness for one; we will not stop to name others now," and she left him to begin her task.

All night long the lights blazed in the cabin and flashed upon the guards and decks. The boat was filled to her utmost capacity—not a vacant spot that was not taken up for the resting-place of some sufferer. Astrea had commenced by passing down one aisle and examining into the immediate wants of the men. The first thing was to feed them for they were ravenously hungry; then began the more trying task of dressing their wounds.

"Boys," she said standing where they could all hear her, "I have taken this ward half way down the cabin under my charge. I am to dress your wounds and try to make you comfortable. Many of you are badly in need of such relief, while others have suffered comparatively little. Shall I begin systematically and take each one in his turn, or select the worst cases first? I leave it to you to decide, because I do not want one of you to think another preferred above you."

"O, take the worst, of course," cried one or two in prompt affirmation. The others responded more stragglingly, but all in the affirmative.

"As I expected," she smiled, "brave men are never selfish."

She knelt beside a heavy, giant-like fellow who lay with his bright eyes wide open and twinkling restlessly. A ball had passed through his right hand; that must be dressed first; then a deep flesh wound in the arm just above the elbow. These done he moved with some difficulty and displayed another flesh wound upon the right shoulder, beginning to canker for want of proper attention. "You see I couldn't git to that myself," he said grimly, "I fixed the others up in some sort o' shape; but this one was too high up."

"Do you tell me that you have had no one to care for you since receiving those wounds?"

"Nary! What's the use? I lost a power o' blood among 'em, but then I was a sight stronger than any of the other fellers round, an' I told the medicine chaps to let me alone an' tend to 'em."

"You are a brave, unselfish man, and deserve to be rewarded! What regiment do you belong to?"

"Berge's sharpshooters. But you never mind. I don't want no promotion; I'm fightin' fur my ole woman an' the chillen, an' don't need to be paid fur it. Guess if we was all officers, thar wouldn't be any men to fight."

"Hurrah! you're a trump!" shouted a wild young fellow, lifting himself upon his sound arm to look at his comrade. "I say, Stevens, you'll wear a Corporal's bars before you know it, old fellow."

Those around laughed; Stevens grunted.

"Don't want 'em."

"A Lieutenant's then; they'll be better."

"Don't want 'em."

"A Captain's."

"Don't want 'em."

"Suppose, then, you take a Colonel's."

"Don't want 'em."

"What *do* you want, I'd like to know."

"Want you to shet up yer jaw an' let a feller alone. If

ye need 'em, I give ye all my chances to put a feather in yer cap."

"Now I think I have finished," said Astrea taking up her sponge and basin. "I hope you feel comfortable."

"Not quite," and he drew one foot up slowly. "I guess the rebs found my heels in spite of me, as they shot one purty nigh off." Astrea removed the bandages and revealed a terrible wound. A piece of shell still remained in it, which must have caused untold agony.

"I cannot dress it until this is out. Can you bear to have a slight operation? It is a wonder it is not past all help. I am not sure, indeed, that we can save your foot now."

"Hope there aint any more," spoke a quiet voice a little beyond them. "I should think a few more shots would have left nothing of you."

"You see the advantage of being big," answered Stevens, stoutly. "It gives more space to work on, an' still leaves something fur the doctors."

"What is this you are saying, my man?" and Doctor Clarke stopped beside him.

"Nothing o' consequence; but I think this lady wants you to do something or other."

Astrea looked up.

"Here is a piece of shell in this wound which must come out," and she displayed it. He looked at the foot and then at the man.

"I think I heard somebody call you a 'trump' a moment ago. That is no name for you, if you have borne all this without complaint. I suppose you would not mind having it out, now?"

"As ye please."

Yet in spite of his stoical bravery, the great fellow winced, and groaned heavily as the Doctor proceeded in the operation. Astrea stood by the operator, a ready and efficient help, closely observing the skillful and tender care of his hands, while his lips smiled and his tongue jested. No touch was lighter than his; no hand more rapid and dexterous. And it was in this that the kind heart revealed itself, making no sign nor boast, but working out its sympathy in deeds that brought relief and rest. He did not leave her after that. Wherever she went he was sure to be beside her, rendering more than aid. Indeed, she came into the position of his assistant, and they worked in unity until the wearisome and painful task was ended.

"Now come out a moment and take the fresh air. The stifling, rank odors of this room will make you ill."

She followed him out and looked abroad upon the still night. Faint and distant, came strains of music upon the moonlit air.

"General Halleck is returning. An expedition went up the river to-night to destroy a railroad bridge, and he accompanied it."

"He was on the CONTINENTAL, then? I heard the band as they started out, and afterwards missed the gunboats. Hark!"

Just below them was a large vessel, upon whose decks were groups of men with lanterns. From the midst of one, came up to them a strong man's sobs and entreaties to spare the arm the surgeon was about to amputate.

"But, my good man, you will die," came in the expostulating voice of the doctor.

"Then let me die. I would rather be dead than maimed for life. Pray go away and leave me to die in peace."

"Rather a hard position to place a man in," remarked Doctor Clarke. "Of course he cannot let him die without an effort to save him. There, it is over!"

Astrea looked. Some one held to the sufferer's face a sponge filled with chloroform, and he had sunk back silently, resisting no more. She turned her face away and walked to the other end of the boat.

"I shall have to see enough without looking at that," she said, a little tremulously. Then steadying her voice:

"What have they done with all the rebel prisoners and wounded, Doctor Clarke?"

"Sent them to various points. We have some of the wounded. The other boats have some, and a number are still ashore."

"Have we any officers?"

"Not here, I think. A number were taken. Do you suppose any of your friends to be among them?"

"None of my *friends*," she answered, with emphasis, and turned abruptly into the cabin. In so doing she came face to face with Mr. Meridan.

"Ah, I was looking for you, Miss Harmon. Doctor Blackman thinks as soon as it is light enough to see our way, we had better go for Major Noble and bring him on board before his wife awakens. It is not necessary, you understand, but it would be a pleasant thing for her to wake and find him here after all her anxiety."

"It would indeed, and Doctor Blackman is more than kind to think of it. Still, if the roads are so bad, I cannot see how it can be done so easily."

She was right, and the sun had risen before they got fairly started. Two horses were brought down to the river, and Mr. Meridan with Astrea were detailed for the duty. She demurred until they insisted that she would be needed to make the Major comfortable; and as it was out of the question for his wife to undertake the trip across the field to where he lay, she yielded and set out cheerfully, leaving her friend still fast asleep. Very slowly the horses labored through the mire, round the narrow road, up the rugged bluffs. As they approached the dead bodies lying in their horrible ghastliness with their faces upturned, Astrea's horse shied and came near unseating her. It was not a very secure seat at best, in a man's saddle with one stirrup shortened and the other brought over the saddle. Had she been a less fearless horsewoman, or valued appearances above the discharge of duty, she could never have ventured to assume it. As it was, she maintained her place steadily, and guided the restless animal with a firm and skillful hand. Presently they reached the summit of the bluffs and struck off in a northerly direction, according to orders from Doctor Blackman. They expected to travel about a mile to a certain point where they were to inquire for the position of Stuart's brigade, then find the Fifty-fifth Illinois regiment's head-quarters.

Though the sun shone beautifully, and the birds flitted joyously all about them, it was not possible for Astrea to rise above the sadness that oppressed her. Their way lay through scenes trying to stouter hearts than hers. Here such strange new phases of life were presented. Now they passed a knot of men burying the dead, who would pause to look at them for a moment, then go on with their work, whistling carelessly. And again they would discover the grave-diggers resting from their labors, and munching their breakfast of crackers and cheese with infinite relish, heedless of the ghastly forms lying so near them! From thousands of camp fires, blue wreaths of smoke curled up gracefully through the trees, and the white tents gleamed dazzlingly pure under the beautiful light of the early morning. As they passed one spot, a group of soldiers were gathered around an enterprising peddler of patent medicines, who mounted upon a huge stump, was crying the virtues of his wares with stentorian lungs:

"I'll tell you what it is, my brave lads of the Army of the Southwest, this medicine is the best ever compounded, and warranted to cure every ill to which human flesh is heir. The wonders it produces are perfectly incalculable. If you are troubled with wakefulness, take a half a teaspoonful of the Magic Cure-All, and it will instantly put you into a Rip Van Winkle sleep that will last a hundred years. And again it is invaluable for headache, that most distressing of all complaints, especially to the man of mental parts, who lives upon his wits. You see, gentlemen, I know from experience, [here a shout of laughter,] and the relief it has brought me I cannot describe. All you have to do is to shave the top of your head, apply a small portion of the mixture to it with a linen cloth, and in something less than a month after the application, your headache will disappear."

By this time our friends were too far away to distinguish what was said, but loud shouts of laughter followed them for some distance. Mr. Meridan smiled rather quizzically.

"Such enterprising men make fortunes" he said "and are admitted into society on equal terms with better people. He can stand up here in the face of death, and vend his vile drugs without thought or care of the thousands slain; then go back to your gay cities and mix with the daintiest of the land, if he happens to be successful in filling his purse beforehand."

"If you knew more about our higher class of society, you would not say this Mr. Meridan. Your prejudices have made you unjust, and you exaggerate the evil. While I have no wish to retaliate, you will allow me to say here, that I think, were you to turn your thoughts back to your native land, you would find that evils of as great or greater magnitude exist socially, as can be found in America."

"Name some of them."

"Take your marriage laws for instance. There is no help for the man or woman who has made the mistake of mating dishonorably. Either may steep the other in the direst shame and you give the wronged one no redress or protection."

"Well, that, bad as it is, is better than the laws by which men may escape from a wearisome connection at pleasure. Marriage in this country has no bonds so sacred they cannot be broken at will. The vilest wretch may marry a sweet young girl and wear her till the first bloom and freshness has been worn away by his own rude handling, then he will neglect her until the tainting breath of scandal has touched her fair name, and taking advantage of this, he applies for a divorce, gets it, and leaves her to the mercies of a cold and cruel world."

"Better that than the daily presence and companionship of such a man," with a warmth almost startling. "With such an one, the fair, pure soul cannot remain spotless, but must be dragged to the dust and made, in part, at least, to mate with his own. Apart, though she be cut off from the world, and her name bandied by the heedless or malicious most cruelly, she may still rise above her wrongs, and live for that better life where such wrongs are unknown."

Mr. Meridan looked at her keenly.

"I never expected to hear a lady, young and beautiful, defend such laws. It sounds strangely to my ears."

"Then we will drop tho subject if you please, sir. It is a scarcely fitting one for the time and place."

Her face had suddenly grown hard and cold, and the large, dark eyes looking straight before her, had a glittering, strong glare which sent a disagreeable thrill through him as he looked.

They were passing at the moment, over a rough piece of ground where the trees had fallen in every direction. Mr. Meridan's attention was drawn necessarily from his companion's face to their road and the horses, who evinced marked dislike to the locality. Being unable to get around the large bodies of the trees from their inextricable entanglement, they were obliged to clear them, a feat which Astrea performed with comparative safety. In this way they had nearly crossed the obstructions, when suddenly Mr. Meridan's horse took fright at a dead body lying directly under his feet as he jumped a huge log, and with a fearful leap to one side, he threw his rider violently from the saddle several yards distant, where he lay motionless.

"Oh, heaven, he is killed!" gasped Astrea, deathly white with the sudden shock. But the next moment she had sprung from the saddle, and was kneeling beside the fallen man, while both horses dashed madly away across the field.

A long, deep cut upon the forehead left the skull bare for two inches. The blood flowed profusely, and Astrea looked about her instinctively for help. Not a soul was near enough to render any assistance, and to call was useless. What could she do? The full extent of his injury she could not judge, as yet, but she put her hand on his heart and found that it beat with a dull, heavy motion; he was not dead; would he die? She could not tell if the skull was fractured, or whether he had received other hurts in his violent fall. Far along the range of her vision, the white tents gleamed, and blue wreaths of smoke curled up toward the sky. If she only dared to leave him until she could procure aid; but to do that would expose him to death from loss of blood. She must staunch that, first, then endeavor to get him to some place of safety.

A small spring bubbled up in a rocky spot a short distance from her, and taking Mr. Meridan's handkerchief from his pocket, she ran and saturated it freely. By the time she could return, however, he had fainted and the copious flow at once ceased. With rapid fingers she wiped the stains away, took from her pocket a little needle case with white sewing silk, scissors, and every thing complete for use, and put several stitches through the edge of the cut—clipped the silk closely, and then tearing her handkerchief into strips, bound it about his head.

All this was done rapidly, and then she ran again for water to restore him to consciousness. It looked very like death to see him lying so pale and still under her chafing hands; and it lasted so long, without any sign of returning life, she began to fear that the vital spark had gone out forever.

"What shall I do? What shall I do?" she said at length in despair. "If he is not really dead, he will die, and no one near to help him."

Not knowing what else to attempt, she went back to the spring, again dipped the handkerchief in the water and ran to him with a tiny stream marking her course. This she dashed over his face and pressed to his mouth. A moment later, to her infinite joy, a faint, but perceptible sigh came through the pale lips. She redoubled her efforts, chafing his hands zealously, until she knew that he was beginning to recover. Assured of this a sudden perversity of feeling seized her. She withdrew from his side, sat down on a log at a short distance from him, and dropping her face in her hands, burst into tears.

Why should she not weep? There had been a sudden and severe shock—a heavy tax upon her powers of action and self-control, following close upon long days and nights of intense care and anxiety. Her sympathies were tender, her nervous system keenly alive to change. Nothing but a wonderful will-power could have upheld a woman so constituted under such trying difficulties. It was natural for intense excitement and overwrought feeling to take this course and dissolve in tears. If she did not weep, it was because she had good reasons for suppressing her tears. Such control over her weaker nature, always cost her more or less of strength, and now there was no reason why she should deny herself the luxury of the relief tears seldom fail to bring. So she cried heartily, in a very womanish way.

Before Mr. Meridan had fairly recovered his faculties, two soldiers came careering toward them on the truant horses. The peculiar arrangement of the stirrups had betrayed a lady's use of one, and they had rightly conjectured some mishap to the riders. Following the direction from which the panting animals came, they had ridden back over the road, and found them just in time to render the assistance so much needed.

Mr. Meridan was soon able, with the aid of the two men, to assume his saddle, while Astrea led her horse to a fallen log, and mounted to her uncomfortable seat and rode slowly after them, and a few hours later, while the crowd gathered and surged around the landing, an ambulance driven by a merry son of Erin, came slowly down the winding path and halted before the Lancaster. Two men rode forward at once and dismounted. Then the back of the vehicle was taken out, and Astrea's little foot was placed upon the steps. Mrs. Noble who had been pacing up and down the guards for what to her seemed an age, caught sight of her, and rushed down the stairs and across the plank.

"Oh, Astrea, how could you treat me so like a child!" she said reproachfully. "Was it not my right to seek my husband myself—and you were unkind enough to keep me here doing nothing."

One look into the grieved face told Astrea how deeply Helen felt what she considered a wrong, and she was for an instant, humiliated, as she thought within herself how indignantly she would have resented a like encroachment upon her rights. But a second thought dispelled the unpleasant sensation, when she recalled her friend's utter physical inability to the task, and the accident which had placed Mr. Meridan beside Major Noble, almost as helpless as he. A smile broke over her face, and she laid one hand upon Helen's arm, tenderly.

"I know I have pained you, but it was farthest from my thoughts to do you a wrong in any way. You will soon come to think differently of the matter when you know all."

Mr. Meridan was lifted out first and assisted up to the cabin. Then they took the Major out and placed him upon a camp cot which they carried up stairs and bore back to the stewardess' cabin. At first there had been only a silent clasping of hands; and then, while the young wife followed with fast flowing tears, the Major's closed eyes held the drops that gathered under the lids. When the men had put down the cot, Astrea made a gesture for them to retire, and taking Helen in her arms for one moment she left a mute kiss upon the quivering lips, after which she went out and closed the door.

And now after all those long hours of anguish, she was alone with her husband. Poor Helen! What a cry went up from her heart as she fell upon her knees by his side and laid her cheek to his, thin and wan already with great suffering. His left hand wandered lovingly over her hair, and now the large tears flowed unchecked.

"Oh, George, they told me you had been killed, and I was rebellious—wicked. The force of my anguish unnerved me, and I could not sooner come to see if it was really true. Even now I am so weak and wan, they have kept me here while they went for you, and that made me more wicked still—I was so ungrateful with all. Now I have you safe, and I don't deserve it. God cannot forgive one so selfish and unreasonable. What shall I ever do to merit this great blessing to my life—to have you back from the grave? Oh, my husband, my husband—given back to me from the jaws of death."

She spoke brokenly, with little impulsive sobs, while he still gently stroked her hair. He spoke now very tenderly:

"Yes, Helen; and you will not quarrel with a wise Director if He has chosen that I shall come to you again badly scathed?"

He lifted her face, and pointed down to the bandaged stump of his poor arm, lying so near her, and which Astrea had hastily covered over with a sheet. Instantly her cheeks and lips turned very white, and again her face fell against his. For a full minute she did not answer. When she did speak, it was in a subdued, quiet yet tremulous tone that betrayed the closing of a brief, fierce struggle.

"How sad is this moment! You have suffered and I have been so proud of you! I did not quite know what it would cost me to be so tried, but I can say now, 'Thy will be done.' I am no more rebellious, I hope."

"Poor little wife! And she has had to bear it alone. The battle has been a hard one."

"Only for her it would have killed me—Astrea—that good and noble girl with whom I have been angry all day because she went for you and left me sleeping. She has been everything to me."

"'Cast thy bread upon the waters,'" quoted the Major, smiling faintly into the eager face Helen lifted when she began to speak of her friend. "This time it has come back, however 'after few days' instead of many. I think no real kindness is ever lost, little wife."

"No, though as she says sometimes, the rewards are a weary while coming in too many cases."

"For our patience, perhaps, but seldom for our real good, if we could only believe it," and then the Major's thoughts took a sudden turn and he spoke quickly.

"I suppose you know Wilfer was taken prisoner. I heard it only this morning."

10

"No! When was it?"

"On Sunday. I am told he fought like a hero, and did more before his capture than any other officer in his division. Now he must be carried down there to languish in those horrible southern prisons! How sad!"

"Poor Captain Wilfer," echoed Helen regretfully, and Astrea coming to the door that moment to see if she was needed, caught the import of his closing sentence and heard her reply. She did not enter, but went outside, crept round a pile of boxes on the side of the boat farthest from the shore, and screened from observation thus, sat some time looking vacantly out across the river. I think she was not conscious of her own depth of feeling. She did not know just why it was that this news had seemed to stun her like a sudden and unexpected blow, because she was so fully persuaded that she did not particularly care for him. Now as she called up scenes of suffering, privation and cruelty in those far off, dismal prisons, she imagined the sick feeling which came with them, arose only from common sympathy, and the remembrance of that last sad good-bye which haunted her very forcibly at this moment. There had been times when she chided and severely ridiculed herself when his name was mentioned, and a conscious growing interest alarmed her. Resolution had banished that, she thought now, and she only felt as she might feel if any one she knew had been captured. He was a brave, good man, and she disliked to think that his useful career had been checked thus abruptly. It might be so long before he could be exchanged; and then his health might be so broken, as to render him unfit for service. Or they might parole him, in which case he could not take up arms again in the defense of his country. But a prompt "no" answered this thought. He would not give his parole. He would either wait to be exchanged or die there, and she did not know that her cheek kindled and her eye flashed with pride as the thought passed through her mind.

CHAPTER XII.

AMONG THE WOUNDED AND DYING.

"Ah, truant, I have found you at last! Will you come and help me?"

Doctor Blackman's face appeared suddenly above her, and his voice quick and sharp, ran along her nerves, with painful discord. She started to her feet confused and trembling, feeling a strong sense of resentment that had nearly expressed itself in words. It was a disagreeable shock to be so broken in upon at that moment, and she turned to him a face which caused him to laugh aloud, then suddenly to become grave and alarmed by its expression.

"You look as if I had struck you," he said. "Pardon my abruptness, please."

"What do you wish, Doctor Blackman?"

"I wanted to ask you to help me with an amputation," he hesitatingly answered. "I know it is asking much, but I am in despair. All the other doctors and most of the assistants have gone ashore and are busy there. Meridan is as helpless as a baby with that ugly cut, and if you cannot bear to see the operation, my last hope is gone, and my patient will probably have to die."

"I will help you."

The Doctor gave a sigh of relief. Her simple, positive tone reassured him, for he knew she would not undertake anything which she was incapable of carrying out. Still the lingering expression of her face made him feel uncomfortable, as she walked beside him down to the deck and back to the place where the man was lying. He again attempted to apologize for his abruptness, but she cut him short in a manner that silenced him at once.

"Do not think of it, Doctor. I have lost much sleep, feel rather weary, and on the whole am rather nervous, I presume. I went back there to find a quiet place, and it was such a luxury, it was something of a shock to be aroused from it and to come back to duty again. I was selfish to feel cross about it, and am heartily ashamed of the momentary irritation. If you can excuse this in me, we will drop the subject."

"Selfish! If you are selfish, I would like to see what you would call unselfish people, for they must be wonders of generosity."

The operation was quickly performed, and Astrea stood by him faithfully, never shrinking to the end. Only once, when the little saw grated through the bone, did she change color and set her teeth tightly together; but there was no trembling or outward sign of emotion. This woman's will was like iron, and would not let the fearful strain upon her powers of endurance, appear, even, much less affect her to the exclusion of the aid she was called upon to render. When they had finished, Doctor Blackman's eyes met hers with a broad stare of admiration and wonder.

"You are the strangest woman I ever saw. Ninety-nine out of one hundred people would swear that you could not bear anything, to look at you; and here you stand like a statue—calm and unyielding. It is not because you have no sympathy or feeling. I know you have that to an unusual degree. It is your will which amazes me, and your strength to endure. I wonder what would happen if another strong will were to come in contact with yours; and prove as firm and steady. I would like to witness the conflict and the final triumph of either party, though I confess I should not like to be the one to oppose you."

Gradually his tone became lighter, until the close of his sentence was playful. She answered him lightly.

"I avoid conflicts. If an opposing will can satisfy my reason, I am always ready to yield. If not, I will never contend. Better separation and safety, than for two hard substances to strike together. They are apt to produce sparks, and from sparks flames are kindled—flames that consume and utterly destroy. Individual battles are both dangerous and degrading."

"Did you never seriously disagree with anybody, in either politics or religion?" he asked still playfully. "Those are fruitful topics for discord, and I cannot imagine such a character as yours separating itself from both."

"Nor do I; but what good can come from conflicts? Others have equal rights to their own private opinions, when based upon a sound and conscientious reasoning of the subjects. I will adopt no creed or theory that I have not first been led to believe right, and from that ground when once taken, no power on earth can move me by mere opposition. Being thus firm, why should I strive to shake from beneath others, their dearly beloved footing? It is far better for each to cherish his or her own 'pets' and go their own way in peace, than for one to try to win or coerce the other into their particular views of things."

"But you know that it is by opposition we rise. If there were no conflicts of opinions and feelings, progress would fall dead, and the world would stand still, moving no higher up forever than its present position."

"That may be, but do we necessarily stand still if we come not to personal conflict in our views? The course we take and the work we accomplish must determine our share in the work of progression. I will have my own way where reason and conscience approve, and I will have it in peace. I do not like to fight for my privileges. If I must do it, the fight will be disastrous to one or the other. I would sooner die than yield."

"I believe it! You ought to have been a soldier. I suppose you could make a better one than either Belle Boyd or

Belle Reynolds—those feminine heroes who are like shining stars in the center of the Confederate and Federal chaplets."

"You may well speak with such sarcasm, sir. I should consider myself deserving of such remarks, if I could even think of assuming so unwomanly a position as they have done. Surely the avenues of usefulness are not so tightly closed against us, as to drive us into unseemly ways to prove our patriotism. A woman may be earnest and enthusiastic; but a true and pure enthusiasm will keep her within the boundaries of her own sphere."

"Undoubtedly. But do you know some people would call you inconsistent? You are womanly—purely so in all your manners; but you act as few women can act, when your aid is required. I may say that you are manly in your strength and capacities."

"Allow me to say that you are mistaken. I am not *manly* simply because I have strength of will and self-control. You base your assertion upon the ground that I have been able to bear more, physically, than any woman you have known, and you set me apart from my sex as 'manly' in consequence. If you will reflect for a little while, you will acknowledge that in all domestic and social ills, the woman is stronger and more enduring than the man, as a general thing. This proves her native strength; and that strength is too often cultivated in the way I have mentioned. The need is more frequent—the causes for its use more numerous. A woman will silently and sweetly walk through a thorny path, where she is pierced and bruised at every step; but who will look on her meek face and call her a heroine? Who will see how she checks the bitter cry of pain upon her lips, and stills the throbbing of her tortured heart lest its pulsations should betray the struggle for endurance? She may go on to the end, die and lie quietly under the green sod, without ever having heard from human lips such words as you have spoken to me. Here my strength is brought out in another way. I am forced to give active and visible aid, which, bringing me into an unusual path, lays me open to your keen and wondering observation. This work is not easy or light—you know that. The tax upon the sympathies and the nerves, is sorely trying. But I tell you the effort for this is nothing in comparison with the efforts that some duties in life impose upon the hardly tried of my sex. Go to any of our city grave-yards, and the thousands of white shafts shooting upwards will bear the name, and recount the gentle excellencies of the dead, touchingly, beautifully. They will not tell you that 'hero women' sleep there forever safe from earthly conflicts. Ah, sir, yonder red field of Shiloh received not the precious blood of more surely brave mortals—openly contending to their death for victory over wrong and oppression, than they. As women, we must suffer and be silent. Men wrapped in their own strength and proud self-consciousness of superiority, have willfully closed their eyes against the truth, until it is impossible for them to see. She is doomed; if she despair not, then is her heroism grander, loftier for that reason. The Jews of old were not more cruel and obstinate in their disbelief of truth, than are men of our own day. And their one great sacrifice of the blessed Son whom God sent to them, was scarcely more cruel, certainly was more necessary, than the thousand meek and lowly sacrifices that are immolated upon the altars of men's inordinate selfishness in the present century."

Her voice had deepened and grown passionately bitter. She was betraying the under-current of corroding personal feeling without intending it, and discovered it only when his curious and intent gaze told what impression had been made upon him. Angry with herself for allowing her emotions to swallow up discretion, she asked him abruptly if he needed her longer, and when he answered in the negative, hastened up stairs without giving him an opportunity for either question or comment further.

A dozen voices called to her as she entered the cabin, and she patiently attended to their wants, answering in a kind, quiet way, all the questions they put to her. No complaint betrayed weariness to them, and they would remark often within her hearing, upon her even, steady kindness and gentle ways. Now, as like expressions fell upon her ear, a sense of humiliation suddenly swept through her heart—a strong, momentary self-loathing which caused her head to droop low over the wounded shoulder she was examining.

"Poor fellows!" she thought bitterly, "in their grateful sense of small kindnesses, they would make me faultless, while every strong impulse of my nature is roused and at war. Longing for good—hating evil—I am still a living lie, and it makes me despise myself to know it. Oh, for escape, for freedom from these galling chains. When can I fling them off and be myself as God intended me?"

Mrs. Noble appeared at the door beyond and seeing her, came close to where she knelt.

"Will you come and help me, Astrea, when you have finished that? The Major's arm has become so painful it must be dressed, and I am so afraid of hurting him if I undertake to do it alone—I'm so nervous."

"Yes, dear, I will help you willingly."

There was a very tender tone to her voice now, as she looked up at the troubled face of her friend. She knew that there was as much dread of facing that foe to her pride and self-control, as fear of hurting the husband's arm, in Helen's appeal for assistance. She could not yet look upon the poor, maimed member, and bear the affliction calmly enough to perform her work well. It would require time to accustom her to bear the sight of the ugly, glaring deformity.

Rest for Miss Harmon seemed out of the question. She had not more than completed the task of replacing the Major's bandages, before a boy came to say that Mr. Meridan desired to see her. He was lying upon a berth in his state-room, and the doors stood wide open to admit the air. He looked up eagerly as she approached and held out his hand.

"It is nearly sundown, and in all this time you have not been near me," he said in a half reproachful tone." You might, at least, have given me five minutes in which to thank you for the inestimable service rendered to me this morning. How can I ever repay you?"

"By never again alluding to it as a service," she answered. "There was nobody else to do anything, and common humanity, if nothing more, would have forced me to do as I did. I hope you feel better."

"Not much, I fear. The blow on my head was violent, and has left me too crazy to hold it up with any degree of safety. I suppose, too, the heat increases its tendency to ache. The air in these rooms is suffocatingly hot."

"Can I do anything to make you more comfortable?"

"I dislike to tax your kindness so much, but if you *would* remove this linen and bathe my head with ice water, it seems to me I might feel some relief."

"Certainly," and the patient face bent over him as readily as it had bowed over others—the untiring fingers worked as skillfully in their ever recurring task of giving relief to the suffering. He closed his eyes and listened to the earnest, irregular breathing which betrayed her absorbed attention to that which occupied her thoughts, while now and then, as a faint pure breath from her parted lips touched his cheeks a delicious thrill ran through his whole frame. How soft and steady her touch was upon the aching brow! No quick, spasmodic movements strung his nerves to that tingling strain of dread which is caused by an unsteady or careless hand. And at the same time he was lingering over the first picture his eye rested on when he woke to consciousness—a slender figure bowed, with a sweet face hidden from sight, while low sobs reached him as he lay helpless and only dimly discerning what had happened to him. He had recalled that picture many times as he listened for her light step that day. Constantly his ear had been strained to catch the sound of her voice; and when she passed his door, he had more than once tried to turn his head to catch a glimpse of her, hoping that she would come to inquire after his welfare.

There was much that was good and generous in Mr. Meridan's nature, though not incapable of stooping to unworthy things, as we have already seen. He remembered the feelings of chagrin which had prompted him both to distrust her and to wish to cause others to distrust her. Recalling these now with her touch upon his face, and that picture of distress in his mind, one great wave of shame swept up and dyed his face crimson. Astrea saw it and thought him in great pain, which softened her manner and increased his uneasiness. If he had wronged her, certainly the swift fading away of a keen delight into the sudden shame and anguish of remembrance, was a sufficient punishment.

"Is that better now? Do you think you will feel more comfortable?"

"O, yes, thank you, Miss Harmon; you are very kind to me. I do not at all deserve it. Will you come again soon?"

"If possible once more to-night. If not I will see you before I get off the boat to-morrow morning. We are about to run down to Savannah where we shall just touch shore for a short time. I believe it is the intention then to go on down the river. Sometime in the forenoon, they will let us off at Paducah."

"And I may never see you again!"

"Probably not. But I hope you may soon recover and be strong again. It was quite unlucky to have met with such an accident just now, when you were hoping to be useful to others."

Another pang of shame. He had not sought to be useful to others for the sake of being useful, but had offered his services in order to secure to himself the privilege of visiting the battle-field and seeing what was to be seen in a new country. He knew that with his small stock of knowledge, he was not competent to undertake what his assurance and curiosity had led him into. Had this lesson been sent to him because of his selfishness and deception? Her presence had been to him a sweet pain, yet he longed to detain her. The sharp torture of self-reproach was better even, than the silence and loneliness with his own thoughts and unheeded longings as he lay there almost forgotten among so many. And what right had he here in the midst of those who were struggling for a noble cause—he who had stood off with a scoff and a sneer, taking advantage of every means of information in the affairs of a great Republic, only to array himself with sharper weapons for assailing its politics, habits and prejudices? Now he was stretched helplessly among their helpless, and at their mercy—dependent upon the kindness of those he had scorned and derided, for every comfort and attention. This was not a very sweet cup for the proud young Englishman to find pressed to his lips, but he was compelled to drink it and be silent, no matter how galling the draught.

She did not come to him again that night, and he waited vainly until quite late, longing for her return if but for one moment. That would have satisfied him—only one minute—just to have her wet the bandages on his head and then say in her quiet, gentle way, "Good-night, Mr. Meridan." Perhaps she would add a hope that he might rest well, and then he would lie and think about it—recall her look and her tone until sleep came, when the sweet vision would be reproduced in dreams. This had been the hope which had fed his fancy until past midnight. He could not hope she would come after that, and turned his face to the pillow wearily, much disappointed and aggrieved. There was some comfort in thinking himself wronged and neglected, as it blunted the edge of his self-reproach. She might have given him a little of her precious time out of pure humanity, since her life was professedly devoted to the welfare of others. How quickly he forgot the recognition of his own false position. Men change in their reasoning as the winds shift from east to west, and from north to south, when inclination comes in contact with judgment. And now, instead of arraigning himself further for deception and unworthiness, he employed the tedious hours in fretfully finding fault with the woman who had suddenly taken a hold upon him so strong, that he had neither the will nor the wish to shake it off.

Meanwhile the little weary feet had trodden the cabin floor back and forth until every limb ached with intense fatigue. She had not been allowed to take needful refreshment. unmolested. Those who made demands upon her, seemed to think only of themselves. Her fair face, and gentle, soothing touch were so much more pleasant than the attentions of another, no one hesitated to call on her, but rather sought to monopolize all the time they could, never pausing to consider that she might need rest and refreshment more than they. Many times after she had crept away to her berth, too weary to sleep, she heard them calling for her and sighed heavily. There was excuse enough for the suffering ones. With those who had faced death and endured evil for her sake, she could be patient. But it was not so easy to bear the unreasonable demands of others. When one after another of the surgeons on board asked for her within her hearing, each wishing her assistance in some work of his own, it was difficult to keep down a keen feeling of resentment and indignation. Why should they impose upon her? How was it that they could not see that she was almost exhausted. Following this train of thought, her mind merged into a state of general dissatisfaction and disgust, and for the moment, all the zeal in her nature faded out. She was sick and tired and hopeless. There seemed nothing to live for or care for. Life was a miserable failure. Nothing but constant snarls, and entanglements, vexations and weariness of mind and body. She thought it would be sweet to sleep out there under the stars, where so many of the unknown and noble of America's sons had fallen and now slumbered dreamlessly. Ah, why could not she have gone in the stead of any one of these? Then came more chaotic thought, followed by a blank after the dire confusion, and she slept.

With the early dawn, the Lancaster stopped at Savannah, and there remained all day. The wounded men were stowed away wherever there was a vacant spot large enough to hold them, and many were in a most lamentable state of distress. Our doctors united in their efforts to give relief and for the greater part of the day, were engaged on shore, leaving the care of those on board to the ladies, one surgeon remaining with them, who was relieved by the others alternately.

A heavy rap on Astrea's door roused her from a feverish, unrefreshing sleep, and she arose to the duties of the day before her, less willingly than ever before. The weight on heart and brain was so heavy, and her physical strength was yielding to the large tax upon her energies so fast. Knowing this, a sort of despairing helplessness came over her and she sank back upon her berth with a half resolve to abandon the effort; but a moment's thought changed her feelings, and with a heartfelt prayer for strength to forget self and remember only the need of others, she made her simple toilet and went forth among the inmates of the cabin. Contact with them wrought an immediate change in all her feelings. Her nerves grew strong—her interest and sympathy keen, while her whole being seemed charged with new life, as she moved among them and heard their glad greetings, and saw their happier smiles on recognizing her presence.

"It is more blessed to give than to receive," she murmured lowly to herself. "Joy like this comes from nothing else on earth; and yet I was tempted to nurse my own unhappy thoughts and leave these poor men to the care of others. Oh, longing heart, be still and learn this lesson well, 'It *is* more blessed to give than to receive.'"

Toward the close of the afternoon she remembered Mr. Meridan and went to look for him. The door of his room stood open, and he sat outside watching the people on shore with a weary desolation in his look that reproached her. His face was so pale and sad, it was a reproach in itself.

"Did you quite forget me, Miss Harmon? or have you taken this mode of retaliating upon me for disagreeing with you the other evening?" he asked as she came and stood beside him.

"I hope you cannot think so meanly of me as to charge me with so unworthy a spirit, Mr. Meridan. If I could stoop to retaliation at all, it would not be possible in taking advantage of your suffering to make you feel any resentment I might conceive of your opinions as expressed in opposition to my own."

"Then why did you not come to see me last night or today?"

"Some one constantly wanted me, and I could not get a moment's leave," she answered. At the same time a peculiar smile dawned upon her face. She thoughtfully regarded some distant object for a few minutes, then held up one little hand before him.

"I am not complaining, Mr. Meridan, but I do not want you to think meanly or unkindly of me. This is Monday. Since Sunday—one week ago yesterday, I have not slept in any night more than three or four hours—sometimes less. Since last Thursday I have not taken one meal uninterruptedly. How much longer do you suppose I can bear this and continue to be useful?"

"You ought not to try it," he burst out impulsively. "We are brutes—selfish and blind as moles not to see that you are killing yourself. Your hand is almost transparent. You must give up and rest."

"No need of that, I hope. If I could only make a fair division of my time for rest and labor, I should do very well. But no one seems to see the necessity, and it is not agreeable to be obliged to tell them of it."

"You would not have told me if I had not charged you with a wish to be revenged on me?"

"No."

"And would have gone on and killed yourself without a sign."

"I could not die in a better cause, perhaps."

"You are very devoted to your country."

"Devoted heart and soul!" with an unmistakable ring in her voice which said, "Before all things else."

"Why is it so?—you are an English born woman. Are there no instinctive yearnings for that land which gave you birth?"

"Mr. Meridan, if a mother should put her child into another woman's arms and turn away from it, laying between herself and that child a gap of silent, unbroken years—denying it the tender love and care of the real parent, while the adopted mother was more than tender, loving and kind, would you call the child unnatural or ungrateful if, when she came to be a reasoning, responsible being, she found no affection in her heart for the one who had abandoned her to strangers?"

"Certainly not."

"Then wonder no more if my heart clings to the land of my adoption. She is 'mother-land' to me—noble, grand, beloved America! Her laws have sheltered me—her children have been my brothers and my sisters and friends. Outside of this land I have nothing—English lips have been silent and cold. Her maternal kiss has never pressed my brow—her parental voice never spoken my name. How can I love or care for England, lying as I lie, in the bosom of an American mother whose lips are ever warm, whose voice is always tender—whose arms are constant to enfold me in a faithful embrace? Oh, fair blue skies of this sun-bright land—I have lived beneath you in joy and pain! I will die beneath you in joy or pain as God wills—faithful to the last."

She spoke the closing words half under her breath, looking up at the cloudless expanse of blue above her. Twenty-four hours previous, he would have curled his lip, and muttered "enthusiast," listening to the fervent apostrophe which proved her love for an adopted land. Now he heard her with a thrill of sympathy, and a dawning sense of honor for her devotion to that which alone she had known in the light of a friend. Her sense of right was both strong and just—even generous. She was faithful to principle and above prejudice—a character set apart, marked and individual, not too pliant, or too plastic to receive impressions unsanctioned by reflection. This was the ground on which he chose to base his love, for he did not deny that he was fast coming to love this strange, lovely woman—he who had laughed at woman's pretensions to character and intellect—who had a thousand times declared her incapable of more than reflecting the man, mirror-like—at best. His theory had been, that woman's mind was like wax to receive every new impression, retaining nothing, but having each impress effaced by the one following after, and changing in action accordingly, as the chameleon changes its colors. The fitful flames of feeling burned in her heart in color suiting that which fed them, but never always the same. Here was a woman whose light was clear, strong, steady and unfaltering. He saw it—longed to reach a point where the rays might fall upon himself and bless him with its pure brilliance. She had started a revolution in his nature already—shattered more than one of his pet theories and forced him mentally to retract much that was detrimental to the honor of her sex for her sake. He did not need to stoop to draw her up by labored efforts to his level. She stood upon an equal footing and looked with clear and steady eyes upon the same objects with himself. If he saw with different aspect those objects, she did not shrink from defending her own views, while she avoided arrogating the sole right of judgment to herself. At times she of her own strength, mounted higher, penetrated deeper than he, conceding to his superiority in other things where her woman's feet might not pass the bounds that necessarily limited her means for acquiring knowledge. She would make no attempts to discuss subjects with which she was not so closely brought in contact as to allow her mind to receive it freely, and digest it in all its bearings. She did not talk for the sake of proving what she knew and displaying her conversational powers. She spoke because the earnest, underlying current of feeling in her nature, forced her to give vent to the truths which she recognized and often saw abused or unappreciated. He recognized in her the only type of Wordsworth's ideal perfection—

> "A perfect woman, nobly planned
> To warm, to comfort, to command—"

and he began to think, as the spell of her presence grew stronger upon him, that it would be the supremacy of happiness to yield himself up to her—her whims, her will, her commands—if he might, in return, have her love undivided.

"Miss Harmon, is it your intention to continue in your present course until the war ends?" he asked, after a considerable pause.

"Yes, if my health does not give way. I have nothing else to employ me."

"You are not so masculine in your tastes as to ignore the usual employments of ladies, are you?"

"No; but just now embroidery or crochet are not precisely the things to employ brain and hands. I must have something more active and all-absorbing."

"Why? Because you are so interested in the result of your national struggle?"

"Partly for that reason—partly for a more selfish and personal object. See, they are casting off the fastenings, and preparing to leave! I am glad, for now we shall have a breath of fresh air, which will be a blessing."

No one could get further into her personal affairs than that. It was tantalizing in the extreme.

"Please do not go yet, Miss Harmon," as she turned to reenter the cabin. "I wish to ask if you will permit me to come back and see you, when I shall have recovered from this unlucky accident. You will still be at Paducah probably, and in the course of a week or two I shall be coming this way again. It would afford me so much pleasure to meet you."

"If circumstances should throw us together as now, I should be pleased to see you, Mr. Meridan," she said politely.

"But I want to come expressly to see you, Miss Harmon.

We do not like to say good-bye forever to those to whom we owe our lives. Your care saved mine."

"O, no; you attach too much importance to that slight service. And I should do wrong to bid you come to see me, when I have no time to spare to my best and nearest friends."

"Shall I then see you no more?"

"Probably never again."

"And you can say it without the slightest regret? We have been thrown together under peculiar circumstances; and such, seldom fail to awaken peculiar interests. I had hoped that I was not so wholly disagreeable or indifferent as you make me feel myself."

"Mr. Meridan, my business is with the duties of life, and not its pleasures, apart from its duties. Engaged in them I forget all else, without wish to remember anything. Speaking of them reminds me that I have remained too long away, and must go back to my patients."

"Am not I a patient also, and will you refuse me a moment and give all to others? Have you no binding sense of duty towards me?"

"I should, were you as helpless as others, but you seem to be doing well, and I cannot do more than talk to you."

"Kind words are better than medicine to some people. They are life to me. Let me share a small portion of your generous store."

He was persistent and she was growing uneasy. Doctor Clarke luckily passing, relieved her with a message from Mrs. Noble, and she escaped gladly from her unpleasant position. He did not see her again until the following morning when she left with her friends at Paducah, and in passing his door, bade him good-bye in a subdued and tremulous tone. Her face was wet with tears, caused by the expressed regrets of those she was leaving behind her, and that last glimpse of it never faded from his memory.

CHAPTER XIII.

PRISON PENS AND REFUGEES.

THE day succeeding the battle was a memorable one to Captain Wilfer, who with several officers and a number of men, had been closely guarded and kept within sound of the strife until the issue was decided. As Beauregard withdrew his forces, acknowledging himself unable, by this act, to cope with the enemy, the Confederate troops who had not suffered in the conflict, became furious and wild with rage. The guards who held the prisoners in charge seemed bent on satiating their thirst for revenge upon their unarmed victims, and drove them forward, with bound hands, like so many animals, sometimes lashing them sharply with whips, and heaping upon them every abuse and indignity which cruel and degraded natures could invent.

In the early dawn, after the Confederate forces had withdrawn from the field, the Captain found himself with a dozen or more unlucky officers, the inmate of a filthy box car, which waited at Corinth to receive and bear them farther south. They were weary and hungry, having eaten scarcely anything for more than twenty-four hours. Sleep had been strange to their eyes while the crisis of a great battle had been pending, and by the time it was past, and our victory complete, they had been hurried away, marching on foot over rough and muddy roads, until Corinth was reached. Here no rations were served to them until after the cars had started, when a man came in and tossed a few hard crackers into their midst—a sorry meal for hungry, almost famished men; but they ate them ravenously, and were glad even for this small means of satiating the intense longing for food.

At every station as they went South, the people gathered around their car, laughing, hissing at and mocking them; indulging in threats, and continuing abuses that were almost beyond human endurance. Children climbed up and peeping at them through the little square windows, threw in pebbles and dirt, pointing their small fingers and spitting at them maliciously. It was horrible to hear the round reckless oaths that rolled from the childish lips, taught to them by those whose religion seemed to consist in their ability to outvie all others in indignity to the "Yanks," whose "skulls they were waiting to convert into drinking cups!" They were regaled with promises of all the ills which heated and lively imaginations could invent, and which were said to be awaiting them at the end of their journey.

Their destination was Selma, Alabama, at which place they arrived after a long and fearfully tedious ride of several days.

The prison was a long, low building, containing neither beds, tables or chairs. A quantity of straw cast upon the floor afforded them the only resting-place they could hope to stretch their weary frames upon; and even this was inviting in their present state of exhaustion. The moment Captain Wilfer found himself in the dismal abode, which he knew might be his only abiding-place for many days, his philosophy came to his rescue, and resolving to make the best of his condition, he threw himself upon the floor, and turning his face to the wall, soon fell asleep. A general smile went round the circle of his comrades as his heavy breathing betrayed his rapid transition to the happy world of visions.

"Cool," remarked one, and another heartily wished he could take the world as easily as Wilfer.

Our friend slept soundly until the hour came round for serving the prisoners with their rations, when a brother officer shook and woke him.

"You must be hungry, old fellow, and our friend, the keeper, says it is time to take our 'grub.' Come and let us see what it is like."

The Captain raised himself upon his elbow, then slowly came to a sitting posture, looking steadfastly at the deep tin plate which contained a sort of soup anything but inviting. Beside the plate lay a huge piece of corn bread which he took up and tasted.

At this moment a black face peered through one of the windows, and the Captain called to the possessor:

"Hullo! uncle! Can you tell me what this is?"

"Dat's a corn-pone, massa."

"Well, will you initiate me into the mysteries of its composition?"

"Dunno what massa means by that."

"Tell me how these 'corn-pones' are made."

"O, yah! yah! dat's what massa means by pomposition. Yah! Well, de way my ole 'oman makes 'em, she jes takes a big wooden tray, an puts in it a lot o' meal. Den she puts some salt, ef she's got any—salt's been mighty sca'ce lately—an' pours cole water in it, an' mixes it up wid her han's till de dough's kinder stiff like. Den she takes up as much as she can hole in bofe hans' an' rolls it ober two or tree times, gibs it a little pat an' souses it into a hot skillet. Den she puts on de lid, cobers it wid hot coals, an' lets it bake. Dat's de way to make nice corn dodgers, massa."

"But you said 'pones.'"

"O, dat's all de same. Don't you nebber hab corn dodgers up nort, massa?"

"Not exactly like this. Do you live on this kind of bread here?"

"Mostly. Sometimes we bakes de pone in de ashes—sometimes pats it on a board and sets it up before de fire—dat's de way to make 'Johnny-cake.' An agin we makes great big loaf, like light bread. When we usen to git holidays, ole massa let us habe biskits. Lor! git away! Dem biskits what my ole 'oman usen to make n'd make yer mouf water—dey would shure!"

Here the darkey suddenly ducked his head and took to his heels, the sentinel yelling after him with loud threats. Our friends were hungry indeed, but more than one laid his bread aside, unable to appreciate the excellencies of its manufacture. A young lieutenant, more hardy than the others, had swallowed a few mouthfuls, and was zealously fishing about in his soup for the small pieces of bacon, which were floating in a mass of smaller objects.

"What have you there, Harding?" asked the Captain.

"What vessels cannot do without, yet seldom boast more than one of. I have floating upon this tide, more than my share of—skippers!"

"And you will not have them? You remind me of the fisherman I once heard of."

"Well?"

"He stood upon the banks of a stream fishing industriously. The fish baited well, and every minute he drew up a plump little fellow which he no sooner saw than he deliberately took them off the hook and threw them back again. Some one who had watched his proceedings with extreme surprise and curiosity, stepped forward and asked him what he meant by throwing his fish again into the stream.

"'When I fish for catties, I fish for catties,' he answered determinedly, and turned his back upon the questioner. I see you are after the 'catties' and will have nothing else."

"And the 'catties' I cannot get because of the pesky little 'minnows' about them! Guess I'll give up 'fishing' for today," and he pushed the plate away from him with a shudder of disgust.

The next day and the next brought no change of fare, and our prisoners found themselves driven by hunger to partake of whatever was brought them, glad of a generous portion of what was served. A hope for escape or exchange urged upon each of them the necessity for preserving their strength; and they were not only patient, but cheerful, as long as health continued. Gradually as the intense heat of the summer came on, however, they began to pine and fall sick under the hard fare, close confinement and suffocating atmosphere. One after another grew pale and feeble, moving about with slow and faltering steps until finally prostrated, only to be carried out in the end, with a laugh and a jest, and buried within sight of the prison—"uncoffined and unknelled." Those who remained behind grew desperate and almost hopeless, not knowing whose turn would come next. Jests no longer passed among the remaining few and smiles were rare indeed. When not pacing the floor or little strip of ground allowed them for exercise, they sat with their faces bowed upon their knees in sad and bitter reflection.

Captain Wilfer found himself growing weaker day by day, and knew that a brief space of time would serve to render him helpless. The thought was unbearable. He was too young and full of hope to give up life without a struggle. And to die thus—cooped up in a miserable southern prison, was terrible. Desperation gave birth to a firm resolve. He would escape or die in the effort. Better death in striving for freedom, than a slow, lingering torture like this, with a grave in the end, unmarked and unhonored!

Many weeks had passed away, and many changes had marked the course of Astrea Harmon. We find her on a sultry August evening, sitting before a small table busily plying her needle—much thinner and more weary looking, but none the less determined than when she stood on the guards of the Lancaster talking to Mr. Meridan. Two tallow candles were upon the table; but with the light of both, the room is still dim—its plain, gloomy furniture looking gloomier in the obscurity. The article upon which she is engaged is but little whiter than the sad face bending over it; and if you look closely, you may at times see the glitter of a tear in the folds. But the busy fingers never cease until the last stitch is finished; then she rises and folds up the long garment, and lays it on the table while she finds a light shawl which she throws over her head. Taking up the package, she opens the door and looks out upon the night, still, calm and radiant with moon and stars. As far as the eye can see, gleam the lights of camp and town, for our troops are now at Corinth, and Astrea is boarding with a widowed woman whose sole dependence for daily bread, is upon the kindness and protective influence of her lodger.

Drawing the shawl more closely about her face, Astrea steps forth, and glides swiftly over the space intervening between her dwelling and the depot. It is a strange place to go, and she has hesitated often, dreading the duty and longing to thrust it away from her; but there is too much already crowded into future hours. The morrow will bring its own and more than she can accomplish of perplexing duties; and, besides, there are haunting memories which will not be smothered, and she is forced to listen to the demands they make upon her—memories of mothers bowed in grief, pleading with broken words and tears, that the children whom God has chosen to take from them, may be "put away decently." How she has toiled to gratify those natural longings! What efforts has she not made to find shrouds and coffins for those little ones! And, now, as she enters the depot and looks around upon the scene, more grim and ghastly in the night time, with the glare of lanterns lighting it up here and there, a great sob swells in her throat, and leaning her head against a pile of freight, the tears fall unrestrainedly."

"Oh, God," she murmured, "to see such sights as this, and to know that there is many a luxurious home where no want is known, no loved form missed! And yet men and women, who have not 'seen' or 'heard,' will stand up with long faces and talk of the 'horrors of war'—moving no hand to help, nor sparing one penny from their generous store to drive starvation from such beings as these! Oh, are their hearts stone, and wilt thou not melt them to pity?"

If tears still lay wet upon this woman's cheeks, and her steps faltered as she threaded her way through the miserable masses lying over the floor of the depot, it was but natural. A maniac's most fearful dream of woe could scarcely equal the reality of misery upon which her eyes rested.

She paused at a group of women in tattered garments, in attitudes of the most abject woe. One, middle-aged, with hair prematurely white and scattered in wild disorder over her shoulders, sat with her hands locked round her knees, and a pipe between her lips. Her eyes were red and swollen with weeping, and Astrea could see that her face was very pale. At her side lay something which was covered over by an old homespun cotton apron, and which made her shudder involuntarily.

"You have come at last," said the woman in a hard, bitter tone looking up. "I thought you'd forgot me."

"No, I never forget or break a promise if it is in my power to keep it," Astrea answered very gently. "I have made and brought this for Annie."

She held up the shroud she had but lately finished; then moving round upon the other side of the mother, uncovered the little one and lifted her up. She did not shrink now, though her hands came in contact with the icy cold form of the dead child in removing her. The divine pity was too deeply stirred in the human heart. With tender, careful touch, she robed the small figure, brushed the silky, tangled hair from the baby brow and composed the limbs for their last, long rest. The small, rough coffin sat there ready for its occupant, and she put the child into it, thinking all the while of the mother who sat there within reach of her hand, her heart filled with hard and bitter murmurings of rebellious grief.

"Do you want to see your baby, now?" she asked softly, when all was finished.

"No, if I do, I shall curse the God who made us an' brought us to this pass," she answered fiercely. "What he made us for is more than I can tell. Rich folks hates us, an' grinds us down in the dirt because we are ignorant; an' they won't let us be anything else but ignorant! Even the niggers despises us an' taunts us, an' flouts at us, callin' us 'poor white trash' an' all other sorts of names they choose. They take our men away from us an' 'script' them in the rebel army, then leaves us without anything to eat, or a shelter to cover us from the storms! Who could help hating them; an' when we hate them, can we help saying so? Then we are druv out of the country, an' sent to wander over the world without help or pity. The federals hates us because our folks are rebels, an' so we are houseless an' penniless an' starving in a strange place; dying by dozens for very want. Much sympathy anybody has! When our tears falls like other people's tears, they tell us that it's silly to grieve, an' we ought to be thankful that God has taken our poor children away from suffering. Oh, put any of them in our places an' see if they'll be thankful! My baby is all I had in the world, an' I've seen her starve to death in my arms! It makes me hate God an' man for the injustice! What have I ever done that I should have my old man an' my son shot down, like dogs, an' my only daughter took away by starvation. An' now, here I am all alone, without anything in this wide world to live for. I wish I was dead."

Her head fell upon her knees, and she sat still and silent after that. Not a softened tone or a single tear denoted a tenderer feeling from the beginning to the end of the bitter speech. There was too much of truth in what she said for Astrea to refute one charge she had made, for she had learned but too well, the combination of evils that made this class of sufferers by far the most pitiable—not even excepting the negroes. And to make the matter still worse, any attempts to comfort them, were looked upon in the light of willful wrongs. They said it was so easy for people who had no grief to say it was wise an' for the best that they were bereaved! If they had ever known suffering and want and bereavement themselves, they would not mock them with shallow attempts like these, to reconcile them to a hard fate.

Notwithstanding her knowledge of this prevailing feeling, Astrea now sat down near the mother and spoke gently, kindly to her, from the depths of a yearning and pitying heart—talked until the woman spoke up sharply and asked her not "to bother her with any more cant." With a heavy heart she rose and turned away, only pity in her soul, and no anger for the ingratitude manifested so openly. She did not remember the hours she had spent in wearisome labor for this woman's sake, that she might take credit to herself and bring a charge against her. Recognizing the true state of affairs, and this event as a natural result of manifold wrongs, she could feel only regret, and sympathy—could only breathe a silent prayer to One who alone could smooth the tangled woof of perplexing fabrics, and go sorrowfully away.

Back through the depot, leaving the sleeping, moaning, suffering and dead behind her, and again out into the night and fresher atmosphere. Walking on slowly toward the lights which burned dimly within her windows, she lifted her face to the blue, serene heavens, and wondered how divine eyes could behold such woe among human beings, and not cover the face of the calm expanse with the blackness of His wrath—how such tender love could exist, and yet suffer such distress among the beings He created. And why, with all that the eye sees and the heart feels, are His purposes so deeply shrouded in mystery? To clear questionings or clouded wonderings, there was silence only in answer. No response, no light, and she was too weak to strive for satisfaction. Reaching her door, she mechanically placed her hand upon the handle, turned it and entered.

Some one sat in her chair before the small table, holding a volume of poems which she sometimes read in moments when compelled to rest from physical labor. And as she entered, he rose, took a step forward and held out his hand—a hand that grasped and held hers closely, while a pair of glowing eyes looked down into her own.

CHAPTER XIV.

ESCAPING FROM PRISON.

"You come as one from the grave, Captain Wilfer. I am heartily glad to welcome you back again."

"Thank you. I am glad to get back. Now what have you to tell me of yourself?"

"Nothing bright or pleasant. I am like a straw in a great murky sea. I battle vainly with the loathsome waters for human life and fail! It is terrible!"

"You feel your own lack of strength too much; it causes you to underestimate what you have. How you have changed!"

"Scarcely more or as much as you. I do not see Captain Wilfer to-night as I saw him months ago, but his shadow, very indifferently preserved. Sit down and tell me about yourself."

He took a chair in front of her, and the two sat face to face. It was true that she did not understand her own strength, as he had asserted. Her manner was so quiet, her tones so even and unruffled he had no thought of how her heart beat, or what strange confusion coursed through her veins. For worlds she would not have suffered him to see how deeply his presence moved her.

"I have much to tell, but will put it into a very brief space. You have probably heard that I was captured on the first day of battle. On the second day we were hurried away on foot to Corinth, and from here sent to Selma, Alabama. What of indignity, privation and distress we suffered there, pass my power to describe. You will see some of it in my face, if you will look—though I have improved much since I came away. I saw my comrades—brave, good fellows whom I had learned to love dearly during our imprisonment, sicken and die, one by one, until few were left. Some were allowed to go beyond the prescribed limits of our walking ground, and were shot down like dogs. We were starved, taunted, and even scourged, if abuse became too galling for endurance, and provoked words in return for words. Finding that I should soon be unable to sustain life under such treatment, and that the Government was too tardy in sending relief, I resolved to make my escape if possible. Exchange seemed far off and uncertain; death appeared very near.

"So, one night four of us succeeded in getting away, aided by an old negro, who was generally conceded to be half-witted, and to whom no one paid any especial attention. He would sometimes come to our windows and peer in at us, chattering his queer, senseless gibberish until we were constrained to scold and chafe at the annoyance. When this had continued until we thought it a part of the plan of the rebels to make us more wretched in our confinement, we discovered that he was neither a fool nor an imp, but a true, faithful friend, to whom I owe my liberty to-night. The others—"

Here he choked and could not proceed for a full minute. The hand which he put up before his eyes to shield them from her compassionate gaze, trembled violently. Astrea saw that it had grown thin, and was covered with small scars, as if it had been torn by brambles and briers in a desperate flight for life.

"The others did not fare so well," he went on more calmly. "I alone of the four, escaped with life, and that was after all seemed utterly hopeless.

"I said that I owed everything to that old negro, and I must tell you in what way he served us. One day when he had almost driven us wild with his chatter, I flew to the window in a rage, and tried to dash my hands through the bars to get at his black face. Usually he would run if he saw us coming toward him, but on that day he remained and as I came up to him, thrust a small roll of folded paper into my hands, saying in a quick undertone:

"'Read, massa, an' don't pay no 'tention to ole Pete's foolery.'

"Then he burst into a yell of seeming delight, ducked his head as if from a blow and ran hurriedly away.

"I comprehended the state of affairs at once, and waited a few moments to hurl at him as he went, a storm of invectives which set the sentinels to laughing uproariously. Having accomplished this, I took the paper into one corner, and read its contents. It was the brown fly-leaf of a book, and had penciled upon it in delicate lines, a few simple words—simple in themselves, but all important to us. I shall never forget them, for they seemed burned instantly upon heart and brain, filling me with new life, and a great hope.

"'You are suffering—dying. I am your friend, and it breaks my heart to see men who have fought under the dear old flag, slowly murdered under my own eyes. My power to aid is small, but my will is great. Believe this and trust me. Uncle Peter is my sole and trustworthy dependence, and to the end I hope to accomplish, I have caused him to annoy you so unmercifully. Watch for him to-night, and if he gives you a key through the windows, take it and let yourselves out. He will then tell you to follow him, and if you can succeed in reaching my house, I have such changes of apparel as may enable you the better to make your escape North. Pray God to help you this night.'

"It has been said that woman from the beginning, has been the instrument of evil to man. If this be true, I am sure it is more than balanced by the good she does him, for all great good seems to come through her hands. I was guilty of the meanness of sitting down and pondering a long time distrustfully over this kind note before I resolved to submit it to my companions. Ten of us were confined together, and six out of the ten were unable to rise from their straw pallets. It seemed a cruel and impossible thing to leave them to the mercy of those fiends in human shape—but their own arguments in favor of the effort decided us. We hoped by a representation of the true state of affairs in the event of our success, to be enabled to have those of our comrades released before it was too late. They preferred the risk to remaining there in endless suspense with a certainty of death before them; and we had all thought the Government had no knowledge of the manner in which our men were treated, else an exchange had been made long before. You know that the imagination has full play in such situations, and we thought of everything, reasonable and unreasonable, then.

"Before night, after much consultation, we had agreed upon our plan of action, and determined to make an attempt to leave rebeldom. A glorious full moon rose, lighting up the earth with the brightness of day, and I felt some uneasiness as the hours waned without any sign of the coming of our deliverer. Standing at the window, I watched long and anxiously, until a clock in the distance tolled the half hour past ten.

"Finally down the dusty road, I discovered Peter swaggering along toward the prison, his long-tailed coat almost reaching the ground, and something like a jug in his hand. He was shouting snatches of Dixie in his own peculiar style, and laughing at intervals in seeming great glee. As he neared the sentinels who paced at the front and rear of the prison, a sudden change came over him. His song ceased, and he grew exceedingly anxious to conceal his burthen, which evident anxiety at once attracted the attention of the first guard.

"'Hallo, Pete, what have you got there?' he shouted intercepting him. Pete shied round and tried to get away, muttering confusedly,—

"'Only 'lasses, massa. Mistess sent me to fetch some 'lasses to ole Miss Blake who's sick—berry sick. Massa wouldn't keep me from fetchin 'em.'

"'Give up that jug to me, you black imp. I'll see what kind of 'lasses your mistress keeps at her house. Give it here this minute.'

"Seizing it from his hands, he drew the cork and lifted it to his olfactory organ determinedly, while poor Pete made a great demonstration of distress. The man uttered a rough oath and drank deeply, then filled a flask which he took from his pocket, after which he handed the jug back to Peter.

"'Carry it over to Tom,' he commanded, pointing to his comrade on duty. 'Quick now, and no foolin'! Tell him I sent it with my compliments.'

"Peter ruefully obeyed, wiping his eyes on the sleeve of his coat as he went. I lost sight of him before he reached Tom, but could hear the sound of their voices for several minutes. Then Peter went away quite disconsolate, and for half an hour everything was still around us.

"How the boy managed to get at our keeper and the key I never knew. But it is quite certain that he did, and while I stood waiting at the window, he thrust it through the grating.

"'Be quick, massa. I'se gwine down de road. You come out an' foller me to de cabin whar missis is ready fur ye,' and without further directions he sauntered off.

"A silent grasp of each hand and low, fervent sighs of kindly feeling which dared not come out in words—then we opened the door and walked out of our prison—passed the drugged sentinels and followed Peter who swaggered along for a short distance, finally crossed an old dilapidated fence and went through an orchard toward a small house surrounded by a little corn-patch and tall bean-poles. All this helped to screen us, and we reached the place in safety, having been observed by no one. A young girl of scarcely sixteen, and very fair, met us at the threshold, pointed to an inner room, and bade us go and change our clothes at once. This done she filled our pockets with dried beef, parched corn and onions. It was all she had, and we took them gratefully. I think no princess royal ever received more grateful homage than we paid to her after she had given us directions where to go, and how to find friends, in her sweet, clear, earnest way. We kissed her hands with tears of gratitude, while she lifted her sweet face upward, breathing an audible prayer for our protection. Oh, she was

FIENDISH AND BRUTAL MURDERS. (See Page 178.)

beautiful and good, and to my dying day I shall never forget her—our kind stranger friend, who would not even tell us her name that we might remember it in our prayers!

"We left her then, and wandered through the woods and mountains according to the written directions she had given us, until we came to an old house where we found rest, food, shelter and a fresh supply of clothing. From thence we carried food and directions to another place of refuge, and so on for a week. After this, the line was broken and we were thrown upon ourselves. Notwithstanding the difficulties that beset us now, we succeeded very well until the last stage of our journey. From that class of the poorer whites, whom you know as refugees, we sometimes obtained food; and always, wherever we could reach a negro cabin without exposure, we were sure to find kindness and assistance. But one day, just as we were beginning to feel greatly elated with the hope of success, a body of cavalry suddenly dashed down upon us where we had lain ourselves for a brief rest, and we once more found ourselves prisoners!

"I cannot tell you anything of the sensation which came over me as they marched us off to the Confederate camp. It was an entire hopeless heart-sickness, such as may be felt only once in a life-time. After all the suffering, privation and mental anguish at Selma,—then the flight and its perils through dreary days and nights of wandering,—to come to this in the end! You will acknowledge that the situation was a trying one. I could not look into the pale, despairing faces of my companions. The expressions were too much for me, and I walked on with my eyes drooping, and a very wicked feeling in my heart, knowing that I could rejoice to strike the death blow of each and every one of our ruffianly captors.

"After traveling for a mile or two, we came to their camp—a small one, for the body when consolidated, was not large,—situated in a valley lying between two hills. What their object was in coming to such a place, I cannot imagine, for to my mind there certainly could not have been any military advantage possible in the situation. Probably they had been out on a raid, or proposed making one.

"Our appearance was much against us. They knew at once that we were escaped prisoners, and as if by common consent, not one of us would give a satisfactory answer to their questions. On reaching the camp we were separated, and subjected to a private examination. I was placed in a little log cabin, such as you will find in a sugar camp, with a few boards for a roof, and no chimney. I did not see where they took my comrades, but I knew they were closely guarded, by the care which they bestowed upon my ungrateful self.

"Late in the afternoon three men came to my quarters and ordered me to come out. I obeyed, and was marched the distance of a hundred yards up the valley, where to my dismay I discovered a rude gallows had been erected, under which stood two of my companions. They looked determined and angry, speaking the moment I came up in defiance of the rebels.

"'Tell them nothing, Wilfer,' said the bravest of the two, in a strong, full voice. 'They have planned to murder us in any event, and if we must die, we will die in silence, for they shall learn nothing from me. I have heard their plans without their knowledge, and they intend to murder us whether we speak or not. Let no false hopes tempt you to open your lips.'

"Almost before the words had died upon the air, a bullet sped whizzing through the brain of my brave comrade. He fell forward without one groan or movement at my feet. The same cowardly assassin again lifted his revolver and shouted in a rage to another who stood erect and glorious now, in his just indignation:

"'Speak, and say you will answer the questions put to you, or the gallows will be cheated of another victim before you have time to call on God for mercy!'

"'Fire,' was the proud response. 'I am ready to die, and would not speak to save myself if I could believe you would spare me!'

"I saw that death, instant and terrible was before him, and

in my agony cried out to him not to be rash. It was not my intention to yield to their demands, but I hoped that if we could gain time, there might arise some means of escape, and I spoke from the impulse of that hope. Doubtless that appeal saved my own life, though it did not save his. The rebel officer lowered his revolver and gave orders to hang him, and he was strung up before my eyes in the most deliberately fiendish manner. They paid no heed to my entreaties for his life, and when he was dead, ordered me back to my place of confinement with the information that I could have until sunrise of the following morning; if by that time I had not made up my mind to tell them where we had been imprisoned, how or by whom liberated, and by whom befriended since, I should share the same fate, and be hung as high as Haman.

"Oh! what a storm of fury raged within me as I found myself once more in the hut, with the guard stationed outside the door."

Here Captain Wilfer rose and paced the floor with excitement; but he went on rapidly.

"I would have given worlds but for one moment's freedom that I might wreak vengeance upon the man who had heartlessly murdered my friends. If ever man prayed wickedly, I did then, for I fell upon my knees and implored God to give that man into my hands that I might take his life. You shrink and look horrified, but you do not know how you would feel, placed in such a position. Even you, tender and merciful and womanly, I believe, could not have borne it with any degree of calmness. And what if I should tell you that prayer was answered! If it was not, mere coincidences are passingly strange!

"Soon after night-fall, a fearful thunder-storm came up, and the rain poured in torrents. I had observed that there was a stir in the camp, too, which could scarcely have been occasioned by the storm. Men passed to and fro talking in excited undertones, and the idea occurred to me that they had received news of the presence of a Federal body in their vicinity. Carefully listening, I ascertained this to be true, and learned also that they were upon the hill, north of the camp. I then resolved to make my escape and capture the whole Confederate band, thus bringing full power of vengeance within my own hands.

"Feigning weariness I lay down upon the ground and soon began to breathe heavily; and the guard thought me asleep. He was now inside the hut, taking shelter from the rain, and was evidently exceedingly weary himself. The light was very dim, but I could just see the outline of his figure as he sat with his head bent upon his knees. His musket lay at his side, and I soon knew that he slept. That sleep I hoped was sound, for the fumes of whiskey were strong from his breath, and I meant to make it sounder for awhile, though I did not intend to kill him. He was an ignorant, thoughtless man, his worst fault lying in the fact of his too great readiness to allow himself to be made the tool of others. He, and such as he, were but plastic wax in the hands of the more scheming rebels; and they were incapable of conceiving any very wicked plans against life or liberty. There was no especial wish to wreak vengeance upon him, and my only thought was to get rid of him until I could make my exit from the place.

"Reaching cautiously for his musket, I succeeded in getting hold of it without waking him, and then after a pause in which I could hear the loud beatings of my own heart, I raised myself and prepared for the last desperate effort to get free. With one stroke on the man's head with the heavy end of the musket, I left him lying senseless, and sped out into the rain and darkness. On my left lay the confederate men; on the right were the horses, whose restless feet favored my approach without discovery. I slipped into their midst, unfastened one and mounted him. He was saddled ready for use, and I felt the breath of liberty on my forehead the moment I had assumed a seat on his back.

"The direction to be taken was a matter for careful consideration, and I was for a moment quite bewildered; but as if fortune had determined to recompense me for the late accumulation of ills, my eyes caught the gleam of a rocket sent up from a neighboring hill, and I knew that there I should find my friends. Instantly I turned the animal's head in that direction, and started, not rapidly because of the darkness, but still with a certain degree of haste which only desperation could give.

"I had gone safely through the very heart of the camp to the outer edge, when I came upon a mounted guard whom I challenged instantly with the instinct of self-preservation strong within me:

"'Who goes there?'

"'A friend!' he answered.

"'Halt and give the countersign.'

"He rode to my side, whispered the word and I answered:

"'All right,' and dashed away. In a moment I came to the outer pickets and in turn received a challenge. As I had the countersign, I gave it boldly and was allowed to pass. Then I gave rein to the animal and we galloped up the valley furiously for half a mile, when I had the joy to discover a faint light upon the hill a few hundred yards above me. How to reach it I did not know, but I made the effort, and dashed through the brush, and over the stones at random, till the undergrowth became too dense for the horse to penetrate, and I left him to try it on foot.

"Finally I came out on top of the hill, and descried the Federal camp where our men were resting calmly, unaware of the close proximity of the enemy. The pickets arrested me and took me before the officer in command, in whom I found a personal friend, well known to me years ago. That meeting was one never to be forgotten. I told him briefly what had happened and what I desired. Immediately the troops were roused, and placed under my command, the colonel taking for the time, a subordinate position. I knew the force and position of the rebels, and we dashed down upon them with perfect confidence, having nearly twice their number of men. The resistance was determined, but they could not hold out long, and the morning sun found us in possession of the entire body of the enemy.

"A few more words will end the long story. My other

comrade had been as brutally murdered as those of whom I have spoken. I suppose it was done after our attack was made, and they found they could not hold out against us. The hope I had cherished of liberating him was thus destroyed, adding to my thirst for revenge."

"And did you take it?" asked Astrea as he paused, looking steadfastly in his face.

"I have not taken it yet," he answered in a suppressed voice. "It was in my heart to hang the leader there, but when I had him in my power and could have done it without one opposing word from a man in the command, I chose to wait. We were joined the day following by a portion of the brigade which had been signaled by the rocket I had seen, and we took up our line of march for Corinth. He is now confined in a house below, and awaiting his trial, which he shall have fairly. But his doom is sealed. My evidence will sentence him to death inevitably, and he knows it. I said I had not taken my revenge; I am taking it every hour of his life."

"What is his rank?"

"A colonel's. He commanded two regiments, and they say that they were foraging, but that is not at all likely. Doubtless their object will come out when we subject them to examination."

"When did you come in?"

"To-night. I arrived, weary and worn, about six o'clock. Our tents are pitched in the lower part of the town, our prisoners safe, and our weary men at rest. It happened that as I sat at supper I heard your name mentioned, coupled with blessings and words of high respect. I found out where you dwelt and came to see you, feeling that you would not refuse to hear what had befallen me since we parted."

"You have suffered much. I am glad to welcome you back among friends, and to feel that you have done nobly."

She held out her hand in confirmation of her words, and he took it, holding it lingeringly—longing to speak, but not daring to pass the limits her manner prescribed.

"Come to see me to-morrow," she added almost immediately. "It grows late, and you need rest as well as myself. May bright and peaceful dreams visit your sleep this night, such as you have not known for weary months. Good-night."

He was obliged to go, and took his leave reluctantly. But he was happier for that interview. Her gentle tones, and earnest expression of pleasure in his safety, sounded pleasantly through all his meditations. He would have been happier still, could he have seen her after she found herself alone, when she had fallen upon her knees in thanksgiving for his safety. A weary weight seemed to have been rolled from heart and brain. As she stood before the little mirror, to unbind the long hair, with tears still wet upon the lashes, she saw that her eyes were bright, and her whole face radiant. The change was startling. Why should she feel so rejoiced at his coming—so glad for that above all else? The question found its answer in her own heart, and her feelings all changed—cheeks kindling, and eyes drooping with shame and anguish, as she admitted to herself the truth which she had never before acknowledged.

"God pity me. I do love him—fervently, hopelessly; and worse still, he loves me as his life. Oh, sun of joy never to shine on me, even while the light streams in my sight, warm and bright and blissful. God pity me! God pity us both!"

The candles burned dim, flickered, and died in their sockets; still she sat with her face bowed in her hands, sleepless and prayerful. The sounds of life died throughout the town, and all Corinth slept, save where a few men paced their lonely beats on picket duty. But she this night thought of nothing but herself and the man who had gone out from her presence, yearning for words she did not dare to speak; dreamed of nothing bright or hopeful in the future. Dull and heavily rolled the current of her life, within dark and dreary bounds—no freshening breeze upon the waters—no tender buds or blooms upon its banks. She saw before her only a rugged, uninviting way—knew that she must tread it, and strove to nerve herself for what was to come.

CHAPTER XV.

PLEADING FOR THE LIFE OF A REBEL PRISONER.

A FEW days after Captain Wilfer's arrival, while talking with General Grant at his head-quarters just out of town, an orderly came and informed the General that a lady was very anxious to speak with him privately. He bade the boy show her into the room, but the latter came back soon and said she would prefer to come again if he could not see her alone. "Then show her into my private office, and I will come presently."

The boy took the message, and she followed him into a small room which no one entered except by the Commander's express orders. It was nearly half an hour before he closed his interview with the Captain and the latter took his leave.

As General Grant entered the room where his visitor sat, she rose and threw back her veil, advancing a step to meet him.

"You do not know me, I presume, General, though I have been here almost as long as you have."

"No, I cannot remember to have seen you before."

"Did you ever hear anything of a Miss Harmon?"

"O, yes. Are you the lady? I am glad to see you, for I can take this opportunity of thanking you for many kindnesses to the soldiers. Sit down."

She resumed her seat, and he took one near her. She was looking wistfully into his face, studying him with an intentness he could not understand.

"Do you really feel as if I have been of any service or done any good?"

"I do, certainly.'

"Enough to entitle me to any consideration, any favor, should I wish to ask one?"

"Perhaps so. What do you want?"

She did not at once reply, but sat playing with a spray of jasmine plucked from a vine in passing, and pulling it to pieces. The General sat very patiently waiting her answer and watching the little thin, trembling fingers.

"Captain Wilfer was with you when I came," she said at length.

"Yes."

"I know him, and did not wish him to recognize me. On his evidence you have condemned the rebel officer whom he brought in a prisoner a short time since."

"Yes."

The General's brevity was worse than any questions or impatience could have been. She grew more and more restless and wild under it, dreading to go on, but driven to it by his patient expectancy. Bursting all bounds of calm control, she spoke with rapid desperation, coming at once to the object of her visit.

"General Grant, I have come to ask that man's life at your hands. He does not deserve it—I know this. His course has been more than cruel, and his punishment should be severe. But I implore you to spare his life. If I have ever done any good to any one, accomplished good to others through weariness and pain, for the sake of this, grant my request. If I could stay away and remain silent while his sentence was being executed without an attempt to save him, I should always consider myself a party to his destruction, and never again know peace. It is in your power to spare him; punish him by imprisonment, anything else but death."

She had risen and stood before him, her hands wrung together in an agony of entreaty.

"I must know why you make the request, and on what grounds you base your plea. So vile a wretch—so wicked, and deliberate a murderer cannot escape from the hands of justice simply because a woman asks his life. You may be entitled by your actions to much consideration from me, but you must know that I cannot do this without a reason. On what grounds do you base your request?"

"On the strength alone of the few services I have rendered. I hope that my care has saved more than one man for his country's service, and until now I have asked no other reward than the consciousness of duty performed. If I have dared to make this plea with hope, it is because the matter is of more importance to me than you can imagine."

"What do you know of him? and what right have you to ask the release of such a villain? You acknowledge him deserving of his fate, and have led us all to believe you a very patriotic, loyal woman. Is there no inconsistency in your present conduct?"

"I may seem inconsistent to you, for you cannot know the motives which prompt me. If you could, you would never charge me with any unworthy action."

He looked at her thoughtfully, then rose and paced the room with slow steps, his hands thrust deeply into his pockets.

"It is true I know nothing of your private motives, and it may be as well to keep them to yourself, for I tell you positively that whatever he may be to you I cannot modify his sentence. He has taken life, and the law of justice requires that his life shall be taken in return. It is a poor equivalent for such blood as he spilled mercilessly; but such a deed shall not go unpunished for any consideration. If he is anything to you I am sorry. Sentence has been passed, however, and to-morrow he must die."

"Can *nothing* move you to alter your decision?"

She stood up, white as wax before him.

"Nothing. I wish your errand had been of a different nature, for I am sorry to be obliged to refuse you. How did you come—in an ambulance? I will see you to it."

She walked out mutely by his side, struck dumb with overwhelming emotions. Could she leave him without one more appeal for mercy? A glance at his cold face checked the words burning on her lips, and she suffered him to place her in the ambulance in silence. Before she could fully realize that he had positively cut her off from all hope, he had touched his hat and walked away, while the driver took up the reins and drove back to Corinth.

Captain Wilfer stood on the porch of the Tishomingo Hotel as she passed, and seeing her, followed the vehicle to her dwelling. Her first thought was to escape him, but a second changed the impulse, and she waited him at the gate after sending the ambulance away. He was alarmed the moment his eyes rested on her pallid features.

"Something dreadful has happened," he exclaimed anxiously. "Can I do anything for you?"

"Oh, I don't know."

She clung to the gate for support. This moment was worse than all that had gone before. He took her hands from where they had fastened themselves, and resolutely put his arm about her form to keep her from falling.

"Come into the house and try to calm yourself. Then, if I can do anything, command me."

Her strength was not great enough to contend with him now. She was obliged to yield and suffer herself to be led like a child. He placed her upon a lounge, got a glass of water and stood by her, anxiously noting every expression of her agonized face.

"Captain Wilfer, if I should ask a great favor of you, do you think you could grant it?"

"I would try."

A long silence.

"Do you think if you were to make the attempt, you could alter General Grant's decision to execute the rebel officer whom you captured?"

"I would not like to attempt it," he answered in great surprise. "Why do you ask?"

"I want you to try. It was your evidence which condemned him, and you may succeed where I have failed. I have been to him. You were there when I went, and I avoided you; but having failed, my last hope lies in you. Desperation has driven me to ask your help, for he must not die, and *you* must not be the instrument of his death."

The last words were spoken so lowly that he could not catch them. After waiting for her to continue, and seeing her silent, he said quietly:

"You fill me with astonishment. Why did you not mention this when I told you of his capture and impending trial, the night I came? It is true that he has not been tried, for it was deemed unnecessary. I gave a written statement to General Grant, and he has acted upon it. I could not now alter it, for my honor is involved, were it alone at stake. You know how I feel, and what cause I have for the feeling."

"Yes, I know it all. Oh, I little dreamed of whom you were speaking then. You did not tell me his name, and I have not known it until to-day, when I heard the soldiers talking about his approaching execution."

"Then he is known to you?"

"Yes. Please ask me no more; but if you would serve me with a kindness that will make me forever grateful, procure his release."

"You ask too much of me. I cannot do it."

"You are bitter! you cannot bear to have your revenge wrested from you! Oh, Captain Wilfer, I thought you more generous. It were nobler to spare his life, and leave him time to repent of his crimes."

"Did he give those poor men time for repentance, before he hurled them into eternity without mercy or the shadow of justice? What is he to you that you can find it in your heart to ask so much of me?"

"*He is my husband.*"

She spoke in a low, heart-broken tone, and he recoiled suddenly as if from a sharp blow.

"That man your husband, and you ask his life at my hands?"

He sat down and leaned his head against the window, while a groan escaped his lips, so deep and bitter it pierced her heart.

"If it is ungenerous in me to ask it, forgive me," she said brokenly. "I have no other hope."

He did not answer and her heart seemed to faint within her. Pride gave way to despair; she forgot everything but the necessity of saving her husband's life. Had another been the instrument of evil, or of justice to him, the case had been less terrible and easier to bear. But she knew that this man loved her. The thought seemed to freeze her blood in her veins. Before he was aware of her intention, she had knelt at his side and clasped the hand nearest her passionately. He felt her little fingers locked closely about it, her brow laid against it in the abandonment of her agonized entreaty. But the struggle was not yet over, and the thrilling sweetness of her touch only rendered it harder to gain the victory over his more selfish desires and act magnanimously. His love grew mighty within him; the temptation waxed strong. Hope and love whispered that it was duty, not affection, which brought her to his feet, a suppliant for the life of a bad, cruel man; and if that man was gone forever from her path, he might win her. Why not suffer justice to take its course, and abide the result. Was he responsible if the man's deeds rendered him worthy of punishment, that the penalty should fall on him? If he escaped the law, and imposed upon his captor this sacrifice, where would the demands of justice be fulfilled?

He lifted his head and looked down upon the woman by his side. That one glance wrought a revolution in his feelings. He might persist in his course, and free her, but in doing so, he would place an eternal barrier between them—dig a gulf, over which he would never dare to stretch his hands and ask her to come to him. Something in the pure, sweet face, stained and agonized with an intolerable woe, called up the better feelings of his nature, and he threw aside the tempter with a thrill of shame for having listened to its allurements.

"Rise, Miss Harmon"—he could not call her by any other name, even now, "and I promise you to do all in my power. How much you have asked, you know; but I will not refuse you, though I may not be able to accomplish what you wish. If I succeed you will grant me one thing in return?"

"Oh, do not impose conditions upon me, Captain Wilfer."

"Do I then still fail to deserve your confidence?" he asked bitterly. "Is it so fearful a thing to grant me the privilege of being called your friend—to be allowed to serve you as your friend whenever you are in need? I understand you now, and your position is no longer a mystery to me. What is due to you, and to myself as an honorable man, will never be forgotten."

She held out both hands frankly.

"If the devoted friendship of a heart-broken woman can be anything to you in compensation for this great service, I shall be proud of the honor of being allowed to call you friend! My gratitude shall be boundless."

He bowed over those hands, drew them together and kissed them reverently. The next moment he was gone—walking rapidly away towards his quarters.

What she felt or thought after that, she could not have told. Lying with her face in the pillows of the lounge, the time sped unheeded until night closed in. She was conscious of a belief that Captain Wilfer would save the man she had called husband, conscious of a deep and fervent gratitude for the nobility of his conduct. Murmured prayers were constantly upon her lips—prayers interrupted by wild waves of thought and remembrances which had the power to make her shrink, and cry out in irrepressible moans. But nothing clear was evolved from the seething chaos of her brain. She did not strive for one distinct idea, suffering confusion to reign until exhausted nature could bear no more, and she sank into profound slumber.

Her landlady, Mrs. Merton, came several times to the door to see if she had wakened, that she might serve tea; but would not disturb her, knowing her need of rest. So she slept on for several hours, until Captain Wilfer came and insisted upon rousing her.

"I have something to tell you," he said as soon as she was able to comprehend him. "After you have taken some refreshment. I am going to beg you to take a walk with me for a short time."

"You have succeeded?" she asked with a gasp, turning white and faint with excess of feeling.

"Never mind whether I have or not. Here, Mrs. Merton has brought your tea, and you must drink it. Do you remember bringing me my tea after that accident on the Mississippi? Now I want to return the compliment, and hold the tray at your side while you drink this," handing her the cup as he spoke. "And now what if I should tell you that I have a great treat in store for you as soon as you have finished?"

"I should say that it is like you to be kind and generous in striving to give me pleasure."

She could scarcely repress the tears which rose to her eyes as she spoke.

"You give me credit for more generosity than I am entitled to," he answered carelessly. "I have just met Major Noble, who informed me that he and his wife arrived here to-night, and she is anxious to see you. The pleasure of the surprise was so great, I could not resist the desire to come and tell you, that you might share it. A man who can come back to service in his condition, is deserving of the highest honor. He looks like a ghost still, but he is as cheerful as a sunbeam."

Astrea's face lighted and glowed with radiance.

"God bless him, and all like him who are brave and true! I will go to my little friend at once."

But when they had passed beyond the gate, he drew her hand within his arm and said with an effort:

"You can see your friend some other time. I spoke of that for the benefit of Mrs. Merton, from whom I supposed you would prefer to keep your private affairs."

"You are right; I have told her nothing, and do not wish any one to know what I have been obliged to tell you."

"I thought as much. And now, what I have to say is, that I have seen General Grant, and that he refuses to make any change in his decision."

She stopped suddenly, recoiling as if about to fall.

"Nay! listen to me a moment. I say he refuses, but I think I can contrive his escape, which will straighten a very tangled web. I came to-night to take you to the prison, if you wish to go—if you have any desire to see him. The permit comes from General Grant himself."

"It is what I would have asked of you as a last favor."

"Are you strong enough to bear it?"

"I do not know; but I *must* see him."

"Then you must go to-night; to-morrow it will be too late."

They walked on slowly, for she faltered at every step, passing through the centre of the town, and on to a large building called the "Stockade," where a large number of rebel prisoners were confined.

Captain Wilfer stepped to the guard and said something to him in a low voice, then as he drew back and touched his cap, the young man half-supporting his trembling companion, crossed the threshold and paused before a small door on the right. To the sentinel who was stationed in the hall, he presented a slip of paper, and another man was called to open the door. Astrea pressed her hands hard over her bosom as the key rattled in the lock, then by a strong effort, recovered herself and went in. Captain Wilfer withdrew and waited on the outside, leaving her alone with the prisoner.

A small lamp burned upon the table in one corner, and by its light the prisoner sat looking at something which he held in his hand, as she entered. His back was toward the door, and he did not deign to look around when he heard it opened, supposing that it was some officer who came to question him. She advanced and looked over his shoulder, drawn by the irrepressible desire of a sudden thought. Her quick eye had caught the gleam of a golden case, and the possibility of its being a miniature, made her act from a sudden impulse. It was a miniature but the features were strange, pretty and insignificant. With a quick, imperious step she passed around and stood before him, throwing off her hat that her face might not be concealed from his view. Had an apparition appeared to him he could not have turned more pallid as he started up, grasping involuntarily at the back of his chair for support.

"You, Eugenia? My God, how came you here?"

She smiled, a cold, scornful smile.

"I might return the compliment and ask how you happened to be here, Mr. Passiver?"

A fearful oath escaped his lips.

"Not of my own free will, you may be sure. I have had the bad luck to get captured, and suppose I've got to die. What hand have you had in the matter?"

"You suspect me of having something to do with your sentence?"

"Why not? You are here, and I am to be hung or shot to-morrow. You would be glad to know me out of your way, no doubt."

"If I could be so wicked as to desire your death, I would not stain my hands with your blood even to meet the ends of justice. By what right do you so falsely judge me?"

"Oh, I did not know but your high notions of honor and patriotism would lead you into making a great sacrifice in the eyes of the world, while at the same time you might rid yourself of an incumbrance. Perhaps you might find a husband more suited to your taste."

He laughed coarsely, in closing the insulting speech.

"Still cruel," she said bitterly; "and this is to be my only reward for all that I have done for you. God grant that I may not be tempted to regret that I have humbled myself to plead for your life."

"You plead for my life!" and he laughed derisively. "I

may believe it when I find myself an hundred miles south of the Federal lines."

"Were I to cause you to be liberated, could you find it in your heart to be merciful to me in return?"

"What would you have?"

"My child. You have robbed me of the brightest years of my life; crushed me to the dust in woe and humiliation; heaped upon me abuses that you would not have heaped upon a dog; driven me from my home under curses and hatred; sunk me from wealth to poverty and toil for my daily bread; subjected me to suspicion, misconstruction, insult! All these I can forgive and make no complaint, if you will make amends for the crowning evil done to me, and give me back my child. You never cared for her; you tore her from me only that you might make my misery complete. Give her back to my love and care, and I will forgive all—will ask no more."

"You *are* magnanimous! What a monster you make me by your generous array of charges. Really, I would like to make some return, but fear I must decline to meet such a demand. My daughter must be reared by persons more fitted for the responsibility than yourself. Considering my own mother to be the best guardian of her innocent years, I have placed her in her charge, and trust that she may grow up a better woman than my headstrong wife, if I may condescend without a breach of honor, to call her by that name."

The spirit of the woman was outraged. All weakness had flown now, and she stood erect and grand in her wounded pride—her just anger. The dark eyes smouldered with consuming passion, and her pale cheeks became crimson.

"Frederic Passiver, are you mad? Do you know what you are doing in your wanton cruelty? In mercy to yourself, listen to me, and heed well what I say. I have been generous, forbearing with you always, but I am no more than human, and there is a limit to endurance. You have wrecked my life, and now stand between me and every hope of happiness in the future. Yet when I heard that it was you who had been captured and sentenced to death for a brutal and inhuman action, I went to General Grant to plead that your sentence might be altered, your unworthy life spared. With him I failed, but I did not yield, and I have the promise from another, that you may be liberated. It is in my power to step outside that door and say 'Let justice take her course,' and the sentence will be executed at the rising of to-morrow's sun. I speak no idle words, and I implore you not to drive me to the commission of a deed that would destroy you, and make me loathe myself."

"Are you telling the truth, Eugenia?"

"*When* did I ever tell you a falsehood? Oh man! so false yourself you can believe in no one—put faith in the integrity of none! Even the remembrance of adherence to principle and truth under tortures as vile and unholy as the tortures of the Inquisition, have not the power to make him spare me now from the insult of his incredulity. Frederic Passiver, I warn you to beware!"

And he did quail as he looked into her resolute, passionate face. She had reached the crisis of an unutterable woe, and his fate rested in her hands. One word of light and mocking import, such as rose to his lips from habit, and he knew by her look that she would mutely walk from his presence, and leave him to his doom. The love of life was strong; his hate and passion were deep and bitter; he panted for freedom and revenge. To gain his wishes he changed his manner and grew humble.

"Eugenia, I have tried you too hardly and regret it sincerely. If you can accomplish what you claim to be able to, I will grant your request, and send your child to you through the lines. At any fixed time, giving me sufficient time to go for her, your messenger may meet mine, who will come with a flag of truce, and deliver her to him, on receiving proof that he has your authority for her custody."

"You will swear to this agreement?"

"If you require me to do so."

"I do require it. Hold up your hand."

He held it up, and she repeated in low, concentrated tones an oath which thrilled him with awe, by its intense solemnity:

"I, Frederic Passiver, do solemnly swear before God, as I hope for his mercy in the day of judgment, to fulfill the agreement made this night to my wife, Astrea Eugenia Passiver, and in consideration for the liberty she gives me by her influence, return to her custody and care, the infant child, whom I took from her in parting. If I fail to fulfill this oath to the letter, may His wrath overtake me, cutting me off from life without a moment's warning, and consigning me to punishment forever and forever after death."

He repeated it after her, hesitating often, and reluctant to proceed. But her eyes chained him, and he was forced to go on to the end. Great drops stood out on his brow, and the moment he had finished he sank to his chair with an oath.

"I hope you are satisfied, madam. And now, if you have no further arrangements to make, be brief, and I will excuse you from wasting upon me any more of your valuable time."

"The Federalists occupy Iuka now. Send the child there with a flag of truce, and I will myself be with the man to receive her. I give you two weeks—ample time for all you may wish to do; and if you fail, the consequences of your oath be upon your own head. I am not responsible."

She went out quickly, without looking back. Captain Wilfer met her at the door, and silently drew her hand within his arm, leading her away without question or comment.

And while he walked restlessly beneath the stars that night, striving to still, by the force of a strong man's reason, the clamor of feelings which kindled the blood in his veins to intense fever, she was lying prostrate upon the floor of her chamber, shut out from all sympathy and consolation, thinking of her blighted life—the years that had teemed with misery—the present, so dark and hopeless—into all of which mingled doubts and conjectures that were in themselves tormenting. Whose miniature was it that she had seen in his hand? Some one whom he loved, doubtless, had given him the semblance of herself. A less worthy woman had won from him what she had never been able to gain, and she would not have been mortal, had the thought given rise to no bitter feeling. Would he keep his oath? He had broken promises almost as solemn, and she did not know if he considered an oath made to her more binding. In her doubt she had been led to make it as strong as possible, dictating the most solemnly binding pledge her imagination could invent. She found it in her heart now to pray that he might be made to keep it—that he might become a wiser and a better man.

Oh, woman, out of the depths of such misery, to remember with humble and fervent prayer one who had only spoken to wound, who had acted to crush! If there be no heroism in deeds like this—no grandeur in the strength which lifts her above self in such an hour of trial—then are heroism and grandeur but names only, idle and meaningless.

CHAPTER XVI.

REFUGEES AND THEIR PITIFUL CONDITION—DISAPPOINTMENT AND FAITHLESSNESS.

THERE was great excitement throughout the town, when it was known that the prisoner who was under sentence of death, had made his escape. He was traced to the picket lines which he had passed about twelve o'clock, giving the countersign; but there all trace was lost, though a company of cavalry was sent in pursuit. Efforts were made to discover who had contrived to release him, for no one thought that he could have made his escape without very efficient aid; but nothing of a convincing nature was educed from the few facts learned, and very soon the excitement died out. If General Grant suspected Wilfer of complicity in the matter, he found no evidence to confirm his suspicions, and did not press the search further than his duty required. Other excitements soon swept this away, and Corinth sank once more into its usual daily routine of succeeding events.

In the days that followed, Astrea had one great consolation in the presence of her friend. Major Noble was appointed to a post of duty which required little exertion, and his wife entered with heart and soul into all the plans to be arranged for the comfort and assistance of the refugees, who were conveyed through the lines every day in appalling numbers. The facilities for sending them north were meagre, and the progress slow. Every spot that could afford them shelter, was crowded, and disease was sweeping them away at a fearful rate—brought on by exposure and want. The ladies were untiring in their efforts to give relief, bringing every possible means of aid to bear upon their dreadful condition, while the officers laughed at them and called them enthusiasts for their pains.

"They are a filthy, ungrateful set," declared one young man with a shrug of the shoulders and an expression of intense disgust. "By the time you know as much of them as I do, you will be willing enough to leave them to their fate."

"And pray, why do you say this? What do you know more than Miss Harmon, who has toiled for them for weeks?" asked Mrs. Noble, while Astrea smiled at his assumption of superior knowledge.

"I happen to know much more than I care to know," he said readily, "having been sent in charge of a hundred to Illinois, where it was proposed to settle them wherever we could find a place. Such things as soap, water, combs and brushes, they hold in high disdain; and they have no more energy than so many pigs. I was thoroughly sick of them before I got through, I assure you. Think of their using the money distributed among them to buy food, for a lot of brassy trinkets and gaudy finery!—that too, when they did not know where to find a roof to shelter them, or a pound of provisions to keep them from starvation."

"But if these things were so scarce as not to be found, of what use could the money be?" asked Mrs. Noble teazingly. "As well spend it for finery as anything else."

"You don't mean that, I know. If they couldn't keep it, why not buy clothing that would have been of some use, and decent in appearance? Preserve me from the refugees forever—those poor people of the south whom the darkies call 'white trash.' I have had my share of trouble with them."

"'Inasmuch as ye do it unto the least of these, ye have done it unto me,'" quoted Astrea gravely, remembering that bitter defence in the depot where she saw the vision of a woman sitting over her dead child. "Major Thornton may declare his disgust, and bewail the thriftlessness and ingratitude of this miserable class; but I cannot think that he would refuse this aid to any one who might come to him in extremity. His lips do his heart injustice."

"Miss Harmon's good opinion is deserving of appreciation, and Major Thornton thanks her sincerely. He feels, however, that he would be taking credit for charity to himself which he does not deserve, were he to allow her to suppose that he would ever take one step further to serve them."

They were sitting in Mrs. Noble's room at the Tishomingo one morning, when this conversation took place, while Astrea was looking over some drawings in colored crayon with General McPherson.

"How do you feel about them, General? Are they not to be pitied rather than despised?"

"I think so, truly. They are not responsible for the ignorance which renders them odious to the more intelligent classes of society, for the circumstances of their lot debar them from all opportunities of improvement. They are born in poverty, and the distinction of position is so great between them and the wealthier classes, there is not one link to bind them together with the first degree of sympathy. The institution of slavery has cut them off from all lucrative employment; tenants on large plantations, they have only an indifferent shelter, and sufficient food from day to day to keep them from want. They are unable to emigrate—incapable of supporting their own schools, and debarred from the privileges of sending their children to those places where the rich men's families are educated. By what means can they rise above the miserable condition to which they are born? Ambition, if it rises, is strangled at its birth, and they must plod on in the same aimless way, year after year, without any visible sign of change. This war has wrought a revolution, and will not only benefit the black by emancipation, but the poor white people also by forcing them into different paths. I sometimes think that it was needed, and is but the course of a wise Providence to lift a portion of his people from worse than bondage."

"But they are all being killed off—the men at least—while the women and children are dying by hundreds."

"Such as may be left will be benefited by the change. The men and women may not, indeed, be greatly changed by it, but their children will come in contact with a different class of minds, and become industrious and ambitious. You may not have noticed it Major Thornton, but I can already see in the result good to them as a people. I could point out instances here in this place, that would force you to the acknowledgment that I am right. And I think it our duty to excuse their faults—make every possible allowance for their shortcomings, and do them all the good we can."

"Then follow out your ideas, and be as philanthropical as you like. I am not a philanthropist, and I beg to be excused from having anything to do with them. There is the whistle of the southern train. You will now have an immediate opportunity to display some of your generosity."

General McPherson rose and excused himself. He was superintendent of the military railroads at that time, and it was necessary for him to be present at the arrival and departure of every train.

Standing at the front windows, our party watched the train as it came in from Iuka, loaded heavily with freight and swarming with human beings black and white. Major Thornton laughed aloud as he saw the comical figures the poor wretches made as they began to clamber from their perches to the platform. They were but half-clothed, stiff and cramped by their long ride in such an uncomfortable position. Huge bundles of clothing and bedding had been piled upon the top of cotton bales, and the smaller children, both white and black, were literally packed between them, as the only mode of traveling safely, never daring to move lest they should fall from the train. The little creatures had become perfectly helpless, and when set upon their feet, were unable to stand. Some cried piteously, while others sank mutely upon the floor, putting on most ludicrously long, grave faces.

"Look at McPherson," exclaimed Thornton suddenly. "I told him he would have a chance to exercise his benevolence."

They saw the General reaching up to aid an old negro who had been vainly striving to descend from his high seat. Catching the old man's arm he steadied him carefully until he was safely landed upon the platform. Then came the old woman, creeping over her bundles and in danger of falling with each new essay, until the General weary of delay, caught her in both hands and lifted her bodily from the train. A shout of laughter from Major Thornton caused him to look up reproachfully, his grave face expressive of genuine pity for the miserable beings thrown thus upon his mercy. That look showed him two other figures, and one face bright with approving smiles, while the other grave and sweet, was wet with tears which rolled slowly down her cheeks. It was enough. Had he needed any other reward than the approval of his own conscience, he found it in that brief glance, and the picture it left in his memory.

"I do not see how you can do it," said Major Thornton, when the General came up again after his duties were ended. "That anybody *can* touch them, is beyond my comprehension. I would not do it to save their lives."

"The time may come when your feelings will be different," was the quiet response.

"It is not likely."

"Suppose you should get captured by the rebels and in making your escape find only negroes to help you," began Mrs. Noble, calling to mind Captain Wilfer's story. "Do you pretend to say that your repugnance to the race is so great that you could not be grateful."

"Not that, but I could not put my hands upon them, or allow them to come very near me."

"As the General says, you may be forced to change your notions at some future time, and feel glad to be touched by them. Think what they have suffered, and how faithful they have been to us and our cause. For this, if for nothing else, they are deserving of our kindness and care. They are homeless and friendless, if we turn from them. Shall we set them free, and then suffer them to starve and die under our eyes, without sympathy or kindness, from those to whom they look for protection?

"As a class, they are not yet fit for self-dependence. It is too sudden. We must give them time to realize that they are free, self-dependent, responsible beings. Not only this, but we must teach them how to be so. They have not known, and cannot learn in an hour, any more than you or I could—thrust at once from one extreme to the other without preparation for it."

"This is all very well now, and does you credit, my dear lady; but just wait until you have been here a month, and tasted some of the nauseous doses they will thrust upon you, and you will talk differently. They will be after you day and night, beg or steal everything you care to keep; tell you numberless falsehoods, and indulge in wickedness generally. You may be able to stand it for awhile, but not long."

"Miss Harmon has stood it, and is not yet disposed to abandon them to their fate," answered Mrs. Noble. "She has been here ever since the occupation of the place by our forces, and has had more to do with them than any one I know of, yet her sympathy is as strong and her desire to aid them, as lively as ever. I hold that the duties which cost us nothing of taste, feeling or inclination are of little worth. If doing good to others led us always through flowery, instead of thorny paths, there would be small merit in choosing good before evil."

"Women are queer in their notions, and always go in for self-sacrifice. Place before them two hard duties, and they will choose the hardest because it will cost them the greatest labor and the deepest pain. They never seem to think that it may be possible to accomplish the same ends without choosing the most difficult means."

Mrs. Noble protested that he was mistaken, and appealed to Astrea, who smiled and answered quietly:

"Major Thornton is nearly right. I have often noticed that it was a trait in the character of our sex to take the hardest of every duty upon themselves in preference to the lighter and easier modes of working to the same results. I think this arises from her keener feeling, and over eagerness to make sure of the right. She is so zealous to accomplish good, so fearful of not reaching the highest standard of right, she is almost certain to rush into extremes and injure herself by uselessly wearing out her own strength."

"Allow me to say, Miss Harmon, that you are an exact type of the character you have drawn," said Major Thornton starting up gayly, at which she blushed and seemed much disconcerted.

"Excuse me, sir; but you are too personal. We were generalizing subjects I believe, and it is unfair to make an application like this to me individually."

"Forgive me if I have offended you, and I will promise better behavior in future, though I confess it does vex me sorely to see you killing yourself over those ungrateful refugees, and exasperating negroes. If I had a sister or a wife who could do so, I would have her sent to a lunatic asylum."

Something like the foregoing conversation came up every day, but failed to produce any effect upon the habits of our friends. They went the same weary round, and performed the same irksome duties; though the sense of right never grew dull, or their sympathies less keen. Mrs. Noble defended herself and friend warmly, when attacked, but Astrea said little. To everything calculated to disparage her protegees and win her interest away from them, she had but the one answer, quoted from the sayings of One who died for such, "Inasmuch as ye have done it unto the least of these, ye have done it unto me," this was all. The time for wasting breath in lengthy arguments had passed, and she strove by steady action to accomplish what words had failed to effect. In those days of toil and trial, the example of this woman's life was grand. But only to one did she assume her just proportions, and that was the one who alone knew the secret history of her life—the ceaseless strain upon her endurance and self-sustaining power. Captain Wilfer watched her with adoring eyes—coming to her side only to serve, and when he could not render any assistance, standing off and beholding with reverence. To him she was something more than human—angelic, in her unselfish goodness. For now that they understood each other, and she could rely upon his honor, her manner became gentle and kind—almost confiding when he was with her. Gradually he arrived at the point when he could feel that it was no presumption to judge of the motives from which she had acted. Indeed the one thought which gave him a keen pleasure in the midst of pain and disappointment, was that her interest in himself had driven her to withhold him from a deed that would have placed an impassable barrier between them. He was not a wicked man, or a selfishly calculating lover. If thoughts of a possibility of her eventual freedom, arising out of the contingencies of war, ever crossed his mind, he banished them resolutely, putting them from him as temptations of the evil one. He looked to the future with no hope of possessing more than she had bestowed upon him—her friendship; but he understood her nobility of character, and almost worshiped her for the goodness, which made her presence a saving influence to so many.

As the fortnight drew near its close, and Astrea was led to realize that her conceded probation was at an end, she became very restless and excitable. Had she tried to conceal it, the truth would still have been manifest to his eyes, and her silence made him inexpressibly sad. He did not know and would not ask the cause. It had grown to be such a habit with her to keep her own counsel, and suffer in silence, the thought had not occurred to her to confide in him until the hour for action had arrived. But when the last day's sun had sunk like a great red ball in the west, and she remembered that its next setting would be upon her joy or despair, the burden became too great to bear alone. She turned to him as they sat together on the porch of her abode, resting after a long, hot walk, and said earnestly:

"See, the day is done, and the night comes once more; and though the sun may rise for you to-morrow, it may be to me a sunless day, I dread it, oh, I dread it!"

"Tell me why?"

"I dread it because it will be to me a day of doom if the promise he made that night be not fulfilled. I made his release, or escape, conditional. He swore to restore to me my child to-morrow, and if he fails—oh, it will be fearful for him and perhaps death to me!"

She leaned her head upon her hand and shuddered.

"You did not tell me that you had a child."

"No; there is much that I have not told you, my friend, because it is too sad, and I have not the strength to bear it. To speak much of my wrongs, would drive me mad. I must curb my feelings as you would fetter a wild animal to keep it from destroying human life. Let them loose and if they do not destroy me they will do mischief to others. I am silent because I do not dare to speak. Yet I must tell you a part of what now fills my mind, for I need your help."

His face lighted gladly.

"You have only to command me."

"I know that. I am undeserving of such ever ready kindness, but I have no other friend in whom I can confide, and I believe that I owe it to you to ask help first at your hands, before going to any other."

"I am glad that you appreciate the position at last," he said with a smile. "Yes, you do owe me this much, knowing how I long to serve or comfort you. Now, tell me all that you wish, and let me prove myself worthy of your confidence."

"No need of further proofs than I have had, but I will explain."

Then she told him of the interview, and the oath she had dictated, ending with the information that she must go to Iuka on the morrow, and see if he had kept his pledge faithfully.

"And this, too, you have suffered! O, woman, so weak, so tender and frail; and yet so mighty! I once told you that I thought you strange; you become wonderful now. I cannot understand how any one with your temperament can bear so much in patience."

"I have been patient only because I was forced to it. Many times my heart has sunk within me, and with all that was dearest lying so far and uncertain in the future, I often grew despairing—would gladly have welcomed the death which could set me free from such a fate as mine. I told you once, when you called me 'strange' the first time, that it sometimes required more courage to live than to die. You did not know how much meaning was in those words; and how often since the tempter has been at my side, urging me to seek that rest for which my soul longs inexpressibly."

"Poor heart; and you would give no confidence—seek from none the consolation of sympathy! Did you not know that, however noble, even grand it may have been to suffer and bear your burthens alone, it was fearfully dangerous?"

"Yes, I knew it; but I did not forget that God was a friend to the suffering, and his mercy has saved me from self-destruction. I hope I am stronger now, and that all sinful thoughts may have been banished forever. But if that man breaks his oath!—oh, then God pity me, for I know not what will follow."

"You will still suffer and be strong," he said, looking at her with his clear, manly eyes, whose glance seemed to inspire her with a new hope.

"I will try, at least," she answered, then added with a change of tone: "How am I to reach Iuka, and what shall I tell Mrs. Noble? I cannot yet give her the story, for when she hears anything, she must have it in full."

"You intend to tell her sometime?"

"Yes."

"Then why not take her with you, and tell her afterwards? Her presence will be a sustaining influence, and you may need her. Besides, if you will allow me to say it, I think you owe it to her to tell her all your history. She will only love you more for it, and never will betray your trust, I feel assured."

"I never doubted her trustworthiness, and you must not mistake my motives in having withheld from her my private history. That she is deserving, I know well, and I bless her every day of my life for her goodness to me and her faithful friendship. I have not told her, because I had not the heart to do it. Her sympathy would have driven me wild, and broken me down. I could not live under a perpetually compassionate gaze, and hear words of tenderness and pity for me in my misfortunes. It was necessary that I should seal my lips and bear my fate mutely, giving no sign, if I would keep my strength for the accomplishment of my one purpose. She could have done nothing for me, and what should I have gained by my confidence? Had circumstances not forced me to tell you, I would still be in sole possession of my secret."

"Proud woman! Obdurate and unwise little being! You know not what you do, when you shut yourself out from pure, true sympathy."

"Tell me what to do," she asked wearily. "I have almost worn myself out, and cannot think with any clearness."

"May I plan for you?"

"Yes."

"We will take the early train for Iuka, and go for some specified purpose which I will arrange before communicating with Mrs. Noble. Leave her to me, and I will save you from all questioning, if you desire it, until after your errand is done, and you know the result. When we get to Iuka, I will see the officer in command, and explain that I expect a flag of truce to meet me with a message. There is no help for this, but if it excites comment, my presence will save you from suspicion of treacherous communication with the rebels, and no one can know more than the fact that you had private business. If you were to go alone with me it would not be prudent."

He spoke with reluctance, and her cheeks crimsoned; but she felt grateful for his candor. He was thoughtful for awhile, then asked if she were absolutely obliged to go herself.

"I said that I would be there, and I could not wait in suspense. Yes, I must go."

"But you trust all arrangements to me?"

"Willingly."

"That is enough. Now retire and take all the rest you can. When morning comes everything will be ready."

She obeyed like a child. There was a sweet sense of safety and reliance in his manner, which set her at ease, and dismissed all fears. She had at once come into an unbounded confidence in his ability to accomplish what he undertook; and hers was a nature that trusted wholly if at all. It was with a feeling of intense relief that she resigned herself to his care, casting the whole necessity of immediate action into steadier hands. He had not promised more than he was able to fulfill, as she found when morning came, and he knocked at her door, in company with Mrs. Noble. That lady walked up to her and clasping both arms closely around her form, whispered in her ear:

"My poor, suffering one, be at rest—trust in my love, and God grant you peace soon. This little wan face, and wasted figure fill me with the deepest sympathy."

"Don't!—don't talk like that," she said brokenly. "I must be strong to-day."

"So you shall be," changing her tone to one of light raillery. "Captain Wilfer approves of strength quite as much as you do, and in order to make sure of it, has filled both pockets. I will wager if you were to empty them, you would find in one a bottle of the strongest and vilest brandy, while the other would give forth a sandwich or two with a very small piece of ham and a great deal of mustard—some stale cheese and some sour pickles. If there is not enough 'strength' in these, you will find an addition in his quarters, where my husband avers that he keeps an old meerschaum that would outrank our Commanding General quite as easily as the butter on the Mississippi steamers."

"I shall have to sue the Major for damages if he continues to injure my character in this way," protested the Captain. To Astrea this sounded heartless and mocking, though she knew that neither felt anything but sympathy for her distress. At the same time, it had its desired effect, and checked the rush of feelings which had threatened to unnerve her. Her head lifted itself proudly as she announced herself ready, and there was a half-angry light in her large eyes. How could they jest so carelessly when they knew that she was suffering such terrible agony of mind? Did they realize what this day was to be, and still find it possible to laugh in her face?

By the time they reached the cars, she had overcome the angry feelings which their manner caused her, and was ready to censure herself severely for the injustice done her best friends. The wrong was all in herself. She would not accept of sympathy, or permit lightness without breaking down or feeling angry and aggrieved. How very unreasonable and exacting does sorrow make us? A better impulse rose with the exercise of her judgment over feeling, and she exerted herself to appear more composed and cheerful, meeting their efforts to aid her with gentleness and a show of gratitude that touched them to the heart. On reaching Iuka, Captain Wilfer sought the officer in command and asked a private interview, in which he stated briefly his business.

"Is not this rather a singular proceeding for a loyal man?" asked the gentleman with a smile, while he regarded the Captain with keen scrutiny. "I should think you would be afraid of finding your motives misconstrued in the end."

"The man who acts from a knowledge of pure motives, is afraid of nothing, sir. This lady has asked me to act for her in a difficult position, and having fully tested her worth by long and close observation, I can vouch for the safety of my present proceeding. She has been unfortunate in her domestic relations, and her presence here is to learn something of a child who was taken from her. This I confide to you as a man of honor, for her history it is desirable that no one should know at present, and as a generous man, I trust to your aid to assist us without exciting comment."

"You expect a messenger with a flag of truce? He will come in from the South, of course. On condition that I be permitted to see that the communication is of the nature you describe, I will order out my horse and go with you, taking no one else as a witness to the interview."

"I will first consult the lady."

Captain Wilfer went to Astrea and spoke earnestly for several moments, then came back and reported favorably. The lady was willing that he should be made acquainted with all necessary details in order to shield her friends and herself from a suspicion of treachery, but it was not an easy thing for her to do this. While Captain Wilfer was completing arrangements, she leaned her head against Helen's shoulder as she sat beside her in a small room adjoining the officer's quarters, and moaned bitterly:

"How long shall I be subjected to such hard conditions? I must bare my heart to the unfeeling gaze of every stranger, else be suspected of evil."

"Is it unnatural, dear? These are times when the safety of our land compels us to be careful. Do not think hardly of the man for doing his duty."

An ambulance had been ordered out ostensibly to drive the ladies over the place, and the two gentlemen were standing outside in conversation, when an orderly rode up and reported a flag of truce at the picket lines. Colonel Heston turned at once to his guest:

"I think I must ride out immediately and see what is to be gained. Would you like to accompany me, Captain Wilfer? And by the way, it would be a treat to the ladies to go. Suppose you invite them."

Ten minutes later, the party set out, accompanied only by a couple of orderlies. Colonel Heston said nothing to any of the other officers, and no comment was made. Such interviews were of too frequent occurrence to occasion any great interest, even had they known of the fact.

"Remain here," commanded Colonel Heston, turning to his orderlies as they neared the spot and saw three men with a flag of truce waiting near the pickets. They at once drew rein a little in the rear of the party, and the two gentlemen rode forward.

"What is your business here?" asked the Colonel of the foremost of the three who had advanced to meet them.

"I come on special and private business with a lady."

"From whom," asked Captain Wilfer.

"Colonel Passiver, lately the guest of a Federal officer in the United States service. I believe that he eluded the too great kindness of his host, and returned to the bosom of his friends. This will probably convey his regrets, but is addressed to a lady, and as two are with you I presume it is to one of them that this must be directed."

"By her authority we receive it."

The document was placed in Colonel Heston's hand, and he rode back to the ambulance, tearing the cover as he went.

"I thought, ladies, you might like to see a rebel document, so I bring it to you to gratify your curiosity, if you have any."

He pretended to glance over it, then carelessly handed it to Astrea. She gave one long look at the few lines traced upon the page and gave it back to him, saying in a low voice:

"There is a reply. Say that as he has dealt with me, so will God deal with him. That is all."

She shrank back and half concealed her face while he lingered to chat with Mrs. Noble for a moment. In a short time he returned to where Captain Wilfer waited him, and dismissed the messenger with her answer. The men turned and galloped back over the dusty road by which they had come, leaving our friends to themselves.

Colonel Heston gave the paper to Captain Wilfer.

"I have not read it and do not desire to do so, feeling assured that your representation is correct. Restore it to the lady when convenient."

"But you have her permission, and I think you ought to know the contents. It may be the safest course for all parties concerned."

The Colonel remained thoughtful for a moment and again took the paper. Its contents were brief and concise:

"Madam,—After deliberate reflection, I have come to the conclusion that my first duty lies in punishing an open rebel to the cause of the South. I took an oath to restore your child, but it was from the lips only and not meant to be kept. 'All things are fair in love and war,' so I am justified. If you had not done so much against us, I would say come back and give your aid to the cause of freedom now, and I will still keep my oath and restore your daughter. But the time is past. You have done too much and it only remains for me to punish you by any means in my power. The child's face you shall never see again, and my constant wish shall be that you may die a bloody and fearful death—such as traitors alone deserve."

"Horrible!" ejaculated the Colonel. "No wonder her cheeks blanched to the whiteness of snow."

The two advanced and saw Astrea sitting upright, her eyes widely staring straight before her. Helen looked frightened and distressed, vainly striving to win her attention. Whenever she touched her, she would, with strong, fierce movements, fling her hands away, shuddering violently.

"Let her alone," whispered the Captain with a face as white as the stony features of the unhappy woman before him. "We will now return home as quickly as possible."

From that time forward, Astrea uttered no word until after they had reached Corinth and she found herself in her own room with only Helen beside her. Not a tinge of color came back to her face—not one rigid line relaxed. She seemed to have congealed to stone under the fearful ordeal, and a terrible crisis had come which filled her friends with the keenest alarm.

"Stay with her and let her weep freely, if she will. Tears may relieve her, and save her from insanity. I will explain your absence to the Major. If I send for a physician, too much will be at stake. Already I have been forced to place both her and myself in the power of another, and I dare not go further."

"I promise you faithfully to do all I can. You had better keep away until I send you word to come to me."

"Then send me word soon. This is torture worse than you ever dreamed."

Helen's ready tears flowed silently down her cheeks, but neither could speak, and he went out abruptly to hide his agitation, while she returned to Astrea.

CHAPTER XVII.

A SERIOUS COMPLICATION AND ITS RESULT.

CAPTAIN WILFER hurried away from Mrs. Noble's presence to the Major's office and informed him that Miss Harmon had returned quite ill, and that his wife proposed to remain with her awhile, hoping that she would soon be better. From there he went to his own quarters and sat down alone to reflect upon all that had transpired.

It may be thought that he had acted without wisdom in what he had done; but it was not so. Fully aware of the danger he had braved, he had boldly planned, and executed his plans, willing to suffer the consequences if he could aid this woman for whom he would have risked his life cheerfully. The step he had taken, owning a knowledge of Colonel Passiver's intentions by meeting a messenger of his according to a previous appointment, was sufficient in itself, to fix upon him a suspicion of complicity in his escape—certainly enough to involve her in trouble should any difficulty arise. He had hope from two things only, to preserve them from suspicion and the affair from investigation. Colonel Heston had been too actively engaged at the time of the rebel's escape to pay much attention to what was going on at Corinth, and might not think of identifying him with the man from whom the message came. If suspicion should arise in his mind, would he consider it his duty to have the matter investigated further? He seemed a kind man, and he believed him to be a trustworthy friend, who would not betray a woman's trust when in deep trouble. Then the nature of the communication was in her favor, proving her loyalty and the suffering it had cost her to be true to the cause she had adopted. After long and serious meditation, he concluded that it was best to let affairs take their own course, and if any difficulty should arise, he would go to General Grant and confide to him the whole story from first to last, and throw himself upon his mercy.

A sharp rap on the door roused him from his reveries, and he opened it to receive a penciled line from Mrs. Noble. Astrea was better, and had fallen into a quiet slumber, after a long spell of weeping, and she hoped the result would be very much in her favor. Captain Wilfer looked at his watch and saw that it was half-past ten o'clock. He had been shut up alone four hours! How the time had sped! But those hours had brought sleep to the heavy eyes of many a suffering one—above all to Astrea, and he was thankful, to weakness. Resuming his chair with the little note clasped in his hand, he bowed his face upon his arms as they lay on the table, and shed the first tears that had moistened his eyes since that memorable night amid the dead and wounded on the banks of the Mississippi.

Morning found him still there. He had not slept, nor had he heeded the hours as they waned, until daylight came. All the night he had thought only of her and her sufferings—had longed intensely for the privilege of shielding her from the ills of the future. He had no hope that such a happiness might ever be his; no dreams were allowed to lure him from the path of honor and duty, even in thought. He was schooling himself to control every impulse which tendered to make him forget his proper position; and with all that great, unselfish love and longing in his heart, he had resolved to keep away from her, save when she needed help. To seek her society was to sap away by degrees, the foundation on which he had built up his resolves; so he would not seek her only in her time of need. Then he would be ever by her side, watchful and faithful to the end, in her interests.

As the sun rose he roused himself for the duties of the day, and after arranging his toilet, he took a little bible from his pocket and read several chapters, then knelt and prayed fervently. His was an earnest and careful nature, out of which faith, charity and generosity rose spontaneously. He lived in the love and fear of a Divine Master, on whom he cast now, the whole burthen of his future, resigning himself to His will without reserve.

A messenger sent to Mrs. Noble, came back with an answer to the effect that Miss Harmon still rested well, though in a slight fever. Doubtless it was only the result of over-excitement, and would soon pass away. This did not trouble him. It seemed natural enough that she should be somewhat feverish after the ordeal of the day previous; but rest would overcome that, and he grew hopeful in thinking that she would soon recover. Taking up his hat and gloves, he walked out and crossed slowly to the hotel where he ordered his breakfast. While at the table, a man came up to him and said in his ear:

"General Grant desires your presence at his head-quarters immediately."

"Say that I obey his commands; I must order my horse first."

"All right," and the man went out without further words.

"Heston has betrayed me," was his first thought, but it was immediately spurned as unjust. Recalling the face and manner of the officer, it was hard to believe that he would take any steps to sink a woman like Astrea Harmon into deeper trouble.

He gave the order for his horse, and by the time he had finished his breakfast, it was at the door. Mounting it, he galloped away rapidly to obey the General's command. He found General Grant in the small private room which has been mentioned, pacing the floor. Colonel Heston sat over against the south window, looking pale and disturbed. One glance showed that whatever the trouble might be, he had not willfully originated it. Another man was present whom he did not know, and who sat with a curious smile upon his lips, closely regarding our hero. Evidently he enjoyed his position with great relish.

"Captain Wilfer, I have sent for you to answer to a serious charge made against you. Are you prepared for self-defence?"

"I am, sir."

"Where were you yesterday?"

"At Iuka, by your permission."

"For what did you go there?"

"To render aid to a lady who was in great distress."

"Will you tell me the nature of the lady's trouble, and why you should endanger your reputation as a loyal man and an officer by such a step?"

"Privately, yes; but I would most respectfully beg that you do not require me to speak of that which concerns others in the presence of strangers." He glanced at the man opposite to him, who answered insolently:

"It is not worth while to be over modest with me, since I know all about it. I have had my eye upon a good many movements that people fancy themselves secure in. But the time will come, when like you, they will find themselves mistaken."

"Will General Grant request this gentleman to make his charge distinctly in my presence?" asked Captain Wilfer, coolly. "Since he knows so much, it is best to hear his charge and put it to the proof."

The General turned toward the stranger sternly:

"Speak, sir."

"I charge you with having aided in the escape of the rebel officer, Colonel Passiver, whom you brought a prisoner to this place, and who, on your own testimony, was condemned to die."

"You must assign some reason for such extraordinary conduct on the part of an officer of Captain Wilfer's standing," remarked General Grant, dryly. The accuser smiled again, following the smile with a short laugh.

"That is easy enough. Adam was tempted in the Garden of Eden to an act of disobedience by a woman; and Captain

Wilfer is not the first and only man in the Federal service, who for the love of woman, has turned traitor to his country."

"Then I am distinctly to understand that you charge me with being a traitor to the Federal cause, and the reason for it lies in my love for some lady, who, of course you charge with being a rebel."

"Yes, a rebel and a spy."

"Are you ready with proofs? Be good enough to state in the first place, on what grounds you base the charge of giving aid to the escape of Colonel Passiver."

"Miss Harmon is known to me—has been for some time—at least, the lady calling herself by that name. That there was a mystery attached to her, I have known also, since I first saw her. The nature of it I could not more than guess until recently. But it was all made plain on the day previous to Colonel Passiver's escape. I happened to be near her when she overheard some soldiers talking about the execution of the rebel's sentence, and when they mentioned his name, she suddenly turned white and threw up her hands with a sharp cry, then pressed them tightly over her heart. This was enough to attract my attention, and I observed all her movements after that. She went immediately home and ordered an ambulance from the Quartermaster's department. In the course of an hour she was driven to this place; General Grant will doubtless remember that visit and its import. When she returned, I saw by her face, of which I caught a glimpse, that she had been unsuccessful. As she passed the hotel, Captain Wilfer saw and followed her. She waited and spoke to him at the gate, then both entered the house together. He remained for sometime, after which he rode out here, and I supposed that he came on the same errand, and was quite as unsuccessful to all appearance. But that night I saw them leave her house together and go to the prison, where the rebel was confined. A few moments later I entered and went into a room adjoining, where I had been called to see a patient, and Captain Wilfer saw me. I heard him ask the guard who I was, and also heard the answer, that I was the physician who attended the sick prisoners. He paid no further attention to me, and while in that room I heard a part of Miss Harmon's conversation. I could only catch fragments, however, by which I learned that he was her hushand and that she promised to liberate him; also that a meeting for some purpose was appointed at Iuka within a fortnight. Until I heard that I fully meant to report proceedings and arrest them before it was too late; but the thought occurred to me that some valuable information might be gained by delay, and I concluded to wait, resolving at the same time to be on my guard and not allow her to convey any important information to the rebels. The day previous to the one appointed for the meeting I went to Iuka and carefully took note of everything that occurred. Captain Wilfer communicated privately with Colonel Heston, and they went with the ladies to the picket lines, taking only two orderlies whom they kept in the rear during the interview. A paper was carried to Miss Harmon to look at, which Colonel Heston has now in his possession if he has not destroyed it. Perhaps if General Grant will demand the paper, it may explain in itself, more than I can of the nature of that interview with the rebel messenger. I considered it my duty to return here as soon as possible and inform the commanding officer of what I had seen and heard. The result was a dispatch to Colonel Heston and an order to yourself to appear before him for the purpose of answering to the charges I have made. If you can defend yourself, do so."

"If Colonel Heston has the paper spoken of, he will be good enough to produce it," said Captain Wilfer, turning to his fellow-officer.

It was produced, and read by the General thoughtfully.

"This matter is more complicated than it appeared at first, and will require further investigation. Doctor Gray, you will consider yourself under arrest and held for evidence, as well as to justify yourself, if justification be necessary. You can now retire until called for."

The two officers exchanged glances as the discomfited informer rose in some alarm.

"I hope, General Grant"—he began confusedly, but the General coolly stopped him.

"Excuse me if I decline to listen to anything further from you at present. You must be aware, sir, that your course has been a singular one, and betrays motives of a personal nature, which it is my duty to investigate. If through any desire for personal revenge, or any hatred on your part, which has induced you to undertake the ruin of loyal men—and place me in the position I now hold towards my officers," looking at Heston and Wilfer, "rest assured, that you will have your reward."

Doctor Gray was pale and trembling with anger and fear.

"Take care, General Grant, that your own course in this affair be not such as to cause you to be suspected of knowing more about it yourself than you would like to have made public."

"You will be good enough to retire, sir, and withhold both threats and advice."

As Doctor Gray went out, the General followed him and ordered him under the custody of the officer of the guard, who accompanied him to the guard-house to await further orders from the Commander.

"Now gentlemen, let me have the whole story freely," said he returning to the room in which he had left them. Captain Wilfer answered him at once.

"Colonel Heston's part in this matter has been trifling, and I beg you to allow me to exonerate him from all complicity. I sought and told him that a flag of truce was expected with dispatches of a private, domestic nature, and that I would vouch for the loyalty of the lady under my care. He accompanied us on condition that he might be allowed to see that no communication of a dangerous character was held, and you have in your hand the only document that was received. To you, privately, I am ready to render a full account of my actions and my motives. But Colonel Heston has done his duty faithfully, and I am sorry to have been the cause of annoyance to him."

"He can consider himself exonerated, and at liberty to retire when it pleases him, though he is well aware that he had no right to receive a flag of truce without my authority."

Colonel Heston, with a few words of thanks and a warm grasp of Captain Wilfer's hand, withdrew.

"Now, sir, what have you to say to the charges made against you, and in justification of your actions."

"Much, I think, if you have patience to listen."

"Go on."

"Doctor Gray is right in charging me with a deep attachment for Miss Harmon. I own it to you, while at the same time I know that I dare not speak of it to her. Some months ago I met her for the first time, and before I was aware of the fact myself became deeply interested in her. It is due to her to say that I never received encouragement from her manner in any way whatever. She repelled me positively, almost with rudeness at times, I think in order to destroy my interest. The last time I saw her was at Paducah, where she had labored day and night for the sick in the hospitals there, after some of the noblest actions I had ever witnessed, during our trip down the Mississippi. At Shiloh I was taken prisoner, escaping but recently, as you know. When I came here I found her engaged as before, wasting her life away in ceaseless toil. Every one spoke of her in the highest terms, and the interest, which with me had never waned, was kindled to as passionate and yet pure devotion as ever man cherished for woman. After that visit to you, she in her despair appealed to me to save her husband. God only knows what that cost me, General Grant, but I could not resist the appeal, loving her as I did—I could not be the instrument of his death, and hope for happiness again on earth! I came to you and asked his life on the grounds of my faithful service and late imprisonment, which you refused. As you are aware, I did not press the matter, lest you should suspect too much, and for her sake I did not desire to commit myself. What you did think then of my strange conduct, you know best. I had been very bitter against him and was suddenly forced to change from severity to leniency, and to try and save his life. Failing with you, I planned to have him escape, and succeeded. As for her, she is innocent of the whole transaction. I took her to see him, telling her that I hoped to set him free, and she could have one interview if she desired it. The nature of that interview I did not know until a few days since, when she asked me to assist her and told me why. She had a child whom he had pledged himself under oath to restore to her, and for that she was to meet his messenger. Can you condemn the woman who has lost home, friends, wealth, and even her child because of her loyalty to the Union? Look at her course amongst us—see what she has done—mark the anguish in her face which has robbed it of much of its freshness and bloom in a few short months, and then see if you can find it in your heart to condemn her. For what I have done, punish me as you think proper. I could not act otherwise, and your duty is open to you. Only spare her from the consequences."

General Grant paced the room for several moments in silence. It was not an easy matter to act decisively just then, for he occupied a very difficult position. He had been appealed to as a man, for mercy towards a loyal woman in deep affliction; and that mercy must extend to her through one who had transgressed the law, and rendered himself liable to punishment. As an officer, he was forced to hold him to account for his actions. Here, the stern discipline necessary for the success of a large army, rendered it imperative for the Commander to be exacting and rigid when enforcing it. Amongst officers, the regulations and laws should be observed most scrupulously for the sake of holding influence over men; and now one of them a highly honored and trustworthy man, was before him under charge of wrong, and making frank confession of the same. What could he do? The question was perplexing in the extreme. Finally he sat down and bowed his forehead upon one hand in deep thought. When he spoke it was with decision, but not in unkindness or anger.

"Captain Wilfer, I believe that you have rightly represented this matter to me, and I am sorry to be obliged to act harshly. You must leave the service. I will not have you tried, but will accept your resignation, and require you to send it in at once. My duty as Commander of the forces here, compels me to one straight course, and this is the lightest punishment I can inflict upon you for what you have done."

The young man turned white and started to his feet.

"And the worst, General, if you intend to make me suffer in feeling, for no man of honor can be thus deprived of serving his country in her hour of need, and not suffer acutely; I accept your decision, because I must, but it is a hard sentence. I would that you could change it without danger of compromising yourself or her. Anything would be better than to be forced to leave the service."

"I cannot change it. Make out your resignation as soon as possible; and if you should ever again find yourself in the service of your country, holding an honorable and responsible position, be more careful in what you do."

With this he dismissed the young man, who went out, looking deeply pained but pale and resolute.

"I have resolved to bear anything for her sake, and will not shrink even from this;" he muttered. "But it is hard—bitter!"

The afternoon of the same day, brought a note to Miss Harmon which Mrs. Noble received and carried to her as she sat in her own room, buried in the depths of a large chair. She took it languidly, looking almost too wan and weak to break the seal. When she did so, a vivid color flashed instantly to her cheeks.

"General Grant desires an interview with Miss Harmon. Send word by the bearer when it will be agreeable to receive a call."

"What shall I do?" she asked, handing the note to Helen.

"I am afraid something is wrong—he has found out something about that trip which may give Captain Wilfer trouble, perhaps you, too, who knows?"

"Let him come at once, the truth is better than suspense, and I do not fear for myself."

"Then give the bearer the message to that effect, if you think best. You are right; I cannot now bear suspense."

The General was at the hotel, and sauntered over before they expected him. When he entered, Astrea was sitting still in the large chair which had been drawn into the parlor, and looking pale and disturbed. He advanced to her and took her hand kindly.

"My call is inopportune, I fear, for you look very ill; but I desire simply to ask you one question, and will not worry you now with a long visit."

"I am at your service, General Grant."

"And somewhat frightened, I think," he said smiling, as he took the seat to which she pointed. "There is no need of being so, however. I only want you to tell me if you know a Doctor Gray, and if he has any reason to dislike you."

"I do know a Doctor Gray, who has every reason to dislike me. He was attending physician at Paducah in one of the hospitals while I was there, and I was so indignant with his way of managing things, as to express myself very sharply. The last time I saw him, he made a threat to revenge himself upon me for some truths that I thought it my duty to administer to him."

"What is his character, and what did you find to censure in his conduct?"

Astrea recounted the condition in which she had found the men, and his mode of treatment, with some of the conversations which had passed between them.

"That will do," he said, rising and extending his hand in a friendly way. "You look weary, and I will not tax your strength longer. It is bad for you to be sick while so many need your care; and it seems that those persons who work so

15

heartily as you do for the good of others, ought to be exempt from suffering themselves."

"Is it not the natural result of our solicitude for others, if our sympathies are warm?" she asked; but the shallow attempt to account for her too plainly speaking looks, woke only a smile of compassion. He went away from her, feeling glad that he had not taken any steps that could add to her distress.

Doctor Gray at this time, held no commission, but was a contract surgeon, who had been permitted to come to Corinth at the time of its occupation by the Federal forces. Seeing Astrea there, he had kept aloof from her, but resolved to watch her closely, and if he ever had an opportunity, to be revenged for those well remembered stings at Paducah.

General Grant desiring to deal justly by all parties, made every investigation in his power, that punishment might fall only on the proper persons; and the facts which came to light concerning Doctor Gray, were sufficient, and of a nature to cause him to be placed under arrest for an indefinite period.

CHAPTER XVIII.

A HOME OF AFFLUENCE—ITS BEAUTIES AND ITS BLEMISHES.

THE village of Florence, a lovely little town in North Alabama, is situated upon the banks of the Tennessee River, and boasts about two thousand inhabitants. On the opposite side of the river, about four miles distant, is the town of Tuscumbia, almost as large, and widely celebrated for the beautiful spring of sparkling water which bursts from the base of a small mountain rising above it.

Tuscumbia had been the early home of Astrea Harmon, and her great wealth, exceeding beauty, and sweetness of disposition, had made her the belle and idol of the place. Being an only child, and heiress to an immense estate, it is not to be wondered at, if from her first appearance in society at a very early age, her path was thronged with ardent suitors, whose earnest endeavors to win her esteem, rather wearied than pleased her. She was too genuinely pure and true of heart, to take pleasure in the pain which she was forced to inflict by repulsing such advances; and too confidingly truthful herself, to suspect that other motives than those of devoted affection could bring so many to her feet. Modest and simple in her regards for self, it was ever a matter of wonder to her why she was sought and preferred above others; but the truth could not be denied, and the days which to most young girls, would have been full of pride and triumph, brought to her much of pain and distress; for while she gave to each of her suitors a friendly feeling of regard, she knew well that no deeper emotion had touched her heart, and she could love none. One year like this, after an education in a fashionable boarding-school in New York, and then an end was suddenly put to all annoyances.

Frederic Passiver returned from Europe to take possession of a large estate left him by his father, and their first meeting had given rise to a mutual interest which resulted in a hasty marriage. Immediately after their nuptials they started upon a long European tour, during which time a magnificent residence was erected upon an elevated site about three miles from Florence, and commanding a lovely view of the river and surrounding country. To this house they came after a year's absence, and located themselves permanently, with every apparent means within their reach, for a supremely happy life. Being the theater of many subsequent exciting scenes, as well as the home of our heroine, Passiver Hall deserves description. The main entrance fronted the Florence road, towering tall and stately amid the green and luxurious foliage of venerable trees, whose boughs waved around the gleaming white pillars caressingly. At the rear of the building, a green slope swept to the water's edge, down the centre of which a flight of steps had been laid, terminating with a small boat-house, containing skiffs and canoes which the young bride might use at pleasure. Upon the east side of the Hall, was laid a most beautiful garden, combining elegance with use, and yielding fruits and vegetables as richly as flowers. From the west, the plantation, beginning with green meadow-lands, stretched away for miles in exquisite and luxuriant loveliness, terminating with long rows of negro quarters, which in themselves, furnished quite a village-like appearance. The young planter took much credit to himself for this last touch to the finest estate in North Alabama. It was such a delight to feast his eyes upon a domain on which were no unsightly blots. He wanted no miserable tumble-down buildings about him, which could mar the beauty of an otherwise perfect landscape. This was not the only reason, however, for the pains Frederic Passiver had taken in the erection of those quarters. He was a proud, ambitious man, and desired to be above his neighbors in everything. His plantation being the finest, and worked by the largest number of able-bodied negroes, must necessarily yield a richer harvest of gain than any other, and, therefore, more would be expected of him as a leading man, universally acknowledged as the most enterprising gentleman in the country. He was not one of that class who, relying upon their wealth and position for absolute power, willingly spend their lives in indolence. Energetic by nature, and more ambitious than is usual in that land, where the warm sunshine seems only to nurture indolence, his course was an entirely original one, promising to place him in a position hitherto unequaled in every respect.

Frederic Passiver loved power as a miser loves money; and he was not content to wield it singly in home or county. Both must come under his undisputed sway, and to that end he began his life at Passiver Hall, fully confident of eventual success. This man was neither good or conscientious, and the principles upon which he based all his actions, were selfish in the extreme. In general objects, he worked with something of a diplomatist's skill, covering deep designs with a frank, fair seeming, which could not fail to win confidence and esteem. And the first instance of this trait in her husband's character, was revealed to her in the erection of the quarters, which he professed to have built solely to please his wife, whose ambition tended only to the alleviation of the hard lot of her people. She looked on them with pitying eyes, as Moses regarded the children of Israel groaning in bondage, and conceived a desire to lift them up, and set their feet in "pleasant places." Seeming to coincide at once with her views, and to enter with benevolent interest into all her plans, he had made the promise on her first suggestion, and worked to a double purpose. One year of marriage had shown to each, the rashness of a hasty step, by opening their eyes to a wide gulf which lay between them. While she was gentle, loving and generous—there was still an element of strength in her nature which he did not like, and vowed not to tolerate, secretly resolving to leave no means untried which might bend her wholly to his will in all things, right or wrong. In Passiver Hall, his power should be supreme, but he had the wisdom to accomplish his purposes by no rash or overt actions. Open tyranny at the outset would have destroyed all hope of sovereignty, and he preferred rather to bide his time patiently for a season, looking to no distant day in the future, when he might reign with the freedom of a prince. On the other hand, the young wife soon began to discern, with a woman's keen penetrative powers, those traits of character which filled her with sorrow and disappointment. But as the chosen instrument of good to man, she hoped with true womanly faith to bridge that wide, unsightly gulf between her husband and herself, with a love that should prove his salvation, and make of him all that a man with such advantages, ought to be. Hundreds of souls looked to them for protection. In their hands rested the burthen of good or ill to those whom fortune had given them as slaves, and she shrank appalled from the greatness of this responsibility, when she comprehended the ease with which it might drag them down in the scale of being. On the evening after their arrival at the Hall, when she had been thinking about it until her bright face was clouded with trouble, he drew her to a large window overlooking the shining river, and asked to know the cause of her unusual gravity.

"I was thinking of the commission that God has given us," she replied without the slightest change in her sober features.

"Commission? what commission?"

"Can you not understand, Frederic? Remember the story of the just and unjust steward, and the disposition they made of the talents which the Master gave them. I have been looking abroad over our vast possessions, and wondering if we shall be able to turn our Master's talents into good account, so as to win His cheering 'Well done thou good and faithful servant,' in the end. Oh, Frederic, I tremble to think of it—the charge is so great. I could find it in my heart to wish for an humbler, less responsible position than ours, for I do not feel at ease, or confident of being able to do my duty wholly."

"You will try, however, and it is better to hold these talents in your own keeping, than to see them transferred to others, who would have no such feelings, and make no efforts to render them back improved."

"Certainly; that is about the only comfort we can have to sustain us under such a burthen. Our people might be in worse hands, and our wealth put to baser uses. Oh, Frederic, we can do much—let us never forget how much, or ignore one single opportunity to give happiness and good to others. Let us try to elevate our servants, and make them better and happier—as well as the poor people by whom we are surrounded."

"What means do you propose to employ in your benevolent projects? What is the first thing to be done?"

"The first thing? Well, let me see! I think in the first place, I would build a large school-house for the purpose of educating our tenant's children, who are most lamentably ignorant, and send North for one of those stirring, energetic New England teachers to take charge of it. Of course, he or she must have a good salary, and here again, we find a good use for a portion of our talents, in affording one self-dependent person, at least, a comfortable means for support. The plantation is large, and will furnish ample employment for such as we have; and as they become more enlightened and intelligent, their self-respect and ambition will increase. The neat walls of their cottages will be covered with vines—their gardens will bloom with flowers, and their children will go to church and school with neat apparel and happy faces. Oh, would it not be joy to look upon such a picture, and know that we had been the instruments, by God's grace, of such good to others! I can easily see how the lives of the rich might be perfect lives, if they would only put their possessions to a proper use."

"But you reason from one side only, and do not consider that you do more evil than good, by this large order of benevolence. The moment you stretch out your hands and lift them above their position, by even one degree, you teach them to forget what is due to yourself as their superior, by obstinately claiming an equal footing. It will never do to let them pass a certain limit, and to establish such a school here as you propose, would be absolute folly. The introduction of a northern teacher, would, in itself, be enough to plant the seed of discord amongst us so deeply it could never be rooted out. Suppose you let this lie over for the present, and tell me what you would do for the negroes."

The sweet face which had grown very bright while devising her own schemes, became anxious and troubled while he was speaking. But now the shadows lifted again when he touched a subject nearer her heart, and she spoke with enthusiasm:

"O, I would build a nice church for them near the quarters, and hire a minister—a really good man—to preach for them. Of course the old patriarchs of the plantation should have the privilege of preaching whenever they desired; but it would be necessary for them to get some teaching themselves, ere they could impart anything of great value to others. And now, while speaking of this, why cannot we resolve to do it? This, and one thing beside, would render our beginning auspicious, I think. I have reference to a plan that was suggested, to my mind by one of the boys, who came to me today and asked if he might have a little strip of ground for a garden patch, lying just in the rear of his cabin. If a small garden was attached to each cabin, it would afford them a great deal of pleasure, and stimulate them to pleasant habits. I promised, if you had no objections, to have the gardens laid out for them, and supply them with seeds for vegetables and flowers, if they would pledge themselves to keep them and everything about them, in nice order and cleanliness. They have an inherent love for the beautiful, and an inordinate desire for praise. Combining the two, we might turn this to good account in more ways than one. Our people would be neater and happier, I am sure, and the produce that these gardens would yield, would go largely towards supporting them. If they choose to sell anything from them, allow them to do so, and make such a disposition of the money thus received as best pleases them. By it we should win their affection and obedience, causing life to flow through harmonious channels."

Mr. Passiver looked thoughtful, and did not answer for some time.

"I see no reasonable objection to such a plan," he said at length, "and feel disposed to try it. But we must not spoil our people, Eugenia."

"Spoil them with simple justice, my dear husband! Surely, for the people whose whole lives are spent in our service, we can afford to do this much, and consider it no great concession of our rights."

"Still, we must not make the mistake of bribing them to do what we can and ought to demand. If we do, incalculable evil may spring from it, and they will give us no peace. If one of my servants should dare to become saucy and insolent, I am sure I should kill him."

"Oh, Frederic!"

"Yes, I would do it, Eugenia. Each and every man, woman and child under my control, shall obey me when I speak, instantly, and without a question. I prefer to be kind, and to have no reason for enforcing my authority; but the black rascal who dares to give me trouble, will never try it a second time if I know myself. Since we are on this subject I will suggest that you make your side of the house fully understand what to expect. From what I have been able to judge in the little I have seen of them, you have been too lenient, and allowed them to take too many liberties with you. Now that the two sets are brought together, the sooner they are taught their places, the better it will be for the future peace and harmony of our life at Passiver Hall."

"Frederic, not one of my servants has ever been saucy or

disrespectful, and they love me devotedly. Such a thing as unkindness is a stranger to them, and I pray you not to misconstrue their actions, and deal hardly with the poor creatures. Comparatively speaking, their's have been very happy lives; but I have had hopes of making them happier still. Do not allow your desire for power to come between me and my hopes. It could only be productive of misery to all."

"Do all the good you can, child, but teach them unhesitating obedience, for that I will have," he answered; then seeing that they were on the verge of an argument which ill suited his purposes, he hastened to change the subject.

Many bright dreams which she had woven and cherished, soon began to fade away, as Mrs. Passiver started in the new path which destiny had marked out for her. The foregoing conversation cast the first chill over her ardent anticipations, and was followed by the utter destruction of one great hope, which served to presage to her heavy heart, all the gloom that the future might have in store for her. After tea had been served, they had taken a long stroll upon the river's bank, and returned just in time for evening prayers before the servants' bed-time. As usual, Astrea took her bible from the little stand placed under the chandelier, and stretched her hand for the bell, when her husband caught it firmly.

"I think you had better dispense with this useless ceremony, my dear. Why waste your time in such a foolish manner?"

"Why, Frederic, they have never known anything else in their lives, and would miss it very much. Besides, it is our duty to do this. Last night I was weary with travel, and the confusion attendant upon our arrival, was sufficient excuse for the omission. But they would wonder at it to-night, dear, and I do not want to sever this strong link between me and my faithful people."

"I do not think it a woman's place to take such things upon herself," he remarked dryly.

"Nor is it, if the husband and master will himself assume the duty. I thought, however, that it might be repugnant to you, and rather than give it up, proposed to keep in the same way as if no change had been made in their circumstances of life. Do you prefer to relieve me?"

"By no means, for I intend to discard it altogether, not wishing to be bored with such nonsense. Think no more about the matter. You will have plenty to occupy your time without it."

"Oh, husband, do not ask this! I *cannot* give it up," she expostulated, with great pain shadowed forth on every feature.

"You must."

"Must!"

The proud blood of her nature flashed instantly up in defiance of so unreasonable a demand. Willing to yield in whatever was right and just, she was not so tame as to bear this without resentment, which she showed plainly in every line and curve of her beautiful form and face. He saw at once that a contest of will was inevitable, and resolved to conquer.

"Yes, I repeat that you must, Eugenia," in a deliberate, icy tone.

"You deal hardly with me, I had hoped for something better at your hands, when you yielded to my request and built those quarters. Have I been mistaken in supposing that you had the real good and happiness of our people at heart?"

"Does it consist in allowing you to make a butt of me, and wear yourself out at the same time, by every night going through a lot of mummery? No, Eugenia, I will be master here, and make them respect me. It is not my pleasure to do what you proposed to take upon yourself—therefore it shall not be done at all. Let this suffice, and end the discussion forever."

"Not yet, dear, my first duty is to you—my next to them. But if an unreasonable whim of yours comes between me and what is required of me, I must consider myself absolved from the promise of obedience to you, by your own act, and do my duty without your sanction."

"Do you mean to say that you will gc through with this folly every evening in spite of me?"

"Not willingly, Frederic. If you force me to it, I must choose a room where the ceremony will not disturb you; but my servants must not think their mistress changed, and careless of their welfare."

"Then listen to me: I will relieve your conscience by transferring every house servant you have, to the field, and putting in their places those who will not miss your over anxious care."

"Do you then care so little for my happiness that you can take such a step and feel no regret for the pain you give me? Surely my wishes are not strange or new to you, and you know how hard it will be for me to give up the cherished plans of a life-time. I have looked forward to the day when I should have it in my power to do these people good, with more than an ordinary interest, and it will be terrible to have you come between me and my hopes. Spare me this grief, Frederic, and I will endeavor to be as good and obedient a wife as a man can wish. You want power—you shall have it; but when I yield myself to your will, and acknowledge your right to command, when I beg of you what I might claim as a right, do not make me feel myself wronged by a refusal. I ask this of you as a favor—allow me to keep my servants around me, and resume the old customs of home. It is not much to grant, when it can cost you so little—but it is everything to me!"

She came to his side and knelt upon an ottoman, bowing her head against him in child-like abandonment of entreaty. All the proud resentment had faded from her face, and left it earnestly pleading and soft. Few could have resisted her then, knowing the noble motives which had enabled her to forget herself and strive only to do right toward both master and slaves. But he cared more for himself and his power, than her happiness and their good; and there was not a pang of regret in his heart as he put her coldly from him, and rose deliberately to his feet.

"It is folly to multiply words since nothing can change me. To-morrow morning I will order the transfer of servants from house to field, and we will begin our domestic arrangements in *my* way, if you please."

He did not look back as he strode in his deliberate, stately way from the room, and saw nothing, therefore, of the effect his words and manner produced. Still kneeling upon the ottoman, she laid her pale cheek against the crimson of the cushioned chair he had vacated, and gave vent to one long, bitter moan of anguish.

"So soon! so soon!" she sobbed. "Has the strife began already, and must I never hope to do good in my life, save through opposition? Oh, my Father, how hardly shall I be made to struggle through life, if my duty to thee must be performed through such obstacles as my husband's will! Why may I not have his interest, his co-operation in the accomplishment of thy work?"

When he returned to the room in which he had left her, she had gone, and, guided by the sound of the piano, he followed to the drawing-room where she sat in the dim light striving to sooth her deeply stirred emotions by music. Very sweet and low was her voice as she sang—sometimes choked and tremulous. The mellow moonlight streaming over the floor failed to reach the point where she sat, but he could dimly discern the outline of her face and figure, and thought he could read her subjugation in their expression of sadness.

"Guide me oh, Thou Great Jehovah," came again and again from the tremulous lips, full of earnest lingering sweetness; but he attached no importance to the words and did not see that he was losing that which he sought to gain most determinedly. He might force her into outward signs of obedience—cut her off from all that was pleasant, hopeful or life-giving. But he could not bend the spirit into willing subserviency, or hold the pure love and respect of the woman whose best feelings he outraged by his unscrupulous assumption of absolute power. He overlooked the fact that the true way to rule a woman, is through her love; and he had yet to learn that fear could not tame a will like hers, where love had no control.

Thus life began for our heroine very inauspiciously, each day that came bringing over the fair young head a cloud heavier and darker than that which preceded it. Struggling and strife were hers from the beginning, and they never ceased. First it was with her own pride and willful spirit, that she might by yielding to her husband's will, win him to more of tenderness and love. Then it was with the outward circumstances of their own unhappy life, that strangers might not see the signs of the grim "skeleton in the closet." She would not allow the world to judge him harshly, and she shrank with a natural dread, from the supposition that the fault rested alone with her. Therefore her smiles were bright and her tone gay, when friends met her—no laugh was more sweet—no step more buoyant than hers in their midst; but when they were gone, and the necessity no longer existed for acting a part, the reaction was terrible. Grief and disappointment and self-loathing tormented her to the verge of madness. It was not enough that all her hopes of a good and useful career within the limits of her own home, were blasted, but each day unwrapped from about the husband of her choice, a portion of that rosy cloud with which love invests its objects, and instead of pure marble, revealed to her aching eyes, clay only! Wearying of arts and strategems to accomplish his ends, as he saw the difficulty of deceiving her growing greater each day, he finally threw off all pretensions to diplomacy, and appeared himself, in all his glaring deformity of character. It was only in the presence of others that he ever strove to appear courteous and kind. When the eyes of friends or strangers were upon him, his manner was perfection itself, winning admiration from all; but alone with her, his chief delight lay in the sharpest cruelty he could inflict, no other occupation affording him half the amusement as that of tormenting her.

It would be difficult to imagine such a character as Frederic Passiver's, without the aid of an original from which to gleam the peculiar traits which set him apart from all other men.

The centre and root of his being was self, and to selfish ends he bent all things within his reach, without scruple. He was proud of his wife because she was, not only the loveliest woman in the country, but the most cultivated and intelligent. Furthermore she was immensely rich, and her possessions added to his own, gave him the precedence over older and longer established men of wealth. His ambition was to have everything better than anybody else, and having the advantage in every other respect, he resolved to tame the proud spirit of his beautiful wife until she had not will or wish, save through him. Had he truly loved her, such an unworthy purpose must have become submerged in the elevating tenderness of that love; but a pure sentiment of affection did not belong to his nature. He studied her tastes and feelings only to add to his power for giving pain. When she expressed a preference for a book, he coolly disapproved her taste and required that she should lay it aside and accept one which his close observation told him was devoid of interest. Her favorite flowers were banished from the vases upon her tables, and the music she loved openly condemned. All that could minister to her pleasure was banished without one regret, while a keen sense of enjoyment was manifested in the actions which distressed her most profoundly.

Existence under such circumstances, would soon become a curse to any woman, and it did become a curse to her, though she clung tenaciously to a hope for change in the future. She strove to bear with patience the ills of her disappointed life—to walk meekly through the thorny paths which had given promise of flowers only, and make no complaint. The magnificence and splendor of her home, mocked her, as the gilded wires of a cage might mock the fluttering bird whose wings beat vainly against the prison bars; but she endeavored not to long for a more humble lot, believing that her Father had chosen to test her faithfulness, and willingness to bear these tests without complaint. The falseness of the hollow life she led, was the sorest trial, and most perplexed her judgment.

It was not easy for so pure and truthful nature as hers, to accept the doctrine of "doing evil that good might come," but it was forced upon her, and the doors of escape tightly closed. Of the many ills that crowded around her daily path, she chose what her judgment sanctioned as least, and hoped on with a hope and faith that find birth only in the hearts of earnest women.

The summer flowers had faded, and the first glowing tints of autumn touched the hills, when a little stranger came to Passiver Hall. The young mother welcomed it with great joy, and said to herself with returning confidence:

"He may learn to love me again for his child's sake."

But all through the hours of her ordeal, his feet had restlessly paced the floor above her, waiting the issue, without once coming to her side, to sooth and comfort her with a word of tenderness. Ever willing to put the best construction upon his actions, she had tried to cheat herself into the belief that his dread of seeing her suffer, kept him from her, until all was over, and no father's face bowed with hers over her daughter's tiny features, as she lay in her arms. Even now, she forced a smile to her pale lips as she lifted her beautiful eyes to the nurse's face.

"Leave her to me, nurse dear, and please go for baby's papa. Poor fellow—he could not bear to come near me, but now he will not find cause for grief."

"How devoted she is," commented the nurse as she mounted the stairs in obedience to her mistress' request. "But I must say that it is queer, and I can't understand it; husbands who love their wives, don't treat them in this way; and she is such a sweet, pretty creature, too. I don't understand it."

Mr. Passiver was still pacing the floor when she tapped lightly upon the door for admittance; her opinion changed immediately when she saw the eager, anxious face with which he rushed to meet her.

"Well, Mrs. Elder, what news have you?"

"Excellent, sir, and Mrs. Passiver bade me ask you to come

down and see your daughter; she is as bright and smiling as a May morning, and looks more beautiful than ever."

He scarcely waited for the close of the sentence, before he left her with light rapid steps, taking his way toward his wife's chamber.

"I will ring when you are wanted, Mrs. Elder," he called from the foot of the stairs, and she smilingly turned to the room where the Doctor sat alone, and refreshing himself with an excellent breakfast. He looked up with a rather quizzical glance as she approached him.

"Why do you leave our patient?" he asked curtly.

"Mr. Passiver is with her, and will ring when I am wanted."

"Ah! I say, nurse, there's something wrong here! What is it? you are a woman, and women are sharp-sighted."

"I think you are mistaken, sir. I imagined so too, until a few moments ago; but if you had only seen his face when I told him that she had sent for him, and how he sprang down those stairs, you would change your mind, as I did."

"I am not so sure of that," he muttered bluntly. "Between you and me, this Passiver is a queer chicken, and I cannot just make him out. I will, though, some day. Now let me give you a small piece of advice, will you? Keep a sharp watch on that fellow, and see if he is the true blue. If not, that little bird of a wife of his will need a friend, and it will go hard with me if she don't find one. I have observed her closely, and if I read signs aright, that child's heart is no stranger to aching. It made me almost forget myself when I saw the eager, intent striving to catch the faint sound of his steps while he paced the floor above her. There is something deeper than we see upon the surface, and I am curious to get at the bottom of it, for I have known her ever since she was born almost, and am sure that the fault does not lie with her if she is not happy."

CHAPTER XIX.

SOME OF THE WORKINGS OF THE "PECULIAR INSTITUTION."

WHILE this conversation was taking place in the breakfast room, Mr. Passiver had entered the chamber where Astrea lay, and turned the key to guard against intrusion. A pale, eager face was lifted from the pillow, and a pair of dark, wishful eyes watched intently his deliberate motions. Heeding neither, he walked slowly toward the fire and stood with his back to her. The white cheek sank again to its resting-place, and the long lashes drooped upon it, closing tightly over the great drops of anguish that had rushed to her eyes.

After a while the dead silence was broken by a low, sweet voice from the bed.

"Frederic."

"Well?"

"Are you not coming to speak to me?"

"What shall I say?"

There was a struggle for mastery over a great spasm of pain; then the voice, more subdued and tremulous, answered as gently as before.

"Surely your heart will dictate one kind word for the mother of your child. Your little daughter lies in my arms; Frederic, come and look at her."

"Deuce take the child!" he answered angrily. "I want no puling girls."

This silenced her. There were no more words, but a smothered sob told of the grief that no effort of will could suppress. Another great hope had been crushed dead at one blow, and she mourned over it with exceeding sorrow. He listened to the stifled sounds for five minutes without comment, then spoke sternly:

"Stop crying, Eugenia, you will put yourself into a fever with such foolishness."

"I cannot help it, Frederic."

"You must. What good does it do you? The strangest thing in this world, is the disposition of women to whimper over everything that does not please them."

"There is no especial delight in tears like mine, Frederic," with a weary, hopeless tone of voice. "I have longed with a womanly longing for sympathy and tenderness which I cannot find. My mother is in her grave, and my dear father far away. Brothers and sisters I have never had, and to admit friends to my heart, would only show the void there, which I have striven to conceal. Life looks very blank and cheerless to me now, for all hope seems at an end."

"Don't be sentimental as well as foolish," he muttered coarsely. "Of all hateful things on earth, it is a soft, sentimental woman."

She answered no more, and he threw himself into a large chair with a half audible oath. Half an hour passed in total silence, giving time to each for resuming the habitual demeanor observed towards each other. Then he rose and drew the curtains round her couch, as if she slept and he would guard her slumbers, while she lay still, with her white face nestled closely against the pillow.

He saw in that face the sickness of an utter despair, but it did not melt him to one relenting emotion of tenderness. Fully convinced that she would suffer on in silence, giving no sign, he left her with her own miserable thoughts, and bore to the breakfast-room where the Doctor sat, a lying face, which wore seemingly proud and happy smiles.

"I was only waiting to take my leave of your wife, Mr. Passiver," said the old physician as the young man grasped his hand with warmth.

"Then you do not mean to congratulate me at all," laughed Mr. Passiver.

"No, because you have kept away so long, it appears like affectation now, I never congratulate young fathers who are not by to receive their treasures first from my hands."

"Oh, you are too hard on a fellow, Doctor; can't you make some allowance for a man's natural shyness on such occasions?"

The old man laughed.

"I cannot imagine you bashful, Passiver, under any circumstances whatever. On the contrary, I think you have more assurance and self-possession than any young man I ever saw. However, I do not so much wonder at this for you have mixed so largely with the world, it would be something of a wonder to find you otherwise than self-possessed."

Mr. Passiver smiled blandly, taking the Doctor's remarks as a great compliment. He had always prided himself upon that especial quality, considering it one of the strongest elements of power.

"I believe you are right," he said, thrown off his guard in his extreme self-complacence. "It has always been a noted trait amongst my friends, none of whom can ever say that they saw me disconcerted or confused."

"Aha! Well, now, sir, by your own confession, it was not bashfulness which deprived you of my congratulations. Come; give an account of yourself. What kept you away so long?"

"Sheer cowardice, I presume," with seeming frankness. "I own that I cannot bear to see suffering by those I love."

"O, fie! that looks selfish. You don't mean to say, that to spare yourself you could leave your young wife all alone in her trouble, without a word of sympathy."

"I am forced to do so, though I see that it does not raise me in your good estimation to make such an acknowledgment!" answered the dissembler in the same frank tone. But his anger was rising fast, and his fingers tingled to hurl the persistent old physician from the room.

"Have a glass of wine, Doctor?" he asked by way of covering his displeasure. "The morning is a little cool, and you have a long ride before you."

"You do not call three miles a long ride, I hope! When I was a young man, that distance would have appeared a mere step to me. I have no objection to the wine, though, and must really take my leave."

Mr. Passiver filled and handed to him a glass of sherry, then escorted him to Mrs. Passiver's door and left him. Shortly afterward, the old gentleman came out and entered the carriage which stood at the gate ready to convey him back to Florence. His young host, still intent upon keeping up the character he had assumed, walked with him down to the vehicle.

"Good morning, sir," began the Doctor deliberately, as he settled himself for his drive. "I hope when I come again to find wife and child prospering. But you must take care of her, Passiver, and don't let her fret about anything. To my surprise I found when I went in just now, indications of uneasiness which had produced fever. She is delicate and cannot bear much, I fear."

Mr. Passiver set his teeth hard to suppress an oath, while his mental conclusion was:

"The old meddler suspects something and is sounding me. By Jove, I wonder if he could have got anything out of her! I was a fool to stay away, and rouse his suspicions."

The moment after the old Doctor found himself alone, his face settled into a troubled gravity which partook largely of indignation. His cogitations ran altogether upon the pair he had left behind him, and were anything but pleasant, for he was a kind-hearted man, and had loved Astrea from her early childhood.

"That fellow is deep," he muttered to himself; "deep and wary. I am much mistaken if that little woman does not already repent the step she has taken in becoming his wife; but she is steel-true, and will bear her lot like a Spartan. Such women are deserving of a better fate than hers promises to be, and I am sorry, sorry! Oh, dear! The old story of mating the vulture with a dove! But in this case the vulture's talons are hidden under the softest down. I must watch closely to see that he does not rend her to death."

Mr. Passiver returned to the Hall, and sought the library, where he remained some time in angry thought. His first impulse was to discharge Doctor Early, and employ some other physician. It was galling to receive a man into his house, who, by his manner, openly expressed opinions that his domestic affairs were not all right. Yet he dared not take so positive a step, and by it, confirm the suspicions which were so apparent. Reflection decided him to let him come, and play out his part to the end. But from that day forth, the good old Doctor had in Frederic Passiver a strong and bitter enemy, who was deliberately planning to crush him.

Mrs. Passiver's recovery was very slow, and it was many weeks before she was able to take her accustomed place at the table, or occupy her little chair by the east window, where she had contracted the habit of taking her needle and favorite books to spend the long hours of the morning. She was too proud, and too earnestly resolute in her desire to do her duty, to make any complaint, and the silent struggle was too great to allow her at once to rise above its weakening influence. While she grieved alone, or sadly toyed with her babe, into whose future she looked with distrust and dread, the kind old Doctor and nurse discussed her troubles in secret, striving in vain, though with the best motives, to gain some indisputable evidence of the cruelty which they asserted was killing her! Finally, however, she grew stronger and broke from their control, sending them both away with gentle firmness, and the declaration that she no longer needed their care. They never knew how she missed them, and the sympathy which she instinctively understood and accepted; nor how fast her tears fell when they disappeared from sight, leaving her alone with her great burthen of woe. But it was a relief, also, to be freed from their watchful regards, while her resolution remained firm to shield her husband from suspicions of unkindness. It was much easier to bear her grief alone and unwatched; scrutiny only added to the difficulties of her trying position.

The autumn and winter months passed away monotonously, varied only by occasional visitors. Astrea was not yet strong enough to go out, had she desired to do so; but there was that in her heart which made her long to hide herself from the world, lest it should guess that she was an unhappy, disappointed woman. If old friends came about her, she laughed and jested as happily as when her place was in their midst; and if they noted that her face grew more infantine in its delicacy, and her figure slighter, ill health was a sufficient explanation. Very few ever suspected that there might be another cause. Doctor Early came to her oftener than any other. He had a large country practice, and always found it convenient to call in passing, to see how "baby was thriving." Mr. Passiver was usually absent, either at Florence or riding about the plantation, so his visits were usually very pleasant and cosy. The young lady learned to look for his coming with eager anticipation, and to see him depart with regret. It was almost like association with a parent, he was so kind and fatherly in his manner, and gave her such wise counsel in the general duties of life. He was too prudent to make a direct appeal to her against the false step which she had taken; but he made her ponder deeply, upon the natural result of certain actions, and by this means, taught her many truths to which she had been blinded, by allowing a high sense of one great duty, to obscure others as important.

Outwardly, the intercourse between Mr. Passiver and his family physician, was of the most amicable nature. Had not the tale-telling features of the young wife betrayed what she never allowed her lips to utter, even the good old Doctor must have been deceived by the man's courteous and attentive manner. With his family and servants, he appeared uniformly kind—with his neighbors, genial and hospitable. The country, for miles around, came under his influence imperceptibly, and he was fast making friends everywhere. Had they analyzed his actions, not one of them could have referred to a real kindness received at his hands; and no man could have vouched for his real opinions, either in politics or religion. The man was too deep to commit himself without some positive advantage could be gained by it, and trusted to one of his favorite theories of the power of one mind over another, for the attainment of any desired object. He did not hint such a thought to others, but his mental resolve was to go to Congress within a year or two. And his ambition was for a seat in the Senate—not the House. That would not at all suit his ambition. Furthermore, he would win such an influence by his diplomacy, that the Legislature should choose and elect him without the expenditure of a dollar by which enemies could say that he had purchased his position. He would work so adroitly to his ends, they should not even know that he desired that position, but consider it a condescension on his part to represent them in the Congress of the United States. Once there he would rely upon the ground he had gained at the outset, and then, by a judicious use of his money, the road to the White House might be easy enough. Perhaps—who could tell?—at thirty he might be a United States Senator; at thirty-five, President! Thus did lofty fancies teem in the brain of our young nabob as he cantered over his fine domain, or sat within his own luxurious room with a cigar between his lips. As the spring advanced, Mrs. Passiver's health became visibly worse, and Doctor Early became alarmed.

"You *must* go out more," he said to her in expostulation. "I cannot hope to bring the roses to your cheeks if you will persist in making a nun of yourself."

"What shall I do?"

"Get a spanking little horse and take a long ride over the plantation every morning. Don't you like to ride?"

"Very much—or I used to like it; I would not care to leave baby so long though, now."

"Nonsense. Nettie can care for Miss Passiver quite as well as you. If she don't, Miss Baby will one day be without any mother at all."

"Do you mean what you say, Doctor?"

"Most assuredly, my dear madame, it is your duty to take care of your health. Let me beg of you to follow my advice."

"I will."

But there was no interest or alarm in her tones, she looked quiet and passive while he planned her daily routine for the future, and he thought regretfully:

"She would rather die than live, poor little soul!"

Old interests became strong, however, when she once more took up an active line of duty. The fresh air and the rapid gait of her spirited little pony, sent the blood coursing through her veins with warmth and energy, rousing her from the dull, morbid state into which she had fallen, and giving place once more to the strong, willful spirit which had never brooked control until the hands of power, and a mistaken sense of duty, had crushed it. Then it was, the leaven of Doctor Early's teachings began to work, and by the time summer came, she was a stronger, firmer and wiser woman.

The change was not sudden or startling. It came gradually, and did not serve to create one uneasy thought, until one evening in midsummer, when her outraged sense of right destroyed the usual tact she had endeavored to employ, and brought them face to face once more on contested ground.

She had ridden down to the quarters to see a girl whom the nurse had reported ill, and came back filled with righteous indignation. Mr. Passiver lounged in a bamboo chair on the veranda, idly glancing over a number of New York papers. He looked up with astonishment, as her crimson features appeared above him.

"Frederic," she began rapidly, "do you know what kind of an overseer you have on the plantation?"

"Perfectly well."

"And do you sanction his cruel treatment of your people?"

"I do."

"Monstrous! You cannot mean to say that he has your authority to beat old men into their graves, and to kill young girls outright."

"Of course not, and he does no such things. A man will not deliberately throw away a thousand dollars; but at the same time, it is necessary for the welfare of the whole tribe, that they should be kept in order, and you cannot do that without the free use of the lash."

Astrea groaned.

"Oh, hearts of stone! Oh, black and bitter curse upon the fairest of nations."

"What is the matter now? Have you taken leave of your wits?"

"No, I wish I had!"

"What the deuce do you mean, then?"

"This—it is fearful, unbearable to see human beings murdered under our very eyes, and have no power to save them! To-day Nettie informed me that one of my girls was sick, and begged to see me; but I had no thought when I started out to visit her cabin, what I should find!"

"Well, what did you find?" he sneered, as she paused in her excitement.

"I found one of my best and most faithful servants dying from the effects of a most brutal treatment—a young girl whose sense of right was too pure and strong to allow her to tolerate the advances of a vicious white man, and whose faithful adherence to the principles taught her, has brought her to her death! I have heard the whole story. She has been married the last six months, to Rufus, one of my boys, and when Ormand insulted Kate, the loyal fellow knocked him down, as he richly deserved. What was the result? Rufus has ever since, been tied up by the thumbs in the direst agony, while Kate was beaten until the punishment brought on premature labor. She lived to see me and to fondle my hands like some faithful animal, then close her eyes blessing me! Oh, she is dead, my poor Kate, and I have remained here day after day, and week after week, in ignorance of the woe to which my people were reduced! I have been blind while their eyes saw rivers of blood—deaf while their wails ascended to God, pleading for the help I did not give them! And they love me still—they trust me still—they can die with my name upon their lips! Merciful Father, the thought will drive me mad!"

Mr. Passiver seized her in his arms as she paced excitedly up and down the veranda, and forced her into a chair.

"Sit still and calm yourself."

"I will not," said she, breaking away from him. "This has gone on too long, and I must put a stop to it. Oh, to think that I should have been tame and passive all these long months, thinking only of my duty to you, while you were killing my people! I allowed you to banish them from the house, and to substitute your own—to break up every cherished custom which had formed a link of unity between us. At night and morning I bore a heart-ache without complaint, thinking of how they would miss me, because I considered peace with you, a duty above that which I owed them, and I thought some time to win you to better feelings. I laugh at my folly now, and hate myself for being made your dupe. You have outraged every feeling that is noblest and best in my nature, and thereby absolved me from my vows of obedience. Henceforth, I do my duty to others in spite of you, and nothing but absolute force can curb my actions."

"We shall see," he answered coolly. "I may teach you that you have, as yet, only seen the shadow of my power. It would not please me to use force with my wife, and attract the attention of other people; but it will please me to tame her, and, by the Lord, I intend to do it."

"You may kill me, perhaps; conquer me you never will. The time for submission, or even tolerance is past."

"You think so, but you will change your mind before I have done with you," saying which, he threw down his paper and walked out to the river. There he cast loose a skiff, and jumping into it, rowed swiftly down the stream. He did not return for some time, and Astrea had regained her usual calmness, though a resolute expression was about her mouth which had long been a stranger to it.

Neither spoke as they sat at the table sipping their tea, and no one would have guessed from his deliberate, nonchalant manner, that anything of an unusual nature had occurred to disturb him. To speak the truth, he enjoyed the prospect of a more stirring life, for the tame monotony of the last six months had become excessively wearisome. He was beginning to long for a change, when this scene roused him with the promise of a rich, spicy harvest, and his first step was calculated to stir the troubled waters to a perfect fury of discord. Something in his face must have suggested the truth to Astrea, who detained him as he was about to rise from the table. The servants had all been dismissed from the room.

"Stay, Mr. Passiver. Will you have the kindness to tell me where you have been for the last two hours?"

"Certainly, my dear; I was down at the quarters."

"What were you doing there?"

"Making some investigations."

"Of what nature?"

"I was curious to know who had told you the fine story with which you entertained me this afternoon."

"I presume you found out?"

"Yes. One of your old men—called Uncle Jacob by yourself, Jake by the other negroes—gave a graphic account of the scene between Kate, Rufus and the overseer, to Nettie, your nurse, whom he met somewhere about the plantation. Of course he designed that she should tell you, and you know what followed."

"From whom did you learn all this?"

"Jacob, himself, who confessed it with a degree of insolence unequaled on any plantation in Alabama. I ordered him tied up and thrashed within an inch of his life."

"And was it done?"

"Yes; I remained to see that my commands were obeyed, before I came home."

Here the self-control which she had maintained through the dialogue, gave way, and she rose quivering with passion.

"Frederic Passiver, are you a fiend in human shape, that you can thus revel in cruelty? Do you wish to make me hate you by this despicable conduct? If not, beware, for I cannot endure this long."

He sat balancing his spoon upon the edge of his cup.

"I don't know that it makes much difference whether you love or hate me, since I am your master all the same. Your bible should teach you that a woman has no positive individuality, except what her husband makes for her."

"The bible teaches no one-sided theories of right; and I deny that you are my master. Make yourself worthy of my love—my superior in anything, and I will gladly own your power! but by such actions as these, you sink yourself to a level with barbarians, and it is my duty to stand between you and your miserable victims. How many more do you mean to murder in cold blood? Last week old Roger was beaten until he fell ill and died—a man of seventy years, whose bent form and white hairs should have saved him from cruelty. Now I suppose Jacob must follow, and a little city of murdered dead will rise up to reproach us! Mark my words, Frederic—sooner or later, retribution must come. Not long can God remain silent and deaf to the cries of his children, and the day will come when he will demand blood for blood."

"Where are you going?"

"To the quarters."

"What for?"

"To see how much injury you have done to old Jacob."

"And sow deeper discord among the others. I forbid such a step. When a wife thus publicly sets herself up against her husband, the result must be disastrous to them and their interests. Let them alone, if you would not make matters worse."

"That would be difficult, for they could scarcely be more dreadful than they are; and to sit still while such things are going on, is utterly impossible. No, if there must be a struggle between us, let it come, and God defend the right. Better to die in a strife for His children's weal, than to wear out my life under a stony-hearted man's tyranny. The hope for happiness died within me long ago, and I have resolved to fill the void, if possible, by a faithful performance of the duties which you have heretofore forced me to ignore."

He laughed mockingly.

"Ride your high horse, my peerless wife, but take care that it does not break your neck."

She stepped into her own room without reply, intending to get a hat and shawl, when he closed the door and turned the key upon her, laughing maliciously, as he put it into his pocket and walked away.

Now, indeed, the struggle between the two strong natures had commenced, each resolved to gain the victory. One was good—the other was evil—one trusted in God—the other in his own strength.

We shall see the result by and by.

CHAPTER XX.

MORE DETAILS OF LIFE AT PASSIVER HALL.

SILENCE, deep and profound, brooded over Passiver Hall. The young master, glorying in his own arbitrary power, sat for hours in his luxurious bamboo chair upon the veranda, dreaming ambitious dreams, while the stars came out one by one until the sky was studded, as with millions of sparkling gems. Then the moon rose large and bright, over the mountain in the distance, and was reflected in the river. The scene was very beautiful, and he enjoyed it—enjoyed it with the more zest, as he thought of the woman he had made a prisoner within her own room, because she had dared to defy him.

Several times he had crept to her door to listen if any sounds might betray distress or anger, but all was silent as death within. Of course she had been obliged to yield, and was crying her eyes out with spiteful resentment, though she would not let him hear her. But never mind. He would let her alone, and keep her there, until she was glad to come and humbly crave his pardon for opposing him. With all her boasted will, she could not hold out very long against him; so he was content to bide his time waiting for the hours of her humility and his triumph. Once Nettie approached her door with little Lillian, intending to put her in her crib; but he checked her with a finger on his lips.

"Carry the child up stairs, Nettie; your mistress is not well, and must not be disturbed to-night on any account. See that you keep her quiet, too, and don't let her cry."

That was early in the evening, and the girl obeyed with ill-concealed dislike. She did not believe one word of what her master said, and rightly guessed that he was "up to sumthin' devilish, shure." But she knew too well what it would cost her to allow him to hear her mutterings, and she proceeded up stairs with a cat-like tread, where she sat for a long time pondering her master's reasons for what seemed so strange to her. Like most negroes, Nettie was fond of sleep, and soon gave herself up to the fascinating sweetness of a nap, which lasted until a light touch upon her arm woke her with a start. Mrs. Passiver stood at her side, holding a small lamp.

"Is you better, missis?" she asked, rubbing her eyes.

"Better? I have not been ill. Can I trust you, Nettie?"

"'Deed you can, Miss 'Genia. Only jes' try me, an' you'll see."

"I will. Do you see this? It is a wax impression of the lock upon my chamber door. I want you to go to Florence to-morrow, and have an extra key made for me. Keep that key in your pocket, and whenever your master takes it into his head to tell you I am ill, rest assured that I shall need your assistance. I depend upon you to take care of Lily at such times, my good girl, and when you know she is asleep, slip round through the picture-gallery to my boudoir, and open the door that communicates with my bed-chamber. When that is done, go back the same way you came, to Lily, and whatever happens, say nothing to any body. Oh, Nettie, Nettie, this breaks my heart, but there is no help, no help for me!"

The girl's eyes glistened as her young mistress leaned heavily upon her shoulder for support. She took one fair little hand in her own and kissed it.

"Trust me, missis, do trust me; I'd die for you an' little Miss Lily."

"I believe you would, good girl, and I intend to trust you. Now keep perfectly quiet, and take care of my child. I am going down to the quarters to see Uncle Jacob."

"Oh, Miss 'Genia, if master should find it out!"

"Never mind if he does; he will not dare to hurt me."

Astrea bent fondly over the sleeping babe and kissed the rosy cheek, then stole with a noiseless tread from the room. Trembling with alarm, Nettie went to the window and listened. Mr. Passiver was still upon the veranda, where she could see the fiery glow of his cigar, quite unconscious of what was going on within. From the opposite window, she could command a full view of the river, and saw her young mistress stepping into a canoe as she drew aside the curtain. One silent push sent the light thing far out into the stream, and in a few moments a sharp bend in the river hid her from sight. Realizing that she had seen her master outwitted, the girl became half frantic with delight, and skipped like a wild thing over the carpet.

"Thar he lies—puffin' away at that roll of tobaccer, an' chucklin' in hisself about havin' her fast in her own room, an' she's done gone spite of him. O, glory! I likes it. I guess I knows now what he's up to! Can't fool this chile! High! it takes Miss 'Genia to match sich smart uns!"

Nettie's delight, though demonstrative, was held within the limits of prudence. She took good care not to make any noise, and after a few more antics, settled herself down again beside the child, and in a short time, was once more fast asleep.

Meantime Mrs. Passiver paddled her little canoe down the river until she came to the landing opposite the quarters. Late visits there had rendered her familiar with the locality of Uncle Jacob's cabin, and she proceeded to it at once. A faint light within, and sounds of distress from some one in deep pain, indicated that the inmates were not asleep, and she tapped upon the door softly.

"Good Lord, is dat you, missis?"

The old woman who opened the door started back upon seeing who the unusual visitor was.

"Yes, Aunt Judy; I have come to see Uncle Jacob; how is he?"

"Mos' done fur, missis, mos' done fur! but dat don't make

17

no difference. Uncle Jake 'd mos' libed long enuff anyhow, an' de good Lord meant soon to take him home."

Astrea knelt down by the old man, and leaning her head against the rude bedstead, sobbed convulsively.

"Uncle Jacob, I did not know it *could* come to this," she moaned in broken tones. "Had I dreamed of such a thing, I would have died sooner than subject you to it; and it will break my heart to think that your faithful love for me, and for those around you, should meet with such a reward, I did not know, oh, I did not know what I was doing!"

"We all knows dat, missis. Many a time when de young folks said Miss 'Genia had done forgot 'em, my ole 'oman an' me said missis hadn't done no sich ting; we know'd dat it wasn't you fault—we seed whose fault it was all de time. Don't cry, missis; it don't make no difference, 'cause ole Jake wants to go home."

Here Aunt Judy sat down upon the floor, and began to rock herself disconsolately to and fro, groaning with each movement of her poor old body.

"Oh, Lordy! I nebber t'ought de dark days 'd come while our young missis libed. We nebber use ter see trouble an' we was sure we'd die in de sunshine. Oh, Lordy, oh, Lordy! I wish de good God 'ud take me wid him. I don't want to lib when my ole man's gone!"

"Stop dat, ole 'oman," came from Uncle Jake as he turned over with a heavy groan. "Is ye goin' to make young missis feel more heart-broke arter she's come all de way here in de middle ob de night to show us dat she don't forgit? Lord bless ye, Miss 'Genia, fur dis great proof ob yer lub. Oh, His glory 'll shine on ye in de las' day, brighter dan de sun, an' de blessed Lamb of God 'll fold ye close in his arms, hol' de cup of life to yer lips which ye'll drink and lib forebber an' forebber."

"You striving to comfort me! Oh, faithful soul, have I deserved this! My Father, help me to bear my punishment, for thy hand is very heavy upon me!"

It was a strange scene, and one a beholder might never forget—the groaning old man upon his hard bed, with the stains of blood all over the coarse sheet where he had lain—the fair young woman beside him with her anguished face uplifted in prayer. The dark cloak which she wore had fallen to the floor and left her white dress uncovered, over which her loose hair fell in disordered masses. In the background, with the flickering candle at her feet, sat Aunt Judy, from whose lips came groans in response to every sound of distress from her husband. Angels might have looked with pity upon so sad a picture of human woe; but, of the three sufferers, Astrea Passiver, mistress of broad lands and stately halls, with gold at her command to exceed the most extravagant desires, was the most to be pitied. Oh, how she loathed the glittering chains she wore! How she shrank from the sweetness of flowers whose breath made her soul faint within her, and under every beauteous hue, concealed a stinging thorn! She had bent her lips to an ambrosial fountain, and the waters of Marah flowed within them; she had stretched her hand for the beautiful garland of hope, and saw it wither within her grasp. One by one the tender petals had fallen, until only ashes of the thing which was once beauty's self, remained. And now, what had she left to make life endurable? A wife, a mother, a mistress of many slaves, and yet, from none of these could she hope to glean a pleasure for her future existence. The husband had fallen from his high pedestal, crushing in his fall both love and trust; and to see her child grow up under such influences as those which now made the curse of her own life, could yield only pain. Despair was in her heart. She put forth her hand and clasping the old negro's burning palm, bowed her brow upon it.

"Oh, Jacob, Jacob, I would I were in your place!"

"Why, dear missis?"

"I should be so much nearer that rest for which my soul longs so intensely."

"Missis must be patient an' bear de cross till de dewine

Marster sees fit to take it away. Oh, we's all poor critters dat don't see what de Lord means by de ways he make us go, an' wee's nebber satisfied. I'se said so many times to de young darkies, when dey's been talking about de rich white folks, an' a wishin' dey 'd been born white. Dey's envied you missis, many a time; jes so blin' is human natur."

"Blind indeed to envy me," she moaned. "Ah, poor things, they cannot dream of how I pine in my high estate. How gladly would I take a crust of bread, and a cup of cold water, if with them, I could have freedom to do good, and love to sustain me in it."

"In de Lord's good time ye may," repeated the old man lifting his faded eyes upward. "An' in his eyes, eben at dis moment, yer deeds, as he sees 'em in yer heart, will bring down his blessin' on yer head. Nebber despair, dear missis, God is berry good to his chillen."

"I hope you will always find Him so my poor old Jacob, and that you will cover me with the mantle of charity if I seem to fall short in my duty to you and yours. I stole away to come to you to-night; if I do not come again, think that I could not—that something happened to prevent it. Never believe that I staid away because I wished to do so."

He looked at her wistfully.

"I nebber will doubt my dear missis. An' don't ye come here Miss 'Genia, ef it is goin' to get ye in any trubble. De angels will come fur ole Jake all de same."

"Never fear me, uncle," she answered as she rose and bent over him. "I have been a coward, and too long permitted my foolish hopes to keep me out of a path where I knew thorns were springing rankly; but that is all over now. Amends must be made. Can't you turn a little further to one side, Uncle Jacob?"

"What ye goin' to do, missis?"

"Try to make you more comfortable. Oh, poor fellow, how you must suffer!"

She had exposed his shoulders and found the skin literally flayed from his body.

"Don't missis, sich work ain't fur de likes ob you. Judy 'll do dat."

"No, I must do it myself."

She took a soft sponge from her pocket and dipped it in the tin basin which Aunt Judy filled and handed to her, then carefully bathed the swollen shoulders of the old man, after which she applied a cooling lotion which she had brought for the purpose. In a short time he closed his eyes with a sigh of relief.

"De Lord bless ye, missis," he said faintly, "ye don't know how good dat feels. Ise goin' to sleep now," and while she gazed upon him pityingly, his heavy breathing assured her that he had found rest.

"Let him sleep just as long as he can, Aunt Judy," she said, preparing to go out softly. "If possible, I will come again to-morrow; if not, to-morrow night."

The old woman followed her to the door with many thanks; but she broke away from her garrulous demonstrations, and hastened to her canoe. It was where she left it, and she took up the paddle with eager anxiety to reach home, for it was growing late. The current was strong, however, and it was slow work going against it. By the time she landed at the foot of the steps and softly drew her frail barque into the boat-house, she was completely exhausted.

Mr. Passiver was still lounging upon the veranda, but happened to look toward the river just as she mounted the steps. She came up slowly, her white garments gleaming in the moonlight, and her hair floating around her shoulders. The dark cloak which she had worn was accidentally dropped into the river as she came up, and before she could recover it, the woollen fabric had filled with water and sunk beyond reach; so, when he now saw her, not a particle of color relieved the glaring whiteness of her apparel. It did not cross his min that it could be Astrea, whom he had locked safely in he room, and a queer sensation crept through his veins as he looked. Suddenly the figure turned off upon the terrace to the left, and was lost to sight.

Filled with curiosity, he sprang down the steps and followed, but the vision had flown. He could see nothing, and after having gone all around the house peering into every nook where it could have hidden, he tried the doors to see if they were fast, and went back to the veranda, by which he entered the Hall.

"I wonder who the deuce it could have been?" he muttered in sore perplexity. "It looked like Eugenia, but that is not possible. I will see, though, if she is in her room."

He approached her door and unlocked it softly, advancing upon tiptoe. There was a regular sound of breathing from her couch, and a mellow light from the east window, showed her figure dimly, reposing upon the pillows. It could not have been her! Who, then, was it and what did it all mean? Mr. Passiver was growing more and more puzzled, and very restless. He stole up stairs to see if Nettie and the child were still there and found them sleeping. The remainder of the night was spent in wandering about the Hall, and making zealous efforts to solve the mystery; but the doors were all fast, the boats and skiffs secure in the boat-house, the windows closed, and all the household quietly locked in slumber. For once, Frederic Passiver was compelled to own himself nonplussed. He was not superstitious, therefore his mind rejected the conclusion to which many others might have been driven. Still it was a mystery which greatly perplexed him, and he determined to solve it at any cost. With the early dawn he unlocked Mrs. Passiver's chamber, and again put the key into his pocket, in order to keep it in his own possession. It was not his purpose to keep her locked up all day, unless forced to do so to prevent a public exposé of the war between them. She met him at the breakfast table with a calm face, poured his coffee, and performed every little duty to which she was accustomed, as if nothing had happened. Only for the clear, brilliant light of her eyes, which spoke volumes of will, he might have thought her subdued. Her manner was quiet enough, and her voice unusually soft. But that was no proof of being conquered. As he regarded her closely during the meal, he became convinced that his task would be a much harder one than he had anticipated. The reed was becoming an oak. He might bend it, but in bending, would it break also? The future must decide that; conquer he would, even if, in proving his own strength, he should bring the pillars of the temple, sampson-like, tumbling about his own ears to crush him.

CHAPTER XXI.

SHARP PRACTICE AND BRUTAL DOINGS.

As Mr. Passiver rose from the table, Astrea stretched her hand to the bell and rang sharply.

"Tell the coachman to bring the carriage round directly," she ordered, as the servant appeared.

"Where are you going?" asked her husband.

"To Florence."

"What takes you there?"

"My pleasure"—then after a moment she added, as if averse to such glaring curtness, "I have a little shopping to do."

"Shall you be gone long?"

"Not very—three or four hours, probably."

"You had better instruct one of the girls and send her for what you want."

"There is no good reason for it, and I prefer to go myself," she replied, quietly. "Lily needs an airing, and I am weary of being in the house so much. It is not often that I feel like driving into town, and I owe some calls that ought to be paid."

"Very well, pay them; but I have a few words to say to you. Hold your tongue about private affairs, and when you come back, see that you keep away from the quarters."

She made no reply.

"Do you hear me, Eugenia?"

"Yes."

"Then why do you sit as if you were dumb?"

"Because I thought an answer uncalled for. You need not have given the order, however. I shall not go there to-day."

"You intend to go sometime?"

"Most assuredly."

"I warn you to beware how you brave me! Do I seem like a man to be trifled with?"

"You could not more than murder me, Mr. Passiver, and I have often thought that death would be preferable to daily torture."

"You may find it sooner than you expect," he answered, hotly. "I warn you that I am waxing dangerous. Where were you last night?"

The random shot failed to confirm a suspicion, if he had one. The beautiful lips curled in scorn.

"I have a remembrance of having been locked in my room last night by my loving lord; and if my ears did not deceive me, he took the key out and carried it away with him. Now he asks me where I was."

"True," he thought; "it could not have been her."

Her calm, cool sarcasm and scornful lip would have been sufficient to disarm suspicion. In the course of an hour the carriage was announced, and Mrs. Passiver entered it with Nettie and the babe. Before they were fairly out of sight, Mr. Passiver ordered his horse, and mounting it, followed them. Wherever she went, his watchful regards accompanied her. He saw every shop she entered, noted the houses at which she called, and, keeping himself out of sight, made a memoranda of her entire proceedings. Not until he saw her enter the carriage at Doctor Early's door, and turn the horses' heads homeward, did his vigilance relax. When she had gone, he made some purchases, ordered them sent home on the following day, and himself took the road back to the Hall. But he did not go straight home. He took another road just before coming in sight of the Hall, and rode round the place, coming in from the opposite direction, triumphant with the thought of the part he had played so successfully. These were the conclusions to which he had arrived after mentally summing up the whole: She had made three calls; they were to cover her real object in visiting Florence. She had made a few purchases; they were to cover the real articles wanted. He had seen her enter a drug store. On the morrow he would go there and ask for his bill, and find out what articles had been purchased, that he might guess her designs. Whatever had been obtained there, furnished the real motive for her trip to town. He thought himself shrewd, and was, undoubtedly. But he had found his match in Astrea, now that her powers were brought into play against him. The necessity for returning to town was obviated by her own seeming carelessness in leaving the bill of sale, which had been receipted, upon her dressing-table. He glanced at it hastily during a brief absence on the part of his wife, and saw that her purchases consisted of some cologne, a bottle of soothing syrup, some fancy soaps, tooth brushes, and rice powder for the baby. There were no poisons, lotions, narcotics or powders. Had he really thought she could be guilty of purchasing any deadly thing for an unholy purpose? If any one had asked him, he would have indignantly denied such an insinuation, but he had followed her, and had scrutinized every action. Why did he do it, and how did it happen that the thought of poisons came into his mind? If the heart of man is filled with evil, his sight is strangely colored by that which he carries with him. And Frederic Passiver was so unscrupulous himself, he could not set treachery apart from others where his interests and theirs seemed to conflict. He was becoming afraid of his wife, and his fears made him unjust in his estimation of the means she proposed to use to accomplish her own objects.

Meantime, Mrs. Passiver flitted about quietly, putting away her purchases and wrappings until dinner was announced, secretly rejoicing that she had obtained what she went to Florence for, without leaving a trace of her errand behind her. While she had been in shops and stores, Nettie, with Lily in her arms, had gone to a locksmith's, by her mistress' order, and purchased, instead of a duplicate, a pass key, by which Astrea could go all over the house without hindrance. This and one other object completed the sum total of her desires. A long, confidential chat with her old family physician, in which she briefly gave him to understand the state of affairs at Passiver Hall, and claimed his promise of assistance in her time of need, made so often while he attended her during her long illness. She had recounted to him the scenes of the night previous, while he listened with an anxious face.

"But how did you get out of your room?" he asked, curiously, when she had told him of being locked up, and her subsequent visit to the quarters.

"Easily enough," she answered, laughing at the remembrance. "There are two doors to my chamber, and when he had secured the one, I heard him go around to the other and try it. Finding that locked, and thinking he had the only key which could open it, he went away. Luckily my closet door key opens this second door, which leads through my boudoir to the picture-gallery, and I went through that, descending to the cellar, whose only exit is upon the north side of the Hall. As we descend to it by a stairway leading from the kitchen, I easily found my way there, opened the cellar door, and went out, locking it behind me. The key is always kept upon the inside, so I thought if a fancy should take him to try it, he would be satisfied on finding it fast. Of course I came back the same way, left the key upon a nail, where it usually hangs, ran up stairs and through the gallery hall to the gallery and the boudoir, then to my own room, which I fastened, putting the closet key back into its place. I had an idea that he saw me as I entered, and hastened to get into bed before he came to see if I was safely housed. He did come, after a while, but I had grown quite composed, and he soon went away satisfied, though he endeavored this morning to surprise me into a betrayal of my nocturnal rambles. It is a dreadful thing to be reduced to such a state, Doctor Early, but what can I do? I cannot let those people die without help, and you see how determinedly he opposes me."

The old gentleman shook his head. "Bad, bad! I don't know what to say to you, child, except that I would do as you are doing; only you must be watchful of your health. You may contract a fever by such exposure to the night dew. Shall I come to see you to-morrow?"

"Yes, and bring with you such things as I may need for the negroes in such cases. I dare not get them myself, lest he should find and deprive me of them. If he knows nothing of it, I may succeed in hiding them about the cabins to use when wanted."

With this she left him, satisfied with having made her arrangements for future operations all complete. As she expected, before night closed in, Mr. Passiver subjected her room to a search. He was too much puzzled to let the mystery go without putting everything to the test, and in his examination of all the keys about the premises—found out the use to which the one belonging to the closet-door had been put. This was what she feared when she conceived the idea of getting a pass-key, and now had double cause for rejoicing, when she saw him go to her wardrobe, and all her drawers to make sure she had concealed none there. Safe in her bosom the little deliverer rested, and she knew that he would not dare to search her person further than the pocket of the dress she wore.

That night after tea, he asked her to sing, and she went cheerfully to the piano, choosing his favorites and singing until he wearied. Lily had been carried up stairs again according to Mr. Passiver's order, and she made no objection to it. Rather earlier than usual, she retired to her room, and he quietly turned the key upon her as before. This time he was resolved to make sure that his bird was hopelessly caged, and after going through every room and locking it, carried the keys with him to the chamber he had chosen for his own use on that side of the Hall, which commanded a view of the boat-house. After watching for an hour without seeing anything, and becoming very sleepy from last night's vigil, he gave up and fell asleep, confident that it was impossible for Astrea to leave the house through all those bolts, which barred her passage to the outer world. But he had scarcely closed the door upon himself, ere she, without any difficulty whatever, succeeded in making her escape by the same route as before until she stood outside of the Hall; but then, instead of going by the way of the river, she glided through the shrubbery and over the meadow lands, walking swiftly all the way until she reached the quarters. In the course of a couple of hours, she had discharged her duties there, and returned safely to her chamber. Mr. Passiver stealing into her room just after midnight, found her fast asleep, and went back to his rest, satisfied of having gained the advantage. But what was his astonishment when morning came, to find that some one had been in his chamber and left its contents in dire confusion. His boots were upon the mantel-piece—his clothes thrown across the foot of the bed, and all the keys which he had left in his cap upon the bureau, laid in a row upon the pillow beside him. He gazed at these evidences of a nocturnal visitor in utter amazement, finally springing from the bed with a furious oath.

"Is the devil in the house, I wonder!" and he tried and found the door fast, as he had left it. There was the key, which he had taken out on retiring with the others upon the pillow, and for any one to have entered by any of the windows was utterly impossible. How, then, could this thing have happened? He had been puzzled before; he was more puzzled now, and furiously enraged into the bargain.

"Before this day closes I will ferret out this mystery, or it shall go hard with me!" he swore as he slammed the door behind him, and stalked down stairs. He began by entering Astrea's room and confronting her with a resolute face.

"I want you to tell me by what means you entered my chamber last night and played the dickens with my things?"

"I have not been near you, Frederic," she replied with unfeigned surprise, while his glance seemed to transfix her with its sharp scrutiny. "What do you mean?"

"Just what I say. I occupied the pink chamber last night, and after entering it, locked the door and took out the key. During the night some one came in and moved everything from its proper place, and I am determined to find out who did it. Will you swear that it was not you who played such tricks upon me?"

"I give you my word of honor that I did not, and know nothing about it. I am just as ignorant as you are."

"By heavens! It is strange," he cried, stamping upon the floor. "I know you are telling the truth, for I could detect a lie instantly. Besides you would glory in making me know that you had outwitted me. Could it have been any of the servants?"

"Scarcely, since negroes are afraid of their own shadows at night, I cannot imagine any of them engaged in anything so daring."

"But some one does it! The question is, *who* dares to play such pranks? Last night I saw some one come up from the boat-house and disappear around the hall; but though I followed quickly I could discover nothing afterwards. Now this other confirms me in the practice of some deviltry upon the premises, and I intend to find out what it means."

"I am sure I hope you may," she answered candidly, for she was herself greatly at fault, having no idea who the perpetrator of such practical jokes could be.

The search began immediately after breakfast and continued through the day. Every servant was closely examined, and as a natural consequence, frightened half to death. It belongs to the race to see evidences of the other world in everything mysterious, and the excitement at Passiver Hall when it became known what had occurred, exceeded all bounds. The young master indulged in some very harsh threats in order to preserve any degree of quiet in the premises. It was unfortunate for the success of Astrea's plans, that such an excitement should have arisen just then, as it opened the eyes of every creature upon the place to exceeding watchfulness, and compelled her to forego her visits to the quarters. Mr. Passiver after having locked all the doors, armed with a revolver, took it upon himself to patrol the house that nothing might leave or approach it unseen. In this way the first night passed without the recurrence of any startling event. On the second, the mysterious confusion was deepened tenfold, the articles of nearly every room in the house, having been transferred from their proper places, and carried all over the building. Astrea was bewildered, Mr. Passiver furious, while the negroes in their affright, did not dare to speak save in mysterious whispers and stifled undertones. And, as if to deepen the fearful impression these events had made upon their minds, Nettie came in from a long walk with Lily, and after making them promise under the most solemn pledges of good faith, not to tell their mistress, imparted the information that Uncle Jacob had died the night previous, which fact accounted for the strange things which had lately been going on at the Hall.

"First, it was old Roger; then Kate and her baby; now Uncle Jake. No wonder the old Nick had come up to the yeth to see after his own."

Nettie always spoke with the broadest negro dialect in speaking to the other servants; but with her mistress, or cultivated people, she usually expressed herself with a purity rarely found in that class to which she belonged.

"Don't ye 'spose missis knows it?" asked the cook from the midst of the group gathered around the girl, upon whose words they hung breathlessly.

"Knows what?"

"Dat Uncle Jake's done dead!"

"No, an' she mustn't know it, 'cause it would just kill her. She know'd well 'nuff marster'd whipped him nearly to def, and dey had a' awful quarrel. Ever sence that, he locks her up every night and puts de keys in his pocket to keep her from goin' out. I tell ye all dese drea'ful things is a judgment on him, fur it's his doin's dat's kill'd mor'n one nigger on dis plantation. Look out dat ye keep yer mouths shet, or some o' you'll go next."

They did not need this warning, but the cunning Nettie thought it quite as well to throw it in to complete the effect, as she took Lily in her arms and left the kitchen to seek her young mistress. She found her alone in her boudoir, deeply pondering over what had transpired. As Nettie came in, she looked up with a sigh, dreading to hear the news she might have to communicate.

"Well, Nettie, have you been to the fields?" she asked, as the girl hesitated.

"Yes, missis."

"What did you learn?"

"Uncle Jake's dead," with a glance of well assumed fear all around her.

"Dead! another one gone!" groaned Astrea, despairingly. "Oh, where will this end?"

"Don't talk so loud, missis; marster might hear you! If he's to find out I'd been thar, he'd skin me alive. I 'spect he hates me now, and only wants to git a chance to take my head off."

"Why do you think so?"

"'Cause he allers looks at me's if he wanted to knock me down. If it wasn't for Miss Lily, I'd ruther go to the fields any day, and take my chances with Ormand."

"Hush, Nettie; you are becoming disrespectful, and must be more careful. Only try to do what is right, and I will endeavor to take care of you."

"Missis means to do all she says, but she couldn't save old Jake or any o' them down at the quarters," answered the girl, slyly glancing at her mistress from beneath her long lashes. Nettie was a pretty, bright mulatto girl, entirely fearless, and loving nothing on earth so well as to get into some mischief that could set everybody in a stew, until she had been appointed to wait on Astrea, when the exchange of servants was made. Then she became very devoted to her lovely young mistress, and at her own request, was allowed to take charge of Lily when she came into the world. For either of these, she would have risked her life; but woe to those whom she might learn to hate. She might not dare openly to revenge herself, but to the secret torments which she devised there was no end. The moment after she had made the answer recorded above, she repented sincerely, seeing the pain it occasioned. Poor Astrea fell upon her knees and burst into tears.

"I know it, oh, I know it, but what can I do!" she groaned, with her head bowed upon a chair. "Nettie, if I could die in their stead, I would gladly give up my life to save theirs; but you must bear witness of all the good intentions which I strive vainly to carry out. Don't let the poor, crushed sufferers learn to hate me. If anything happens that I cannot go to them in their troubles, you must manage to tell them how it is. I am almost in despair."

"Oh, missis, get up quick! Marster's comin'!" cried the girl in alarm, hearing a step in the hall, and Astrea rose to her feet as he entered. The traces of tears caught his attention at once.

"What's happened now?" he demanded roughly.

"Not much," she replied with bitter sarcasm; "it is nothing of any consequence at all, I suppose, if another of my negroes died last night from the effects of the beating you gave him the other day!"

"Who says that he is dead?"

"It does not matter; I know it, and that is quite enough."

"Did you tell her?" turning furiously to Nettie, who shrank back in alarm.

"How'd marster 'spose I know'd it?" she faltered.

"It was you who brought tales to her before. Jake told you about Kate, and you told your mistress. Now look here, my girl; I will let you off this time, but if I ever hear of your carrying tales again between the Hall and the quarters to anybody, I'll give you fifty lashes! Mind that you don' forget this."

"Yes, marster."

She crept humbly from the room, but the moment she was out of sight, lifted her clenched hand and shook it spitefully.

"I'll not forgit—never think it! I'll not forgit, young marster! So, you look out, y'll catch it wuss'n I will. Some night the devil hisself'll come fur one o' his imps! Mind, I tell ye!"

Unconscious of these threats against his welfare, Mr. Passiver threw himself moodily into a chair before his wife.

"I cannot find out a thing that can help me to solve this infernal mystery! If you have the slightest idea, you had better give me the benefit of it, or something awful may happen. I am resolved to shoot the first person I see prowling round inside of this house, or outside of it, after ten o'clock. This shall not go on any longer."

"I assure you that I cannot tell you. If I had possessed the power to open the doors which you took such pains to fasten last night, I could affirm upon oath with perfect truth, that I did not do it. How, then, can you suppose that I know anything about it?"

"I don't suppose you do," came reluctantly from his lips. "It is impossible!" springing up with an impulse that sent his chair tumbling upon the carpet. "But, by the Lord Harry, somebody does know, and I want to find out who it is. This thing is driving me mad!"

"Abandon your attempts to solve the mystery, and let things take their course. The culprit will betray himself after awhile."

"Yes, abandon it, and get strangled in my bed! No, I'm not such a fool!"

"As you please; I only made the suggestion," she answered indifferently.

"You would not care if I should be found dead some morning, I dare say," he said angrily.

"Perhaps you judge me by yourself."

"I judge you by your actions. No wife who loves her husband, will do as you have done and are doing."

"Very likely."

"Then I am to understand that you do not love me?"

"Certainly."

"A beautiful confession, truly!"

"It cannot affect you, since you care neither for my love or hate. You only want to be my 'master!' I object to the last, and do not intend to own you as such, though you may lock me up, starve or even beat me. That man is my master who makes me respect him, and you cannot do that."

It was her turn now to be cool, while he literally foamed with passion.

"If you value your life, take care!" he gasped, catching her arm and shaking her with violence. I'll crush you into atoms before I'll submit to being brow-beaten by a woman, and that woman, my wife."

She grew more cool as he became more enraged, and preserved the most stolid calmness.

"Crush me if you like; resist I always will—if not in action, in spirit. But if you fail to finish your work, and keep me in torture, I will leave your house forever. This cannot last always."

"Dare to try it! I would track you to the ends of the earth, if you dared to leave my doors; and then all purgatory could not devise a punishment like that which should be yours. You may give me untold trouble in my own house, but you shall never disgrace me—make my name the theme for gossip through all Alabama, by deserting me."

"Better that than to be hung for murder," she answered quietly. "I feel assured if I do not go, you will kill me yet."

"If I do, it will be so well done, the sharpest detective in Christendom would fail to fasten proofs upon me. I am not a bungler, rest assured."

"O, I beg your pardon! Perhaps practice has perfected

you in this delicate work. I forgot that you were not a novice in taking life, without laying yourself open to the just punishment of your crimes."

"Repeat those words, and I will knock you down."

"If you choose to be a coward as well as a murderer and a tyrant, strike! No one but a coward would strike a woman."

She stood with her calm, fair brow uplifted, and in his brutal passion, he brought his hand down heavily upon it. She sank at his feet without a moan.

"My God! I *have* killed her!" he gasped, as the mists cleared away from his eyes and reason began to return to him. In an agony of alarm, he snatched her up in his arms and carried her to a sofa, where he laid her hastily down and began to dash water in her face.

Several minutes passed without a sign of returning life, and, as if to complicate confusing affairs at that moment, Doctor Early was announced. Frederic Passiver ground his teeth with rage as the old gentleman advanced into the room with the air of one who had no need to wait for an assurance of being welcome. But the moment his eyes fell upon Astrea's pale, motionless features, his whole expression changed to one of alarm and distrust.

"What is this?" he asked quickly, coming to her side, and the man's ready instinct for self-preservation prompted a falsehood without stopping to consider.

"My wife has met with a serious accident, I fear, and has fainted with the pain. She stumbled and fell, striking her forehead in her fall."

"Were you in the room when it happened?"

"Yes, standing near her. Pray see what extent of injury she has received."

His face was pale and anxious enough to have won pity from any other than Doctor Early, who made no reply while he examined his patient. Suddenly he put out his hand and caught Mr. Passiver's, saying passionately:

"I knew it, sir! I knew it! Look at that hand, and then

dare to say that you did not strike her with it! Oh, man! what are you made of, that you can find it in your heart to abuse a woman like this? A blessing for her if she never wakes again, and a blessing for the country, since it will rid us of so desperate a character by treating you to a dance in the air!"

"Hold! Doctor Early; no more of this, or you may be made to repent it in a manner you do not expect. This hurt to my hand was purely accidental, and in my affright at her fall, I did not even know that I had hurt myself until you called my attention to it this moment. If my poor wife recovers, she will bear me out in my denial of so brutal a deed. When that happens, I will deal with you as you deserve, but now for God's sake, attend to her."

Doctor Early was staggered. Had he been too hasty, after all? Frederic Passiver's proud, resentful air, mingled with that anxious, and at the same time assured expression, made him waver in his opinion. A few moment's application of restoratives brought her back to consciousness, her senses returning very slowly. When her eyes opened upon the two anxious faces bending over her, she gave one moan and closed them again with a shudder.

"Why did he strike you?" asked the Doctor in her ear. She did not move, and both gentlemen waited breathlessly for her reply.

"Who said he struck me?"

Mr. Passiver's eyes blazed with triumph.

"I said so."

Her white lips moved with difficulty.

"You are hasty, Doctor; I fell."

Loyal woman! This after such an indignity, to spare him from the public exposure of so brutal an act. Had the heart of the man been human, he must have loved her for that one brave and unselfish defence, but he thought only of himself, and drew up his fine figure haughtily.

"I am ready to accept your apology sir, or to settle the

matter with you elsewhere, and in a different way," he said coldly.

"If I have wronged you, Mr. Passiver, I am exceedingly sorry, and beg your pardon in all sincerity," answered the old man with a huskiness of voice which betrayed deep emotion. The excitement of the moment had nearly unnerved him, and Astrea's deathly features did the rest. He turned his head aside to conceal the large tears which ran down his cheeks as the young planter bowed his haughty acceptance of the apology, and crossed the room. In answer to the Doctor's ring, a servant came, and was ordered to assist her mistress to bed.

"No, no, I will not lie down except on this sofa," said Astrea rousing. "Please let me be quiet for awhile; that is all I need."

"As you like, my child; but you must not talk. Can you sleep?"

"I think not. Where is Mr. Passiver?"

"At the window. Do you want him?"

"No, I only asked. How did you happen to come here, Doctor?"

"I was passing and thought I would stop a moment, which was quite lucky, for you had just met with this accident. As soon as you feel a little better, I must leave you again."

"It is scarcely worth while to detain you, I think," she answered with an effort. It was so hard to bear his presence, with the fear she had of betraying what she desired to conceal from him. He saw that she preferred to have him depart, and rose at once.

"Then I will say good-bye now, and call as I return, if I have time."

Mr. Passiver followed him to the door.

"Do not trouble yourself to come again," he said in a low voice, "we can dispense with your services in future."

The Doctor bowed, and went slowly out into the hall.

"Recall your words, or apologize for them, else you may be sorry for what you have done."

Mr. Passiver turned and saw Astrea at his side, her eyes flashing with a sudden passion. His eyes questioned her.

"Yes, I will expose you," answering his glances as if he had spoken. "Deprive me of my only friend, and I shall not strive to shield you from the consequences of your actions."

He knew that he did not dare to trifle with her then, and hastened after the Doctor. The manner with which he approached him, was ingenuously frank and engaging.

"It is my turn to apologize now, Doctor Early. I have followed to beg you to forget my hasty words, and to come again as usual, when needed, or socially. You must acknowledge that the accusation you made, at a moment when I was in an agony of distress over the accident which threatened to deprive me of my wife, was a hard thing to bear—especially for a man of my naturally resentful temperament."

"I frankly own that it was hard. When a man has apologized for a wrong, however, I do not well see how he could do more, I am willing to make any reparation in my power."

"Let it pass then, and we will try to forget it, you will not allow what I said to keep you away from us?"

"No, for Mrs. Passiver's sake I will not."

Both gentlemen bowed with stiff formality, and the Doctor rode away. Mr. Passiver looked after him with clenched hands, and teeth set hard.

"My turn will come sooner or later, and I shall have full pay for all this, my old friend! When I yield to mortal man, it is that my final revenge may be sweeter. Never yet have I been forced to record a failure, and in your case success will be doubly sweet."

When he returned to the Hall, Astrea was lying upon the sofa again, looking very faint, with her face turned from him as he entered. He brought a chair and sat down near her, his mood being relentless in its will to torture.

"Well, madam, I hope you have learned by this time, that it is dangerous to brave me with impunity. You have only yourself to blame for what has passed here to-day, and it will be your fault if it is repeated in the future. Let this lessor suffice; it will not be pleasant to me to have a frequent recurrence of the same scenes. I am disposed to be kind and peaceable in my nature, and only demand obedience. Give me that without question or hesitation and this will never happen again."

"It never will happen again."

"Very good; I thought you'd come round at last. Pray why did you tell Doctor Early that you—fell?"

"I did fall—after you struck me. The reason I chose to conceal the truth from him, was because I knew that my self-respect would force me to leave you the moment a knowledge of such abuse went beyond our own doors; and I have reasons for preferring to remain at present."

"What are they?"

"I must be excused for withholding them now. Time will show."

"So! you are not conquered yet! All right, my lady; you will find me more than a match for your stubborn will. After all, I don't know but I prefer to have you keep it up as long as you can. It will afford me infinite amusement, and quite a triumph in the end, to have tamed such a shrew. The spice of life consists in the breaking down of barriers which impede the will of man."

She was silent.

"You have chosen to place yourself in my way with a stubborn resolution which really does you credit," he went on coolly, "seeing that you are only a woman. Women are usually very weak and inconsistent, and will give way with the first slight scratch they receive in a contest. You are spunky, and can stand pain; but you have very false ideas. Now, those niggers you make such a fuss about! There is no earthly use in it. Ninety-nine men out of every hundred will tell you that it is a real advantage to get rid of those old and useless ones, who are only an incumbrance to the estate. There are heavy taxes to pay upon them, while they cannot earn their board, and are only fit to hobble around and spread dissatisfaction among the others by their complaints and misrepresentations. The sooner they 'go home,' the better; and where such events as that affair with Kate, occur, the result serves to set an example to others that is very salutary in its effect. To be sure, one does not like to lose a valuable woman like that, but then an occasional loss in that way is absolutely necessary."

He might as well have talked to a stone for all the sign she gave. She lay motionless as marble, with closed eyes, but with an anguish of heart that she strove with all her soul to conceal from his sight. Seeing that he failed to make any startling impression upon her, and growing weary of argument without opposition, he rose and left the room.

CHAPTER XXII.

FLIGHT OF "GOODS AND CHATTELS."

After this last event, which served not only to excite the secret fears of the young planter, but to threaten his reputation, and fasten odium upon him, matters went on rather more peacefully at Passiver Hall. Astrea fell into a fever which lasted for some days, rendering a daily visit from her physician necessary until it was broken, and she began to recover. During this time, without directly questioning her upon the subject, he endeavored to ascertain whether his accusation had been really true, as he suspected, in spite of denials; but she invariably parried his attempts either to trap her into a confession or to win her confidence on that one point. She would not betray him.

Passiver Hall, during this time, was very quiet. The ghostly demonstrations which had perplexed all and frightened many, ceased to disturb them, and a stranger might easily have imagined this the most peaceful and luxurious home in the South, judging by its appearance. But the master was ill at ease with all his assurance, and the mistress lay thinking, day after day, of her people, and grieving over their wrongs while her hands were powerless. She thought of what had passed with a heavy heart; of the present with many doubts; of the future with fear.

"Oh, Doctor," she said one day while speaking upon the subject with him, "when I think of all that ought to be done, I feel so small and weak, it fills me with despair. It is like attempting to overturn the world, for one woman to put her small strength against so mighty an evil as this evil of slavery. I stand alone in my views, and might preach against wrong and oppression till my breath was spent, without making one good impression. They will laugh at me, who hear, if they do not angrily call me a fool; and if you should ask them why slavery is a divine right and an absolute necessity, they will coolly ask in return, if it is necessary to eat, or to breathe, in order to live. When it comes to such unreasoning tenacity as this, what can we do?"

"What would you do with your own slaves, if you had the ability to act just as you pleased with them?"

"Free every one," she answered quickly; "and if any loved me sufficiently to desire a home with me still, they might stay, and I would pay them fair wages for their time and labor. Those who preferred to go, should be provided with homes wherever they chose to live. I would give them houses in which to dwell; lands to cultivate, and implements to work them. They should then have schools and churches of their own, and the opportunity for becoming reasoning, self-dependent beings. The poor creatures have no privileges, let those who will, make assertions to the contrary. A negro cannot hold property; he cannot vote; he is not allowed even to read and write, there being rigid laws against it. For him ties are but names, without meaning, save in his own poor, tortured heart. Marriage is but a farce, the proceeds of which go to swell the size of the master's purse. Wife and children are torn from him as mercilessly as you would separate animals. He cannot call the blood which courses in his veins his own, much less that which flows in the veins of his children. It is subject to the will of any cruel monster who may choose to let it, until the wretched victim faints from its loss, and perhaps, even dies!"

"How is it that you are so bitterly opposed to slavery, owning slaves, and reared from infancy in the midst of them?" asked Doctor Early with much curiosity. "Mr. Harmon certainly never taught you to view it in such a light; and if there are others in this country who do, I am ignorant of it. Among the young especially, the love of power is so great, none will stop to question whether it be right or wrong. Slavery is the foundation of family pride, and a man's pretensions to aristocracy are regulated according to the number of negroes he owns."

Mrs. Passiver's hands shaded her eyes, but her full lip curled.

"Yes, we have, indeed, fallen so low! It is the natural result, however, of such deeds as ours. We send our vessels to a distant shore, and steal the people from their native lands to bear them here in spite of cries and prayers and groans, that we may lay our burthens upon their shoulders. We cry that their ignorance renders this bondage a blessing to them, by giving them the light of divine truth. But when we teach them of God, we take greater care to teach them the necessity of obedience to men, who have constituted themselves their masters. Every word that seems to justify the master, falls glibly upon the ear of the man; but not that his soul may be benefited by it—only as a rein of power by which he may be driven with more ease in his chains. If we so much desired to enlighten the African race to God's beautiful truths, why did we not send to them faithful ministers, as we have to Burmah and other places, instead of countenancing that fearful trade which has entailed a deadly curse upon us! You will say that we have sent missionaries to Africa, and that the slave-trade has been suspended, but these come too late to save us from the consequences. Already we are beginning openly and excitably to talk of State rights, with secession in view, and the result will be a deep and deadly plunge into civil war."

"You really think that we shall have war? Why?"

"I cannot tell precisely; but you know that woman's instinct is sometimes better than man's judgment. Our hot-blooded southern politicians have begun the work of spreading dissatisfaction throughout the country, and are constituting themselves leaders in the contemplated faction. A conflict is inevitable, and whatever we may think, we are not strong enough to win. Secession would be wrong, and will not be tolerated."

"I advise you not to talk this way to everybody," said the Doctor gravely. "If your predictions *should* be realized, it might go rather hard with you, unless I have mistaken your character. With your present views, if you make them known, and any subsequent actions which might be construed against you, the day may come when you may know what it will cost to declare yourself independent."

Astrea searched his face earnestly.

"Then there is more than even I imagined, afloat. Tell me frankly, Doctor Early, just what our people are doing."

"No, my child, I will make no predictions, and take no steps to spread the evil. Time will develop purposes fast enough, and I am too old to embroil myself in such difficulties. As for you, there is plenty now in this little heart and brain to wear you out, without any addition. Be quiet, and if the time comes when it is necessary to take a position on either side, choose the one which you conscientiously believe to be right, and give all your strength to the maintenance of your choice. Of course you know your husband's views?"

"Mr. Passiver avoids speaking to me on these subjects, and will not do it in my presence, if he can help it. Still I know perfectly well what his course would be," and she sighed heavily.

Several conversations similar to the above, took place during her illness; but when Doctor Early ceased to come, though she thought much upon the subject, no word ever passed her lips that could indicate the presence of an idea concerning the political events of the times. In a few days she was able to drive out, and then as she felt herself becoming stronger, began to think about resuming her visits to the quarters, when another startling incident occurred to completely cut her off from her designs. She was sitting by her window in the mellow moonlight, gazing at the long, narrow stretch of meadow lands below, when her glance fell upon a figure which advanced slowly, stooping and dodging with every indication of fear. The figure followed the course of a little winding brook until it crossed the road leading to Florence, then left it, and came directly to the gate which it opened, and closed carefully. The nearer approach proved it to be the figure of a man, and he came up the graveled walk, turned abruptly into the shrubbery, and made his way to her window, pausing beneath it. Astrea's heart beat wildly. What was coming next to torment her? Evidently something unusual had happened, and she dreaded to hear it.

"Missis," called a voice softly, "oh, missis." She threw the window open with as little noise as possible.

"Who is there?"

"It's me—Rufe, ye knows Rufus, missis?"

"My poor boy, what brings you here?"

"Ise come to say good-bye before I goes away," and his voice was husky.

"Going away, Rufus! you cannot! you dare not! Oh, boy, they would kill you! Don't make the attempt."

"Must do it, missis. Ise stood all I can stand, an' I jes' as soon die tryin' ter sabe myself, as ter be beat ter def by inches. Dey's done swor'd ter whip me to-morrer, an' I aint goin' ter take it, 'cause I don't 'serve it."

"What did you do that made them threaten you?"

"Massa Ormand, he found me cryin', an' wanted to know what's de matter wid me. I couldn't help it missis, fur it was de trufe, an' I telled him 'twas about Katy who's done dead, an' my heart's broke. Den he went into a' awful rage, an' swor'd he'd skin me alive. Massa, he's down dar now, an' I saw 'em dribe a great big stake in de groun' whar dey said dey's goin' ter tie up all de bad niggahs for ter whip 'em, an' de fus chance I got, I slipped off ter say good-bye ter my dear missis. I mus' go now, 'fore he comes home."

"Rufus."

The moon streamed upon the beautiful, resolute face of his young mistress as she leaned from the window.

"Well, missis?"

"You are sure you are telling me the truth?"

"Berry shure."

"Then come around to the north side of the house and hide yourself in the shrubbery there until you hear the cellar door open. I intend to hide you in the house until I can get a chance to send you North. If I let you go, they will catch you and bring you back again—then God help you, for I could not!"

"But missis 'll git inter trouble."

"Never mind, I can take care of myself. Do as I tell you."

"I will, Miss 'Genia."

He crept softly away, and she closed the window, thankful that he had gone before any one discovered him in conversation with her. It was not late, and the servants had not been long enough in bed to have fallen asleep, but with the necessity of immediate action before her, she dared not wait, lest Mr. Passiver should return and discover the fugitive. He had not omitted the now usual ceremony of locking her doors before going out, yet that did not disturb her. With the key that never left her possession, she swiftly passed through all the rooms, pausing only to look through the gallery window, if perchance her husband might be returning. No sign being visible, she stole through the hall into the kitchen, and through that to the cellar below, which she soon opened and admitted Rufus.

"You must sit here in one corner, perfectly still, until I come for you," she whispered as she put out her little hand to guide the trembling fugitive to his place. "Trust me, Rufus, and if it is in mortal power to save you, I will do it."

"God bless ye, missis!"

"I hope he will," she answered in an unsteady voice, as she withdrew her hand and groped her way back to the stairs. "I hope he will bless me in allowing me to free at least one soul from bondage," she added mentally, as she mounted the stairs. In a few moments she had safely regained her own room, and threw herself upon the bed to think, and plan what ought to be done next. The most feasible plan, seemed to center upon the attic for a hiding-place at present. Having determined upon that, she immediately stole forth to carry such food as he might need, and some blankets to make him a bed. While the search was being made, which was certain, as soon as it was known he was gone, she might find time to make the supply more liberal. Carefully keeping watch of the river for her husband, she made several journeys to the attic, and succeeded in conveying everything that was necessary. By the time he came back, she had made all her arrangements, and was snugly ensconced in bed. He did not pause to enter, but after listening for a moment at the door, went up stairs with a weary tread unusual to him. She only gave him time to retire, when she stole from her room and with a wax taper to guide them, that he might not stumble in the darkness over strange objects, descended to the cellar and brought Rufus up by the back stairway to the attic. Thrusting him into it, she bade him keep still, whatever happened, and never fear; then leaving him the taper, locked the small door and hastened back to her own room.

If Astrea had known anxiety before, it was doubled now, when she had taken such a responsibility into her own hands. Thinking over it, kept her awake until the dawn of day. Then she fell into a troubled slumber, from which she was awakened by a fearful scream, proceeding from the room directly above her own, and followed by a great confusion all over the house. Her first thought was of Rufus, and that he had in some way betrayed himself; but she had locked the door upon him, and charged him earnestly to remain quiet. Surely he could not have become frightened and disobeyed her. Had her door been opened she would have rushed out to ascertain the cause of the alarm, but she had presence of mind sufficient to restrain her from the use of her key, which would have exposed her at once. The half hour which succeeded before any one came near, seemed an age of suspense. Finally Mr. Passiver burst into the room, foaming with passion.

"I will know—I *will!* what has got into this house to turn it upside down with its deviltries! What! am I to be defied under my own roof, and subjected to all sorts of tricks? Look at my hair, madam! just look at my hair, and see the shocking condition it is in! Every lock of it will have to be shaved off close to my head, before this infernal wax can be got out of it! Shoe-makers' wax—all through! And that is not all; when I woke this morning, there I was, tied hand and foot, fast to the bedstead, with strong ropes, and could not get loose until they came and untied me! Now, tell me who it is that dares to brave me in this manner! Woe be unto that fool-hardy mortal if I find out who it is, for life will not be worth a straw!—and know I will, by Heaven!"

"How is it possible for any body to tie you without waking you in the operation?" asked Mrs. Passiver, relieved in finding that Rufus had not been discovered. She had great ado to keep from laughing, as her husband stamped up and down the floor with his hair sticking out all over his head like the quills of a fretful porcupine. Necessity forced her to control her amusement, and assume the gravity she really felt in a considerable measure. She was as curious as he, to know who the real perpetrator could be, and was not easy in knowing that such things were constantly occurring in the house, without the slightest clue being left behind by which the mystery might be solved. Her questions seemed only to deepen his exasperation, and a stool which happened to come in his way at that moment, went flying across the room with a crash.

"How? Go up there and you will soon understand! The whole chamber is charged with the odor of ether! That's the way I am treated! The infernal thieves steal into my room, by what means the devil only knows; and then they dose me with ether while sleeping, and leave me tied fast to my bed. Furies! won't I have my revenge sometime!"

He ground his teeth impotently, at the same time attempting to thrust his fingers through his hair. Failing, from the state into which it had been rendered by the wax, he could endure no more, and rushed out of the room with a perfect volley of oaths. In hastily descending the steps, he ran against Ormand, who was coming up from the fields with an anxious countenance. The young planter recovered himself, and demanded the reason for his presence very angrily. Bad, and hardy as the man was, he quailed before the flashing eyes and passion-inflamed visage of his master, dreading to impart the news he came to bring.

"Why don't you speak, and not stand there staring at me as if I was a ghost? What do you want here this time in the morning."

"I came to say that one of the boys had cut sticks an' left."

"You don't mean to say that he has run away?"

"Yes, sir, that an' nothing else."

"Now, by the Lord Harry, things *have* come to a pretty pass! One of *my* slaves gone! We'll fetch him back quicker than lightning, and then make an example of him. Which one is it?"

"Rufus."

"That rascal? Whew! went to escape a thrashing. Aha! my fine fellow! we'll see how far you will get before we come down on you! When did he go, Ormand?"

"Last night, I reckon."

"Have you made any search for tracks?"

"Yes, sir. I missed him when the horn sounded fur the hands to come out, an' as soon as the others was set to work, I began to hunt fur signs. All I could find was some tracks on the banks of the river, an' if he swum acrost, he must be hid in the woods over thar; but I took a skiff an' went over, an' couldn't find no tracks thar."

"He must be there, however; he could not swim far, and that seems the most likely hiding-place he could find. We will try ourselves, to-day, and if we fail to find him, will get some help to-morrow—and such help as can't fail."

"D' ye mean dogs?"

"Yes."

The man's eyes glistened with a brutal delight.

"That's the talk, but I didn't 'spose you'd want to use dogs."

"Why not? Every other planter in the South will use them when it comes to a pinch—why should not I? Things seem to be culminating, and there will be a grand explosion pretty soon. I can't stand it, and I'll show everybody that I am master at Passiver Hall, and on the Passiver estate."

"Hope nothin' else hain't gone wrong, sir," began the overseer deprecatingly; "leastways, if it has, I hain't been to blame."

"When I accuse you, it will be high time to deny. You had better go back to the fields now, and make preparations to begin the search. In the course of an hour I will join you."

Mr. Ormand was obliged to obey, and went doggedly back to the fields. His master's anger and curtness had given him a very uneasy sensation with regard to his own welfare, and he knew that he would not dare to trifle with him. At the same time, he was averse, as bullies usually are, to having any man talk to him with such an air of authoritative independence, and for some time, Mr. Passiver had shown an utter carelessness of his feelings which galled him sorely. If he could not retaliate openly, he could at least give him some trouble, and he resolved to do it. While he was sulkily plodding his way to the quarters, Mr. Passiver returned to his wife triumphantly. The last event had exceeded the night's adventure, in importance, and he began to grow cooler over the prospect of tangible satisfaction.

"So, one of your boys has taken it into his head to run away! How do you like that and the prospect of seeing him flogged as an example?"

"I would not witness such a thing."

"I intend that you shall, so that you may see the need of teaching them sounder doctrines in the future."

"He will have to be caught first."

"That will be easy enough. If we do not find him to-day, we'll try the blood-hounds on him to-morrow, and see if they won't bring him to light. I'll hunt the whole State of Alabama but I'll ferret the rascal out at last."

"In the meantime, what do you propose to do about these mysterious nocturnal visits?"

"I will let that matter stand over for the present, as it may take some time to get at the bottom of it. The first and foremost thing to be done, is to find Rufus—after that every other perplexing thing *shall be* made straight."

What to do now, was more than she could divine; our heroine was in a straight, with no apparent means for escape. A search through the house for the cause of the disturbances would have been disastrous to her schemes, and place the poor fugitive within the power of the destroyers. That immediate danger having been averted, the one which was to follow was equally, if not more terrible. No power on earth could save him if the blood-hounds were put upon his track, and to have those creatures rushing through her house, tearing the boy to pieces before her very eyes, would be horrible! How could she save him? Get him away she *must*, but how?

Mr. Passiver had breakfasted hastily and departed, leaving her in an agony which surpassed words. She walked back and forth through the rooms with an intensity of feeling almost akin to despair, as no chance of escape seemed to present itself. She might get him out of the attic, but where could she send him that they could not follow? She was in danger of exposure herself, but she cared little for that. They would trace him beneath her window, then to the cellar and up stairs; and it would be difficult, if she tried, to convince her husband that she had not done it. She could not convince him, for the same dogs, if put on her trail would trace her to her room, and fasten with their panting breath, proofs of her deeds upon her.

In the midst of her reflections, Doctor Early stepped in upon his patient, and found her pacing the room like a caged lioness. Instantly she resolved to confide in him, and ask for help in her difficulty. He listened while she rapidly recounted the events of the past night, wearing a very troubled expression.

"Oh, my child, you are rash indeed," he expostulated when she had finished. "Now it will be impossible for you to conceal your mode of exit from the house, and at the same time, you have lain yourself open to greater abuses than those which you have been made to suffer already. You ought to have sent him back, and told him to bear his lot patiently."

"Doctor, you cannot mean it! Send him back to be flayed, as old Jacob was, because God has created him with loyal blood in his veins—because he dared to love his poor wife so much, that her loss left him with a hopeless heart-ache! I will die, sooner than see him punished for the tears he shed. It is cruel, inhuman! and I will save him if it is in mortal power!"

"I trust that you may be able to do it. Yes, I will even help you, if I can, though you know the risks I run. If I fail, it will ruin me throughout the whole country, and I shall have to leave it. I am not rich, and depend upon my practice for a living. If I was a young man, it would make little difference; as it is, the matter becomes serious."

Mrs. Passiver wrung her hands.

"I know it, but what shall I do! There is no one to help me if you do not, and life is at stake! God help me, but I know there is no hope if they get hold of him! Too much blood has been spilled already for me to feel in the least safe. Doctor, I cannot let him be taken. Help me, and as long as I have a penny upon earth, you shall not want."

"I will help you, my child, without money. There must be no pecuniary interests mentioned between us, or the sanctity of our deeds is destroyed forever. No, come what will, I can bear the consequences of my own actions, and I choose to help you in your dilemma. Perhaps you will need a shelter for yourself ere the matter ends, for he will find out that you have aided in the boy's escape."

"Yes, I do not expect to be able to conceal that; it will not make much difference, though, when once he is safe. I could brave a whole army, then, and never fear for myself."

"Why, because you have always escaped without hurt?"

Astrea blushed crimson.

"Ah, my child, why try to deceive me so persistently? I know too much not to see that you are striving to hide the truth."

"I did tell you the truth, Doctor Early."

"The whole truth? No, you will not say that! You fell when he struck you, and then refused to expose him. I admire your loyalty, but at the same time, you need a friend, and if I am to be that friend, you owe it to me to make me acquainted with all that occurs in which you are personally interested. If your father was here, I should make no such demands upon your confidence, and leave you to his care; as he is not, I dare not stand aloof and see that man kill you, without lifting a saving arm. When Mr. Harmon returns, he will thank me for it."

"Dear father, so far away while his only child is in such terrible trouble," and her tears began to flow fast. "Still, I am glad," she added, "for it would break his heart."

"Have you never written to him about it?—never told him anything?"

"Not one word, and would not for the world. Time enough when he comes, to crush his gray hairs into the grave by a grief that cannot longer be concealed."

"You are a strange girl—shutting yourself out from everybody, and striving to bear your griefs alone."

"It is my duty, since few could help me, and might only add to my burthen by injudicious uses of my confidence. Better to sacrifice one's self than to crush the innocent, who love us too dearly to know that we suffer without grieving for us. But we must not talk about such things now. How shall we manage with Rufus?"

Doctor Early sat buried in thought for several minutes.

"Do you remember a little creek which crosses the road about a quarter of a mile above here?"

"Yes; it is where I go to fish for trout."

"Well, that empties into the river a little way above the Hall. Can Rufus swim?"

"Rapidly; he is one of the strongest and smartest boys on the place."

"Then if you can manage to get him out of the house to-night without being seen, tell him to swim up the river to the mouth of that creek and enter it without landing, so as to leave no trail for the dogs. The water is not deep, and he can easily wade along the course of the stream until he reaches the road. There he must wait for me without leaving the water, and as I drive along, I will stop in the middle of the creek and take him up in my carriage. He must keep himself well in the shadow of the overhanging boughs until he hears me give a low whistle, then come out, and while I water my horse, get into the carriage. I am going down the river some twelve miles, to see an old woman who has dislocated her leg, and the young sprig of a doctor, who has been attending her, will let her die for want of a little common sense. When I come back I will let it be after dark purposely, so that I may reach the creek about ten o'clock."

"That seems a splendid plan, and now that you have mentioned it, I remember that he followed the bed of the creek last night, and must have thought of the dogs at the time, though I did not. Wait a little while, and I will get a suit of Mr. Passiver's old clothes for you to put in the carriage."

"What for?"

"Rufus; you don't want him to enter it dripping wet. You can take the clothes with you now, and I will tell him to sink his in the river by rolling them around a stone, at the mouth of the creek. He can don the others when safe with you, and they will do him some good. You will need money for him, Doctor, and you must take this to provide for his comfort," she concluded by slipping a well filled purse into his hand.

He did not refuse, since it was not for himself, and put the purse into his pocket, saying:

"If I can use it for him, I will do so; if not, it shall be returned to you."

Soon after this, he drove off down the river, leaving Astrea to the completion of their hazardous plans. Mr. Passiver did not return to dinner, and nothing was heard from the search until tea-time, when he came home with three great, rough fellows, whom Ormand had sent for at his master's command. They were professional negro-hunters, and looked fitted for their calling, with their coarse, ruffianly manners and uncouth faces. Astrea sickened with disgust when summoned to do the honors of her table for such guests, and saw her husband treating them with the politeness due to better men. Had he known her complicity, and desired to punish her for the part she was playing, he could not have done it in a more effectual manner, as he seated them, after having gone through with a formal introduction, and began to talk in his most pleasant and kindly manner.

"My dear, these are the gentlemen of whom you have often heard, and who are the best men in the whole country, since they are the guardians of our highest interests. If anybody can find that ungrateful boy of yours, they certainly will do so, and will, therefore, be entitled to your highest consideration."

She inwardly writhed under this speech, remembering the poor, trembling creature lying above them, unconscious of what was to come. He was totally unprepared, however, for the calm and even smiling face she turned to them, asking the one nearest to her if he did not find his mode of life very exciting.

"Tole'ble," was the answer. "At fust a man feels a good 'eal excited, but he soon gits used to it, an' finds it ruther tiresome. Once'n awhile a smart chap comes along that knows how to dodge purty well, an' then thar's some fun in a chase. Ginerally, howsomever, niggers is very stupid an' can't hold out long. How's that boy a' yourn?"

"Really, I cannot say how he will manage to effect his escape; but I should not be surprised if it were to take you some time to catch him."

At this moment Nettie came in and whispered something in her ear. She rose hastily.

"Excuse me for a moment, gentlemen, my child needs my care," and disappeared within the adjoining room. The moment she closed the door behind her, Nettie caught her arm whispering hurriedly:

"Miss 'Genia, don't be 'fraid, an' don't touch the wine when it comes on the table. I heerd marster order some put in ice, an' I fixed one bottle of it so's to make 'em all sleep good. It won't hurt 'em."

"Nettie, are you crazy, girl! You might kill them!"

"No danger; trust me missis; I know's all 'bout everything, an' I'm bound to keep 'em out o' your way to-night. If I don't, poor Rufe 'll die to-morrer. Now go back, please, an' let 'em do their wust. Tell 'em I got skeer'd an' thought Miss Lily'd swallered a button, if they ask you what's the matter. I did think so awhile ago, but she hadn't."

Mrs. Passiver returned to the tea-table, looking a little flushed.

"Pray, what was the matter, my love?" asked Mr. Passiver, anxiously.

"Only a fright of Nettie's. She says she thought Lillian had swallowed a button, but was mistaken."

"Niggers does love to git up a row," remarked one of the guests who had not before spoken. "They're allers seein' things whar they aint to be seen, an' makin' the biggest mountains out'n the littlest mole-hills. I git so cussed, all-fired mad at 'em sometimes, I could knock thar tarnel heads off."

Even Mr. Passiver winced at this speech, glancing furtively at his wife who answered in a very quiet manner:

"I believe it belongs to the race to magnify everything into importance, because of their enthusiastic and imaginative temperaments. They love excitement because it is a relief to the severe monotony of their lives. They have not the constant changes and interests of the whites, who can find enough of change in the world without seeking to magnify events."

Her guests sat staring at her in unfeigned wonder to hear her using what appeared to them, "big words," many of which were Greek to them. The timely entrance of a boy with the wine, covered the smile which she could not quite suppress, and gave her an excuse for leaving the table. They remained talking and drinking for some time, and Nettie who was hovering round, peeping occasionally through the doors, saw that Mr. Passiver filled his own glass more than once, from the important bottle, while he urged the others frequently to drink, until it was empty. It was not his habit to drink much wine, and she knew it, at the same time guessing with a shrewdness for which no one would have given her credit, that his excitement, weariness, and desire to please his tools by appearing to stand more upon an equal footing with them, would prove a sufficiently reasonable excuse for an unusual indulgence. To Astrea's infinite relief, they were ready to retire very soon after tea, and were soon by the watchful Nettie reported asleep, under the effects of the drugged wine. Had she been less anxious on the fugitive's account, it would have been impossible to have tolerated a thing of this kind in her house, and planned by her own servant. The case was an extreme one, however, and required extreme measures, which she was forced to accept for the present without questioning. Taking advantage of Nettie's stratagem, she hastily brought Rufus from the attic by way of the rear entrance to the hall, and gave him instructions how to act. Fortunately the moon had not yet risen, and by the dim starlight it was impossible to discover who they were, had any one seen them as they stood on the lower steps of the flight in the moment of parting. They did not dare to speak aloud, but her tears fell fast upon his head as he seized her hand and pressed it to his quivering lips in a mute farewell.

"God bless you, Rufus," she said stooping to his ear. "Put

your trust in Him, and never forget to do right. Sometime we may meet again on earth—if not—the Heavens are open to those who choose to enter."

"We's shure to meet dar," was the low, husky reply. "Oh, missis, I hopes no trouble 'll come to you, an' I'll pray fur ye wid all my soul—you's so good to a poor niggah dat's got no odder frens!"

"Hush! Go now, quickly, and remember all I have told you."

He lowered himself into the water without noise, and swam away. In a moment she had lost sight of him, and ran back into the house. Nettie was in the hall with a huge bucket and scrubbing brush.

"Why, what are you doing, child?"

"Washing the steps; they'll be dry before mornin', an' nobody'll see what I've been doin'. When I've finished outside, I'll wash the hall and stair oil-cloths, and the stairs up to the attic. You go an' put away the things, Miss 'Genia, while I do this; then I can destroy your trail as well as his'n. We mustn't let them dogs git inter the house."

Astrea stood gazing at her in amazement.

"I cannot imagine how you have found out everything so clearly, Nettie," she said in an undertone. The girl smiled shrewdly.

"This chile's got eyes, missis, an' they aint in her head fur nothin'! I'll tell ye all about it when the trouble's over."

Her mistress left her then, and went up stairs to remove all traces of what had occurred from the attic. For hours the girl toiled indefatigably, scrubbing, or rather washing and wiping every stair over which Rufus had passed, even down to the cellar. The cellar floor being damp, a row of planks were laid from the foot of the stairs to the door. These, after wiping with a wet cloth, she turned over; then opened the door and scrubbed the sill. This done, the trail from the cellar door outside to the creek, was all that remained. It was after twelve o'clock before she reached that with a strong solution of salt, into which she dipped her brush and drew it over the grass until thoroughly wet. Under the window where he had stood, she poured a quantity of the water. But here the greatest difficulty of her task began. She had seen Rufus leave the brook and come under his mistress' window, and had heard their conversation, but she did not know precisely how to follow his trail through the grass to the graveled walk, he had dodged about so much through the shrubbery. She did the best she could, however, treating the gate and latch to a vigorous wiping with her drying cloth, dipped into the salt water, then pouring the remainder over the ground at the outside, as if spilled accidentally. She could do nothing further, and crept wearily back into the house, to find her mistress sitting upon her bed, looking very pale.

"I have crept two or three times to the doors of their rooms, and cannot hear a sound," she whispered. "I am afraid you have given them too much."

Nettie looked frightened.

"I'll go an' see myself," she said after a moment, rousing up resolutely.

"How will you find out?"

"Very easy, if they hain't left the keys in the doors on the inside," and as she spoke, she drew a key from her bosom which she exhibited with a grin of delight. All at once the truth was revealed to her mistress.

"Nettie, it is you who have been playing the ghost! you got that key when I sent you for mine."

"Didn't ye never 'spect it afore?"

"No, indeed! The thought never entered my mind. What was your object in such tricks as you have been playing upon your master?"

"I thought he'd think it a judgment on him for his bad doin's to the darkies, and wanted to skeer him. I got a little 'fraid when he went to huntin' so, 'round the house, an' wouldn't 'a done it any more if it hadn't been fur last night. When I heard ye tell Rufe to go to the suller door an' wait,

I know'd what you's goin' to do, an' I waited till you'd done it; then I played them tricks on marster. I knowed he wouldn't hunt fur the ghost to-day, 'cause he'd be huntin' fur Rufe, an' I was sure that the tricks 'd skeer all de niggers an' keep 'em out of the way. That's mostly what I done it fur."

She might have added with truth that she did it to vent her spleen upon her master, for she hated his handsome face with an intensity almost deadly; but she dared not tell her mistress that. Astrea waited for her to go up stairs and investigate the condition of the sleepers, and in a few minutes she came back declaring that no harm had been done, and urged her mistress to lie down, which she was glad to do, being completely worn out. No sleep came to her eyes that night however, notwithstanding her weariness. She could only think of Rufus, and pray for his escape, while that thought was varied at times with Nettie's faithfulness and singularly artful management. She felt that everything was due to her if she did succeed in eluding a suspicion of the truth; but it was deeply painful to her to find the girl so deceitful and full of tricks. There might be danger to those who roused her opposition, for Nettie had a very intense nature, and loved with a whole-heartedness that had often struck her as unusual. Might she not hate, as well, and in her hatred, prove unscrupulous? These thoughts were calculated to banish all hope of rest, which rose out of this, and once more she watched the day dawn, with weary eyes and heavy heart.

CHAPTER XXIII.

BLOOD-HOUNDS AND HELL-HOUNDS—BANISHED FROM HOME.

Everybody was astir at an early hour of the morning, eager for the chase to begin, not even excepting the negroes, whose love of excitement kindled a deep interest in the proceedings, while, at the same time, they hoped that Rufus might escape unhurt. Wine was ordered upon the breakfast table, and partaken of with high glee by all. The stately, elegant Mr. Passiver, for the time, was sunk to a level with his colleagues, and drank as freely as they, so that by the time the meal was ended, they were all ripe for their unholy work. They left the table noisily, and went out with great confusion, taking their way to the quarters amid loud talking and laughter, in which the young planter's voice was loudest. Mrs. Passiver covered her face with her hands, sickened with disgust and fear. Soon after their departure, a message came from Doctor Early, to the effect that all was safe, and his charge hidden under his own roof. He had a plan by which he would soon place him beyond reach of capture, and bade her be at rest. The note was wrapped in a little package of medicines, and as soon as read, was immediately destroyed. She saw it burn upon the hearth, while glad tears coursed down her cheeks, and a leaden weight seemed rolled from her heart. To be sure the danger was not all past, but the most imminent cause for distress was removed, and she confidently waited the remainder of what was to come. Her own part might be discovered in the transaction, but they could not force her to reveal his hiding-place, and before they could gain any clue to it, the boy might be safe beyond their reach.

The hunt began from Rufus' cabin where the dogs were let loose upon his trail, and followed it rapidly to the river. There it was lost, and though the banks upon both sides were searched for his landing-place, no further traces were discovered.

"Shouldn't be surprised if the black rascal 'ad drownded hisself," said Ormand once when they paused about noon, wearied and heated with the fruitless search. He had all day indulged himself in like remarks, calculated to annoy the young master whose cloudy face betokened a storm every moment. Mr. Passiver answered him with an oath, and a peremptory order to hold his tongue and cease prating. "He never yet saw a nigger who was not too great a coward to destroy his own life," whereupon an animated discussion rose in which all the others joined, each having his own particular examples to cite in proof of a superior knowledge of the disposition and habits of the race. During this time, the young man was forced to chafe and fret silently, allowing them to have their own way, until the subject was exhausted, when he suggested that the search should be resumed.

"I'm agreed," answered the largest and roughest of the three "professionals," and who had the reputation of being the shrewdest of the "company." "Howsomever, it seems to me we're on a wild goose chase, an' not likely to git off'n it very soon, unless we change our course."

"What do you propose?"

"Well, to go up the river to the fust crick, an' foller the course o' that till we find a landin'. He'd be obliged to take the dirt sumtime, an' I 'spect he must 'a' done it sum'ers nigh the road to Florence."

"Why did we not think of that before?" asked Mr. Passiver, a light breaking over his moody features.

"Well, I did."

"Why the deuce, didn't you say so then?" was the impatient answer, "and not keep us all chasing through the hot sun for nothing!"

"Well, ye see I look out fur our own interests, consid'able, mister. We're not paid by the job—but so much 'a hour," he answered facetiously, drawing a laugh from his comrades.

"I would rather double your wages, and pay you by the 'job' and be done with it," was the curt response. "You cannot think this waste of time very pleasant to me, and I protest that it is not fair."

"That's a fac'," spoke up another of the three; "it aint fair, an' I vote that we go to work without more palaver."

Here the colloquy ended, and the hunt began again with renewed vigor, taking the course of the little brook which Rufus had waded through to the Hall. The negroes heard the noise and made a stampede which attracted Mrs. Passiver's attention and drew her to a window from which she saw the approach of the party, accompanied by the dogs, which they were now leading on each side of the stream. Now, indeed, the most trying moment for her had come, and hidden behind the curtain of her window she waited with suspended breath and a fast beating heart for the issue.

On they came, the animals sluggishly and unwillingly, until they reached the point where the brook crossed the road, when one of the brutes gave a sudden bound and uttered one deep, prolonged cry, which announced his finding the trail. The excitement was now intense, and being freed from the chains which bound them, the three animals bounded forward to the gate, where they paused, baffled and at fault. Astrea saw it from her hiding-place, and uttered an audible prayer of thanksgiving.

"Dear Lord, it *has* succeeded! I thank thee, oh, I thank thee!"

"Open the gate," shouted a voice, "and let 'em through! Perhaps they'll find the trail agin on the inside."

The gate was thrown open accordingly, and here again the

dogs gave tongue to a simultaneous yell. But in a moment they were again baffled, and dashed over the yard without finding further evidence of the fugitive's presence. Convinced that the animals would have followed the trail had it existed, the men stood amazed and at fault.

"It's the infernalist, strangest thing that they can't git on the back track," growled the leader, whose name was Perkins. "Here we have it from the branch (brook) to the gate, an' then from the gate to a certain spot in the yard, whar it's lost. I can't see through it. Thar must be a back track; but why can't the dogs find it! It beats me all holler!"

"Take them around the house and see if a trail can be found anywhere else," said Mr. Passiver; but half an hour was spent fruitlessly, and they were forced to yield.

"I 'spose he couldn't a' got into the house any way?" remarked Perkins at last, as he stood wiping the perspiration from a very red face with a yellow silk handkerchief.

"Impossible! still, you may see if you choose. Turn one of the dogs loose in the hall. I suppose there is no danger of his attacking anybody?"

"No, but they'd better all clar out'n the way fur all that."

Mr. Passiver shouted to the negroes to vacate the house, and they all scampered pell-mell into the kitchen, where they fastened the door, while the dog was turned loose in the hall. He trotted through the halls and up the stairway, snuffing at everything without any satisfactory result. Seeing the uselessness of the search in this quarter, the animal was called out, and consultation held as to what was to be done next.

But the remainder of the day was a heavy drag upon all, and night closed in upon a baffled and moody party. They slept at the Hall that night, and resumed the hunt upon the day following, without any better success, and finally were forced to give it up as useless after having scoured the whole plantation, and followed the course of every stream for miles.

While this was going on at the Hall, Doctor Early had taken Rufus about twelve miles down the river on pretence of visiting his patient there, and under cover of night, put him in a skiff well provided with food enough to last him a fortnight. He charged him to travel as fast as possible at night, taking pains to tie up during daylight in some obscure spot where he might not be discovered. To secure him against detention in case of being discovered, he gave him a paper which professed to be a pass from his master, stating that the bearer was sent upon business to Paducah, and was in every way trustworthy. This done, he was committed to the mercy of the stream and his own shrewdness, while the Doctor drove hastily back to Florence.

Poor Rufus now found himself adrift upon the water, with many dangers before him, and no one on whom to depend but himself. There was a blanket and plenty of food in the bottom of his frail barque, and a purse well filled in his pocket; still he felt sadly afraid and despairing at times as he whirled along over shoals, and through the swift current, with the broad expanse of stars overhead, and no other companionship than his own distrustful thoughts. Just as day dawned, he paddled his skiff into the mouth of a small creek, and drew it snugly under cover of a dense clump of water-willows. This done, he breakfasted from his store of eatables, and creeping among the leaves under a small cliff, laid himself down to sleep until night, when he might pursue his perilous journey with a greater degree of safety. In this way he traveled the whole length of the Tennessee River to its mouth, and there paddling across the Ohio to the Illinois side, found himself free!

We say free! He was comparatively free, though the fugitive slave law provided means for his recapture by his owner, could that owner succeed in tracing him to his place of refuge. But as if fortune had wearied of tormenting him, she turned a smiling face upon the poor wanderer, and guided him safely to friends, where he found shelter and protection. The farmer who kindly took him in, was soon induced to give him employment at what Rufus thought very liberal wages, and from this place, one week after his arrival, went forth a queer little messenger, which was destined to bring gladness to more than one heart. It was written by the farmer's daughter, badly spelled and filled with blots; but the evidences of a generous nature shone through every irregular line. It was addressed to Doctor Early, Florence, Alabama, and was read by him with much satisfaction, and passed over to Mrs. Passiver, to whom it was even more welcome than to the Doctor. Being an evidence of a dangerous nature, against her friend, she was compelled to destroy it, and thus fared Rufus' first and last letter home. It was long before she heard from him again.

And now, for a time, exciting scenes were at an end at Passiver Hall. The young planter, baffled in everything he undertook, changed his excitable course to one of watchfulness, which brought, however, no mysteries to light. From that memorable night forth, ghostly visitants disappeared, and the negroes were so well behaved, there was no excuse for flogging them. Consequently there was no need for stolen visits by night-time, and their attendant risks. But the young couple were hopelessly alienated, and lived apart under the same roof, one full of hatred and brooding revenge, while the other was sorrowful, and went on her lonely way without one gleam of hope for the future, since her husband's course had forever destroyed all respect and affection.

This was the state of affairs until the political excitement previous to the Presidential election roused all the country to a ferment. Mr. Passiver, being one of the most prominent men of his section, was chosen delegate to the Charleston convention which nominated Judge Douglas as Democratic candidate for the presidency. As it is well known the proceedings of this convention were unsatisfactory, and ended in the downfall of the Democratic party—Mr. Lincoln being elected to the high office of the Chief Magistracy of the United States.

This would have been a bitter cup for men like Frederic Passiver to drink, had it not been in accordance with their own purposes. One of the first to secede in the convention, he hotly promulgated the confusion, going with the minority whose purpose was to suffer the Republican party to elect a candidate, thereby furnishing a pretext for the secession of the Southern States. They wanted an independent government, and had for years looked forward to this epoch, when they might find an excuse for the consummation of their evil designs. Being of a sanguine and excitable temperament, Mr. Passiver had easily fallen into the views of this factious party, and from taking a lively interest, soon became one of its most prominent leaders. The excitement which now pervaded the South was terrible. South Carolina was first to secede followed by Georgia and Alabama. The Governor had called an election for members of a convention, by which Alabama could pass an ordinance of secession, a law having been passed by a previous Legislature from which he took his authority for this bold and dangerous step. The purport of this convention, was alleged to be for the consideration of the best course for the State of Alabama to pursue. The parties were about equally divided in the State, and the convention consisted of one hundred members. Fifty of the elected were pledged to resist secession, but through fraud, the certificates of election to the two Union members from Shelby County were given to the secession candidates which gave the latter the majority. The Union party were headed by Jerre Clemens, while the secessionists looked to William L. Yancey, with whose name and abilities the country is only too well acquainted. By this man and his party, no efforts were left untried to accomplish their purpose, and pass the ordinance, which was finally effected through the treachery of the Union leader and some of his closest adherents. Having succeeded, the names of every member of the convention with the exception of some half a dozen who were steel-true to the last, appeared upon this ordinance, and Alabama was declared an independent and sovereign Government. Foremost among those names which must go down to posterity dishonored as traitors, was that of Frederic Passiver, whose career began with the first mutterings of a long brooding faction, and was doomed to end ignominiously, as our readers will see.

With the first call to arms, he responded by placing himself and a large sum of money at the service of the Confederate Government, which evidence of loyalty was rewarded by a Colonel's commission and command. Meagre as this seemed to one who had taken so active a part, he was not displeased, and he resolved to win for himself a reputation unequaled by any in the Confederacy.

And now again, began the ills of Astrea Passiver's adverse life, when she saw her husband actively engaged in the downfall of a government which she had always looked to with the hearty pride of a true American citizen. She was not a born American, having been reared in Alabama only, from her third year; but it was the home of her adoption and she was true to it because it had afforded her wealth, friends and a happy home up to the time of her marriage. Mr. Harmon's only brother had early settled in the States, and amassed a considerable fortune, which in dying, he had left to Astrea's father, who sailed from England immediately upon receiving intelligence of the fact, to take possession of this unexpected fortune. Uniting his own previous possessions with this, he found himself in a fine position pecuniarily, and setting aside the prejudices of his race, had easily fallen into the ideas and habits of the slave-holder. It is a wonder that Astrea failed to imbibe from him and those around her, the same false ideas of right and justice; but we have seen with what views she grew up, and into what troubles they involved her. In those days, to oppose the popular current, was to immolate one's self upon a sacrificial altar, and the worst was yet to come.

It was no small trial to look from her windows over the long stretch of meadow lands below, and see the men drilling for the field of action, especially when she knew why that spot was chosen. Nor was her discomfort relieved by being obliged to see those men whom he called his officers, seated at her table and lounging through her rooms when not thus actively engaged. A very little while served to betray her real sentiments, and the work of persecution began the moment his sanction, by manner, was obtained. He made a great show of grief over her degeneracy, and an attempt to win her back to allegiance to the southern cause; but she stood firm, at length openly asserting that she had never been with them in any respect whatever. From this time the demon of hate was roused against her to a degree beyond description, and all sorts of stories set afloat which served to increase her danger. Amongst other things it was asserted that she had "run off one of her husband's niggers," and attempted to run others out of the country, which, while it partook only partially of the truth, seemed a sufficient ground for her banishment, and when at length she was called upon to take the oath of allegiance to the South and firmly refused, it was decided that she, with all others who cherished sentiments of a like nature, should be sent North, with a penalty of death attached to their return within the lines, which act would subject them to the trial and punishment of spies.

Against this summary measure, Frederic Passiver made no protest, and in the midst of seeming grief, declared himself equal even to this great sacrifice for the good of his beloved country, "which he would purchase with his own blood, ere it should fall into the hands of the northern vandals!" Forthwith he became a hero in the eyes of his blinded colleagues, and received their condolences with an admirable assumption of grief and self-sacrifice, while his sweet young wife was taken from her home, bereaved of her child, and sent North among strangers.

By Colonel Passiver's direction, she was escorted to Louisville, where she was bidden to take care of herself, and from thence with her scant fund of money and jewels, she went to St. Louis, carrying a sick heart within her bosom—having lost home, friends, husband and child through her loyalty to the Federal Government.

And now began her struggle for subsistence, having as its

sole motive, a hope of eventually recovering her child. Some one incidentally spoke in her presence, about correspondence with the papers, and she immediately conceived the idea of becoming a correspondent. Her first letter was to a New York paper, detailing some of the exciting scenes through which she had passed, and which meeting the demand of the times, being largely copied, brought her, not only a liberal price, but an invitation to let the editors "hear from her again." In this we have revealed the mystery of her independence at Paducah, which so much troubled Major Noble, and caused him for a while to suspect her of dishonestly appropriating funds placed in her hands for the benefit of the soldiers.

The substance of the foregoing history was given to our friends at Corinth by Astrea, herself, who could no longer withhold from them the story of her life; and which she told them in fragments as her strength permitted. With the novelist's privilege, the events have been woven together as the reader sees, the author vouching for the truth of the history, as confirmed by subsequent proofs.

CHAPTER XXIV.

THE BATTLE OF CORINTH, AND SOME OF ITS HORRORS.

The evening succeeding Captain Wilfer's last interview with General Grant, found him a guest in Astrea's little parlor, where he had begged to see her alone. Helen, who would not leave her until she could take care of herself, put her into her easy chair and ran home to "see the Major," giving him the opportunity he desired. He took a chair and sat down beside her, saying in an unsteady voice:

"I have come to bid you good-bye, Miss Harmon."

"You are not going away?"

"Yes."

"Why, how can you leave at this time? I heard an officer say the other day, that it was difficult to get a leave of absence."

"I have not found it so," he replied with a sad smile. "To tell you the truth, I have resigned, and am going North immediately."

"What to do there? Oh, how *could* you resign your commission now?" she expostulated reproachfully. "Have you so soon wearied of the good cause?"

"No, I have not, and shall not abandon the service. When you hear from me again, it will be of a man, who, in spite of everything, intends to serve his country. I am going to the Army of the Potomac."

"Why, pray!" was on her lips, but she paused before the words were spoken. A sudden thought flashed upon her which dyed her face and throat crimson. He was going away from her, and her lips were sealed. The truth had not entered her mind, and he would not enlighten her as to the real cause of his departure, knowing that it could only add to her pain unnecessarily.

"I hope you may be successful," she faltered, as the only thing she could say under the circumstances.

"You will know it if I am," he answered quietly. "I mean to write to you sometimes, and I shall expect you to reply to my letters. Surely you cannot refuse me now?"

"No, I will write," but she thought the request inconsistent, if he was going away to avoid her.

"And you will tell me everything about yourself—all that concerns you?" he urged again.

"Certainly, if you wish it."

"I do, as I would wish to know about a dear sister, if she was in your place. If I dared I would even go further, and say that I would be glad if you could make up your mind to leave this part of the country altogether; you are too delicate to bear all these hardships, and I shall constantly dread to hear of you, lest you may be sick or—dead!"

"If I am ill, it will be no wonder—if I die, it will be a blessing. If you do hear of the latter event, rejoice in your heart, for I carry a heavy burthen in carrying my life."

"Nay, you are too despairing. Have you abandoned all hope of recovering your child?"

"I scarcely know if there is any hope left for me, so much has been done to destroy it. While General Halleck was here, our forces, as you know occupied Tuscumbia and Florence. I came to him and told my sorrowful story, to which he listened in all kindness, but would not give me a pass to revisit the place, and try to ascertain where my child was. He sent a message to the commanding officer, however, who returned an answer that Colonel Passiver had removed his family and effects to Tuscaloosa, within the Confederate lines, and I was forced to wait, there being no help for it. The only attempt made since, you are familiar with, and know if I have any reason for hope."

"I do not think you need to despair. He says the child is with his mother. Will she not be kind to her?"

"I do not know, for I have never seen her more than once or twice. About the time he took possession of his father's estate, a disagreement of some unpleasant nature occurred between them, and she went to some friends in New Orleans. I have never seen her since, and do not know what her disposition may be."

"Has Colonel Passiver any brothers or sisters?"

"One brother only, whom I have never seen. He is an artist, and has spent the last ten years in Rome, Venice and other places. About the time we went to England, he went to Germany, and it so happened that we missed him everywhere. I have always suspected that these apparent accidents were intentional, and that some cause for a feud existed between the brothers, though Mr. Passiver would never acknowledge it. Perhaps, if my suspicions were true, the same thing which caused the breach between them, was the cause of his mother's departure for New Orleans. I once heard that his brother shared but sparely of the family estate, while the division should have been equal, which is probably true."

They sat talking over events for half an hour longer, when Captain Wilfer rose and held out his hand.

"I must go, my dear friend."

"So soon? I may never see you again."

"You will if God spares our lives. This war cannot last always. When it is ended, if not before, I will find you. Promise me, in the meantime, to take care of your health."

"I will try."

"Very reluctantly spoken! Oh, Astrea, be wise and be faithful as well, little sister. God created you for a noble life, and you must not waste it in useless pining. Trust Him, and hope for a brighter future. I do believe that it will surely be your lot to know happier days. Probably I shall never see you again, as you have just said. May I kiss your hand in this my last good-bye?"

She held up to him a pale cheek instead, and he touched it with his lips lightly, reverently. Tears coursed down her cheeks, as they parted, and she fell back in her chair and sobbed as he strode away with hasty steps, striving to keep down the emotion which was unnerving him.

When morning came, he was gone. Corinth was now dull and quiet, nothing of importance occurring to disturb the usual routine until Price advanced upon Iuka and made some hostile demonstrations which resulted in small loss upon either side. The chief excitement which arose out of this little episode, was in the war amongst northern papers, which canvassed the movement of Rosecrans and Grant with much warmth. The weather was intensely hot, the roads dry and full of dust everywhere. All Corinth, and the country for miles around, began to look like a desert, while the streams dried up, rendering it difficult to find enough water for the use of the animals. The green leaves became crisp, and covered with a fine, white dust which destroyed every vestige of freshness, while scarcely a blade of green grass was to be seen. In the midst of this dull, dead, unpleasant picture, burst the vivid battle-fires of Corinth.

The enemy made the attack on the morning of the third of October, just after daylight—not this time upon an array of unsuspecting troops. They had been expecting, and prepared for him in time, bravely contesting every foot of ground from the beginning. That was a terrible day at Corinth, and before the sun went down upon the struggling masses, many of our best, and some of our prominent men had fallen. Neither side could be said to have gained any decided advantage, though the odds may have been upon the Confederate side, when the battle was suspended for the night. During the day our friends, Astrea and Mrs. Noble, had been forced to remain within the sheltering walls of the Tishomingo Hotel, where the wounded were brought to them for attention, until the place was full of the mangled and groaning sufferers. Many died, and were drawn into the kitchen and wood-house, until the floors were literally covered with lifeless bodies. There was scarcely a spot below stairs where they could step without treading in blood; and yet neither shrank from the task, though both sickened many a time over the horrors of that scene. They could hear the thunders of the cannon, and the hissing of the shells which sometimes crashed against and through the walls, but never once thought of leaving the spot. During the first two hours they had suffered greatly with affright, especially when the sound of the strife seemed to come nearer and nearer toward the town. After that, however, they had grown accustomed to the noise, and being occupied with things immediately around them, became calm and self-possessed.

As night closed in, Astrea sought and found a couple of lanterns, two buckets and some tin cups which she immediately appropriated. Helen regarded her curiously as she lighted candles to place in the lanterns, and hung an empty bucket with a cup inside upon her arm.

"Where are you going?"

"To the field to carry water to the wounded. You will go with me?"

"Yes, but who will take care of these people here?"

"There are one or two doctors, several women and all the negroes. Surely among them, they will find attendants until we return. Think of the many who lie out there bleeding, thirsting, dying, with none to help! Come quickly."

Helen tied a handkerchief over her head, and they went out together, crossing the town and fearlessly pressing on to the battle-ground where the wounded lay. On arriving there, they found the ambulance corps busy picking up the wounded, their lanterns gleaming from every point. But a few moments served to show them that their services would not be useless, and at once they began to search for water, which they had much difficulty in finding. At length they came upon a well near a small log-cabin, whose fast-decaying windlass made it almost impossible for their united strength and skill to raise enough to fill their buckets, yet they toiled perseveringly, and carried their burthens back to the field with rejoicing. As soon as the buckets were emptied, they were again refilled by the same wearisome process, until an end was put to their labors by Major Noble, who insisted that they should return to the house and leave the remainder to those whose business it was to care for the wounded. Helen expostulated with him, unwilling to return.

"Only think, George, how you would feel, lying here in the dreary night, with the dead and dying all around you, thirsting vainly for a drop of water, while none was near to give it to you! I cannot think of it and go home, leaving them behind to suffer."

"I would not ask it, if I did not know it to be necessary. You must not exhaust yourself at the outset, for the battle is not yet over, and there is no telling what demands may be made upon your strength. Neither of you are fit to remain longer now. Come home."

"Astrea, tell him we cannot go yet."

"No, dear, we must go," she answered sadly. "Your husband is right; we ought now to go home, and save our strength for to-morrow. It is dreadful to be obliged to leave one sufferer *here* uncared for; but if we stay and exhaust ourselves to-night, many may suffer to-morrow in consequence, which we might be able to relieve."

"Why do you not add that you need relief yourself?" asked the Major. "Not one person out of a hundred would say that you ought to be here, with that pale face and those hollow eyes. You are not fit to be out of your bed, much less in the midst of a scene like this."

"I cannot help it, and this is what I am here for. Perhaps if I take pity on these, and give one beloved one back to his friends, God will take pity upon me and restore to me that which I have lost. I must do my duty."

"My dear child, you have grown too morbidly exacting upon yourself, and fall into the common error of striving for too much. Be content with less, and you will not fall short in your duty. You owe something to yourself as well as to others."

"Major Noble, this is a point which I cannot argue with you, especially at this hour, and in such a place. As long as I can stand up, I will not cease to strive in the path I have chosen. I will go home now, because I feel that it is positively necessary."

They went back into town almost in silence; the Major and Helen saw Astrea safely to her own door and left her there, knowing she could get no rest at the hotel. With the early morning she was again at her post, much refreshed by three or four hours of sleep, and a substantial breakfast. Her face was almost bright as she entered the long dining-hall, now converted into a hospital, and began the task of relieving the wants of the wounded.

If the first day's strife was terrible in that memorable contest, the second was more fearful still; for now the Confederates gained ground and penetrated the town to the very center, pressing hotly around the Corinth House, and over the railroad bridge just above the Tishomingo. Nearly every inmate of the latter house was forced to abandon it and seek for shelter in the woods; but our friends refused positively to go, remaining in the midst of the strife, while the battle raged hotly around them. A shell had crashed through the wall just before noon, killing a man who lay on a cot close to the spot, and badly wounding Major Noble, who, being unfit for duty on the field, was doing all he could inside the building, until the blow left him senseless upon the floor. Helen ran to him, and gathered his head into her arms, with a frantic cry of anguish:

"He is killed! Oh, my husband, my husband! he is dead!"

Astrea heard that bitter wail, and hastened to her, followed by a surgeon, who examined the wound. A small piece of shell had buried itself in one side of the head near the temple.

"He is not dead, but this wound is fatal," said the surgeon anxiously. "Let us move him down stairs as far from the strife as possible, or you may be killed as well."

With the assistance of one or two others, the Major was borne to the wood-house in the rear of the hotel, where there was less danger of stray shots, and laid upon a cot. Helen threw herself beside him with a burst of frantic grief that was terrible, and no one could comfort her. The dead were strewn over the floor, and her garments brushed against their white, cold faces, but she did not even see them, with that one beloved face beneath her eyes, whose lips might never more syllable her name in accents of endearing affection.

"You can do nothing," said the surgeon to Astrea, who lingered beside her friend, and would not leave her. "He is past all help, poor fellow."

"Can he not even be restored to consciousness? May nothing be done to give him relief?"

"Nothing. In less than one hour, he will be beyond the possibility of pain. Hark!"

A woman's scream rang out upon the air, and they looked upon a fearful scene just outside the door, where lay the fragments of a human body. A soldier's wife had fled from the camp into the town, and concealed herself in one of the negro cabins, until the advance of the rebels frightened her from her hiding-place. Frantic with alarm, she rushed out, and was vainly essaying to find some other place of refuge, when a shell hissed down before her and exploded with a crash, dashing her to pieces.

To the young wife, the horror of this was as nothing to the scene before her. The brave, noble heart of her darling was growing cold—the mute lips white in death, and he would never again open his eyes upon the world which he had made so beautiful for her. She sat there at his side, heedless of everything but him. Her hands wandered over his face, through his soft, dark hair, and to his heart where they sought for the lingering signs of life, fast fading away. And when the faint breath ceased to pass the cold lips, and she realized that he was dead, she grew so calm and white, her stony grief was worse than shrieks and tears would have been. Finally, throwing herself upon his lifeless body, she laid her cheek to his, and refused to be moved from him.

"I have nothing to live for now," she moaned. "Let me die with him."

"Come away and let her alone for awhile," said the surgeon to Astrea. "It is the best thing you can do, for she will soon exhaust herself, and then become passive."

Astrea obeyed very reluctantly, following him into other parts of the building. When she came back half an hour later, Helen had sunk into utter unconsciousness, and she had her carried away to one of the chambers, where they laid her upon a rude bed and left her to the care of her friend. Astrea looked down compassionately upon the still, pale face.

"Poor, stricken one! shall I strive to restore you to life and misery, or let you sleep on forever?" she said. "I could find it in my heart to let you go with him—yet I dare not without an effort to save you."

Night closed in once more upon wearied and exhausted troops; but now a victory had been won, and the Federals were triumphant. The Confederates had been repulsed with great loss on both sides, and left the ground covered with dead and dying.

At Helen's request, after recovering consciousness, Major Noble's remains were carried up stairs and laid upon a bed in one of the chambers, where she would allow no one to come near him. With her own hands, she bathed his face and smoothed the hair over his unsightly wound, composing him for burial with the faithful tenderness of a matchless love. Mrs. Hemans tells a touching story of a faithful wife, who remained beside her husband, and ministered to his wants, until he died upon the wheel; but that instance of devotion scarcely exceeded the devotion of this more modern sacrifice. She seemed transformed, and from weakness, had risen into power passing credulity. Her face was very pale, and the brown eyes looked black and burning with their silent pain; but she neither trembled nor faltered in what she did, and after all was complete, and she had kissed the cold lips and brow, she spread a covering over him and turned away to join Astrea.

"You are again going upon the field?" she asked.

"Yes."

"I will go with you."

"Would you not prefer to remain with him?"

"No, he does not need me now, and others do."

Remonstrance was useless, as all saw by her rigid features, and no one lifted a voice against it, as they proceeded together to the battle-ground.

Now the dead were strewn from the Corinth House far back beyond the belt of woodland that skirted the town. They pressed on past the groups of men busied in the streets, and entered the bushes where a number of wounded men had crept for shelter, and lay groaning piteously. Occasionally the foot would slip in a pool of blood, or a groan from beneath their feet would startle them with a sickening sensation at heart, hard to sustain; yet they would not give up. Each sought forgetfulness of their own sorrows in ministering to others; but it was a sad, yes, a startling picture to see those two pale women wandering at night through the darkness, their dreary path lighted only by the flickering beams from the lanterns they carried, and the dead all around them. Less suffering women could not have passed through such ordeals. It is the magnitude of woe, which words cannot express, that makes us unselfish. Once Helen had stooped to peer into the face of a dead man, and saw that a wound in the left temple had caused his death. A short, sharp cry escaped her lips, as if, suddenly from the midst of the dead where she wandered, that one beloved face had started, ghastly and cold. Sick and trembling, she gazed down at it with pitiful eyes, not heeding the gray uniform which clothed the still figure, in the thronging, bitter memories it called up

Astrea had wandered farther and farther, toward a denser portion of the brush, unaware of the fact that she was leaving Helen behind, absorbed as she was in her occupation. Once, as she stopped to closely examine a body, to discover if life remained, the rays of her lantern fell upon the figure of a man only a few yards in advance of her, who was upon his knees, busily engaged at something, she could not comprehend at first. As her light flashed upon him, however, he turned, hastily thrusting something into his pocket with a very guilty look. His features were now exposed to full view, and the truth forced itself immediately upon her mind.

"Doctor Grey! you here, and rifling the dead?"

The exclamation escaped her lips almost before she was aware, and startled him into a confused attempt at denial. Failing to get through well with a self-defense, he blurted out roughly:

"And you—what are you doing here, I'd like to know? This is no place for women."

"My business is apparent, and if my pockets were to be searched, surely they would not be found full of dead men's property. Doctor Grey! oh, for shame to stoop so low."

"You'd better take care, Miss Harmon, or rather Mrs. Colonel—what's-your-name! Do you suppose I don't know all about you, and that you are the wife of a rebel—the worst kind of a rebel, too! You ride a mighty high horse—passing yourself off for a young lady, and trying to trap some young sprig of an officer! Captain Wilfer, maybe!"

Astrea's hand shook so violently with suppressed indignation, that the lantern sent shimmering streams of light along the ground to the Doctor's feet. He saw his advantage, and went on mercilessly:

"Aha! it makes you tremble, does it? You see I know too much for you to take a high hand with me. I promised you payment at Paducah, and I've given you a taste of it already. What got Captain Wilfer into trouble, and who caused him to be dismissed the service for meeting flags of

truce with a rebel officer's wife? The next thing you know, you'll find yourself in prison as a rebel spy,—if you haven't sense enough to hold your tongue where your own interests are at stake, and keep dark."

Astrea understood it all now. That which had before perplexed her was all made clear by this man's attempt to intimidate her. This was why General Grant had questioned her concerning Doctor Grey, whom she afterwards learned he held under arrest for some cause, and subsequently discharged, with the friendly advice that he should leave Corinth at once, and not venture back again. Everybody thought he was gone, she with others, until she came upon him now, engaged in his loathsome occupation.

"If you think to frighten me, and thus seal my lips upon this night's deeds, you are mistaken, Doctor Grey," she said, straightening herself up resolutely. "And I think that you will soon find the time past for meanly striving to put others between yourself and just punishment. If Captain Wilfer was dismissed the service, what befell you afterward, and how does it happen that you are here to-night? Whatever he has suffered, it has been through his own generous goodness and nobility of heart. Never a deed of disloyalty or meanness has stained his name. If your own history, from the time I first knew you up to this night, could be revealed, what a contrast it would form to Captain Wilfer's career! You told me when you left Paducah that you held a Colonel's commission, and that was untrue. You were a Major only; but why were you afterwards drummed out of the regiment? To this place you came by contract, and have done what better men would not willingly do—attended the sick rebels whom we had confined here. By that means you obtained the power to injure Captain Wilfer, and attempt to cast suspicion upon me. But had you accomplished your purpose, I think this night's work might have given me cause for a new hearing on account of the character of my accuser."

At this moment a group of men were seen approaching with

lanterns, and Doctor Grey broke away through the bushes in alarm, knowing that Astrea would not spare him in the presence of others. She looked around hastily, and was about to call them, when the sight of Helen sitting upon the ground with her head bowed upon both hands in an attitude of utter forgetfulness, won her from her purpose, and she went quickly to her friend. Helen had taken off her mantle and tenderly placed it under the dead man's head for a pillow, sitting down beside him immediately afterward, and losing consciousness of everything but her crushing grief.

"Helen, dear, look up."

Astrea touched her bowed head compassionately, gently bending to lay her cheek against that of the bereaved wife. The action revealed the dead man's face, and brought one long, wild scream from the lips of the beholder. Helen started up in affright and grasped Astrea's arm convulsively.

"What—what is it! oh, what has happened now?"

But Astrea did not heed her. With quick, gasping breath, she had commenced tearing the contents from the dead man's pockets and examining them with wild, eager eyes, until the positive proofs she had sought were in her hands.

"The curse," she gasped,—"the consequence of his oath! He has met a fearful death, and doomed himself to punishment forever and forever!"

By this time Helen had roused sufficiently to comprehend what she was saying, and stammered tremblingly.

"But you may be mistaken!"

"No, no! See—a letter—'F. Passiver, Tuscaloosa, Ala.'—and his hat with his name inside—under it 'Fourth Alabama Cavalry.' And see, a Colonel's stars on his collar."

As Astrea's excitement increased, her companion became calm and self-possessed. With an arm slipped supportingly around the excited woman's waist, she took the letter from her shaking fingers and opened it.

"Be quiet, Astrea. We must put this matter beyond all question. I will read the letter."

The eyes of both were bent upon the delicate, irregular chirography of the pages, but Astrea only listened, seeing dimly what her friend read in a steady voice. It was a brief, strong appeal to do his duty as a man and a soldier, in the cause of freedom; and breathed the relentless spirit of a Spartan mother, sending forth her son to battle, with but one object at heart—to conquer the foe. The reader got on very well until she came to the last page which was written in a still more irregular hand, and was touched with a deeper feeling of tenderness. It bore the date of several days later, and closed with the crushing words:

"And now, my noble boy, how can I add to all you have suffered, this last terrible blow! You have known how the delicate plant committed to my care, has drooped and faded each day—but can you bear to know that she is dead? Yes, like the fair petals of the flower whose name she bore, she drooped under the scorching rays of the southern sun, and I have laid her away under the church-yard sod with many tears."

"My child! Lily! Gone! dead! Oh, my God, my God!"

Down upon the dead man's breast she sank, stricken, crushed, and Helen's strength was barely sufficient to draw her up to her own bosom, where she pillowed her head with a strange sense of resentment that it should have touched a thing which she loathed as the cause of all the great woe which had fallen upon the poor victim of an adverse fate. She struggled up passionately and drew her aside, beyond the possibility of contact. Then taking her head upon her knees, she sat looking at her in a sort of bewildered helplessness. Their positions were now strangely reversed. Only a few hours before, she had been the helpless one, while the woman in her arms stood over her, pondering the question of life and death, as she now vaguely pondered it. Was it here a career like hers was to end, after all of hardship, self-sacrifice and mental suffering she had borne? Had the angel of death put forth his hand and smitten her from the life preserved through fears, and struggling hopes that were little better than despair? It looked strangely like it. No signs of life lingered about the blue lips and waxen features, and the heavy eyes were sealed as though never to open again upon the world and its tormenting phases of suffering. She was almost in hopes they never might open again, though a keen sense of yearning awoke in her own heart with the thought. Loving Astrea so tenderly, it would not be easy to give her up now, when her own life was like a vine suddenly torn from its support, with quivering tendrils broken and prostrate, feebly reaching out for some object around which they might twine.

An end was put to her meditations by those whom Astrea had seen a few moments before, and who now came upon the strange scene with loud exclamations of surprise. A shower of questions were poured upon Helen, which she answered drearily, in a cold, passionless tone. The strain upon her had been too great, and they saw that she was upon the verge of insanity, forbearing, when this became apparent, to question her farther. But while they forbore to annoy Helen, it did not seem out of place to grumble among themselves, over the "trouble these women were making them. They had enough to do, without that, but supposed it would not do to let them kill themselves after that fashion." Considerable discussion was indulged in during the time Astrea was being transferred from the ground to a stretcher, that she might be carried home, one or two openly censuring the commanders for allowing ladies within the lines under such circumstances. Mrs. Noble heard, but with stolid indifference, seeming to care for nothing until a movement of Astrea's announced her return to consciousness. Then a sudden reaction set all her blood tingling through her veins, and she came to Astrea's side with a sharp decision of manner that was startling from its suddenness.

"You may go away and let us alone! We do not need your care, and will not have it. I can manage this lady myself!"

She stooped, and passing her arm around her friend, lifted her to her feet and held her there until she could steady herself

"Come, darling, and I will take you back to the house. These people are moles, and can see—understand nothing."

They were moving slowly away, when Mrs. Noble, remembering that the dead man lying there was the husband of her charge, turned hastily.

"That man is a rebel—a villain, who well deserved the fate which has befallen him; but for the sake of this woman, whose life has been devoted to those who suffered in our cause, let him have a Christian burial. Whatever you may say of her, she has at least earned this at your hands."

"Follow them in case they should need help," commanded the chief of the ambulance corps; and as they slowly picked their way through the tangled brush-wood, two soldiers kept near until they reached the hotel.

On the afternoon of the following day, Colonel Passiver was buried apart by special orders from General Rosecrans, and the day succeeding that, the early morning train bore Astrea and Helen, with the remains of Major Noble, from Corinth.

CHAPTER XXV.

THE CLOUD WITH A SILVER LINING.

A BREAK of a year lies between the present chapter and the events chronicled in our last. The scene has changed from the battle-field to a quiet residence in New York, where we find our friends together, occupying the same apartments, and inseparable. Very little change has come to either, personally. We have seen them in suffering and danger, and known that they have had cause for the loss of early bloom and freshness, so strongly apparent now in the face of each. Perhaps the deep mourning robes in which they are habited, serve to make the pallor of their faces more striking; but a serene, calm resignation has come to each, not altogether familiar. They have had a hard battle with the Inevitable, and have been conquered. Their resignation partakes more of despair and helplessness than submission; and the wounds left in the conflict are still too tender to bear any rude pressing. They have sought and found refuge from the world, where they may pass their days in peace, at least, if the nights still leave wet pillows where each have lain.

Helen has grown much slighter than when we last saw her, though, of the two, her face retains more of life and hope. They have just returned from a walk to the Battery, and laid aside their wrappings to sit by the window in the gathering twilight; Astrea, roused by some sudden thought, turns to her friend.

"How strange it seems that in all this time, we never should have heard of Captain Wilfer. He made me promise to write to him, and I have not had a line yet. Do you suppose he has quite forgotten us? or is he dead?"

"Neither!" answered Helen rather warmly, rising to take a package of papers from a drawer which is usually kept locked. From the packet she extracts a newspaper and hands it to Astrea, and watches her narrowly while she reads a marked passage, noting the promotion of Harry Wilfer to a Colonelcy for meritorious service. The article is very complimentary, and the reader's delicate cheeks flush warmly, kindling to a vivid crimson.

"Why, Helen, when did you get this?"

"Three weeks ago. He sent it to me."

"And you never told me! Was that kind, Helen? Remember what he has done for me—what he has suffered through me! Am I no longer worthy the confidence of either of you?"

"Oh, no! no! don't think that!" cried Helen, hastily. "I did not speak to you of him, because—because—can't you guess, Astrea? He was afraid to write you because he could not write as a mere brother or a friend, and he dared not write otherwise. No such reason existed between him and me, and I have sometimes penned him a little note to comfort him in his loneliness and distress."

Astrea's head drooped a little, while the color faded slowly.

"Forgive me, Helen; I did not mean to reproach you. Has he written you often?"

"Yes, quite often. Would you like to see the letters?"

"I think so. Where are they?"

"Here in this package. But, darling, can you? They are nearly all about you, and—he loves you, Astrea, 'desperately.' Can you bear it?"

"Not yet! not yet!" covering her eyes with one hand, while she puts the package away from her with the other. Then, after a long pause:

"How did he find you out, Helen?"

"He sent me one letter, it seems, just after entering the army of the Potomac. Receiving no reply, he became alarmed about you, and wrote to me to ask what had become of my friend. I answered his letter which followed me here, sent on, I suspect, by General Rosecrans' order, for he asked me the morning we left Corinth, where we should go, and I told him. In my reply I told him all that had befallen us both, and begged him not to write to you for a while yet. I thought that it might be painful to you, dear. But he has kept up the correspondence, and his letters were so good, they have been to me priceless treasures in my sorrow. I have longed to have you share them, but dared not until some sign from you should open a way to the subject. These are more yours than mine, and they will do you good," slipping the letters into the hand which had fallen upon her lap, and clasping the slender fingers around them. "Keep the package, and look at them when it pleases you—not before."

With this Helen rose, and, leaving a kiss upon Astrea's forehead, glided into the adjoining room and closed the door between.

Long after Helen's head had pressed the pillow that night, her cheek wet with the tears she bravely hid from her companion, Astrea sat in a rocking-chair in their little parlor and unbound the package which she scarcely had the courage to open. Her eyes ached for the sight of those lines which she knew were full of the tender sweetness for which her heart had yearned hopelessly, and yet something in the memory of the past made her shrink from what she most wished to see. Whenever she had thought of Captain Wilfer, it was always with that dead face between, as she saw it on that terrible night at Corinth. The wide-spreading gloom of night had seemed to settle into a yawning gulf, while the pale stars faded out, leaving only an impenetrable darkness into which no ray of light could strike, and she had striven to keep away those thoughts which were so fruitful of pain. But now! now a bridge seemed laid across the chasm, and she pressed it with trembling feet, longing to rush over into the light and warmth beyond. Was it a temptation? Dared she venture out of her gloom so soon, almost before the grass could spring greenly upon the dead man's grave? Her heart was struggling for the light, and rose up from that strife to throw off the sickening bonds of conventionality. What was the world to her that could care now, whether it criticised her or not? And what had her past been, that she should shield it so tenderly for her own weary eyes, not yet drained of the tears it had wrung from her?

"I have nothing on earth," she said mentally. "Shall I shut myself out from all hope of future peace and joy as well? I live now because I must, but shall it always be so? Were it not better to let something slip into my life that can give it an aim, or an interest? The saddest of all things on earth, is an immortal soul encased in an unwilling body; and that body slowly dragging its burthen from day to day because it dares not set it free, and the time has not yet come for death to open the prison doors. No warm, sweet motive for life links the soul with its casket. Only a dull blank, and a vague, ceaseless yearning to lie down to dreamless sleep on the part of the one—the other, at times sharply struggling to be free. Oh, no, I cannot live on in this way!" with sudden energy. "If I do not find something to hold me to life, the tempter will sooner or later, woo me to self-destruction."

One after another the broad, generous sheets were unfolded now, and her eyes drank in their contents hungrily. The clear, bold hand gave character to the manly sentiments of affection which he must breathe to some one, and which delicacy forbade that he should pour into the ears of its object. He longed to fly to her and hold forth his arms, offering her the shelter of their strength, and the love that was like a broad, deep stream in its mightiness. But he feared to come to her in her deep and bitter woe, lest he should cause her to shrink away from him, and destroy the hopes he had dared to cherish in his secret dreams of the future. Thus she read on, page after page, sheet after sheet, filled with that one theme, and as she read, she saw that the hope grew in stature as it seemed to come nearer to her, claiming their mutual friend as a link between which might soon unite them with the blissfulness of actual presence. The last letter was of very recent date, and said: "I only wait your bidding now, to come and stand face to face with my love, that I may ask her to let me take her little hands and draw her up into the warm, rich light of a matchless devotion. Oh, my friend, how much longer will you make me wait? Be quick! I grow impatient, and if you do not hasten to bid me come, I shall break through restrictions, and, perhaps destroy all hope by throwing myself at her feet unawares."

Soft tears fell upon the page, slowly dropping like shining dew upon rich verdure. The lips smiled with a touch of the old sweetness as the little hands clasped their treasures in kneeling down beside the chair she had occupied. Through the open shutters a shower of silvery rays filtered through the locust boughs over her head. She had extinguished the light, and now for a long time knelt there in silence, mutely whispering in her heart all that she was learning to hope for. The soft, sweet smile had not yet faded when she crept to her place at Helen's side, and lingered there through the hours she slept. The latter woke from a troubled sleep, with the first bright rays of morning, and seeing that rare expression upon her friend's face, read it joyfully. Stealing from her side, she sat down before her little desk, and with glad tears in her sweet, brown eyes, penned a hasty note to Colonel Wilfer. As she was sealing it with a dainty touch of her delicate fingers, Astrea lifted her head from the pillow where it had rested and spoke.

"To whom are you writing, Helen?"

"To—" then she hesitated.

"Whom?"

"Colonel Wilfer. To whom else should I write?"

"And you have told him that he may come, I suppose?"

"Yes, darling mine. Was I wrong?"

She left the letter, and crossing the room, laid her arm tenderly over Astrea's shoulder.

"Did I not read aright the sweet smile that I saw upon your lips when I awoke this morning, and which has not gladdened my eyes for so many weary months? We have become more than friends, Astrea, in our unity of trials, and have been forced through love and necessity to share each other's burthens until neither can stand alone under a storm without the other's support. Shall we be divided in the coming sunshine? Shall not I, who have learned to love you with a sister's devotion, share some of the joy that lies in your future, by asserting to place it in your possession? If I seem over-eager and officious, pardon me, dearest, for I am very desolate, and must have something to ease the aching void in my heart. For me there is nothing else in this world, than your happiness."

"Helen, darling!"

Astrea's eyes had filled, and her arms closed impulsively around the figure which trembled at her side, with the sobs that broke an effort to suppress them. She was touched inexpressibly by the tone of the sad words, as well as the unselfish devotion of the poor desolate one, who, as she had said herself, had no other now to care for than her friend whose path had been marked providentially to run parallel with her own. For a few moments they wept together, then Astrea's hand stole caressingly into Helen's brown hair as she added softly:

"Sister dear, you have not done wrong, and I thank you, oh, so much, for the care you bestow upon me. I do not deserve it, for I have been a gloomy companion, chilling you with the shadow of my own hopelessness all this weary while, when you had more than enough grief of your own. The only objection I would make to the step you are taking for my sake, is its haste. It seems so strange, so sudden, and—

so sweet, after so much of suffering and dread. It is no wonder if I thought he had forgotten me; men are so unlike women. And then he had never spoken his love, for he could not, honorably, and I did not suppose he could know what had happened. I must do myself the justice to say that I did not even wish it, Helen, for I was too crushed and remorseful to look to the future of this life with anything of hope. I was wrapped up in grief for my lost Lily, and sorrow for the curse I brought upon his head, when he took the oath which he broke so fearfully. If I thought of this man at all, it was with a feeling that made me tremble, and shrink away, for I could never separate the two, which is but natural, after all, when we remember how strangely they were brought together and associated in my mind. That Harry Wilfer loved me once, I knew only too well, and that was a part of my torture when in spite of right, honor and pride I was forced to acknowledge that his love touched a responsive chord in my own heart. There was no fear, for we were both wise through sorrow, and our lips were sealed upon the words we dared not speak. But I would not do him the injustice to thrust aside the friendship he so nobly offered me, warm and true from the ashes of his own lost hopes, and I could have been his friend always, had not fate changed the circumstances of our lives. After what happened at Corinth, I more than once recalled his promise to write to me, but always with dread, for I had pledged myself to tell him everything which befell me, and it seemed as if I could never tell him *that!* As time went on and no message came, the thought that he might have been wounded or killed annoyed me; but at length I reasoned that in such a case, I should have seen the news in the papers, or heard it from some one. This idea banished, the only way left to account for his silence, was that he had become interested elsewhere. He was so young, needing the sympathy and affection, in his strong nature, which he never could hope to win from me as he wished, and it would not have been wrong or unnatural for him to reason the matter more calmly, with a great space between us, and decide it the wisest course to forget me. Perhaps you will think it very strange if I tell you that I even hoped it might be so. I have so long felt that I could not summon courage to own my affection for him, and I loved him so truly that I desired his happiness above my own. Ah, how noble he has been! My heart grows so warm and glad now, to think that *he* had nothing to do with—his death! I could not have borne *that!*"

Helen had grown calm in listening, and now said, more to herself than to her companion:

"I am rejoiced to hear you say so frankly that you love him. *He* deserves to have the woman he loves, to avow it with that noble independence which you show in owning it to me—and would to others, were it necessary. But it seems so very strange, yes so *very* strange that you could ever dare to love again after that experience. I think if I had ever borne such suffering through such a source, I should be afraid to trust my happiness to any man's keeping."

Astrea's eyes deepened and dilated, then settled into a calm expression as she answered slowly:

"I have always thought so until lately—that is, within the last year, or a little more, perhaps. But I have gained something of wisdom through my bitter experiences, and I can now see that something more of the fault was mine than I knew. I was too young to know what I required in my husband. I took too much for granted, and did not wait to study the character of the man whose handsome person and polished manner seemed to mirror everything that was noble, manly, and calculated to hold a woman's love. I ought first to have understood what my own nature required that I should find in a companion, whose being must be so closely woven with one's very self; and then I ought to have known if he had the nature to meet those requirements. Here is the secret of the mistake so many unhappily make; and when our golden idols change to clay, and we vainly yearn for the flown brilliance which dazzled our sight, and can come no more, whom have we to blame most? Few of us will acknowledge our own share, and yet, alas, the fault lies largely at our door. It is human nature to find every other explanation for our woes, than that which would betray our own blindness, folly, rashness or carelessness. Oh, if the lessons we receive, could only teach us wisdom in our own actions, and turn our critical glances more within ourselves and less to others for the true causes of our sufferings, how much might be spared us that is not."

"So of course you are taking the blame upon yourself for all that has ever happened to break your heart and darken your life with misery!"

"No, I am not. That would be injustice and affectation. But I am not blameless. I was very proud and self-willed, and I thought I owed it to my self-respect to say bitter and cutting things against the evils which exasperated me. Often, I might have done my duty, maintained my dignity, and yet left unsaid words that sank deep and rankled in a nature wholly opposed to mine. Yet, if my mistakes were many, bitterly have I been made to atone for them. Looking upon my bereavement as a part of the atonement, I have been able to bear it; otherwise I could not. Oh, Helen, my heart is opened now, and I can speak as I have never before spoken to any one. The habit has so grown upon me to keep my thoughts and my yearnings to myself. But I loved my child as I think few mothers can love, for all loves seemed centered in her. My mother was dead and my father gone beyond reach of my great needs. In my husband I had been disappointed, and while my grief was boundless for the little one who came unwelcomely, to find no place in her father's heart and arms, I gave her that which was strong enough to supply the loss. Day after day I sat with her in my arms, looking at the rosy lips, soft, velvety cheeks and fathomless eyes with a deep love that was idolatry in itself. At night I would steal her from her crib to my bosom, that I might feel the wandering touch of her baby hands, and the precious head nestling close against my heart. The very grief she caused me, strengthened the nature of my love—the fears that arose for her future, drew me nearer to her with an instinct for protection only a fearful mother can feel. With all this, I was so proud that I did not complain when he sent her away from me, and made her nurse sleep with her up stairs, while he kept me locked in my room. I would not let him see the suffering he caused me in robbing me of her presence. But I had some relief in being able to steal to her as she slept, and kiss her warm, soft cheek. If I could not have done that, perhaps my pride would have yielded to my longing."

Here Astrea paused, and Helen's wistful eyes begged her to go on, though her lips would not frame the request, as she saw the color fading swiftly from the mother's cheeks which excitement had called up.

"You want to know all," she said at last, with a short gasp. "Oh, I can't, I can't! The memory of that last act will make me hate the dead, if I dare to linger over it! I see her now, with her little arms stretched to me, her sweet mouth quivering with pain and affright as he bore her away, leaving me bound fast to my chair until he could send her beyond my reach! Poor Nettie had been sent off to Tuscaloosa on pretense of punishing her for some misdemeanor, and that was the last I saw of her faithful face, for she did love me, poor girl! And Lily!—I heard her give a sobbing cry for 'mamma'—the last thing for sight and memory, the grieved little face and heart-broken cry! If passion had not given birth to a desire for revenge, I should have gone mad then and there! But I thirsted for the day to come when I might claim and keep her in spite of him! It bore me up, and I lived for that until other objects came in my way and helped me with the burthen of my life, as I began to faint and grow despairing. Oh, you know it all—all! and what it has all come to. How the future suddenly seemed to become blank, and I no longer looked for each coming day to bring me nearer to the only joy that could be mine. I *had* a great hope while she lived, if I did at times long for death in my seasons of despairing helplessness. But now one little grave holds it all!"

"One little grave holds it all!" repeated Helen with a sob. "Oh! God! that so small a spot of thy earth, should hold all the world for so many of thy creatures! and leave them so desolate and lonely."

The sound of weeping broke the stillness of the room painfully, dying away only when they had exhausted their tears. Then a softer, tenderer mood followed, and they knelt side by side, pleading in their loneliness and sorrow, for that comfort and strength and resignation, which One alone can give. After that both grew more cheerful, and prepared for the duties of the day with lighter hearts than usual, though their manner was very subdued as they partook of their breakfast, which was always served in their own room, and afterwards turned to their respective occupations. Helen's was at her easel, where she painted the rarest little pictures of still life that ever grew under the brush of artist. Astrea's pen and her brush, supplied them with more than enough for their simple wants, and served to pass the time in which neither had held any keen, warm interest until now. But out of the blackness of the cloud overshadowing them, a soft, bright light was breaking, and would soon reach down to touch those young faces back to life and hope and beauty. Thank God, it is the blessing of life when bereavements that must come, visit us in youth, for then we may hope to outlive them, and build up new interests upon the ashes of those which have passed away.

CHAPTER XXVI.

LOVE FROM AN UNEXPECTED QUARTER.

It was the custom of the ladies to walk every afternoon when the weather was pleasant, and through this custom they one day came in contact with an old acquaintance. Sometimes they went to the Park, where they could sit quietly with a book for an hour, or watch the living stream of humanity as it flowed past, but afterward, it was to the Battery they bent their steps, where they could watch the vessels skimming over the water, with their snowy sails spread. One day as they walked down Broadway, just after passing the St. Nicholas, they became aware that some one was following them, and quickened their pace in some uneasiness, but the man pressed forward more rapidly still, and in a moment had gained their side.

"Miss Harmon, I owe you an apology for the rudeness of following you, and perhaps giving you a fright. But I saw you pass, and could not resist the pleasure of a word with you. Am I forgiven and made welcome? I have so long wished for such a moment as this? Mrs. Noble, I presume," bowing to Helen. "You see I do not forget names, though I scarcely had an opportunity to speak to your friend during that trip up the river. Pray tell me of yourselves and your fortunes since I saw you. I have heard something, but not half as much as I wish. You are living here now?"

"Yes," answered Astrea, laughing at the breathless rapidity of his long speech. His manner was so heartily cordial, and he looked so manly in his evident delight, she could not resist the keen sense of pleasure she felt in meeting him. "But, do not my eyes deceive me, Mr. Meridan? It cannot be possible that you are in the service?"

A rich, warm glow mounted to his forehead as he answered:

"Yes, it is possible, as you see. I met with an old friend of yours, Captain—now Colonel Wilfer, who persuaded me to take a Captaincy in his regiment, and it is the best thing I ever did in my life. We have pleasant times together, I assure you, and are as happy as larks. But you have not told me one word about yourself, and Mrs. Noble does not look as if she was sure that she has ever seen me before at all."

"O, yes, I remember you now, very well," answered Helen, "and that I should still owe you a grudge for conspiring with Miss Harmon against me, had not Fate taken your punishment into her own hands. You got rather a serious fall that day, did you not, Captain Meridan?"

"Rather. I am not sure but it would have terminated my erratic career altogether, had it not been for the very prompt assistance of your companion. I have always held myself indebted to her for my life," with a shy glance at the pale, sweet face, shadowed by its weeds so somberly. "And yet, do you know," he added more pointedly, "that she would not give me even the poor privilege of thanking her for what she had done? To see or hear from her ever again, was not to be thought of, and I owe it to accident that I have once more had the grateful pleasure of clasping her hand. Was she not cruel to me, Mrs. Noble?"

For a moment Helen was at a loss how to answer, knowing why Astrea had chosen to repulse his advances; but with a woman's usual tact, she smiled and said lightly:

"O, you know she could never tell one day where she might be the next, and it would have been rather a difficult matter to keep sight of her. How long have you been in the city?"

"Only a very short time, and must be off again in a day or two. When I go back, Wilfer talks of taking a little rest, and will probably run over to the city. I will tell him that I found you here."

The ladies exchanged glances, but walked on without remark, listening to his spirited stories of army life, until they had reached the Battery. Here, after being seated, he continued to entertain them with his adventures until the low sinking of the sun warned them that it was time to return home. Captain Meridan begged to be allowed to accompany them, and when they reached the door, did not hesitate to accept the invitation to enter and remain to tea. But he had the grace to make a short visit only, and contented himself with asking permission to "run in again before he left town."

Astrea accompanied him to the door, remarking:

"Of course we shall be pleased to see you whenever you are at leisure. I am as much interested in what you have to tell us, as I am surprised to see you in uniform. I never expected it, for I never quite forgot that conversation on the Lancaster, in which you expressed some uncomplimentary sentiments."

He laughed, coloring deeply, then lifted his eyes to her face with a wistful glance.

"Ah, you might forget that portion of it! I don't know, either! You see it is all owing to the softer influences which are brought to bear upon a man, Miss Harmon. I did not have a very exalted opinion of things in general, until I met a dear little woman who was the soul of patriotism; and in learning to love her, I learned to love the country she cherished. She taught me true manliness, and for her sake I took up arms in behalf of the Government she risked everything to serve. If she ever condescends to smile upon me, I shall be more than repaid for the little I have been able to do."

He did not look at her, and no thought entered her mind of his true meaning. Her face beamed sweetly bright as she answered:

"I hope you may have your reward, Captain Meridan. It is noble in you to give America the strength of your arm in her need." Then, as he took her hand: "We shall see you to-morrow evening?"

"Yes, if allowed to carry out my own inclinations, most assuredly, Miss Harmon."

"Pardon—I must correct your manner of addressing me. I am known here as Mrs. Passiver."

"Ah, pray excuse me! I *did* hear something about—but I did not remember, and am so accustomed to the other name! Good-night."

She saw him spring lightly across the street and walk quickly down upon the other side, his face uplifted in the moonlight with a joyous expression. He had not thought it a sin to tell her an untruth, but through Colonel Wilfer he had learned the whole of her history, and drawn his own secret hopes from the facts, though he did not yet dare to hint them. Several days passed, and Captain Meridan had not yet returned to his regiment. He found it very convenient to be always expecting to go at any hour, and presumed upon the liberty of "running in whenever he could before leaving." Never a word was allowed to escape his lips to give her any alarm, but the spell of her presence had deepened upon him, and he found it harder, each day, to leave her side. The prospect of a final parting, with a doubt of ever meeting again, rested very heavily upon his spirits; but he concealed the oppression, and kept up his gay, cheerful exterior to the last day of his stay. He was to have called upon them for the last time in the evening, intending to take the night train for Washington. But as he came up Broadway in the afternoon, he saw Helen entering a store, and the temptation for a few moments' chat with Astrea alone, was too strong to be resisted. He turned quickly, and in a short time found Mrs. Passiver engaged at her desk in the quiet parlor. She received him with some surprise, but cheerfully left her employment to entertain him. He "regretted to disturb her, but found that he must go earlier than he had anticipated, and had hastened to say good-bye. Where was Mrs. Noble?"

"She is shopping a little," answered Astrea innocently, "but will soon return. We shall miss you, Captain, our lives have been so very quiet and retired until you came. It is like seeing an old friend leave us."

He was "sure that the regret of going must be much deeper on his part. He had spent some charming hours with them," and then he grew so very uneasy and restless, Astrea could not avoid remarking it, with a hope that nothing unusual had occurred to disturb him.

"Nothing at all, thank you. And yet I *am* troubled, Mrs. Passiver, and do not know whether I dare explain the cause of my distress. May I tell you something that very nearly concerns my happiness? I have no lady friends beside to whom I can speak, and I need sympathy."

"Certainly, if you desire to honor me with your confidence, Captain Meridan," she answered, but her manner was, unconsciously, a little constrained and cold. Nevertheless he brought a chair nearer, and began earnestly:

"It will not take me long to say what I wish, since I am a man of plain speech and manner. I came to this country quite young, and for my pleasure, taking more delight in criticising what I considered its faults and weaknesses, than in the vast and matchless array of beauties it presented to my gaze. I had an Englishman's pride, and something of an Englishman's bigotry—the latter trait being owned now with shame, and out of which arose a disposition to exalt my own native country, while this was depreciated in proportion. I went everywhere, saw everything, and made light of everything American, often against my better judgment, and out of pure perversity, until it was my lot to be shamed by a woman into a more just and earnest observation. A fair young creature was thrown in my way, who combined in her character all the lovable traits of human nature. She was very singular—at once strong and gentle, earnest and sweet, and so pure and lofty in her principles, I never had been forced to acknowledge woman's true worth until then. When I first saw her, I tried to laugh, for she was at once called 'strong-minded' after the fashion of all intelligent American ladies, and I was sure that I should hate her. But though she was self-willed and unbending, she was too purely womanly to answer my idea of a 'masculine woman,' which I thought 'strong-mindedness' meant. She had dared to step into a self-chosen path, and walked it with a courage that was grand. I was amazed the more I studied her, for she had the face of a child, and a manner as simple and natural, except when some perverse spirit crossed her own and her maturer strength was forced out. I saw, too, in my closer scrutiny, that she suffered, and would fain have offered her my sympathy, but she made me see that she would walk alone with her grief, putting it from her own sight whenever it was possible, and I did not dare to intrude my sincere compassion. This little woman—strange, beautiful thing that she was!—never showed herself arrogant or over-eager to thrust her own ideas prominently before others. On the contrary, she was rather retiring, inclined to keep her own counsel and never meddle with other people's pet foibles. But when pressed for opinions, and closely driven within her lines of defence, she would rally and fight for the victory with a warm, earnest, deliberate air that was enchanting.

"Day after day, though they were not many, I watched her with increasing interest, until an accident happened to me which nearly cost me my life, and when I woke to consciousness, the first thing I saw, was her slender figure a little distance from me, trembling with emotion. The keen, wild sense of delight that ran through all my being at that moment, when I thought she cared enough for me to shed a tear over my misfortune, taught me what I would not have been willing to acknowledge to myself before. I knew then that I loved her, and that love grew mightily every subsequent hour passed in her society. But she kept me afar off, and I did not dare to utter a word—not even when we parted, and I knew she was going from me with the intent to see me no more. She did not care to be troubled with me, and would never know that I would willingly serve for her with the faithfulness of a Jacob for his Rachel, if she had only given me one smile upon which to build a hope for the future. Ah, well, she went her way and I went mine, but I could never forget her. She haunted me like a sweet, wild dream, and turned all other pleasures to nothingness. The world had become blank. I wearied of everything, and like *l'homme blasé*, could nowhere find a 'sensation.' At length I resolved to give up my roving, useless life, and be a soldier. I could not make up my mind to leave the country she loved, so I determined to win her respect, at least, by fighting for it, and good luck threw me in contact with one of her best friends, who got a commission for me, and often pleased me with the high, earnest, manly praise he uttered of her whom I loved. I did not tell him the name of her who claimed all my thoughts, but I told him that I loved, and for the sake of that love, took up arms hoping to win her favor, and he told me to go to her with my tale of devotion, and she could not fail to smile upon me. Do *you* think so too, Mrs. Passiver? Do you think I dare to tell her of my love and beg her to give me one hope for the future? I would not be impatient, but await her pleasure in all things. All I would ask would be the sweet privilege of coming to her in the end, with permission to strive to win her affection."

She sat pale and embarrassed, painfully at a loss how to answer this man without deeply wounding his feelings. His wistful glance never left her face now for a moment, and forced her to hasten.

"The lady gave you no encouragement in the beginning, you say; and if she had reasons then for repelling your advances, what reason have you for supposing they do not still exist?"

"Ah, she was not then free! I know all that now! But she is no longer bound to repel me except from choice. Oh, Mrs. Passiver, this is mockery! You know whom I mean, and I cannot rest until I have had your frank reply. Tell me if there is any hope that I may one day win you. Without your love, life will seem very dreary and desolate."

"Captain Meridan, this is unexpected and out of place," she answered with difficulty. "These weeds I wear might have won me your forbearance in such a declaration; but time could make no difference. I cannot now, or ever, give you reason to hope for more than a friendly regard, which you have deserved richly in your frank and manly course of action."

He rose to his feet, mortified and deeply distressed.

"Forgive me for my unseemly haste. I had not intended to thrust such a declaration upon you now, had not the thought of coming danger forced me into a forgetfulness which I cannot myself pardon. I deeply regret the pain I have caused you."

All the sweet womanliness of her nature was touched by his tone and manner.

"Captain Meridan, no true woman can be indifferent to the sincere love of an earnest man, and I thank you for the honor you have bestowed upon me in such an affection. I even may go so far as to say that I regret my unworthiness, and utter inability to give you the hope you desire. In remembering you it will always be with the kindest sentiments of honor and esteem."

"Thank you for this much. It is like you to speak frankly, and I am comforted in knowing that I have not wholly forfeited your respect. If we never meet again, believe that I will most sincerely hope that your future life may be happier than the past has been."

He took her hand, bent over it for a moment and was gone, leaving her bewildered and heart-sick with the suddenness and singularity of the painful interview. When Helen returned a short time after he had gone, she was once more busy with her pen, and said nothing about his visit until the non-appearance of the expected officer as the evening advanced, caused Helen to exclaim against his want of punctuality. Then she told her all that had passed, and was rewarded by a burst of uncontrollable merriment over the Captain's manner of wooing. A touch of the old playfulness had come back to

Helen during Astrea's ingenuous recital, and now she began to tease her most unmercifully, until Astrea's gravity and gathering tears, warned her that she was pressing upon sore wounds.

"Oh, but you must learn to be less sensitive," she cried regretfully, putting her arms around her shoulders with a tender, caressing touch. "I know that life has few sunny spots for us, but we must try to rise above the darkness, and take more reasonably whatever may come. We have each courted the shadows too long, and I know it is not right. I try very hard to break through them, every day, and I have not your promise of hope and joy to make my future bright."

"I try also, dear, but it is not easy to control our feelings where we have suffered so much of pain. I feel very sorry for Mr. Meridan, for I think him sincere, and it is not in my nature to feel no regret over wounds I am forced to inflict."

"O, I'll tell you how to manage it, then! You may reward the gallant Captain's devotion with this little hand and turn Colonel Wilfer over to me. A man—especially an Englishman, who can voluntarily set himself up as a target for rebels to shoot at deserves some reward—" But here Helen broke down under the pain self-inflicted by her light speech, and wept with womanly shame and regret.

"One would think me heartless," she said at length, wiping away her tears. "But I never forget my husband and how faithfully he loved me. I cannot imagine what can be the matter with me to-night—so nervous, restless and foolish, like a hysterical school-girl! I must learn to control myself better. Oh, dear! I wonder what we are all made for, and whither we are tending! Whatever we may think and resolve, it all comes down to this perplexing question at last. I wish I could see my way, or hope that the peace I crave may ever reach me."

Astrea took her well-worn bible from the desk, and read in a sweet, clear voice from the fourteenth chapter of St. John:

"Let not your hearts be troubled. Ye believe in God, believe also in me." Helen listened to the close, and sighed wearily:

"That is not for me; that was to comfort His disciples under a coming bereavement. At times we can apply such terms of consolation to ourselves, but oftener, they seem afar off and unreal. We cannot grasp them as meant for us—because, perhaps, we know ourselves unworthy—and must go on our weary way mourning hopelessly. Human nature is weak and very inconsistent."

Astrea was silent. Helen had but too well expressed her own feelings. Yet they knelt together and earnestly prayed for the faith which alone gives hope for earth or eternity.

CHAPTER XXVII.

A DAWNING AS OF BRIGHTER DAYS.

THE last lingering tints of autumn had faded away into the dull, leaden dreariness of winter, ere Astrea yielded to Helen's entreaties and Harry Wilfer's prayers that he might be permitted to visit her. Even then he was delayed in his arrangements, and it was Christmas eve before he found himself in the city, eagerly hastening to the abode of his friends.

A private letter to Helen informed her what hour he might be expected, and she, guessing his wishes, had made an excuse to go out for some forgotten purchases, in order that their meeting might be freed from the restraint of her presence. The good little creature hastily threw on her cloak and hat as the hour drew near, and had just time to reach the corner when she saw a carriage whirl past and stop before her door. Then she went down the street slowly, with a smile upon her lips and her hand pressed over her heart to still its excited throbbings.

The streets of the metropolis were thronged, and ablaze with light. Continuous streams of human life poured from all directions, while the rear of Babel-like Broadway seemed each moment to grow deeper and deeper, until the "holiday noise" became stunning. Bright and happy faces passed her, heedless of the leaden sky above and the sloppy pavement beneath. They had homes and friends to be made happy by what they carried to them, but in the midst of all this, she felt her desolation as never before. No husband—no children waited her return! The one friend left her, was forgetful now that she existed, probably, in the deeper joy of another presence; and while her faithful heart rejoiced in her joy, there was a heavier sense of desolation and loneliness that made her wander aimlessly up and down, with humid eyes and a swelling in her throat that must have terminated in sobs, had she been anywhere else than in the open street. The air was chill, sometimes sweeping up against her rudely with wintry violence, and scattering the clouds above, until a few pale stars blinked faintly from momentary glimpses of blue sky. She did not want anything, and so wandered away, looking at everything—caring for nothing—often jostled, and many times hailed by ragged children who shivered and held forth their little cold hands for pennies "to buy bread." She gave mechanically until all the loose change in her pocket was gone, then vaguely wished herself away where she could no longer hear the pitiful sound of their voices. Occasionally the notes of a street organ penetrated through the harsh confusion of sounds; and once a child's clear, sweet soprano in accompaniment, smote her with a keen anguish which brought an involuntary sigh from her lips as she turned to look at the poor little wanderer, standing at the side of a blind father shivering in the blast. When the song was ended, she timidly strove to gather a few pennies from the passers-by, but no one seemed to notice the little outstretched hand, and she finally took the organist's arm to lead him away. In a moment both were lost to sight in the human stream, and Helen turned to other scenes, repeating the sad sigh:

"How prone we are to think ourselves alone in wretchedness! I was thinking that in all this great city there could surely be none other so desolate and wretched! Oh, blind! oh, selfish! when there are thousands who may not even have food to satisfy hunger, or a shelter to cover them from the cold of a winter night! Shall I ever learn to be less careful for myself, more thoughtful of others?"

In the meantime, Astrea, left alone, had stirred the coals in the grate to a vivid glow, and ordered tea to be served immediately upon Helen's return. This done, she sat down to indulge in the luxury of a quiet revery, though that revery could not be otherwise than sad at such a season, contrasting the mirth and joy around her with her own loneliness. Once she had been merry and gay in the Christmas time, but that was past now. Wrapped in the thoughts which thronged upon her, she did not hear the bell, or the quiet step in the hall, until some one advanced into the room. Then she looked up to see Harry Wilfer with both hands outstretched, and looking down at her with loving eyes. A quick, keen throb of pain ran through her sudden joy, but she rose and put her little hands into his broad, soft palms, saying no word, but suffering him to draw her to his bosom, while he bent his head with proud and eager gladness to kiss the pale lips of his love.

"Can it be that I have you at last! The future gave so little promise of a joy like this when I said good-bye at Corinth! But now!—oh, God is very good to me, and I think no man was ever so supremely happy!"

She felt it in the quick beating of his heart, and saw it in the warm tears which dropped glitteringly upon the sable folds of her dress while he held her tightly, as if he would never again let her go from his arms. If she was silent, he did not chide her, for he knew all that she must feel in an hour like this. Yet he longed to have her express something of the delight he experienced, and could not forbear the question as she drew herself gently from his grasp.

"Are you happy, my Astrea?"

"Happy? Yes, Harry, in the midst of sadness. How happy, I cannot tell you. This hour brings me an untold joy. It is the glory of a spring-time season bursting suddenly out of the stormy depths of winter. Imagine a scene! Where stretched long reaches of trackless snow magically appear bright fields of living green. Frozen streams that struggled beneath their fetters with a sullen murmur, have suddenly burst their bonds and laugh in the sunlight, happy and free! Green buds and bursting blossoms grow from the forest boughs, while through them run the glad wild notes of singing birds, making blissful melody. Clear and blue and cloudless, stretches overhead the lately leaden sky. From her white winding sheet the earth has risen radiant with living beauty. Do you like the picture, Harry? Oh, love and hope, what marvelous works do ye create in human hearts!"

"And do you love me like this? I have not deserved such happiness! You make me afraid that it is but a wild, sweet dream that will fade with the sound of your voice."

They sat down before the grate and talked quietly, wrapped in a more serene and confident joy. They had much to say, and forgot the passage of time in relating and listening to each other, until a sudden remembrance made him ask for Helen.

"I am looking for her every moment," Astrea answered uneasily. "She ought to have been home half an hour ago."

"I might have been here a week without your knowing it," came cheerily from the adjoining room where Mrs. Noble was removing her wrappings. Then she came forward with a soft, warm glow upon her face, and gave both hands to Colonel Wilfer in cordial greeting.

"How long have you been in there?" he asked.

"Not long," she returned archly. "I found so much upon the streets to be seen, it kept me longer than usual, and I have brought a present for each of you. See!"

She took a little package from her pocket and opened it, while Astrea asked if she was not rather too fast in assuming to have bought a present for Colonel Wilfer. The two exchanged glances, then both laughed.

"No, I am not too fast! You see, *I* expected him, if you did not. He and I each have a *penchant* for surprises, and we thought we would initiate you into the pleasures of the same, so you were left to receive the visitor which you did not expect, while I went off to hunt something to give you on Christmas morning."

To the trio, that Christmas eve was passed with a sober, quiet joy that few could understand, for the same experiences never tend to like results in the lives of different people. Perhaps, in all the city of New York, such a scene as that which was passing in the little parlor, could not have been found. After a dish of tea, and a long chat in which all took a part, Astrea handed her little bible to Colonel Wilfer, who unhesitatingly took it, found a chapter suited to the season, and read aloud while they sat listening upon either side. No false modesty kindled his cheek or caused his voice to falter. He closed the book with simple reverence, and knelt with them in earnest, fervent, grateful prayer.

"I never knew before how good he is," said Helen when he had bidden them good-night and gone back to his hotel. "There are few young men who are so earnest, yet so bright and cheerful. His mood is never trifling, yet seldom gloomy. I like him better than ever for what I have seen and heard to-night."

Astrea's face was radiant with a proud happiness, and she stooped quickly to kiss Helen's cheek in acknowledgment of her praise. Neither had known such a sweet sense of joy as that which dwelt with them when their heads lay side by side upon the same pillow, with cheek pressed to cheek in loving confidence, as they sank to rest. They had only time to breakfast and prepare for church on the following morning, before Colonel Wilfer made his appearance with Christmas greetings and a small present for each. Helen's gift in return, was a miniature of Astrea painted by herself, and handsomely set in a little golden case. Astrea put a pocket Testament into his hand, beautifully bound, with his name written in clear, free characters upon the fly-leaf; but while he thanked them for the remembrances, holding the miniature with hearty pleasure, he stooped and whispered to his betrothed secret thanks for the more priceless gift of her love.

The walk to church was very pleasant, though the day was cold and stormy. Seated far back in the church, where the mellow light from the stained glass windows fell upon each subdued face, they were still serenely happy, and enjoyed the solemn, impressive sermon with the sweet and cheering sense of right to possession in the promises made through the lips of the old white-haired pastor. Never had words seemed so nearly intended for individual comfort and acceptance. Each felt as if the kind voice was directed to them, with words of cheer fitting the peculiar need of their natures; and they rose with a feeling of regret when he spread his hands above the congregation in benediction.

Then there was the walk back, pleasant but quiet. Once in their own room, however, they seemed to have brought with them the spirit of the season, and vied with each other in striving to make each other happy. Colonel Wilfer remained to dine with them, after which he opened his budget of amusing reminiscences for their amusement, until it grew quite late; so it happened that he did not mention the subject nearest his heart till just before he took his leave. He dreaded to cast a shadow upon the bright face by pleading for an early day to call Astrea his own, and feel that he had the right to shield her from all future ill. And he had not mistaken the effect it would have upon her to mention the subject of marriage. She turned pale and shrank tremblingly from his touch, speaking in a quick, sharp tone:

"Wait, Harry, wait! I cannot quite bring myself to that yet. Be content with knowing that I love you, and let me have time to forget the past."

He looked troubled.

"But I want to be able to care for you. It troubles me sorely to see you in these small rooms, and to know that you must toil from day to day for your bread."

"That is foolish, for we have more than we want. Helen has some property and her pension, while I can make what I need easily enough, with my pen. It is necessary for us to be employed with something, therefore we work; but we do not labor more than is good for our mental health. No, Harry;

there is no need to worry about us. Wait until you are out of the service, then I will make no further objections to your wishes."

"It is hard to wait for so long a time! It may be many months yet ere this strife can cease, and I must in the meantime endure the eternal fear of losing you."

"Why should you fear? Can you not trust to my affection?"

"It is no doubt of that which makes me impatient, but the uncertainty of things. I must go back to duty, always under the probability of danger; and if it is His will that I should fall, I could die easier to know that you had a legal right to what I possess, and that a wife's tears might sometimes fall upon my grave."

"Don't talk of death, Harry! That is a subject too fearfully familiar to me, and horrible in connection with yourself."

"You value my happiness, Astrea?"

"God alone knows how much."

"Then hear me. I shall know neither peace nor rest until you are my wife beyond possibility of loss."

"Come for me in the spring, then," she answered quietly, and he was obliged to be content.

When he had returned to the army, life flowed on for the two women in the same quiet, monotonous way as before. Amidst thousands they were alone, seeking no society whatever, but they had ceased to be unhappy, though it was impossible that they should yet cease to be sad at times. Colonel Wilfer's letters, which came regularly twice a week, were always like visitors, and filled with a variety of news which served them in the stead of gossip. They talked over them with the freedom of sisters, and planned for the future with undivided interest.

Thus the winter passed, and the spring came with bursting buds and bloom. Colonel Wilfer had begged the middle of May for the promised visit, and received Astrea's permission; but the early month saw the campaign upon the Wilderness opened—beginning on the 3d—and all his plans were shattered. This campaign lasted until late in June, and at its close, our hero was detailed for special duty, which threatened to keep him engaged for an indefinite period.

During this time Astrea suffered greatly with anxiety, knowing but too well the dangers to which he was exposed. And there were long weeks of silence unbroken by a line of intelligence, which were followed by a number of letters all together and of dates far back, calculated to tantalize her sorely when she saw how faithfully he had striven to keep her advised of his welfare. His missives were often penciled upon the pommel of his saddle, or a drum-head—wherever he chanced to be—and breathed an all-absorbing devotion very grateful to her longing heart. And yet, though they made her desire his coming with an intensity that was almost irresistible, she was still glad that circumstances conspired to detain him—so strange and unaccountable was the dread of his coming! It was in vain that she chided herself for her foolish and unfounded fears. The thought would haunt her that some great sorrow would follow his advent, and she had suffered too much not to shrink from any new phase of woe.

To Helen the reason for this dread seemed plain enough, remembering the past life of her friend; and she chided her seriously for allowing it to rise up between her and the happiness that a wiser Providence had ordained. But she told Harry nothing of Astrea's fears, in the little spicy letters which he had loved to read by the flickering light of his tent lamp; and thus he knew nothing of her uneasiness until months had passed, and the second expedition against Fort Fisher was forming, in which he was to take a part. Then he had resolved to get a leave and go to New York, if but for one day, that he might claim his bride before rushing into this new danger.

"I am to have a command under General Terry," he said as he sat in their little parlor after the flutter of his unexpected arrival had subsided. "And I could not go on so dangerous an expedition without having seen you first. I have suffered much of uneasiness and suspense, and now want the comfort of knowing if I fall, that I shall not leave you destitute. I have come to claim your promise, Astrea."

She placed her hand in his.

"I am prepared to fulfill it, but fear it will bring you little of joy or peace. I wish the fulfillment might ensure to you all you deserve."

"I ask no more than this, and am willing to trust a kind Providence for the future. Do you know I have been haunted most cruelly with the fear that you would find some excuse for again making me wait?"

It was well that Helen had left the room, or this speech might have made her forget her prudence and expose Astrea's unreasonable forebodings. As it was, the latter only hid her face against his shoulder and allowed him to have his own way in the settlement of affairs.

"I must go back this very evening," he said, "for I could only get away with the greatest difficulty, as every man is needed to hasten the completion of arrangements for the enterprise. The annoying delay of the Baltimore train for some hours, has cut me off for a whole day which I hoped to spend with you. Therefore I shall go now and find a clergyman, and immediately afterwards, we will drive either to his house or a church and be quietly married. Our parting will not be so hard for me, if in leaving you, I know that I may come back to my wife—should God spare me for that great happiness."

No objections being made, he carried out his plans, and at mid-day they drove to a quiet little church in the upper part of the city, where the minister and three or four persons awaited them. It seemed like a dream to her as she listened to the solemn, beautiful words of the service, and heard Harry Wilfer's earnest, manly response. Then, when all was over, when Helen's impulsive kiss and her husband's close warm pressure of the hand, to which were added the congratulations of the few witnesses, assured her that she was once more a bride, a mist gathered over her eyes, and she leaned heavily for a moment upon her husband's arm. But the cloud soon lifted, and it seemed as if a rich, warm flood of light had fallen around her. For one brief, bright hour, our heroine was happy. She did not know how very soon it must end, as she sat with him for a few moments alone, after they had partaken of a hasty dinner. He was to leave on the two o'clock train for Baltimore, whence he would go to Fortress Monroe, and when he had urged her earnestly to lay aside her pen, and try to find a more agreeable home in a more cheerful part of the city, they entered the carriage with him and drove to the depot to see him off.

Until the last moment, they maintained a degree of cheerfulness which none felt; but when they stood upon the wharf and bade him good-bye, not knowing if he should ever come again, the bitterness of a coming woe seemed to have fallen upon all. Harry Wilfer thought it no shame to his manhood that others saw the tears that ran swiftly down his cheeks as the boat left the wharf with him, looking at his wife, who, bathed in tears more copious than his own, was supported by Helen until he could no longer see the two figures. And we know that it is well we are not permitted to look into the future. A wiser power than we comprehend has ordained that we shall see each purpose of His own as He wills to unfold it to our sight. We cannot more than conjecture what the future may bring, though it is in human nature to look forward rather than back, forever upreaching for that which is beyond our grasp. Often the appreciation of the present is lost in the eagerness with which we look past our actual possessions to that which we hope to possess in the future; so, we drift onward, rarely if ever content.

When the boat was out of sight, Helen gently urged Astrea to return to the carriage which awaited them, and the latter was about to enter, when the uneasiness which is often felt when closely regarded by unseen eyes, caused her to look up questioningly. Standing a little apart from the crowd, was a man who came forward the moment he met her glance.

"You will not deny me the pleasure of offering you my congratulations, Mrs. Wilfer? Judging by the scene I have just witnessed, I may be excused for presuming that you must be his wife."

"Yes, sir, she *is* his wife," said Helen sharply; "but I think she can dispense with your congratulations. Please to stand aside, sir."

"Not so fast—begging your pardon, madam. I am a little curious to know how a lady of Mrs. Wilfer's high principles can reconcile it with her sense of right to marry one husband while the other is still living."

"Doctor Grey is not well informed," Astrea answered with quiet dignity. "If he had found it convenient to wait a short time longer on the night of our last meeting, he would not now have found it necessary to intrude such a question upon me. Have the kindness to let us pass, sir?"

He stood out of the way while they drove rapidly from the wharf, but almost immediately after they had gone, he entered a hack and instructed the driver to follow. When they reached their home, he took down the street and number, muttering to himself as he put the address into his pocket:

"A lucky day for me, and one which will furnish me with both money and power—power to pay her back for all the daring things she has said to me!"

CHAPTER XXVIII.

THE CAPTURE OF FORT FISHER.

NOTWITHSTANDING the dispatch made in the preparations for moving a second time upon Fort Fisher, it was as late as the fifth of January ere the fleet left Old Point Comfort and steamed out of the lovely harbor into the broad, blue expanse of the Atlantic. Colonel Wilfer's letters up to the day of starting were long, frequent and cheerful. But after that there were long days and nights of silent and anxious watching, until the glad news swept over the land that "Terry had captured Fort Fisher," which was followed soon after by a long epistle from the proud and happy absent one, who had been permitted to take a part in the glorious enterprise. The letter came just as the gas was lighted for the evening, and we will take the liberty of looking over the reader's shoulder for a share of the stirring contents. It was dated January 16th, the day succeeding the capture of the fort, and gave a glowing account of all that had been done from the time they started up to the date of its fall:

"My Wife,—I scarcely know how to begin, where there is so much to say, and with the powerful scenes that mark this day, all around me to shame the weak efforts of my pen at description. We set out upon our journey under unfavorable auspices, encountering a heavy storm almost as soon as we found ourselves fairly launched upon the trackless deep. It was with great difficulty that we were able to double Cape

Hatteras, and many of the smaller transports were compelled to heave to and await the sinking of the tempest. After a few hours, however, the wind changed, and we steamed rapidly towards Beaufort over a smooth sea. We found Admiral Porter already at this place when we entered the harbor, with his co-operating fleet of gun-boats. Fort Macon frowned upon us like a stern sentinel, but we laughed in its face on beholding the glorious array of strength about us, and lifted our faces with a proud consciousness of power that was in itself, a surety of the success which is now our own.

"I do not remember ever to have seen a more beautiful day than the ninth of January. Beaufort seemed to lie in quiet and peaceful repose upon our right, its lines softened by the distance. Upon the left, Fort Macon rose nearer and more formidable, with its bristling artillery and grim walls. Afar up the harbor, Morehead City shone like a speck of life in comparison, but it bore its important part, and therefore deserves mention. Looking seaward, we find the Carolina coast, which here breaks into an opening and is called Cape Lookout.

"Tuesday dawned with a threat of storming. The clouds were heavy, with a raw, wintry wind and misty rain, while great, angry waves rolled up from the sea upon a dismal shore. Such dense clouds of vapor brooded over sea and land, we could not even discern the outline of Beaufort, lately so beautiful under the dazzling beams of a glorious sun. One of the heavy storms peculiar to the latitude and season was upon us, and our largest vessels were forced to throw out additional anchors, while the others sought a more sheltered spot. In the afternoon, a brig was driven near us in a disabled condition, and we sent to her relief as soon as possible, tugging her to a place of safety, while the gale increased to a hurricane, as the day wore on. The steamers were obliged to keep up steam to keep from being blown ashore, and the ocean was one vast sheet of snowy foam. I cannot describe the horrors and discomforts of that night, especially for the troops on the transports, exposed to the beating rains, driving winds and icy spray from the sea. About midnight the fury of the storm somewhat abated, and by morning it had gone down sufficiently to allow the fleet to reassemble. At one o'clock the order was given for the squadron to make ready to sail, each vessel having its position assigned to it. By sunset the war vessels were under way, and under the careful directions for the order in which the advance was to be made, the others followed. The vapor had disappeared as the sun sank in the gorgeous splendor that succeeds a storm, and a full moon rose majestically over the blue waters.

"As the fleet swept on over the great, sublime wells of the sea, a populous city seemed suddenly to have sprung upon the waves. From the peak and flag-staff of every vessel, the suspended lamps shot out their rays into the night, creating a scene of more than earthly beauty. By morning the ocean had sunk to a perfect calm. A sail of about seventy miles brought us to New Inlet, where the fleet which was to enter from the Atlantic Ocean would pass within the mouth of Cape Fear River.

"Thursday morning, the 12th, dawned perfectly beautiful. The wind was low, the ocean smooth, the sunshine glorious. Fleet and sea and frowning fort were bathed in a flood of splendor. General Terry, in command of the land forces, crossed the bar in the flag-ship McClellan, and fired a signal for the transports to get under way; Admiral Porter took his position in the Malvern, at the head of the gun-boat fleet, and before noon the entire armada swept gracefully on over the unruffled waters. Such a scene as that never before greeted mortal eyes. Here peace and power seemed to clasp hands under the brilliant splendor of a matchless day. The glossy blue of the ocean mirrored still bluer skies, dotted over with the varied vessels of the fleet—every size and shape rising clearly relieved from the shining surface of the waves. Over these vessels streamed the dark swarms of men, into whose hands our lives seemed to have been committed, and from every side shone the bright colors of our fluttering flags and pennons, while through the midst burst wild, sweet waves of martial music from the bands. The forward ships could not be seen by those in the rear, and the monitors which could not sail with the other vessels, had to be taken in tow to keep them in line with the squadron.

"We advanced thus, with good speed upon the fort, which in its grim and massive power, commanded New Inlet upon the north. A grand sunset closed this lovely day, and four additional steamers from the east were joined to the squadron. The vessels in advance halted slightly, giving those in the rear time to close up, and as the twilight deepened into night, the lights once more swung from the mast heads, kindling the scene to a wild and picturesque beauty. Now, as the moon rose about nine o'clock, lighting up the land, signal lights were exchanged upon the water, indicating that the hour for some important movement had arrived. From the walls of Fort Fisher flaunted the rebel banner, while in the rear great billowy waves of ruddy light thrown up against the starry sky, signaled to the inhabitants of Wilmington the unwelcome approach of the Union forces. At eleven o'clock the squadron came to anchor where it could shelter the approach of the transports by its guns, allowing the troops to land, who were to storm the fort immediately the ships had done the duty assigned to them of bombardment.

"The 13th of January was a propitious day for our undertaking—a refreshing breeze from the sea—clear sky and glorious sun overhead, and everything heart could desire to give us the inspiration of exterior surroundings, for success. The frigate Brooklyn, leading a number of war vessels, slowly skirted the shore, tossing their enormous shells into the forest, and wherever it was supposed any rebel troops might be concealed. Not an answering gun hailed our approach, and after thus reconnoitering the ground, preparations were made to land the forces. The transport boats were flung out as with one impulse of will, and the water swarmed with the fairy-like flotilla. O, how the cheers rent the air—how keenly the bugles piped their joyous notes, and the bands crashed into their weaker music with their exultant voices! Hundreds of strong hands grasped the oars, and myriads of diamond-like drops flashed from their glancing blades in the sunlight.

"While this was taking place, the new Ironsides, afraid of nothing, and accompanied by the monitors, took their places defiantly in point-blank range of the fort, and opened upon it with a daring, destructive fire. Cowards were transformed into brave men that day, and the blood leaped like fire through the coolest veins. Before three o'clock, the land forces, with the exception of the 'reserve,' were all ashore and ready for action. We made the landing upon a line of hard beach about five miles above the fort, and were drawn up in military order for the length of two miles in extent of line. The bombardment was progressing bravely, and about half-past four, Porter signaled for the remaining gun-boats to move into position and take part in it. Thus far the Ironsides and three monitors had done their work so well with their deadly shot and shell, the rebels were forced to take refuge in their casemates, rarely venturing to return the compliments paid them. When they did fire, it was at the intrepid monitors, who did not even take the trouble to smile at the pigmy attempts to annihilate them. At length all the ships were engaged in the action, however, and then, indeed, the scene took a sublime and awful aspect. From the midst of dense clouds of lowering smoke, which had settled upon the face of the waters, great tongues of flame leaped up, followed by a crashing, as of mighty thunders. The roar was incessant, and as night advanced, and the gloom of smoke and moonless sky made more vivid the battle-lights, one might be pardoned for recalling Milton's sublimely awful picture of the infernal regions. Vast flames of lurid light ran through the whole wide expanse of action, and as the missiles hissed through the air, the explosions seemed to shake both sea and land. In the meantime, the land forces had diminished the distance by more than two miles between themselves and the fort; and after a time the flash of camp-fires along their lines, added to the breadth and beauty of the singular scene.

"Saturday morning, showed Fort Fisher without a visible flag-staff, it having been shot away in the night. But about eight o'clock the rebels ran up another to show that they were still alive and defiant as ever. General Terry had landed and established his head-quarters on shore in the very foremost ranks of his men. By this time, two parallel lines of breast-works had been thrown up, extending across the peninsula from the ocean to Cape Fear River. One of these was to prevent the approach of any re-enforcements to the beleaguered fort, and the other, the escape of the garrison by land.

"On Sunday, the bombardment continued during the morning, but the rebels succeeded in running down six steamers from Wilmington, and landing about three hundred men in the fort. It was done amidst such a shower of shells from the fleet however, the steamers were compelled to retire. At noon such a breach had been made in the sea face of the wall, it was deemed expedient to attempt a charge, with a strong hope for success. No one thought the rebels would not make a desperate resistance, and yet the determination to make the charge gathered force from consideration, and we began at once to prepare for it. The boats, filled with men, were lowered upon the outer side of the ships, thus screening them from observation, while at the same time the land forces advanced in a resolute attack upon the land side. The land forces, almost in rear of the fort, with Generals Ames and Curtis to direct them, made the first move upon the fortress, met by a furious resistance. But they never faltered or paused in their onward path, hewing down the stockade and chevaux-de-frise, until they had pressed on to a lodgment in the north-east corner of the fort. Here General Curtis sent the national flag proudly floating upon the breeze from the ramparts, and was greeted by deafening cheers. While the uproar and carnage was at its height—while the fleet kept up its deadly fire upon that portion of the fort which the patriots had not yet penetrated, the sailors and marines burst into the arena with their cutlasses, revolvers, and muskets, to take part in the daring conflict. They had come in the face of the bristling cannon, running up the beach into the very jaws of death, while great gaps were swept through their ranks as they ran. By the time they reached the ramparts, the whole beach over which they had passed, was strewn with the dead and wounded. And now, three of our national flags rose above the rear walls of Fort Fisher, followed by the bravest and most resolute effort ever made to seize a stronghold. It was the grandest spectacle that ever moved under mortal eye, to see nearly two thousand men running through the most pitiless storms of shot with loud, defiant cheers upon their dauntless lips. Each boat's crew carried its own ensign and distinguishing flag, and these glittering banners moved gorgeously, while the flames flashed in their faces, and great billows of smoke rolled up over and around them. The ground under their feet was shaken by the heavy thunders of artillery, and over which they trod with unfaltering steps, and spirits determined as death.

"This combat was waged for six fearful hours, and often hand to hand, ere a decided advantage was gained. But the storming of the fort by the naval brigade had been effective, and served to aid the troops in gaining a foothold from which they could not easily be dislodged; yet how long this foothold might be maintained was a question which would probably be solved by the loss of hundreds of brave men. The rebels could sweep the entire interior of the fort with both musketry and artillery; and from Fort Buchanan in the south-west, they now opened fire upon us, also. Yet our undaunted General (Ames) never gave way in his forward pressure, until nine traverses had been captured. Being now almost night, and the troops nearly exhausted, General Terry sent forward reinforcements, consisting of one brigade and a colored regiment, then the whole force was again pressed forward, and the conflict renewed with tenfold fury. Traverse after traverse was taken in rapid succession, and finally the victory won! But it was past ten o'clock at night ere the fort was actually in our possession, and purchased by the lives of hundreds of men who had fallen to rise no more.

"But oh, what an hour was that for those who had fought around and within those walls, when General Terry announced to the Admiral by signal, that the fort was ours! The whole sky seemed one vast blaze of light, from the meteoric shower flung up from the fleet amid loud shouts of rejoicing! When the rebel flag went down, and the star-spangled banner was run up in its place, such cheers were never before heard from the throats of men! The order had been given to stop firing, and their cheers rang over the waters in long, almost demoniac yells of wild and fierce delight."

Astrea dropped the letter upon her lap with a deep breath, while the proud glow of cheek and eye expressed the excitement to which she could not give words. Helen's clasped hands relaxed as she uttered thankfully:

"Oh, to have come out safe and victorious from such fearful carnage! How grateful I feel, that *our* world was not sunk in seas of blood. But when is he coming home?"

"He cannot tell—soon, he hopes," answered Astrea, reading from the concluding page; "we need not be surprised to see him now at any time. Ah! here is something else! Our good friend, Captain Meridan, was badly wounded in one arm, while fighting with the heroic coolness of an old soldier. He will send or bring the Captain here for us to nurse back to health again. Very well, I will not object now."

Helen laughed.

"Nor I. It will seem natural to have some one to take care of again, and you are now proof against his fascinations, being the sole property of his gallant commanding officer. They cannot come too soon. I am growing weary of this tame, uneventful life."

"Tame! Uneventful!" cried Astrea, laughing in her turn. "To me it seems anything else!"

"O, I mean comparatively, of course. You know it is very different from that which we have experienced in the past, and it frets me to see uniforms out of their proper places. One might think New York a battle-field, counting the number of officers that may be seen upon the streets, only for the unexceptional cut of their coats, and the splendor of their buttons, bars, eagles and stars! I long for the sight of a rusty coat, tarnished bullion and the smell of gunpowder, once more. I hope the Colonel and Captain may both be as rusty as an old copper before they reach here, if only to shame the others."

"Doubtless they will be rusty enough," said Astrea absently, having only half heard Helen's remarks, and the latter quietly left the room, leaving her alone with the letter and her own thoughts.

CHAPTER XXIX.

AN UNLOOKED FOR DENOUEMENT.

SOME days after the receipt of Colonel Wilfer's letter, Astrea sat alone before the grate, listening to the dreary sough of the wind outside. It had been a stormy day, and was now drawing to its close sullenly, sobbing itself to rest with a fretful moaning, like a willful child. Helen had gone next door to see a sick girl to whom she had recently become much attached, and Astrea, on finding herself alone for the evening, had taken a chair in front of the grate, where the ruddy light fell brightly upon her sweet face, now growing rounded and lovely once more under the inspiration of more hopeful days.

It was a pretty picture, as she sat there with her head against the dark blue velvet lining of the chair, which brought out her face in strong relief, and made it look fairer by contrast—her hair softly rippling over the dazzling whiteness of her brow, and the full lips parted just enough to display the gleam of pearly teeth. The large, dark eyes had grown very soft and tender with some lingering phase of thought, and the little hands lying upon her lap moved gently as she toyed with the wedding ring upon its slender finger.

The door opened and a light step fell upon the carpet, but she did not look up, and spoke as one who was but half conscious of what she was saying. "You have returned early, Helen. I thought you intended to spend the evening away. What brings you home so soon?"

Instead of Helen's voice, it was a short, dry laugh which answered, causing her to spring to her feet and grasp the back of her chair for support, gazing with wild, distended eyes at the cloaked figure of the intruder. He took a step forward and removed his hat, suffering the warm red light to fall upon his features, while the steelly glitter of his blue eyes met her intense gaze mockingly. Thus they stood, face to face, until she reeled and gasped in a broken voice:

"It cannot—be—Frederic! I must have gone mad!—am dreaming some wild dream of insanity. Frederic was killed! I saw him—dead on the field, and buried him—forgivingly—pityingly! How could he come out of his grave to find me here?"

The intruder laughed again, tossing the hair back from his handsome forehead, with a movement full of careless grace.

"You may as well come out of your maze and know the truth, for I am here to prove that you never had the pleasure of burying me, as you thought. I was not in that battle of Corinth."

She could not speak, but still stared at him fixedly, and he went on in the cool, deliberate manner characteristic with him:

"I suppose, since you see that you are mistaken, you would like to know who it was you took for me, and buried with such sublime 'pity and forgiveness.' Well, that was my twin brother, Ferdinand, who had been so long in Europe. As soon as he heard of our national troubles, he hastened home and came to me to offer his services. The spirit he manifested, made me forget some old scores that were between us, and I got for him the vacant Colonelcy of my regiment, on being promoted to a higher rank. But it happened that I had other work to do just at the time of that battle, and was not there. My brother fell, and you buried him, really believing, I suppose, that it was your beloved husband! But you will have hard work to make others believe it when all this grand story comes out. You have gotten yourself into a pretty tight place, if I know anything about it."

Astrea took no notice of the last remark. From a host of bewildered ideas, but one of importance was evolved. Seizing his arm with passionate vehemence, she cried out in quick, short gasps, while life and death seemed struggling within her:

"Ferdinand!—he had a child! It was *his* daughter of whom your mother wrote—who is dead! Not my child—not Lillian! Oh, speak!"

"Yes, it was his child—Lillian also, as both were named for our mother. His wife died in Italy, and he brought his daughter to her grandmother to be taken care of. By the Lord Harry, all this is better than a play! Talk of novels, romances and that sort of thing! It beats them all to see what a string of events has been made."

His tirade was here cut short by the heavy falling of poor Astrea, who sank without a sigh at his feet, and he stood looking at her for a minute without moving. With the first signs of life, he lifted her up and placed her in a chair, then took another for himself, and sat facing her, coolly waiting until she was able to speak.

"Lily!—where is she?" soon came faintly from her lips.

"O, never mind her now; she is safe enough. We have other things to talk about. You don't ask me what especially brought me here."

She was silent.

"I have come to claim my wife," he continued in slow, measured tones.

She started as if from a severe blow.

"No! no! I am not your wife!" she faltered, putting out both hands as if to shield herself. "You cannot take me!"

"We shall see. You will quietly go with me wherever I choose to take you, or stand a trial for bigamy. Will that suit you any better? You see I have a very strong case against you, and fancy that I can make a rare old time for you before I have done. It will not make the matter any better for you, certainly, to have married the rascal who captured me and had me under sentence of death! Now I understand how you got your power to release me—played sweet on him and won him over through his love for you! Good! by the Lord Harry. But, why the devil did you not let them hang me and get me out of your way then! Suppose, however, the *idea* was not quite agreeable, to let him hang me, then turn around and marry him. Then you wanted to get the child, and knew you would not dare to go after her. Its all very well for me, as things have turned out. I owe both of you a grudge, and having you under my thumb, can pay it off with interest. Your most noble lord will be home in a few days? Good! I shall be on hand; the condition of my revolver is always perfect, and she never hangs fire," saying which he took a small, silver mounted pistol from his pocket and examined it caressingly.

For a moment, Astrea's blood coursed coldly through her veins; but reason was slowly rising above emotions of pain and fear, and her eye was kindling with its old, steady, scornful light. He was surprised when she demanded in a totally changed voice:

"Being a rebel officer, how does it happen that you dare thus boldly to venture into the enemy's country?"

"O, I was captured again by the Feds, and being rather tired of the service, concluded to take Father Abe's amnesty oath and look around the North a little for a change. I had been to Richmond for a special purpose, and in attempting to return, got picked up by Phil Sheridan's cavalry. Then, as I said before, I thought I'd like a change."

"So you find yourself at large amongst us. I suppose, of course, being a general officer, you were specially pardoned by the President, according to the requirements, before being permitted to take the oath?"

He darted a quick, keen glance at her, and replied rather hastily:

"Yes! That is all right. I got a special pardon, and came here to 'crack nuts' with my sweet and dutiful wife. By the luckiest accident in the world, I came across an old friend of yours—a Doctor Grey, who informed me that you were here, and gave me your address. He sent his most respectful compliments to 'Mrs. Wilfer,'" following this speech with a triumphant laugh.

She sat still, looking at him with a gaze that made him change his position uneasily, and ask her why she looked at him in that fashion.

"Because I see that in trying to deceive me, you have betrayed yourself, Frederic Passiver; and so far from having me in your power, have placed yourself hopelessly in mine. I understand the whole thing now. So bitter a rebel as you, could not change without some purpose in view, and you went to Richmond to apply for leave to come North on secret service. Then you allowed yourself to be taken by our cavalry, took the oath and came on here for the sole motive of playing the spy. Have you not already proved to me your estimation of the binding character of an oath, and shall I do wrong to judge you by the past? As self-preservation is the first law of nature, I do not see why I should not be justifiable in giving you up at once to the proper authorities as a spy!"

While she was speaking he had turned fearfully pale, staring blankly at her resolute face. But almost immediately he recovered himself and put on a defiant manner calculated to mislead her.

"You can try it if you like, but the result will be a notoriety that cannot be much to your credit, since the object for such a step would become too apparent for doubt—to get me out of your way! I am not such a fool as to thrust my head into the lion's mouth without first seeing that all his teeth are rendered powerless to hurt me. Come," and he rose to his feet. "What is your decision? Will you go with me now, or is there to be open war between us—the charitable public umpire, to decide who wins?"

"War, if you will," she answered with a sharp ring of unbending will in her voice. "I shall have no fears for myself if the public is left to decide my case—a loyal northern public which shall know the nature and course of the antagonist with whom I have to deal. Every loyal soul in the land will rally to my side; and every tender mother's heart will bleed for the anguish you have caused me to suffer through my child, of whom I am so cruelly bereaved! Yes, let it be war, and let it come quickly!"

Her face glowed, and her eyes flashed most gloriously now. A crushed, helpless woman was no longer before him, but a heroine, grand and strong in her sense of right and innocence. He changed his manner of attack and approached her with fiendish strategy.

"Not just yet! I can wait a little while, since time brings fullness of revenge. This little friend of mine," tapping his pistol, "and I, have an account to settle with Colonel Wilfer. I am going to wait for the gallant Colonel, and see what he has to say for himself, looking out for you in the meantime."

"I know you would not hesitate to murder him, if your own personal safety did not prove his strongest safeguard," she replied, while a shade of color faded from her cheek. "But you will not dare to harm him save in secret, and if you do that, I am still left to give you into the hands of justice. You cannot escape."

"Humph! What will prevent my serving you the same way, if I choose? Let me tell you that mortal man or woman cannot escape the law of my revenge! Listen, and I will give you a little piece of news that will serve to confirm what I say. Do you remember your good old friend, Doctor Early? I had a long score laid up with him before the war, and I resolved to pay it off with interest. I suspected him of a great many things that I could not prove until after the war began; but then I watched him, and found out very soon that he was a regular Union man, out and out! That was enough for me, and I set a trap for the old fool, into which he ran his head straight off. He was up to all sorts of tricks, and I caught him in one, which gave me a chance to seize him for trial. I sent a squad of my own men to arrest him, and he could not bring up one item of self-defence. I charged him, among other things, with running off that boy Rufus, and he stood up like a hard-headed fool and owned to everything, thinking it heroic, I reckon! But he got his neck stretched in consequence! I had him strung up right there, and saw him die the death of a traitor to his country, and a d—— scoundrel! Now what do you say to that?"

"That it is like you to revel in cruelty and injustice! Oh, Doctor Early! dear old friend, to die such a death and at *his* hands! Frederic Passiver, are you *all* bad? Is there not one soft or humane spot in your hard heart? Have you no fear of the consequences of your deeds? Beware ere you pass wholly beyond the pale of God's mercy, if you have not done that already!"

"Don't worry about me in that respect. Plenty of time to get 'good' after I have had my revenge. Now, my fair wife, I am obliged to take my leave of you, but would suggest that you keep it in mind that my eyes are ever upon you; and that, through the many I shall employ to watch your movements, it will be utterly impossible for you to do anything of which I shall not immediately become cognizant. Good-night, and pleasant dreams."

Ere his closing speech had died upon her ear, he had passed out into the hall and opened the street-door for himself. As he ran down the steps, a figure came out of the gloom upon one side and joined him familiarly.

"Well, Grey, I've got her frightened almost to death;" and he laughed a cold, hard laugh that grated harshly upon the ear. "But she's desperate, too, and as spunky as a worried cat. We will have to work with caution. Have you any news?"

"Yes, you are to report to Thompson immediately."

"The deuce I am! I am not partial to leaving the city just now, with all this prospect for fun before me. Before I can get back, she will have had time to get away."

"Leave me to watch her movements and keep you advised

of what is going on. It will not take you much over a week, and then you can remain here until the signal is given to move on to Washington."

Passiver was thoughtful for some moments.

"I suppose I must, but I don't like it. When am I to go?—to-night?"

"Yes, you had better. And as for her, an invisible foe is worse than an open enemy. She will suffer much more anxiety if you keep entirely out of sight."

"By the Lord Harry, Grey, you and I ought to have lived a few centuries earlier! Our ingenuity will fail to be appreciated in these times. You are right! It is better to let the leaven work while we accomplish that which has brought us here. I'm afraid I made a mistake there once to-night. I had forgotten that she was as sharp as steel."

"Why, what did you do?"

"Told her I had been especially pardoned by the President. Afterwards she made out a pretty clear case against me, coming much nearer the truth than I relished. But I braved her out with a little bravado, and think I shook her faith in her own judgment. I don't know, however, that we need to fear any way, even if she knew all about it. She's a queer one—conscientious, etc."

"Tell me just what was said by each of you," asked Grey anxiously, and Passiver repeated it as correctly as he could from his memory of the interview.

"You *have* acted the fool for once. Pen up a woman in a place like the one you have her in, and then talk of trusting to her "conscientiousness!" What's got into you, man! Wait till your work is done, before you give her the chance to put a halter round your neck. You can't play with her and do the other at the same time. Let the—*trap-door* fall first, then do what you please."

Here the Doctor cut short his lecture and beckoned to a hackman. He followed Passiver into the vehicle, after giving the order to be driven to the Hudson River depot.

"I am not to see any one here before I go?"

"No; you are to go straight to Thompson for orders. At Albany you will take the New York Central to Rome; there change cars, and go by way of Ogdensburg to Canada. Keep a sharp look out for friends, and carry nothing about you that could be construed into evidence against you, if anything happens. What have you now about your person or in your baggage?"

"Nothing but some few letters, with all the envelopes bearing address destroyed. My clothes are not even marked. You need not fear for me, Grey. I am not quite such a fool as you think me; and I did not venture up here with my eyes shut."

"All right. Good luck to you, old fellow!"

Half an hour later, Frederic Passiver was being rapidly whirled along the bank of the Hudson, while Grey walked back up Broadway to his hotel.

It was sometime after the former left Astrea, ere Helen came home and found her pacing the floor with hands wrung together in agony, and an expression of suffering upon her face that was startling.

"Oh, what has happened, Astrea? Something dreadful has occurred. It is no ill to Harry?"

"No, not Harry! But oh, Helen, even the grave deceives me!" she groaned. "Frederic Passiver has been here—has threatened everything terrible—to kill Harry—disgrace me—claim me as his wife!"

"Frederic Passiver! Astrea, *are* you mad, child?"

"Alas, no! It would be a mercy if I could lose my distracted senses. Sit down, Helen, and listen to me, for something must be done quickly. You must try to help me."

Helen sank into a chair, dumb with affright. Astrea took a stool and sat down beside her, leaning her head against Helen's shoulder until she had gained a little composure. Then she related all that had happened.

"Now you see there is no time to be lost," she said in

conclusion. "Will you go to Washington and find out if his statement is true? He says he will watch me, and I dare not try; but I must have something to hold him in check until I know what to do further. This seems my only hope."

"I will go to the ends of the earth for you if I can be of any service to you, as you well know. But how can I feel sure that something dreadful will not happen to you while I am away? Oh, I wish Colonel Wilfer was here. Let me telegraph to him to come to us at once! Shall I?"

"Not for worlds! Would you have him come here to be shot down like a dog by a hidden foe? Frederic Passiver would not put himself into such a dangerous position without some desperate, deadly purpose at heart, and he goes armed all the time—has emissaries employed as spies, if he spoke the truth, which is likely. Besides, dear, even if we knew where to send a dispatch, he must not come here now, until—"

"What?"

"Until I am legally free! There is but one course left for me to pursue, and until I accomplish my purpose, Colonel Wilfer must not come to me again. You know he is not—my husband!—not legally my husband now!"

"But oh, child, you thought him dead, and *I* can testify to your truth and goodness! Your proofs are all too strong to give you any uneasiness as to the result, and it is Harry's right to stand beside you in trouble. Think of all Passiver has done—what he is! A cruel man, a bitter rebel—a willful murderer who was under sentence of death, and made his escape from prison only in time to save his neck! How much sympathy do you suppose he would find in a northern court? He would not even dare to come forward and oppose you!"

"But Helen, this must not come before the public if there is any help for it. If we can only get any hold upon him to keep him quiet for awhile, I hope to find some way out of this wretched entanglement, without actual harm to any one. If what we suspect should prove true, his life is in danger, and you know that *I* cannot be the instrument of harm to him, however deeply he may have wronged me. I will not do more than strive to protect myself, and must be very careful in this, lest I should betray him."

"Why should you strive to shield him—a rebel—murderer—spy!" cried Helen with dawning indignation. "He is doing his best to crush you, after all that he has caused you to suffer in the past! I cannot understand your forbearance!"

"Whatever else he may be, I dare not forget that he is my husband—the father of my child, and I will not stain my hands with his blood! 'Vengeance is mine, saith the Lord.' I will leave him in his hands. Oh, Helen, do not add to the weight I bear! Come what may, I will not injure him even to save myself. Only do what I ask, and let me alone in this matter. The end will come, and in my Father's time I shall be justified."

"When shall I go to Washington?"

"To-night. Take the express train at twelve o'clock, and go through. You will not return until you have ascertained the truth, and learned whether he was really pardoned. That is all that is necessary now."

Without reply, Helen made her few hasty preparations, and took leave of Astrea tearfully. She had but little time left before the departure of the train, and, as soon as she could be ready, drove rapidly to the Jersey City Ferry. But when the train went out, she was safely seated in one corner, and thinking very earnestly upon the business that was taking her thus unexpectedly to Washington.

Left alone, Astrea was naturally anxious and feverishly watchful, but nothing of an alarming nature transpired to add to her uneasiness. There were no signs visible of a watch having been set upon her actions. Still this was no surety against the evil intentions of a man like Frederic Passiver, and she had scarcely eaten or slept when Helen returned two days later. She was almost ill with weariness from her journey, and looked worn and haggard. Yet there was that in her heart which she dared not show to Astrea, and she refrained from putting a cheerful tone upon the face of the news she brought.

"Whom have you seen, Helen?"

"The President himself. I was lucky, and obtained a private interview, in which I learned enough to destroy that daring man inevitably. A man of the name, and answering his description, claiming to be a private, was captured by Sheridan's cavalry, and took the oath, as he stated; but no man of rank has received a special pardon. Evidently he threw himself in the way of the cavalry, and allowed himself to be captured—in which the soldiers only saw a desire to leave the rebel service without the odium of desertion. But we know there must be deeper reasons for such a daring course. I suspect a great deal that I cannot put into any satisfactory shape. Help me to solve the mystery. What did Frederic Passiver leave Richmond, get captured, come here, and take the oath *for?*"

"To find me, certainly."

Helen shook her head.

"How did he know anything about your being here? What reason had he to suppose you were not still with the army?"

"You have forgotten that he claims to have learned from Doctor Grey, who, you are aware, is no friend of mine. You remember our meeting, the day Harry went away last."

"Ah, yes, and it is this thing which so puzzles me, Astrea! How did Doctor Grey know just where to find Frederic Passiver the moment he discovered you in New York? There is some mystery here that must be unraveled. Just as surely as we live, that man is not here merely to torment you. Of course, that is a part of his purpose, but there are other and dangerous reasons, and they are leagued in them. I believe Doctor Grey's discovery of you to be purely accidental, and probably he then saw a chance to turn his discovery to some personal advantage. But he did not come here originally to find you. Think of his strange, unprincipled course throughout the war, and how many things we know against him!

Doctor Grey was in the prison that night of Passiver's escape, and how do you know he was not there for the purpose of releasing him, on pretense of attending the sick? Accident may have furnished him with what was really about to take place, and it is probable he then allowed Wilfer to do the work and himself dodge the risks, at the same time giving him a hold upon poor Harry. You know how closely he followed us up, and how skillfully he worked until Captain Wilfer was dismissed the service! If we could only get at the whole truth, I have no doubt we should find that they are leagued together, and engaged now in some terrible plot against the country."

Astrea's pale, thoughtful face was turned to her now with wistful questioning.

"Yes, Astrea, some terrible plot. But they are digging a pit for themselves, and I shall rejoice to see them fall into it! Forgive me for taking steps against your will. I love you too much to stand by and see you murdered by inches, and all that I have done was to save you."

"*What* have you done? Oh, Helen—"

"Nothing except what was right. I told President Lincoln the whole story—all that we have done, seen, suffered, lost—and he could not doubt my truth. He stood up like the good, noble soul that he is, and declared that you should be protected from persecution and danger. He has ordered detectives put upon their track, and, sooner or later, the truth must come out. I furnished a full description of Grey, thinking he must be in the city, and now we will have to leave them to the mercy of the law. Don't look at me as if I had broken your heart, for they deserve it—they do deserve it! and God knows I have striven only to serve you faithfully, because in all the wide world I have none other to care for me."

"Oh, Helen! Helen! I know that you are good and true, but you do not know what you have done! I did not want his life!"

"Well, you have not taken it. The whole responsibility is upon *my* shoulders. If he is innocent, there is nothing to fear.

If guilty—why, let him suffer as he deserves. I say he *shall* not longer worry you with his diabolical hatred. Already you have allowed him to take too many liberties with your peace. It has got to end here, or he must suffer the consequences."

Helen was becoming more and more excited each moment, but Astrea, who was calmed by the magnitude of her troubles, wisely remained silent. Notwithstanding her distress at the step Helen had taken, she could not deny a sense of relief at the thought that no blow could reach Colonel Wilfer through the secret machinations of her enemy. The strict guard set upon his actions would prove a safeguard for the intended victim, at least, and she should not feel now that he was hopelessly exposed with no sure protection against unseen dangers.

Still the days passed very heavily after these events, until another letter came from Colonel Wilfer, saying he could not be in New York probably before the last of April. This removed her last fear, and turned her thoughts back from fears for his safety to things more immediately connected with herself. Helen begged her to advise the Colonel of what had transpired, but she firmly refused, resolving to keep the matter a secret from him until he came, or she was forced by some imperative circumstance to reveal it.

"It would only hasten his coming," she said, "and perhaps prove his destruction. Wait."

In the meantime nothing more was seen or heard from Passiver, and they were utterly ignorant of his movements. Once they caught a glimpse of Doctor Grey hovering in the vicinity of the house; but after that he seemed to disappear also, and they were left to await the future in anxious suspense.

CHAPTER XXX.

THE LAST ACT IN THE TRAGEDY, WITH BRIGHTER CLOSING SCENES.

ON the morning of the 15th of April, our friends were awakened from feverish sleep by the sound of hurrying feet, and wild confusion upon the pavements. Helen sprang from her bed and ran to the window to listen to the shrill, sharp cry of a boyish voice which was repeating with startling distinctness:

"Here's th' Her'ld—all about the 'sassination of Mr. Lincoln! Third edition. Seward's throat cut an' General Grant killed on the cars! Here's th' Her'ld."

"Oh, merciful God, it *cannot* be! Killed! dead! murdered—that brave, good man! Astrea, President Lincoln has been assassinated!" and with the fearful announcement she reeled through the room and sank down like one crushed beside the bed. Astrea sprang up with a scream of anguish, catching Helen's shoulder and turning her face to the light. The thought that had instantly crossed her brain had come to both in the same moment, and now they gazed mutely into each other's eyes, struck dumb with horror. Helen was first to break the dreadful silence.

"Oh, *that* was it! I seem to see it all now. Mr. Lincoln assassinated! It was he they came to murder! Horrible, horrible!"

"Wait! For God's sake do not hastily condemn!" gasped Astrea, hoarsely, then she fell back upon the bed and lay motionless as if her heart was breaking with its weight of grief and fear.

What a day was that for them in mutely bearing the burthens as if by tacit consent, and moving about in bewilderment of woe, robed in black from head to foot, with the same sombre signs of grief floating heavily from every window and door. Wherever they turned their eyes, sable drapery and flags at half-mast, with slow, mournful sounds of music breaking through the deep, heavy murmur of life on the streets, seemed to add to the oppressive load that was crushing them to the earth; and in the midst of this, came a secret summons, calling them immediately to Washington.

"Oh, my God, it is true," said Astrea, "and there is no escape for me! They are calling me there to consign him to death by my evidence!"

Helen wrung her hands hopelessly, overwhelmed with the fearfulness of her position. Not until she found herself seated beside her stricken friend on the way to the Capital, did she fully realize the importance of the step she had taken, for she could not know what was to come when she confided her story and her fears to the President in her appeal for protection. She could not know that she was then arming the doomed man against his secret foes, though retributive justice might not reach them until the life at which they aimed had been smitten from the earth.

They arrived in Washington just after daylight, and were conducted to a hotel, where after hasty refreshment, they were taken before the Secretary of War and required to "state what they knew about the prisoners, Frederic Passiver and Doctor Thomas L. Grey, who had been arrested under suspicion of having been cognizant of, and engaged in the plot to assassinate Abraham Lincoln."

They gave their evidence briefly, saying no more than they were obliged to say in answer to the questions put to them, and were then dismissed and ordered to be sent to the Old Capitol Prison to identify the prisoners. Oh, with what heavy hearts did they re-enter the carriage and drive away toward that gloomy pile where the two conspirators had been confined. Helen was almost frantic with grief, and sobbed unrestrainedly.

"I did not know it would bring you to this, darling! I was thinking only of you," she whispered, "can you ever forgive me!"

For answer, Astrea slipped her arm over her neck and kissed the tear-wet cheek, but she could not speak, and the gentlemen who accompanied them, turned their faces from the two wretched beings, touched almost to tears by their uncontrollable distress.

The two men had been confined in separate rooms, and they were taken first to Doctor Grey, who lost all hope at sight of their faces, and shook his fist at them in impotent rage. Up to this moment he had been cool and defiant, seeming to care for nothing, but on their appearance, all his hardihood and assurance suddenly changed into a fury of rage and despair. On Frederic Passiver the effect was no less striking, and he reeled the moment they appeared, as if he had been struck a heavy blow by an unseen hand. He had counted upon Astrea's peculiarly forbearing temperament, and hoped that their arrest had arisen from no action of hers, until her presence seemed to prove that she had not been as scrupulous as he deemed her, in taking steps to compass his ruin.

Three days of untold anguish followed that first visit, and the investigations had developed a strong circumstantial evidence, but no proofs, and the authorities were at fault whether they were really in the conspiracy or not—though plenty of treachery and mystery had come to light to render their imprisonment a matter of justice. In order to keep down unnecessary excitement, the proceedings were carried on secretly, and Astrea had striven in vain to gain any knowledge of the result, or to get permission to visit her husband in the prison. Now, however, the desired leave was granted to her, and with a sense of relief most grateful to her feelings, she went with Helen and one gentleman, who was instructed to see that she was admitted to the prison. Helen was not to be permitted to enter, but remain outside while Astrea sought the interview.

"I can at least convince him that I did not betray him willingly," whispered the poor wife as she left her at the carriage door. "It would be terrible to let him die believing that it was I who caused his apprehension through personal motives."

The gentleman who accompanied her, saw her to the door, then, as she passed inside, softly drew it together after her. Frederic was sitting upon the bed, looking most wretchedly pale and haggard; but the moment he saw her, he gave one bound from the couch and caught her by the arms, holding her as in a vice, while he hissed through his set teeth:

"Demon! devil in woman's form! How dare you put yourself into my power after betraying me into the hands of these infernal Yankees? I shall murder you in spite of myself!"

Her dark eye met his unflinchingly, and her voice was low, almost tender in its mournfulness as she answered:

"Frederic, as I hope for God's mercy, I did not betray you. What I charged you with was mere suspicion, and I would not have used proofs against *you*, if I had possessed them, even to save myself from your unjust cruelty. When you left me that night, the friend with whom I lived came home from visiting a sick child, and in my extremity of woe, I told her what had occurred. I only wanted to keep you from taking any rash steps that might give publicity to my painful position, and what you had said of yourself, made me suspect that I might gain some restraining power by sending here to ascertain if you had told me the truth. She came only to see if you had been especially pardoned, as you claimed to have been, and in her eagerness to serve me, was tempted, when she learned your deception, to tell the President everything. She had known me long, and we have suffered—borne hardships, dangers, everything together! She wished to save me from your cruelty, and her efforts in my behalf was the means of putting the detectives upon your track. From that time forth you were watched, and you, not I, know how much you have to fear! But oh, Frederic, it is not by my will or wish you have come to this! I was willing to leave your punishment to a wiser power than my own, and it is justice, not fate, that has overtaken you! Oh, Frederic, your oath, your oath to give me back my child! Why did you break it—for see! now it has come upon you! If I could save you even now, I would, but I cannot!"

He had relaxed his hold upon her, and sank back upon the side of the bed, white and trembling. The woman's truth was incontrovertible, and the grandeur of her nature overpowered him. There were no forced, false tones of sublime pity, and the tears that fell over her anguished face were too genuinely the signs of an inexpressible grief for his scoffing. Anger and defiance faded into despair, for he thought his fate sealed, and that she had come to bid him a last good-bye. Crushed by the magnitude of the fearful dangers he had brought upon his own head, and seeming to see himself upon the borders of death, all her great goodness, forbearance and suffering—all his own wrong, cruelty and deceit, came up before him overwhelmingly, and his heart was filled for the first time with a sense of remorse.

"Eugenia," he faltered after a long pause, "you have much to forgive. Are you sure it is not more than you are able to do?"

"More than I am able to do to forgive you? Oh, no! I can freely pardon all you have done to me. Perhaps if I had not suffered so much, I could not do it so easily, but suffering teaches us to appreciate the great sacrifice of the Son of God for our sakes; and he taught us to pray 'forgive us our trespasses, *as we forgive those who trespass against us.*' If we could more fully comprehend what we ask for when we utter that prayer, we might be more generous in forgiving the wrongs committed against us. Oh, if God should measure out his mercy to us *only* thus far!"

"There would be no hope for me," he answered, dropping his head heavily. "Eugenia, have they sentenced me—am I to die soon?"

"I do not know—no one will tell me, and I fear the worst. Show some signs of repentance, Frederic—speak some kind, regretful words, or this will kill me! Oh, to die as you have lived would be too terrible!"

"What shall I say? I can ask you to forgive me, if—"

"Oh, no! not that! You have my forgiveness! Ask God now, and may he forgive you as freely as I do! I have forgotten all wrong to me in the terror of your punishment."

"I have lived a sinner, and will not die a hypocrite at least, Eugenia. I cannot fall down upon my knees, and own all my sins repentantly, for I am more angry at being detected than sorry for my sins. I went to Richmond on purpose to get permission to come North on secret service, and this was my object, for I had seen Grey who told me of the movement on foot, and we hoped to have an active hand in Old Abe's death, which we have helped to plot—"

"Frederic! Frederic! Oh, for the love of heaven cease! You are condemning yourself by this confession, and if any one has heard you, no power upon earth can save you. Oh, what are you thinking of!"

She sprang to his side and laid her hand over his lips, and now stood holding to the bedstead, white and quivering, as the keeper pushed open the door and called out:

"Time's up! Must come out."

Astrea reeled forward with a moan, but rallied and asked desperately:

"Have you been there all the time? Have you heard—"

"Everything," answered the gentleman who had accompanied her, stepping forward. She struggled as if for strength to stand, then threw up her hands with a cry that rang through the room!

"Oh, my God, lost! lost! lost!"

Before any one could catch her, she had fallen heavily to the floor, and the prisoner with a cry as bitter as her own, would have snatched her up in his arms, but the keeper put him aside, while the gentleman lifted and bore her out. With one long, bitter groan of despair, Frederic Passiver sank down upon the bed as the door closed upon them, leaving him once more alone with his maddening thoughts.

Astrea recovered to find herself in Helen's arms, fast driving to the hotel; but the bitterness of death was upon her.

"An inexorable fate seems to have decreed that I shall place the halter about his neck," she groaned hopelessly. "Now they will make me testify to his confession of complicity in the murderous plot."

All night she lay wakeful and moaning in her anguish, fearing and dreading that last act in the terrible tragedy she was called upon to render, but when morning came a message was brought to the effect that Frederic Passiver had anticipated the ends of justice and committed suicide. Then all struggling ceased, and she passively submitted herself to the hands of her friend, who, as soon as possible, started back to New York, after ascertaining the whereabouts of Colonel Wilfer and telegraphing him to return home immediately.

That Doctor Grey met his deserts we know, but just in what manner is not here to be recorded. Certain it is that he never appeared again after he had once gone within the grim walls of the Old Capitol Prison—consequently passes from our sight forever.

Once more Astrea's weary feet pressed the threshold of her quiet refuge, with Helen at her side, daring only to express her sympathy in silent and faithful services. It is said with too much of truth, that misfortunes never come singly, and it had not been proved exceptional in the case of our heroine, on whom the vials of wrath seemed to have been poured out pitilessly. Amongst Frederic Passiver's effects, which had been given to her, were found letters from England informing him of Mr. Harmon's death more than a year previous, and the mystery of his long and torturing silence was explained. Now she knew why the letters she had been constrained to write after her arrival in New York had never been answered, and the secret fear that he, too, had cast her off, was sunk in the deeper woe of her loss.

It is no wonder if she seemed utterly crushed under all these sorrows combined. Strength to battle with grief was gone, and she lay passive and helpless while Helen fluttered around her sofa grievingly, hoping and praying that Harry Wilfer would soon come to rouse her from that dreadful apathy into which she had fallen. She had only a little while to wait. Two days after their arrival he came worn and haggard with grief and alarm. Astrea turned her face from his caress to bury it in the pillows with a moan of anguish, and Helen was forced to tell him the story of all that had befallen them. He listened until she had finished with pale, rigid features.

"And all this has been willfully kept from me!" he cried at the close. "Helen! Astrea! Oh, was it kind!" and he stooped to gather her head to his bosom with pitying tenderness in spite of the reproach.

"You forget that we did not know where you were," Helen hastily added, but Astrea gently lifted herself from his embrace to say calmly:

"I would not summons you here to be murdered, and I could not let you come while *he* was here. Do you not yet know me, Harry? But you are here now—and safe!"

In a moment she lifted her pale wistful face with a glance that touched him almost to tears.

"What is it? Ask anything of me that I can do, and it shall be done!"

"I may seem impatient—unreasonable, but you will pity me, Harry! I want my child! I am dying for her presence! Oh, if you value my life, do not keep me waiting! I have suffered so much!—so much!"

"Only a little while longer, dearest one! I must get my 'leave' extended for the trip, and then after one thing is done, we will go together and seek for your little one."

"What do you mean?"

"Can you not guess?" he softly answered touching the ring upon her finger. "This must be replaced," and he drew it off. "When may I put it back again, Astrea?"

"Whenever you please. I am too weary to think."

"I will think for you, then. This evening I will bring a minister here—to-night telegraph to Washington to get my leave of absence extended, and if you are equal to the journey, we will start to-morrow. Oh, Astrea, my dear wife, shall I ever see smiles again upon these pale lips, whose weary whiteness breaks my heart!"

"Only give me my Lily, and with her and you, I can be happy. Happiness brings smiles naturally. I cannot but suffer for awhile, but it will pass sometime—soon, I hope, for your sake."

"And for your own," he answered fervently. "Yours has been a sad and wretched life."

"But it has passed now," said Helen, whose presence they had forgotten. "I suppose God has some purpose in making his children suffer so much, and after the darkness he will show the light. I am sure I hope so."

Astrea put out her hand and drew her friend toward her lovingly.

"Faithful one, you have done well your part, and I can only love you for it. Never think that I cherish one hard thought of my best little friend."

Helen's face was instantly hidden upon her shoulder while glad tears coursed down her cheek.

"Oh, thank you for those words. They are very, very sweet to me!"

That same evening a quiet ceremony was performed in the little parlor, the pale, feeble bride supported by the strong, sheltering arm of the husband. Neither she or Helen had known until he removed his overcoat that a star had taken the place of the eagles on his shoulder-straps, but now they shone brightly in the light of the chandelier as he stood up to repeat again those words so lately uttered without a thought of what was to follow.

The day succeeding, they set out for Alabama, Helen, accompanying them as nurse to her friend, and after a few days' travel, found only ruins where Passiver Hall had stood. They learned from some of the citizens in Florence that the negroes were all scattered abroad, many in the service, while others had gone from one place to another—no one knew whither. Rufus had come back once in search of his young mistress, but finding that she was gone, had again disappeared. Mrs. Passiver was in Mobile, and probably had taken her granddaughter with her. There was no other reasonable inference to be drawn, and with this information, they set out for that place impatiently. Astrea's excitement as she found herself in old familiar scenes, was becoming a source of alarm, and as every delay could make it only worse, General Wilfer hastened with all the speed he could command, to Mobile.

There, after nearly a whole day's fruitless inquiry, they found the house where the old lady had taken up her abode, and was approaching it with breathless suspense, when a colored girl ran down a long flight of wooden steps with a fairy-like little girl in her arms. Astrea gave one wild cry of delight.

"Nettie! oh, Nettie!"

The girl turned and looked at her for a moment as she came toward her with both arms outstretched, then with a scream that rang sharply on their ears, darted forward and placed the frightened child in her mother's arms, falling at her knees and clasping them round with frantic joy as she sobbed out:

"O, bless the Lord for this day! I kep' her for you, Miss 'Genia, tho' I thought you was dead, may-be; but I know'd you'd come if you wasn't. Old missis said you'd never come back any more, and that made me take better care of Miss Lily, for I thought if you was an angel, it'd please you to see me; but if you wasn't you'd come to her. Anyway she needed me, and she's the beautifulest child that ever was!"

RECOVERY OF THE LONG LOST CHILD.

Here the poor breathless creature was forced to stop, as Mrs. Passiver coldly marched up to the group, having been attracted by Nettie's scream. She found Astrea holding Lily in her arms, kissing her passionately, while both she and Helen wept freely; General Wilfer stood near, making no effort to conceal his emotion.

"I presume you are Mrs. Frederic Passiver, my son's wife," she said stiffly addressing Astrea. Remembering that her son was dead, and pitying the gray hairs of that mother, blanched white with sorrow already, the young lady answered very gently:

"Yes, I was his wife—" then paused.

"Was? was? What are you now? Where is Frederic?"

"Do you know that he went to Richmond?"

"Yes, all about it—but now?"

"He went to New York, and—and after Mr. Lincoln's death—"

"What! not suspected of that—not arrested!"

"Yes, and would not wait to stand his trial. He anticipated the law, and—and—destroyed himself!"

The poor old mother looked bereaved indeed. Personal wars had crushed much of the fierce spirit with which she had entered into the rebellion, and now it was pitiful to see her bend to this new blow.

"He too! he too!—both gone. Oh, my brave boys! my twin boys whom I loved so much. Has God sent this in judgment? Have I been wrong and needed to learn the truth in this way? I suppose you have come for Lily? Well, God took Ferdinand's daughter, and you will take yours, and I shall be left desolate!"

The sorrowful pathos of her voice was irresistibly touching, and Astrea gave one quick, prayerful glance at her husband's face. He answered it with a sad smile, and she laid her hand gently upon Mrs. Passiver's arm.

"Not if you will go with me. I have never known much of you, but you are old, lonely and bereaved of everything you love. If I can in any measure supply a part of that which you have lost, come to me and share my home."

"No, you are kind, but I cannot," she answered turning away. "If you will take the child, send Nettie for her things and I will try to live without her. It will not be for long."

Very sorrowfully the little party saw her move away, but a something in her carriage, a proud lifting of her head that spoke of will and unconquerable spirit, made them leave her alone, and they now returned to the hotel where they had been stopping, Astrea clasping her lost treasure in her arms. Before leaving Mobile, one more attempt was made to persuade the old lady to go North with them, but she firmly refused, and they were obliged to leave her in her loneliness. Nettie, proud and happy as it was possible to be, went with her young mistress to her northern home, never again to return to the South where she had known little else than suffering.

In the city of New York, on a very pretty street, and very handsome in its exterior, stands the home of our heroine. Around her fireside gathers a very pleasant circle with each closing day, of which she is the center, sharing her honors generously with her long-tried friend. If Astrea is not joyous, she is cheerful and quietly happy, while a little golden-haired, fairy-like creature, darting everywhere, makes the life of the house, and is a great pet and favorite with all, in her merry, happy ways.

Sometimes a guest whose face is familiar to our readers, sits at General Wilfer's board and shares the pleasures of his fireside—a man with a long scar across his forehead, and heavy English whiskers with which Miss Lily takes great liberties. It is whispered that this gentleman, who lost an arm at Fort Fisher, is about to sail for Europe with an American bride as the reward of his devotion to the Federal cause. But we cannot vouch for the truth of this, as Helen Noble declares herself too devotedly attached to the memory of the brave, good Major ever to take a second husband, even if she could leave her friends.

www.ingramcontent.com/pod-product-compliance
Lightning Source LLC
LaVergne TN
LVHW020111110826

845151LV00001B/127
9781425544195